BARE your
TEETH

TWOONY

BARE YOUR TEETH

Copyright © 2023 by Twoony

All rights reserved.

No part of this publication may be reproduced, distributed, or transmitted in any form or by any means, including photocopying, recording, or other electronic or mechanical methods, without the prior written permission of the publisher, except as permitted by U.S. copyright law. For permission requests, contact

sarahroberts4313@gmail.com

This is a work of fiction. Names, characters, businesses, places, events, and incidents are either the products of the author's imagination or used in a fictitious manner. No identification with actual persons (living or deceased), places, buildings, and products is intended or should be inferred.

Book Cover by M.E. Morgan

ISBN: 9798344287423 (Paperback)

Imprint: Independently published

Warning

This story takes place in a fantasy version of the early 1800s during a violent war. There will be occasions of homophobia, misogyny, gore, body dysmorphia, dead naming, sexual assault (off page,) violence, and general unpleasantness. It won't overwhelm the story but will be present so please consider that before reading.

Prologue

WILLIAM AUGUSTUS VANDERVULT WAS the fourth son of Viscount Robert Vandervult, raised by luxury and love. William's mother, Lady Matilda Vandervult, brought her boys up to be poised and fine gentlemen. Though they did not want for anything, Matilda and Robert ensured their children took nothing for granted, either.

The Vandervults were known for their charity endeavors spread across the Heign kingdom. Orphanages and clinics mostly, so young William learned not to be disturbed by missing limbs or the sick. He found the work of doctors pure in a sense, crucial and hopeful. They possessed the Sight, a gift of magic from the Holy Soul, allowing them to tug on the strings of the world. In a flick of the wrist, doctors healed the injured, calmed the sick, or made peace for the dying.

After a hot day toiling among the clinics, Matilda often said to him, "There are many less fortunate than us, and so it is our duty to share that fortune and rid the world of a little sorrow each day."

He thought the world of her, and his father, who shared those beliefs. His parents met in a clinic on a summer afternoon tending to children suffering shimmer sickness, in fact. However, the Court of Lords his father was a part of were not all known for charity. Occasionally, he eavesdropped on their conversations over the suffocating stench of cigar smoke and liquor. The court gentlemen laughed over atrocities and barked at those who dared to suggest charity.

"If we took pity on every poor bastard, there'd be more pity than gold," Lord Hornbill loved to claim.

William found so-called gentlemen such as Lord Hornbill to be awful company and never quite understood why his father invited them over for supper.

"There will always be those among society who do not see past their own desires. Those same could rule this world if we allowed them, so occasionally we must invite them for tea and find compromise," Robert explained to his boys, the oldest of which understood, but William did not. He found many of his father's phrases peculiar, though that could be because he did not have the same aptitude as his brothers.

He did not know business like Arthur. He could not charm like Richard. He could not absorb knowledge like Henry. William was sensitive, so others loved to remind him. He preferred the company of flowers and animals over people. He could not stomach a hunt alongside his father or brothers. An act many gentlemen found concerning, though he couldn't fathom why.

Matilda doted over him, though, their youngest and a spitting image of her; fair skinned, a dimpled smile, hair of spun gold and emerald eyes of promised spring.

"I would not stand another dull conversation of proud men spouting nonsense a moment longer if I had my way," she proclaimed over an afternoon of knitting. He quite enjoyed knitting, finding the repetitive motion soothing while his brothers would have nothing of it. His mother smiled, comforting as morning sunlight. "You, my sweet child, always have interesting tales and thoughts to share. I find that far more fitting than an overly confident man who can wield a rifle or smoke a cigar."

Matilda was the singular person who found his interest fitting. Though Robert never spoke ill of his boy, he did not expect William to follow in the footsteps of his brothers.

As the eldest and wisest, Arthur would take the title of viscount. Richard held galas across the kingdom to raise money for their charity ventures because, as Matilda once claimed, the boy could charm the britches off the king himself. At seventeen, the Holy Soul blessed Henry with the Sight. He earned a position within Heign's Magical Society. To study magic among the most renowned mages of Heign was an honor few Vandervults had been offered before. Then there was William, the fourth son who tended to birds with broken wings and cried over books unbefitting of a boy.

"Do not let others find you reading such things," Henry chastised after catching William huddled at the back of their house library with his nose in a romance novel. "Such books are for ladies."

"Why?" he asked. "They are poetic and sweet. They tell of love. Can gentlemen not enjoy love?"

The bridge of Henry's nose wrinkled. Concern trickled through his words. "Do not speak like that to others, either. They will not treat you kindly."

"Why?"

Henry ruffled William's hair. "Because it is not the way of things, my dear brother."

He thought perhaps the way of things were wrong, for no one should be deprived of a marvelous book. They allowed one to explore a thousand worlds in a single lifetime. What could be more magnificent than that?

He would become increasingly grateful for the many lives spent among books, for the life he knew came to an abrupt halt at sixteen.

"He cannot go," Matilda argued. Her voice carried through the cracked door to Robert's office. William kneeled and dared to peek inside.

The fireplace was not lit on the mild fall afternoon and the maids had shut the windows. Dusk light glistened against the glass, revealing the warding spells marking the panes to protect against beasts and unwelcome intruders. Fae placed the wards there long before his parents were born, although his family rarely spoke of them. Many believed anything from fae would cause tragedy, but their wards and spells became necessary evils over the last few decades.

However, William found the wards eerily beautiful. They always gave off a faint glow, like dawn barely waking over the skyline, and had yet to fail in their protections. Matilda weaved stories of days before their lifetimes, where monsters didn't roam the lands. He couldn't imagine a world without worry, just as he couldn't fathom how either of his parents stood the smell of the office. Robert's guests caused the room to reek of tobacco and brandy. A glass cabinet containing a dozen foul tasting beverages lined the wall. He would know after Richard convinced him to taste one and he hardly made it to the open window in time to empty his stomach in the bushes outside.

Deep navy wallpaper circled the upper half of the room, designed with twisting morning glory flowers stretching to the ceiling. Ebony wainscotting completed the lower half, save for one wall where a stack of shelves contained dull books that rotted the brain.

Robert stood at a wide black desk, leaning against the same colored cane tipped in silver. His opposing foot tapped impatiently against the floor. Matilda sat on the sofa, a hand against her heart and the other pressed to her head.

William had never seen her so troubled, never witnessed such horror in her eyes.

"This is not our war," Matilda whimpered.

"This is everyone's war," Robert argued and threw the crumpled letter in his hand onto the floor. "The shadowed disciples have plagued our realms for too long. Their summoned beasts are no longer rats dying in cages. We, and our children, have not known the world without their curse, without their fleshed damnations. Should this war continue, an unholy plane may spill upon ours. Calix Fearworn will cast this world in shadow, ending all life as we've known it."

"Do not speak that name in our house." Matilda pressed two fingers against her heart, as she taught William.

He begged the Broken Soul not to punish his father and prayed to the Holy Soul to forgive him for uttering a blasphemous name. The name of a murderer like the world had never seen, who would never march through the healing sea of Elysium. The Broken Soul would drag his horrors to the depths and the damned.

"Not speaking the name of evil will not defeat it," said Robert. "Fearworn, and his shadowed disciples, cannot be ignored. The kings of Terra and the lords of Faerie agree: this is no longer a divided war. Our kings require each family to send one man of their direct lineage to the front." Red faced and ruffled, Robert slammed his cane against the floor. "Richard and I have been deemed unfit to serve. Arthur and Henry offered themselves, but the king denied their enlistments, arguing Arthur is our heir and Henry is studying magic that our soldiers will use to survive. They're needed here."

"Does that not count as serving?" Matilda argued.

"No, as Henry will not see the front lines. William must go, as ordered by the king," Robert said in the stern tone he used on the boys, the one that wasn't as authoritative as he needed it to be. His expression was even worse, anguished and guilt-ridden.

Matilda wailed like William had never heard, sharp, bitter, and utterly broken. "He is too young. He is our baby."

"He is sixteen."

"William is not like our other boys. By the Holy Soul, Robert, he cannot hunt. How can any expect him to take a life? Why would His Majesty choose our William?"

"You know why," Robert whispered.

Matilda leaned over as if that would grant her more air to breathe. Robert kneeled in front of his grieving wife. He grasped her hand so tightly William worried he'd cause harm, but Matilda returned that force. Her bottom lip trembled, so did Robert's.

"William will do what he must to protect himself." Robert's voice cracked. "He'll learn to survive. He'll come home."

That was the first time he heard his father cry. Both of his parents wept, and once he returned to his room, so did he.

William Augustus Vandervult went to war at sixteen, where he became who he needed to be to survive.

1

William

No one knew Death like William. He danced with her most nights, sometimes dared to defy her, though ultimately no power prevented Death from reaping her fill. She was queen, eternal, limitless, especially so here where the stench of death hovered over agonized screams and smoking entrails.

William knelt among mud, gore, piss, and shit. They seeped into his stained trousers. The scent of burning leather seared his nostrils through the cloth wrapped tightly around his face. A soldier laid before him, insides painting his outsides. Slaughter and stench, vomit and copper, wafted from the open wound. Snow flurries clung to his frozen hair and frostbitten uniform.

Every corpse-to-be he stumbled upon reminded him of years ago, a child listening to war stories told by foolish gentlemen with nothing to do. The fantastical tales high society spoke of never painted reality. They gossiped of heroes and adventures, of glory and the Holy Soul guiding brave soldiers through Elysium's waters, not shit stained trousers, maggot infested abdomens, and gouged eyes.

"Did we win, Doctor?" the soldier croaked in a puff of white smoke. Blood caked his bruised and chapped lips. His left arm lay a foot away, revolver clutched between blue-tinted fingers.

"We did. The monsters of Lockehold are vanquished and the road to the Deadlands has opened. The war will be over soon and we will return home," William replied in a carefully crafted voice perfected over five years. The serene and collected tone of a physician meant to ease the pain, and passing, of patients. Some patients.

Blood gurgled in the back of the soldier's throat. "And I will join them, won't I?"

"After such a marvelous battle? Of course. King Ellis shall mark this day in history, our names laid among golden plaques within his castle walls. Children will sing of Lockehold's fall and write of our accomplishments in history books. You will return home a war hero."

The soldier whimpered a delirious laugh. The dying didn't want the truth. They sought hope, for Death had her claws in them. Her brisk breath nipped at their necks. A temptress guiding them to the other side, wherever that may be, and so the dying sought comfort, a ledge to uselessly cling to.

He tightened the leather strap securing the rifle to his back. The worn gray leather bag of medical supplies he carried would not be of use. The Sight revealed the interior of living beings, a series of glistening silver strings coalescing to expose the soldier's torn muscles, blood bursting from his lungs, and a heart fluttering fruitlessly.

Slipping off a glove, he flexed his fingers among the unforgiving cold, then set his hand atop the soldier's chest. The strings of the world curled around his fingers, gentle in their caress, even if he willed them to strangle the heart beneath his palm. The soldier offered a curious stare.

"Comfort will greet you in a moment," William said.

The soldier's heart slowed, weak as an injured mouse caught between a starving cat's fangs. With a few short breaths, the soldier's eyes glazed over, and all went still. Tranquil. An end to suffering. Death swept another away although William knew not where.

He had long since discouraged the idea of Elysium, of the Holy Soul shepherding the compassionate dead to their next life. He couldn't fathom joy after brutal deaths or supreme beings watching over their miserable existence. If the Souls were real, if all the so-called godly beings ever uttered truly existed, then they were malevolent bastards and he wholly despised them.

He didn't glance at the dead man's tags. In his line of work, he needn't feel for these men, merely care for their wounds, end suffering to those who deserved it, and move to the next. As he did now, shifting through corpses of beasts and man alike in search of the next wounded or dying, but his gaze defied him by traveling north to Lockehold, a midnight black thorn bleeding upon the horizon.

Towers sharpened to deadly points prodded at the gray sky, defiant to the world above. Smoke rose from fires scorching upon terraces and crumbled ramparts. The Dread Peaks, a range of monstrous mountains, ran along either side of the fortress, tips coated in white, casting a looming umbra over the field of dead. A single path sliced through the mountains. The fortress of Lockehold protected that path for decades, until today. They had won this battle.

If the dead could argue, they would say otherwise.

Snow crunched beneath William's boots. His medical bag swung from one hand and a revolver in the other. A soldier knelt among the grim ahead. Head bowed; the soldier clutched the hand of another man long dead. The corpse of a spion lay nearby, belly ripped open and green guts spilling out, reeking of rotten meat baked in a summer sun. The grotesque creature was an amalgamation of a spider and a scorpion. Eight-legged, two pinchers, a stinger, too many eyes, and a hard indigo tinted outer shell. The webs suffocated prey or pinned them for a spion to drain them of blood. The spion's stinger had embedded itself in the deceased soldier's chest. That close to his heart, the poison worked swiftly.

"Doctor," the grieving man rose and wiped the snot from his nose. A recruit based on his boyish face, plump cheeks, and bloody, albeit uncalloused, hands.

William tugged the cloth from his nose and gazed at the soldier's name tag. "Do you require medical attention, Oscar?"

"I feel alright, but this cut was bleedin' horribly earlier, sir." Oscar revealed a wound on his arm. Out here, infections took more lives than fangs and claws.

William retrieved a mixture of herbs from his leather bag. The Sight granted wondrous magic, but magic had always been wild and unpredictable.

The strings connecting the world didn't always obey commands. They disliked taking orders and preferred kind suggestions. If one pushed too hard, if they pushed themselves too far, requested too much, magic replied and the response was rarely good. He, and all others with the Sight, knew to use assistance when they could, something to ease the pressure of their abilities. For his healing, herbs and potions worked wonders.

After crushing the herbs between his palms, he ran the green paste on Oscar's arm. The young soldier winced while admiring the wound, stitching itself together.

"How does it feel?" He ran a finger over Oscar's arm, checking for abnormalities.

"Great, sir."

"Good, now follow me. You do not wish to be here if there are unfriendly scavengers. The medical tents are over there." He nodded toward the flickering fires. He did a thorough walk through. Nothing could be done for the remaining bodies, and one on his list had been taken care of.

Oscar shut his friend's eyes and hurried after him. The cold stole the color from one's skin, making Oscar white as winter itself. Snow clung to the thin layer of brown hair atop his head and his full lips trembled from chattering teeth.

"The bodies of the dead will be returned to their loved ones, won't they, sir?" Oscar whispered.

"Perhaps. Did he fare from across the sea?"

Oscar's sniffle gave the answer. Many, like William, were not born in these lands. During the first year of his recruitment, he remained in the Heign kingdom for training. Then came the days of battles that dragged him, and many others, across the sea, closer and closer to the Deadlands behind the Dread Peaks and the monsters summoned within.

"Priests of Soul will retrieve the dead to grant proper burials," he explained, eyes shifting to the crunch of snow at their back. He feigned looking at Oscar to glimpse their follower; fae scum. He clutched his revolver tighter, and muttered, "Fear not. Your friend may not be home, but he will rest in peace."

"May the Broken Soul find him true and the Holy Soul see to his rebirth," Oscar whispered, with two fingers pressed to his heart.

He struggled not to roll his eyes. A friend told him it was uncouth. He didn't need a lecture from her over his needlessly boorish and unlikable nature. Her words, not his.

"So many dead." Oscar's gaze lingered on the decapitated head of a debrak. Titanous monsters, muscled and red as an open wound. They ate men like midday treats and snapped spines easier than flower stems. "At least we ain't like these poor suckers. Ran himself right into a trap."

Oscar kicked the debrak. The head rolled and released a gurgled whine of breath. Oscar cursed and stumbled. William caught the oaf prior to falling into the fatal trick that killed the beast, a fairy ring. Traps created by fae with varying degrees of torment and death laid within, warned only by a ring of mushrooms.

A dry chuckle crept upon them; the pointy-eared vermin William spotted following them. The fae brushed by donning a grin of villainy. She wore a beauty that stole hearts. Complexion perfect even beneath the mess of battle and eyes breathtakingly beautiful, a shade of eternal obscurity against rich ochre skin and black braids woven by sterling silver. The allure of fae drove one mad, and their personalities were another hoax entirely.

"Watch yourself. We are not immune to fae trickery," William warned. "Fae are allies, not friends, and it is easy to die at the hands of an ally out here."

"Y-Yes, sir."

Oscar shuffled behind William, who kept that hand tight around his revolver, eyes trained on the fae's back. Waiting. Expecting the worst.

Though mortal kings and fae lords spent months toiling over agreements to prevent the races from slaughtering each other, they did little in the face of a fae's murderous wrath. Agreeing to fight together didn't prevent those like Oscar from stumbling into traps. Unfortunate deaths, not murder. The fae always found ways around deals struck, even those that benefitted them.

"A woman," Oscar remarked with a soured expression, like a toddler sucking on a lemon. "I've always known fae to be a rotten bunch, but to send a woman to fight ain't right. It is a horror waiting to happen."

"You did not witness their battles today?"

"They were not the ones I was paying attention to."

"You should. Always." He gave Oscar a stern look. "The stories spun about fae are tame at best. They torture and curse so as not to kill us with their own hands. Most humans take their lives once a fae is through with them. Do not believe for a second their women aren't equally vicious. They expect mortal men to underestimate them, and I've met many who did not live long enough to regret such decisions. Do you understand?"

Oscar nodded vigorously, then followed to the medical tents without further incident.

A dozen tents had been pitched along the outskirts of the battle, away from filth and along the line of pine trees. Oscar took to helping others outside while William entered.

Heat suffocated the interior. Orbs of flames lit the chaos and stole the chill. The injured spilled from cots to makeshift floor beds of hay and damp cloth. The stench of charred leather and excrement burned the corners of his eyes. Nurses hurried to attend to the worst injured while soldiers scurried past carrying corpses to make room.

"William," a cheerful voice called.

Charmaine Tuckerton hurried forward, her military uniform seared up to the elbows and caked in crimson. A bandage wrapped around her bald head, and remnants of healing remedies stained her cheek.

Towering over most, Charmaine had little trouble shoving through the masses to wrap William in a tight embrace. "What a relief, you're alive," she muttered against his temple.

"I am relieved to see you, too. Has anyone looked at your head injury?" He settled a hand on her temple, catching the strings that felt too tight. She had a concussion.

"Yes, there is nothing to worry about, and we need our medics to tend to the others. I have nothing more than bumps and bruises otherwise. What about you? Are you injured? I wanted to join the initial search, but—"

"Tuckerton!" Charmaine jolted at the shout of the Head Medical Officer, Marsha Montgomery.

Montgomery went by her last name only. Never liked being called Marsha because the men scoffed at her before she entered a room. One of the very few female medical officials of her status, she had to be stern and borderline cruel to survive here. That's probably why she was barely forty and already gray as a grandmother. She glared from across the tent, wrinkled tawny brown hands covered by the blood of a thrashing soldier she kept pinned to the table.

"Cauterize this wound, now! Move it, man!" Montgomery bellowed.

Charmaine's expression fell. William squeezed her hand. That was the most either of them could do here. Others would see Charmaine as sick for daring to say she identified as a woman. No one could fathom why one born a man, supposedly mortal representations of the Holy Soul, would want to be a woman.

"Yes, sir!" Charmaine hurried to the back of the tent. Fire crept over her fingers. An anguished cry followed the hissing of flames and smoke.

Removing his jacket and rifle, William joined nurses at a nearby cot.

Hours passed. Darkness settled. Those meant to die, had. They laid in droves outside. Forty among them wore silver shrouds to represent lost fae. Resilient rabble. Forty had been the most fae lives lost in a single battle. Once a man spoke of an assault where seventy fell. No one believed him, and as expected, the fae cared little for their dead.

A group of the rotten dregs converged by one of the supply carts, belonging to the human troops. They had no issue stealing, and mortals ceased arguing. Fae were easily outraged and impatient to seek revenge for the smallest slight. A selfish lot. William despised them. Their nonchalance, their disdain, the general lack to feel outside their own greed and lust for mayhem. War was troublesome enough. Fighting alongside the fae made war worse. They were good for one thing and one thing only—

Fuchsia light burst through the camp, followed by a wave of blistering heat. The fae cried out. A series of victorious chants grew in the face of shadows closing in. The fuchsia flames dimmed to flickering sparks within the palms of a pompous fae.

The bastard and his entourage stepped into their kin's circle. His raven hair sat a glorious mess atop his head, wound loosely at the nape, and roseate eyes brighter than gems. His tattered clothes hung against a muscled form. When he laughed, it was joyous and evil and proved what the fae were good for; fearsome power. Fae wielded magic better than the air they breathed. The pink tinted fire danced between his fingertips, illuminating his suave features. A face that most would look enviously upon.

Perhaps fae were good for two things. They had always been charming to admire, flawless and magnificent. Everything anyone could yearn for, and even what they wouldn't expect. As much as William, and many others, hated working alongside fae, none denied their grace made the sun shy. Yet another weapon in their long arsenal, a way to deceive lonely and desperate souls.

Charmaine appeared carrying the heavy aroma of disinfectant, wafting from the towel wiping her raw hands clean. "Nicholas Darkmoon," she whispered, awestruck.

"You speak his name as if we are to be impressed," he said.

"We should. He's the son of a High Fae who holds tremendous power. The fae revere him, in their manner, and thus revere his son."

"All I see is a cursed jackass who likes to show off."

Sweat dripped from his brow thanks to Nicholas' infernal flames. The sparks danced over his broad shoulders, flickering at his back like feathered wings. Such magic was unnatural, tainted, and wielded by the enemy they battled against. Thus, the sight of Nicholas put him on edge.

"Lockehold must have had something." A hopeful gleam caught in Charmaine's down-turned eyes. "I heard Nicholas was sent more as a delegate, but he has been appearing frequently during important battles. Rumors say he throws tantrums after a boring siege."

"Only a fae would call any siege boring."

"If I had to wager, he is in a good mood. Lockehold is the key to the Deadlands. We've broken through. There must be little more left to do. We can go home. I can..." Charmaine said no more, less she risks unpleasant interactions with the simpleminded.

"Albie," William whispered. He hated using that name, but they agreed it was different enough from her deadname that it wasn't an utter torment to use. He pressed a finger beneath her chin, gentle and nurturing, to break that hopeful gaze away from creatures intent on snuffing it out. "Do not trust hope. She's a painful and disappointing mistress."

"Hope has never failed me. Hope gave me you."

"A group of ruthless boys with a lot to prove and a pained cry brought us together. At most, a dose of dumb luck."

"Such optimism, William. Where ever did you acquire it?" Charmaine sank to the floor. "I want to sleep through the night and have three meals a day with snacks in between. I want to... be myself. I want this damned war to be over. I want to go home," she whispered in a breathless voice others shared in the middle of the night when they believed no one listened. William, too.

He wanted to hope. He dreamed of home, of afternoon tea, his favorite asiatic lilies in the garden, a soft bed, a mother's comforting embrace, his brother's teasing laughter, and his father telling him long-winded stories. What he remembered of that, anyway. What he hoped he still loved about normalcy.

He craved the life before suffering, war, and cursed fae, like the annoyed one heading their way with fuchsia flames at his back.

2

NICHOLAS

POWER SURGED WITHIN NICHOLAS, a potent chaos forever his promising mayhem, threatening an infinite destruction. He desired to give in, to give Power everything she wanted. Shatter bones. Burn forests. Dry the oceans. Hide the sun. Break the world. Make every beating heart beg him not to take tomorrow and all the days after. This energy, this need, could not be holed up forever, but he was taught to temper the beast. Let her out when necessary, then tighten the noose and don't let go or she'd take him, too.

The Dread Peaks sat before him, overrun by beasts of another plane. An unholy plane, the humans called it. He did not believe in the folly of humans, their foolish morals, and wrathful religions. However, he believed in repaying debts. Calix Fearworn declared war against Faerie years ago and Nicholas would eagerly engage.

Lockehold, the shadowed disciples' citadel of horror, held more than the path forward. Tonight, he had a job to do, and he couldn't wait to let go. The fae and mortal armies stood at his back. They shared a breath when he held out his hand. The eternal flame burning upon his center spread from his fingertips. Mortals called magic the Sight, something gifted from their mundane gods. Nicholas saw it as nature, as natural as rivers and mountains and the bleeding heart within his chest.

Fuchsia flames lurched from his hand through the sea of monsters and the battle for Lockehold began. The siege lasted hours. He long lost track of the bugs he crushed. Prey wailed. Bodies dropped. Limbs shattered. Gore and death always followed power and he couldn't get enough. Those were the hardest times to strangle the destructive need for all he wanted was to unleash.

But as he gazed upon the remnants of his mission, a shadowed disciple barely more than blood and ash at his feet, his power diminished, ceasing the turbulent air and rampant flames that charred the ruined room. The air sparked with life, flames flickered in and out of existence. They settled atop his skin, then withered into lines of smoke. His eyes opened, the fierce hue of pink dimmed.

Around him, his kin watched. They clutched daggers and swords, tips pointed at him, for none knew when one like him—a shade—would lose themselves entirely. When Power took hold and wouldn't let go, they had to be ready to strike that down, if they could.

"The generals will be pleased," Nicholas said while digging through the remnants of the shadowed disciples' robes. He tracked the bastard for nearly two months. His mission was about what the disciple carried, a book of weathered pages stitched together by glistening spion silk.

The half dozen fae around him eased the hands from their weapons, now aware that Nicholas was himself. Snow filtered in through the collapsed ceiling at the edge of the room. Corpses lay strewn about, crushed by debris or splattered against walls. Their stench carried over the heavy musk of the citadel. Nicholas loved the scent of a good slaughtering and the taste of copper on his tongue. He knew little more than that over the last decade, always yearning for a fight, for fun and games, anything to ease the pressure of energy gnawing at his core. Anything to prevent a change that all said was inevitable.

"Our sources were correct. A general of Fearworn's shadowed disciples carrying a book of monsters," Duke said. The mortal mentor, forced on him by his father's orders, surged forward.

"May I, sir?" Duke asked. Nicholas dropped the book into his grasp, smirking when the mentor flipped through the pages and his expression sank. "What language is this?"

"Not one a dense mortal would know." He snatched the book. "This is the ancient tongue of High Fae."

Which Fearworn knew, as a High Fae himself... and a shade, same as Nicholas.

The greedy gazes Nicholas received during childhood changed when Calix Fearworn fell to the storm within him. When he threatened to recreate the Collision that opened gateways between the realms of Faerie and Terra. Fearworn yearned for a sinister power, to unleash monsters from another world and seek all realms that may be after, even if that meant destroying their realms in the process.

Though others wanted the power Nicholas had, they also came to fear it, to expect him to fall to Fearworn's corruption as shades were cursed to self-destruct, one way or the other. Truthfully, he considered following Fearworn's path more times than he could count.

Fearworn sought knowledge and power. This book proved that. One flip through the pages and he glimpsed decades of Fearworn's curiosities for the unknown. Among Fearworn's ranks, he would be encouraged to lean into the worst monster that lived within. However, even his desperation for a good time knew better than to risk throwing himself to madness. He would not be himself afterward, and he quite liked himself.

"I was taught this language before any other. It is a complicated tongue. Translating will take time, however, I am eager to determine how fucked Fearworn is now," Nicholas added with a chuckle.

"The generals appreciate all the work you've put in, Lord Darkmoon," Duke said. "We would not have won this battle without you."

"Lord Darkmoon is my father, and save your piss poor pleasantries for one who cares."

Duke bowed in the typical obedient manner.

Nicholas' father, Lord Laurent Darkmoon, sought to maintain a relatively civil connection with humans for the time being. Nicholas wasn't known for civility, so a mortal mentor followed to ensure he didn't prove a hindrance by teaching him mortal ways.

Duke had been a constant annoyance. Laurent could have at least hired a fuckable annoyance. But Duke had the curse of all humans; age. Wrinkled skin and thin, graying hair that sprouted out of his ears, too. He always thought about tying the man down and ripping out all that affronted him, although there wouldn't be much left of Duke afterward.

"We should hurry back to the generals," Duke said. "They have likely sent scouts into the Deadlands by now. The generals will want to move, too, now that Lockehold has been taken. This book is no doubt going to be of great value to us. This war may be coming to an end at last."

Nicholas couldn't say he shared Duke's excitement. If there was one mortal creation he found marvelous, it was war, and mortals were exceptionally prolific at it.

"Look at this," Blair called. Nicholas' sister stepped into the light from a shadowed hallway. Her teeth, jagged as a predator, unsettled any unfortunate enough to gaze upon her. With limbs long as a willow branch, ocean eyes narrowed and cold, skin a pale blue, and hair black as midnight, she was vicious in both words and appearance. Her blood-stained fingers snatched the book out of his grasp. "Well, well, won't Father be pleased about his little pup performing so excellently at playing fetch?"

"Do not act as if you wouldn't be swift to obey had he not given you the same orders," he countered.

"Then aren't I lucky to know he would never give me such orders. You're his favorite leashed dog, after all."

He hated that she wasn't wrong. Blair came for war first, zealous for the slaughter, and of her own volition. He would have joined, but he did not have the same freedoms as she. He was more of a delegate than a warrior, meant to monitor and ensure Fearworn fell to the hands of a fae. Laurent wanted the mortals to be grateful, to show the capabilities of his lineage, but Nicholas couldn't stop running into the fray on the occasions when he could get away with being disobedient.

Duke cleared his throat. "Shall we return, sir?"

"Oh, this one's still here." Blair clicked her tongue as if Duke's presence offended her. It probably did. She said she preferred her men to be pretty and pathetic. Duke only fit one part of that criteria.

Ignoring her, Nicholas set off. His kin traversed the citadel at his back, searching for any potential survivors. The fae lunged at any sound. There was no life left in Lockehold. Even the structure withered, burnt, and broken. The mortal generals would be displeased. They had mentioned wanting to use the stronghold against Fearworn, but Nicholas wanted to unleash, needed to, really. He thought little of the consequences. Besides, he gained the book, and that would satiate any potential anger.

Approaching the military encampment, he cast the world in a blaze of pink light and announced, "Let us celebrate this victory till morning!"

The fae crowded around a supply cart, clutching the neck of liquor bottles. Blair skipped ahead to join them, linking arms with another woman. The group cheered and raised those bottles high. Arden stood with them, eyes more brilliant than polished rubies. The fair color of his skin made snow appear gray, and the white of his hair drifted over his shoulders as if a constant wind followed. After a long day of bloodshed, the white shade took on a soft red tone.

"Congratulations, Nicholas. You fought well today, as always," Arden said.

Nicholas captured his waist in a lewd gesture and relished in the hungry kiss he received.

"Lord Nicholas." Duke cleared his throat, souring his mood in a single sound.

"What now?" Nicholas barked.

"After such a trying battle, is it not prudent to speak with the soldiers?" Duke nodded at the med bay adjacent to them. "You are a delegate of Faerie, sent by Lord Darkmoon himself. The generals, and kings, would appreciate your attention toward the wounded, especially now when we are getting so close to the end. It may set the mortal soldiers at ease, seeing you so clearly on their side."

"Send Blair for such trivial matters. She loves toying with mortals."

Blair laughed. "I don't think so. This is your duty as the oh-so-special delegate of the Darkmoon family." Caught between two of their kin, she wiggled her fingers dismissively. "Have fun."

The three scurried off with booze in hand, leaving him with Duke's expecting attention. He snarled. "What attention would I give those ailing bastards struggling against the inevitable?"

Arden placed a hand against Nicholas' chest, fingers toiling with the buttons of his blouse. "Nicholas has done more than enough. We have earned an evening of celebration."

"I do not disagree," Duke said. "But this will only take a moment. Speak to the soldiers, let them know how grand this victory is, that you slayed a shadowed disciple considered of great importance and we're far closer to catching Fearworn than ever."

"Mortals and their cares will always elude me." Nicholas pressed a kiss to the base of Arden's neck, whispering against the shivering skin to wait for him. Arden slipped away, and he waved a dismissive hand. "So be it. I'll speak to the wounded, then you will leave me. If I see your vile mug before dawn, there will be severe consequences."

Duke bowed and Nicholas stormed toward the tent reeking of human filth. They had an uncanny ability to carry the aroma of rotting fish wherever they went. Their weak bodies lay out on cots, broken, bloodied, and bandaged. The medics and nurses toiled over them. A useless endeavor, he always thought. Mortals passed with such ease.

"Mortal filth!" Nicholas twirled his hands dramatically.

Duke pursed his lips in disapproval.

He meandered by the cots, speaking in a high tilted voice like a parent coddling their children. "If you are somehow unaware, I am Nicholas Darkmoon, a delegate of Faerie and your soon-to-be savior. I've come with great tidings. As you may have known, Lockehold was of great importance. Some gave their pathetic, insignificant lives to the cause. I've been informed that it is a tremendous honor. Though nothing compared to my achievements. I burned one of Fearworn's shadowed disciples to a crisp, someone high ranking among his wretches. Thanks to that, we're one step closer to defeating the bastard. Although I doubt most of you will survive to see it, this remains a blessed day." He cast his gaze from one silent cot to the other, then added, "This is when you applaud."

No one did, though a disgusting bastard made the mistake of clutching his wrist. A frail voice sputtered from a man with blood-stained bandages over what little remained of his melted face. "Please, sir, water," the mortal croaked.

Nicholas felt life slipping away, the mortal's energy fading like a forgotten fire. Nothing the medics tried would prevent this soldier's demise.

The Collision Treaty stopped fae from taking the lives of mortals and making deals with them during war times, but there had always been loopholes. Mortals could offer to make a deal first. Fae could kill mortals already bound to death since their religions found it merciful to end suffering. Most mortals didn't believe souls left this world forever. Eventually, they returned, so their medics were ordered to ease the passing of those incapable of being saved. To fae, that meant a little torment could happen prior to a final breath.

"I will give you something, but it won't be water," he chuckled and reared his arm back. Power twisted around his hand, forming a sharp saber intent on relieving the dreg of a limb.

A gun fired. The iron bullet pierced his shoulder. He cursed. The skin sizzled and burned. Coral mist seeped from the wound, accompanied by bubbling blood, then the bullet slipped out to clatter on the ground. His guttural growl grew when gazing upon the smoking revolver held by a soon to be dead dunce.

"Get out of our tent," the medic spoke, based on the crimson stained shirt clinging to his muscular form. Sweat clung to the short ends of his blonde hair, carrying the sun's first rays of dawn. Those jade eyes did not share the same fervor, as wild and feral as a starving beast. He stepped out from behind a cot to the center of the tent, gun raised.

Nicholas hated how he admired the man's tone figure, long legs and cool white skin. What a waste of looks on a mortal who would be eaten away by time and death. "You shot me," Nicholas hissed.

"You were about to dismember one of my patients. If you try to do so again, I will aim for the head." The gun clicked in warning.

A nurse gasped and knelt by the cot of her patient.

Duke stepped forward. "Let us all calm down. This is unnecessary and the Collision Treaty—"

"Is a load of bullshit," the medic interrupted. "Written by halfhearted kings and lords with no care or mind for what happens here. Now, get out. We have enough work on our hands. We needn't care for an arrogant child, too."

"An arrogant child. You better tell me I heard wrong." Nicholas rolled his shoulder.

Nurses and patients gasped, shocked to witness the bullet wound closing. Nothing remained but a dull throb.

"Let me correct myself then, an arrogant and hard-of-hearing child utterly incapable of thinking of anyone other than himself. He comes raging into camp without thinking of the consequences of his fire." The medic nodded toward the muddy ground. "The snow was cold, but at least it was sturdy. Our medics shouldn't have to worry about twisting their ankles while attending to the wounded. Then you come in here spouting bullshit and daring to put your hands on anyone. I don't believe I've ever met one as dull as you."

Nicholas clutched the throat of the disobedient bastard. His claws pierced skin. The medic kept his haughty chin high. Blood followed the slender curves of his neck, painting the skin a lush red.

"You have quite the tongue on you. I would love to rip it out," he snarled and squeezed harder.

"Go on." The medic smirked when Nicholas grunted from the head of the gun digging into his crotch. "Let us determine who is quicker."

"That is a game you don't wish to play, mortal scum."

"I'll decide what games to play myself, arrogant jackass."

"My Lord." Duke shot an arm between them, attempting to separate the two. "This is uncalled for. You are on the verge of going against the Collision Treaty. No king, and especially not Lord Darkmoon, will tolerate this."

But he couldn't tolerate smug mortals and this blonde dolt made him want to snap necks.

Though, truth be told, the combat medic was not worth the torture his father would set upon him for causing trouble. The one fae he listened to, in a sense, and for good reason. Laurent knew pain and dealt it like no other. He didn't take disobedience well. Even with all of Nicholas' strength, he never won against his father, because Laurent always knew what made him tick. What made him cower. What to use and how to use it. Laurent's long years of life made him invincible.

Nicholas reluctantly released the medic. The stranger fell to his heels and retreated; gun pointed between Nicholas' legs.

"You should learn to hold your tongue before you lose it," he warned.

"I don't take the advice of fools," the medic replied.

He wanted nothing more than to burn the medic and listen to his shrill screams through the night. But a glimpse of Duke reminded him of what would happen if he dared, so he stormed out of the tent, leaving a trail of flames in his wake. He overheard Duke apologizing for the disturbance, then the mentor approached him outside.

"Who was that?" he growled, catching sight of the medic through the slaps of the tent.

"Nothing more than a combat medic," Duke replied nervously. "Forgive him. He didn't know to whom he spoke. Tonight is a victorious one. Please, enjoy your evening with your kin."

Nicholas was sure to do so, drinking the night away and spending an evening in bed with Arden, all the while dreaming of gouging out a pair of smug green eyes.

3

William

No one knew what to expect of the Deadlands. The generals sent scouts as soon as the battle ended. They didn't waste time browsing the ruined Lockehold citadel. When the scouts returned, speaking of a better location for encampment, the generals called for a march. The Medical Corps agreed the wounded could not stay on the battlefield or follow through the pass. Come morning, soldiers guarded the caravan of the injured south to the last city before the Dread Peaks. There the wounded could heal, then catch up later. They may pass a few friends along the way, too.

Soldiers celebrated too enthusiastically that night. Three made life ending decisions and found their corpses hanging from trees. The word traitor had been carved crookedly into their bare chests, no doubt while they were still breathing, and their severed hands lay at the ground beneath their feet.

"Were we truly in need of more dead?" Charmaine muttered, teeth chattering from the morning frost.

Oscar huddled close to her. The young soldier followed William around most of the night, then Charmaine upon realizing she spoke more than her friend.

"They laid with fae, didn't they?" Oscar sniffled and rubbed his hands against his flushed cheeks. "During training, everyone said fae and mortal ain't meant to be together. Folk said you'd meet a bad fate, but I never expected that."

"The consequences aren't always so bad," she explained. "Sometimes it's nothing more than being ignored, but after this battle, I am not surprised by the violence. I doubt the men were fond of their friends laying with those known for treating us worse than the dirt beneath their boots."

"Mortals have always found the act more egregious than fae," William contributed. "I've overheard the lying scum treat bedding mortals as a game, seeing who can deceive the most in a single evening. I wouldn't be surprised if the fae they laid with were the ones who revealed to everyone what had transpired."

"Well, I ain't going near one of 'em with a twenty-foot stick," Oscar grumbled. "I never saw much of the lot till now. Never had fae in our ranks, only heard they were no good. I would rather not learn that the hard way."

"No, you certainly do not."

Although it would be inevitable. Fae ensured any who crossed their paths had fearsome stories to share. Nightmares plagued William concerning his.

"But you stood up to one." Oscar sounded awe inspired. "To a shade, no less. You are brave, doc. I never learned much about shades, but I know they're not right, corrupt."

"They have strength we, and even their own kin, cannot fathom," Charmaine said, then swung an arm around Oscar's shoulders and pointed accusingly at William. "Do not take notes from William. He shouldn't have done that last night, so you should rethink idolizing his moment of insanity."

"Idolize? I, no, I just thought it was brave, is all."

William nodded. "Albie is right. Such behavior shouldn't be idolized, but never let a fae walk over you, either. Once you do, they will end you."

Oscar repeated the advice as if his words were gospel and the march continued on.

The Deadlands had a fitting name, for they came across nothing living, save the trees. A sea of evergreens stretched far and wide. Snow piled high. Clouds blocked out the sun, coloring the world a dull gray. Soldiers coughed and hacked. Medical officers ordered everyone to cover their faces. There was no telling what they inhaled, and the scent of sulfur grew during their trek,

"We've yet to cross any monsters," Charmaine said, voice muffled by the cloth wound around her face.

"With how many protected Lockehold, Fearworn likely assumed they didn't need more near the keep," William replied.

"Or they fled," Oscar said. "After what happened, they could have retreated and regrouped elsewhere."

"That could be true. I've heard Nicholas Darkmoon gained a tremendous artifact from Lockehold," Charmaine whispered, as if this gossip hadn't already spread through the troops. "A tome, of sorts, something very secret. The beasts may have known this and fled to their master. We're close. Not just to Fearworn, but to the end of this damned war. I can feel it."

"Are you sure that feeling isn't indigestion?" He winced when Charmaine pinched his earlobe.

"Don't mock me. Your optimism may be dead as a poisoned rat, but I carry mine wherever I go."

"I am more than aware of that, though that will not prevent me from reminding you we've been told for years that the war is almost at its end."

"And we never had a genuine reason to believe that until now."

He allowed Charmaine her hope. Not as if he could ever douse it, nor did he truly want to. However, Calix Fearworn went two decades with no one paying his devious plans any mind. Then almost another decade before he attacked both Terra and Faerie. Humans and fae finally agreed to fight together. Within all those years, Fearworn showed himself only when absolutely necessary. It's how he survived this long.

Even if they defeated Fearworn, the world changed forever. There are more shimmers, portals that once joined only Terra and Faerie. Fae call them scars, probably because they considered humans a scar upon their lives. Now, there are shimmers to the unholy plane Fearworn opened to summon monsters. Those portals will never close. Their lands will forever be infested.

Even his Mother, across the sea in Heign, suffered from an increase of monsters invading their backyard to steal cattle, ruin crops, and kill innocents.

William pressed a hand to his chest. Beneath his jacket, tucked in one of the interior pockets, was one of her many letters.

Matilda wrote to him often, far more than he replied. He knew that hurt her, but he ached after reading and asked himself if he remembered her voice correctly.

Am I terrible son if I struggle to remind them? He wondered.

Matilda always sprayed the letter with perfume, too. By the time the letters reached him, the scent had dulled. He barely got a whiff of honeysuckle, but when the aroma hit his nostrils, he had the urge to cry, to scream, to beg, and to run home. Fear overtook him because his family would not recognize who he became. He'd be reminded home hadn't changed, but he did, and life would never be what it once was.

Plucking the letter from his pocket, he flipped open the pages to read a fifth time. Matilda shared updates of their family. Arthur married two years back. They recently welcomed a daughter. He ached over missing his brother's wedding and the birth of his niece, but Matilda always wrote in great detail. Even that charming dolt, Richard, started courting a lady. Matilda and Robert hoped to receive news concerning an engagement soon.

The brief moments reading over her letters set him at ease. She did what she could to remind him of the home waiting for him. She ensured he didn't feel left out, that he knew his family and what they were up to, that he had a home to return to, and they were waiting for him.

Any comfort brought on by the letters shattered when a set of horns blared proclaiming the troops were to make camp.

The scouts discovered ruins of an old village once inhabited by the unfortunates who farmed these lands before Fearworn claimed it as his domain. Two of the buildings became the medical bay where William inspected soldiers suffering from fever, fatigue, and potential shimmer sickness.

Although the army didn't come across a shimmer for days, some were more sensitive than others. The affected became dazed and loopy, stumbling over their feet, forgetting to eat and drink. These were simple cases where giving them more food and water eased their symptoms. The more severe cases left people lying motionless in bed, as if the shimmer called for their souls and trapped them in limbo. The only solution was to take them far from any shimmers and hospitalize them. Most woke up eventually. Those who didn't passed slowly.

Between inspections, he took breaks to write Matilda back. He never shared much. It was doubtful his mother wished to know how many limbs he severed or fingers he reattached. The least he could do was let her know he was alive and pretend to be himself.

With the sun about to set, he worried he couldn't find the postmaster. Another soldier explained the postmaster refused to pass the Dread Peaks. Two soldiers volunteered to cart letters to the nearest town, but that would be the last of any letters. The generals wouldn't risk sending men on their own or force anyone to retrieve letters. Birds didn't work, either. All the messenger birds died when entering the Deadlands, an ominous omen for certain.

The soldiers in charge of tossing duffle bags into a rickety carriage were kind enough to allow him to write a swift note, informing his family they may not hear from him for some time. Then the carriage departed. He watched with an ache in his heart, wondering how he would survive this torture without news from home. In truth, he knew he would be fine, that he may even forget about not receiving the letters at all. And once more, he wondered what sort of son that made him, if he was an awful person.

"The insubordinate medic."

William rolled his eyes at the sound of Nicholas' grating voice, then faced the shade, smiling viciously as a rabid dog. "The little lord with a weak stomach," he replied. "How's the shoulder?"

"We'll see how weak my stomach is when I split yours open and wrench it out," Nicholas growled.

"Always resorting to violence, your kind never changes. You trick and deceive. Such pathetic minded creatures."

"Says the mortal living among those who make little sense."

William tilted his head. "Do you care to elaborate?"

"You send your men to war and leave behind half an army because of their genitalia?" Nicholas laughed, a low and foreboding sound reverberating in the back of his throat. "Are your men frightened that the women may outperform them? I heard tales of mortal men beating girls for going against your arbitrary rules."

"Don't speak of arbitrary rules as if fae don't have their own. Your kind isn't known for their caring demeanor toward anyone. They harm for the sake of it, even their own children. I would bet a shiny silver that daddy never hugged you, did he?"

"The constant need for so-called affections is a disease laid upon your kind, not mine."

"You consider any kind of affection a disease because you're incapable of it."

The tension between them was palpable. Though they marched with an encampment of thousands, not a soul stood nearby. Any who stumbled upon them surged in the other direction. Seeing the roseate embers of Nicholas' eyes and coral mist twisting about his form told all that he wasn't to be trifled with.

"I hoped to see you again." Nicholas took a step forward, allowing the heat emanating from his figure to wash over William. "Though I wanted it to be under different circumstances, preferably with you as a corpse at my feet."

"Is that what you're interested in? Corpses?" he chuckled. "Fitting for fae. You're as disgusting as you are delirious."

When Nicholas went for his neck, he caught the fae's wrist. The Sight revealed Nicholas' convoluted strings, blinding and blazing to the touch. He never witnessed anything like them. The world itself struggled to withstand Nicholas' presence. One brush of his finger against the strings and his skin hissed similarly to touching a heated kettle, but he caught that string and made Nicholas' arm fall limp. A swift shove from the shade's opposing hand sent him rolling across the snow.

With a few twists of his wrist, Nicholas' arm moved on command again.

"Numbing my arm? How quaint," the fae remarked, then snapped his fingers. The snow rose high and shifted into spears of ice. "The Collision Treaty prevents me from killing, but I've always been curious how far I can bend those rules."

"Bend them too far and the magic of your people will render you as a corpse you so love."

Nicholas' light raged. The shade called to magic as if he were made of nothing else. Power, pure as can be, circled him in violent waves of coral sparks.

"William!" Charmaine called, rushing into the mix. She skidded to a halt, brown eyes darting from the ice to Nicholas. "Uh, Lord Darkmoon, excuse us. We've been summoned to the medical bay."

"Tell your officers that William and I have important business to attend to." Nicholas clicked his tongue. Two spears flew. William rolled, dodging both, then a third struck near his head. The tip of the ice sliced his cheek.

"I fear we are needed immediately." Charmaine clutched his arm. She lifted him to his feet. Three spears of ice fired, hitting the ground where she nearly stepped. She cursed.

"Answer my riddle first and I'll let you go," Nicholas said with a wild glint in his eyes.

Typical of fae to be obsessive over one thing, then get distracted by other possibilities.

"Fine," William replied, but Nicholas waggled his finger.

"Not you." He pointed at Charmaine. "Him, and the medic cannot assist."

Charmaine stiffened. William bit back the urge to correct Nicholas. Oddly enough, fae honored the request of pronouns, but Nicholas would let the whole camp know about Charmaine's identity for the chaos.

"Okay, what is it?" Charmaine muttered.

"A mission I can have, but do not choose. I can save, provide, defend, or kill. What am I?"

Charmaine's attention drifted back and forth.

William had the answer, having been fond of riddles as a kid. Normally, a book of riddles called his bedside table home, but after being around fae all these years, he came to despise them.

"Tick tock." Nicholas sent another spear of ice that clipped her leg.

William grabbed the revolver at his waist. The next spear slammed beside him in warning. Charmaine's shivering intensified.

Nicholas took two steps closer. Snow drifted about his form. He became the center of an ice storm, little more than a pale silhouette in a wintery gale.

"You are boring me," Nicholas growled, eyes a sea of rose quartz. No longer beautiful, but deadly.

"A blade!" She screamed. "You're a blade."

The corner of Nicholas' vicious lips quirked, and he laughed.

William shoved Charmaine out of the way before the knife Nicholas formed hit her. The blade embedded itself into a crate behind them, and with that, they sprinted. Nicholas didn't follow. With the riddle solved, the fae relented.

They rounded a couple of tents, rotted fences, and old huts, panting from the sudden run. William stifled an idiotic laugh. Now wasn't the time for it, and yet, he often found his pulse racing in hazardous situations. That frightened him, and not in the way one may expect.

Charmaine pushed farther forward and hissed, "Have you gone mad? Why would you pick a fight with him? By the Holy Soul, I was almost impaled!"

"For starters, he picked the fight with me, and he wouldn't have impaled you, though he seemed insistent on testing if he could hurt you." He dusted the snow from his uniform while Charmaine slapped a hand against her chest.

"I suppose he is the mad one, but the moment he showed up, you should have excused yourself and be done with it. Treating a fae, let alone a shade, like that is not a good idea. He wished to torture you."

"Nothing he does could ever be worse than what I've already gone through. We both know what happens when those like us don't stand our ground. I'd sooner he torture me than bow to another ever again."

Charmaine frowned. Her words muted upon her lips.

He hadn't meant to stir up old memories. He didn't want to think of his training days, either. All he wanted was to forget. However, so long as they were among the desperate and dangerous, they couldn't let their guard down.

"Sorry. I didn't mean to raise my voice. Just...we especially cannot back down from fae." He set his hands on Charmaine's shoulders. "Those with haughty heads, like Nicholas, will perceive us as weak and they will do as they wish. I don't want to be put in that position again, do you?"

"Of course not," she whispered, gaze lowered. "But I don't want to attract their attention, either."

"It is too late for that. I attracted his attention the moment I shot him."

Her eyes pinched shut. "That was rather dramatic, wouldn't you agree?"

"No. You saw how swiftly he healed. He would have cut off that man's arm otherwise." Though the man in question didn't survive the night, anyway. William assumed Nicholas could sense death on the man, somehow, that it was why he risked injuring the soldier because he understood The Collision Treaty wouldn't harm him.

"Do be careful." Charmaine gave his arm a firm squeeze, then let go. "I can't lose you."

"Nor I, you. I promised to meet Charmaine in all her wondrous glory. I hear she's a lovely woman."

Charmaine giggled, sad yet hopeful. "She is, and she'll adore you."

"How splendid. After all, there is nothing I want more than a lovely lady on my arm."

With a playful shove, the tension dissipated, although he was not foolish enough to think that was the last he'd see of Nicholas Darkmoon.

4

Nicholas

Hovering spheres of fuchsia illuminated the tent. Nicholas brooded at a desk constructed of contorted tree roots, smoothed by his command. Papers lay scattered, notes he had taken, instructions from the mortal generals, and letters from his father lecturing him on taking drastic measures they never agreed upon. Nicholas' purpose was not to wade into the war zone but to give the generals dainty smiles and advice until the right moment. Laurent saw no reason to waste fae lives. Let the mortals wage war and the fae play their games, then end it all in one fell swoop.

Though Laurent never admitted this, Nicholas suspected he aspired for his family to end the war because that would look good on him, on all of Darkmoon. Laurent may have made bets with other fae, who would then owe him a terrible favor. Laurent loved nothing more than to be owed. Then there were the mortals who would view the Darkmoon family as saviors, perhaps even trustworthy enough to make deals with. They would be fools to think so, but mortals are damned by their foolishness.

It never mattered what Nicholas did though, his father always had complaints, so he never strived to listen. He tiptoed the line of a good beating. That was the only way he had ownership of himself. Besides, those letters couldn't hold his attention when battling against Fearworn's book of monsters. He began the translations the previous morning and barely made it thirty pages in. The language of High Fae was ancient, a tongue spoken by the first fae. A rare few remained, such as Laurent and Fearworn. Many offed one another in their violent display of strength or fell to a grave deal with another, more intelligent opponent. Laurent taught his offspring to speak the ancient tongue, if only to remind them of influence.

Fearworn's notes were indecipherable ramblings at first, but his focus returned when he opened a new scar within the Deadlands, though they weren't called that at the time. Nicholas couldn't recall the previous names, nor did he care. He sought how Fearworn fed life into his creations.

Arden entered the tent, a stack of papers clipped between his clawed fingers. "I have them."

Nicholas snatched the papers. "Did Blair catch wind of our snooping?"

"I do not believe so. I haven't seen her."

"Not seeing her doesn't mean she isn't watching."

"Do you want me to hold on to the papers until later, then?" Arden asked.

Nicholas pursed his lips. "No."

Smiling, Arden explained, "William Augustus Vandervult is the youngest son of Lord Robert and Lady Matilda Vandervult. He has three older brothers and was recruited at sixteen, thus serving in the war for five years. He was born and raised in Alogan, the capital of the Heign Kingdom, attending military training at their recruitment camp for a year where Marsha Montgomery, the current Head Medical Officer of the second battalion, surmised he had the Sight, specifically for medical purposes."

Arden chuckled at the terminology. Mortals had strange beliefs that he enjoyed berating. They believed magic to be so simple, gifted by mystical beings in their made up afterlife and ever so limited. To fae, magic simply was, no different than mountains, trees, and rivers. Magic is not a gift, it's a part of nature, and the limit was one's imagination and determination.

Nicholas sat the pages on his desk to flip through them. "How useful that power must have been for him. He was in the infirmary more often than not. A sick and weak child needed to heal himself lest he fall in the war to a mere infection."

"I believe there is more to it than that. I conversed with a few who served alongside him. William is known for standing up for himself and others, sometimes in violent manners. He has been reprimanded."

"He started fights?"

"I believe his past, combined with his lack of hesitation in shooting you, speaks volumes."

Nicholas' nail dug into William's portrait, scratching out the eyes, then tearing off the picture entirely. "Let us test how brilliant or violent of a mage he supposedly is."

Typically, Arden was always in for good fun. They met years ago at a revel that lasted a full thirty days and nights, hardly exchanging names before taking each other to bed. However, at this suggestion, Arden hesitated. Nicholas wasn't a fool to imagine why.

Laurent and Arden never mentioned a deal, but Arden greeted Nicholas first upon his arrival in Terra. Arden shadowed him ever since. Many owed Laurent and he always waited until the opportune moment to be repaid, so Nicholas suspected Arden's true concerns lied elsewhere. Even in another realm, his father tightened the noose around his neck, reminding him who had control and who would snap if they stepped out of line.

"What of the Collision Treaty?" Arden asked. "The consequences of breaking it are severe."

"We won't push too far. I merely wish to play a game."

"This game must be played with the utmost care."

Lest Laurent bring down his wrath on both of them. Nicholas considered his father's punishment if anything was taken too far. He thought of a cold, dank cell crushing him, walls too close, and little air to breathe. The sensation of being crushed, consumed by the earth itself, broken down into nothing and forgotten in the damp soil, little more than food for the worms. No one would mourn his loss. They would forget him easily enough, even his resting place, and he'd be lost to more than life, but also memory itself.

Nicholas choked back his thoughts. "Neither of us will cause any true trouble. Do not worry. I want my father's attention as little as you do. So, why don't you find us something fun to play with?"

Arden's concern shifted into intrigue. "I will be sure to impress."

Nicholas fell back in his chair of thorns, picking the spikes off one by one to pinch between his fingers. The blades drew blood that he wiped away with a flick of his finger. The dull prick of pain kept him occupied, otherwise he may break that cursed treaty.

After decades of Fearworn and his shadowed disciples not being taken seriously, they attacked Nicholas' home of Darkmoon and one of the mortal's capitals. All learned these were points where the distance between realms was thin. Fearworn sought to tear through them, to open pathways to a new realm, one potentially far worse than a plane of monsters. The shadowed disciples, followers of Fearworn as both mortal and fae-alike, dealt a devastating blow. Countless lives were lost on either side, but Fearworn didn't succeed in opening a portal that could condemn them all. That was the moment fae lords and mortal kings met and agreed to fight together. They devised the Collision Treaty between fae and mortals, ensuring one race did not kill the other. Though mortals have always been dimwitted, there were dozens of loopholes in the treaty.

So when Arden returned a day later to confess that soldiers were given a pint of wine as part of their daily rations, Nicholas knew he could cause a little trouble. The soldiers guarding the stash wouldn't deny him. They stepped aside when he approached the rations. He grabbed a random bottle and slipped two crushed amaryllis plants within. A poisonous flower that caused vomiting, diarrhea, and tremors, unpleasant but not fatal.

"Do you know of the medic William Vandervult?" Nicholas asked the guards.

One nodded and took the pint, aware of what had to be done unless he risked a fae's wrath. Some believed fae would snatch their firstborn, which could happen, but Nicholas wasn't all that interested after meeting a couple with three dozen babies that wouldn't stop crying and spitting up on the carpets. He never led any of the mortals to believe otherwise though since the possibility made them so compliant and he wasn't the type to forgo a good laugh.

Nicholas returned to his translations. He progressed slowly from the complicated text, accompanied by the excitement of what was to come. When Arden retrieved him later that day, he slid the book of monsters beneath his waistcoat and leapt. Together, they traversed the campsite toward the medical bay.

Through the windows of the old hut, William toiled between the soldiers with aching limbs or running fevers. Blood and dirt stained his uniform making the once dark green nearly brown in color. His pint of wine sat on a crate used as a makeshift table. Nicholas and Arden shielded themselves behind crates and an old fence across the pathway.

William sauntered over to his pint, but didn't drink. The medic set both hands on the mug, observant in his reticence, then stalked outside. Nicholas didn't bother hiding. His plan had gone amiss, so he stood and let William approach. The bastard's fingers twitched, then he downed the drink in front of Nicholas' vexed face.

Smacking his lips, William said, "Amaryllis. You'll have to do better than that."

He stifled the urge to grind his teeth. "I wanted to determine what you were capable of. I ensured you wouldn't taste or smell anything peculiar, so you're quite young to be such an adept healer."

"I'm a quick learner."

"Cocky, too."

"Says the little fae lord, playing games rather than working. Didn't you get your grubby hands on some important tome? That should have far more of your attention than a mere combat medic who spoke truthfully to you, probably for the first time in your life. Must be why you're so sensitive about it."

William grunted when Nicholas' nails formed a sharp blade to press against his neck. Arden barked a reminder of the treaty that Nicholas craved to burn, if it meant he could carve the skin from William's bones.

"You continue to bare your teeth at me. One day, I shall pluck them from your mouth one by one," he warned.

"One day? Why not cut my neck here? You so clearly want to," William goaded.

"Stop testing me. You don't have a gun this time."

"Don't I?" William grinned defiantly. He was an annoying beauty, like an ugly portrait one couldn't cease admiring for the longer they look, the more intrigued they became. Bewitched, even. Nicholas had the abrupt urge to grasp his neck and bite those treacherous lips. It was a strange thought, delirious even.

"You have your oaths," William continued as Nicholas' eyes swept over him in search of a weapon. The only visible tool was a knife all military personnel wore. "As imprudent as the fae are, the one thing they will not break is an oath, especially a magical one. I hear the results are unpleasant."

To say the least. The Collision Treaty marked fae for death if they slaughtered mortals, so William was not wrong. Fae made their deals and stuck to them. They simply found ways around their rules and Nicholas was already compiling a list of torments for William.

In Faerie, one did not speak ill of another without the thrill of knowing they may retaliate in a far more violent manner. It was part of the game they all played, waiting for a moment to strike, to rip and tear and break.

"This has gone too far," someone said, a face that had Nicholas squinting. Right, the one who interrupted them the other day.

Charmaine settled between them, forcing him to release William. She stood taller than all of them, glaring down at Nicholas with her lips set into a grim line. "Continue this and I will inform the generals. We are allies in this war. Start acting like it," she demanded.

"Lord Darkmoon would not be pleased to hear of any trouble," Arden whispered, even if his fingers twitched from the same chaotic yearning coursing through Nicholas.

William stood defiantly beneath his glower. A defiance others rarely showed. When they did, Nicholas' wrath followed them, swift and agonizing, neither of which he could do here. The challenge enthralled him and brought about a vicious wanting. William had this energy, a sensation he couldn't put his finger on, a magnetic pull now taut between them. He wanted to break it. He might have tried if a howling gale hadn't swept over the encampment.

Nicholas smelled the creatures first, a stench of sulfur, then two massive beasts, gray skinned and yellow-eyed with leathered wings, plummeted toward them. William cursed when two nails caught his left shoulder. Nicholas would relish in the sound if his torso hadn't been grabbed by the beast, too. Through the chaos, the second creature wreaked havoc. From the sky, Nicholas witnessed a leather hide swatting at soldiers becoming ant-sized in his vision. Two shadows battled the monsters that grabbed them, too, then lurched skyward to follow.

Wind hissed in Nicholas' ears. Drums rang. The world shrank. The camp disappeared, replaced by endless evergreens, then overcome by ashy clouds. Power surged within him, blinding and white hot, screeching like a dying animal. His elongated nails, harsh as steel blades, sliced the beast's front leg clean off. The beast yowled. Nicholas fell. The beast surged forward to catch him in its jaws. The serrated teeth crunched through his abdomen. Blood gushed. Bones cracked. The edge of his eyes watered. Each nerve sang in agony.

He jabbed the blade through the bastard's eye. The beast thrashed about, throwing Nicholas from side to side. The teeth tore further through his flesh. Skin hung from his bones in thin threads. He pressed both hands to the monster's cold muzzle. Fuchsia flames lit his fingertips and overtook the creature.

Among the blistering winds, William's petulant curses echoed. Then they fell and rose and fell and rose. The beast corrected itself, but the flames kept burning and Nicholas started tearing. The monster's wings gave out. They plummeted. Nicholas sunk his nails beneath the monster's mouth and yanked. The monster's good eye opened, gaze fierce and deadly. He leapt free from its maw, scarcely missing the snapping teeth.

One wave of his hand and the soil below lurched to meet him. A scream left his throat from broken twigs and thorns tearing at his leaking wounds. The earth settled, sparing him from the fall, but the creature flew at him. A figure dropped behind the beast, then those jaws came upon him.

Snapping, drooling, and bloodied, the monster stumbled forward on three legs. Blood pooled beneath a brawny body not set right, as if the creature's spine had twisted at the middle. The head cocked to the right and its wings were large, albeit slightly different sizes. A tail rose over its head, reminiscent of a spion. Acid spat forward.

Nicholas waved and a wall of thorns burst from the soil. The power of the acid disintegrated the roots. The acid burned the skin from his right shoulder and chest, now a festering wound of oozing puss. Darkness overcame his vision. He imagined falling asleep for a long nap to ease the suffering, but the guttural growl of a monster kept his eyes open. He would not die here to a mere monster hardly capable of a coherent thought.

Power danced over his fingertips. Roots slithered from the dirt to grasp the beast's legs. In the monster's moment of panic, Nicholas shot flames into its jaws. The beast reared back, screeching so loudly his ears bled.

Snow shifted to form a cloud of blistering wind around him. He sent a blast of ice that tore the beast's singed skin. Spears pierced limb and abdomen, but the beast wouldn't stop. It lunged at Nicholas, claws and teeth bared. He rolled out of its path. The ground shook when it hit. Trees toppled from its large body. Nicholas called for them. Trunks shattered into shards of bark, thousands of them all pointed at the animal. In a single swing, they skewered the monster.

Nicholas lay in the snow, resting a hand over his bloodied abdomen. The serrated teeth tore him to shreds, revealing muscle and bone. Then a gunshot rang through the air.

He jolted, wide eyes narrowly catching the beast's stinger writhing about. A green substance oozed from a wound along the head of the stringer pointed at him. William appeared from the forest, revolver moving from the stinger to the beast's head. He fired into the monster's skull. The beast twitched, then stiffened.

"You survived," Nicholas chortled.

Blood flowed from an injury on William's shoulder, where the beast grabbed him. Dirt and twigs got caught in his mussy hair. A bruise blossomed on his cheek and his uniform had been torn. Those eyes, as frigid as these lands, turned to Nicholas. William held death in his eyes, eerily beautiful. He glanced at his gun. William's finger twitched on the trigger.

"Nicholas!" Arden's voice spared him from the fate William planned. Dashing out of the forest, Arden slid to Nicholas' side. Grime covered his form. Behind him, William's friend followed, limping on a bloodied leg.

The breaths Nicholas took caught fire in his lungs. That fire roared, nothing like Power that gave him a twisted form of comfort, this bit and gnawed on his nerves, like a dog with a bone it wouldn't release. Colors blurred together. His consciousness bled out into the snow. Even his natural healing couldn't spare him, and Arden could not heal him. Most fae were not known for magic that helped others. His body battled against the acid, scarcely preventing the substance from eating clean through his bones.

"We can't travel with you like this." Arden turned his attention to William. "Medic! Be of use and help Nicholas."

"Why should I?" William knelt in front of his friend to inspect her leg. "That pointy-eared bastard burned that creature and almost myself in the process. Then he jumps on his own, leaving me to die, and you," William's deadly glare caught Arden. "Did you leave Albie to die, too?"

Arden didn't respond.

"See?" He scoffed. "I find it only fitting that we do the same. If he dies, he dies."

"William," Charmaine huffed. "We were brutally attacked. We're alone in unknown territory with no rations and another of these beasts trying to kill us. Four heads against that is better than two, wouldn't you agree?"

"Listen to your friend. He speaks sense," said Arden.

"Keep those vile lips of yours sealed," William spat. "The more you speak, the less inclined I am to listen."

Charmaine and William whispered to one another. Nicholas blinked, trying to focus. The world became a haze, silhouettes blurred and discolored. Then a shape loomed over him with eyes of dreamy green. The last thing he remembered was pain, a vexed medic barking orders, then silence.

5

William

They couldn't risk staying by a reeking carcass with a living beast searching for them and an injured fae. Even while Nicholas was unconscious, William's Sight struggled against his obstructive light. The strings tethered through him burned hotter than a campfire. Catching the strings between his fingers, William retreated with a frustrated hiss. No doubt the bastard would survive without help with that kind of energy swirling inside of him, protecting itself, but they couldn't risk waiting around.

"We can't stay here." William grasped Nicholas' shoulders. Charmaine took the fae's legs. Arden moved ahead, searching for a safer place to make camp.

Once they found a thicker grove of trees, Arden searched for a water source under William's orders. He didn't have his satchel full of herbs and potions. He had to rely on the Sight alone, hoping Nicholas' power would ease up so he could stitch the fae together.

"Will he live?" Charmaine asked from where they perched beneath towering pines.

"Yes, but I am not risking pushing myself for him. We will do some of this the old-fashioned way," he replied.

Those who didn't have the Sight saw magic as limitless. Those with the Sight understood magic as a muscle. The muscle needed to be worked, tended to, eased into strength, and used regularly or it would lose that strength. But like any muscle, push too far and that muscle shreds. Mages died reaching for more power than they had. That's why many used balancing agents. Fire mages carried lighters or matches to build flames rather than create a spark from nothing. Healers used natural healing remedies to enhance their abilities.

Arden returned carrying two full buckets made of smooth stone, a conjuring of strange fae magic. Water sloshed over the sides. He dropped them at William's feet.

"The water must be clean. Start a fire and boil it," William ordered.

Based on his snarl, Arden didn't take kindly to his tone, though did as instructed. Waving a hand, branches snapped from trees. Arden gathered the wood to build a fire. Charmaine snapped her fingers and fire sparked, biting at Arden's fingers. He cursed and may have shared a tart remark if he caught her cheeky smile.

Roots sprung from the soil to link above the fire, creating a pole to hang the buckets from. Charmaine encouraged the flames until the water boiled. Then she tugged the bucket over to where William situated Nicholas on his side, preventing the dirt from gathering in his wound. This wasn't ideal, but he had to run water over the wound to remove any remaining acid. He ripped the edge of his sleeve off to use as a rag. Also not ideal. He wet the makeshift rag and dabbed at the wound, then rotated Nicholas on his opposite side.

"What are you doing?" Arden bit when William retrieved his military knife. He held the blade to Charmaine. Fire crept over her fingers to heat the metal.

"I must cut the infested area out first. A scalpel would do better, but you fae heal quickly. I imagine a shade heals even faster." He took the blade from Charmaine and got to cutting.

"What is the purpose of healing mages who cannot heal?"

"I will not hear of that from a fae, creatures capable of almost purely destructive magic."

Stories said a rare few could heal among fae, typically those of such ancient lineage, all had forgotten from whence they came. The average fae naturally healed, capable of surviving deadly wounds, even regrowing limbs, so long as the injuries weren't from iron. For whatever reason, iron burned the fae, made their skin blister and wounds fester. Fae had such unnatural dispositions, but that disposition saved Nicholas' life. He would have died the moment the acid hit otherwise.

Arden muttered about worthless dregs, then fell silent. He should be more grateful. William did not intend to spare Nicholas. He was damn lucky Arden arrived, and Charmaine made an excellent point. They needed each other out here, even if he believed the world didn't need someone like Nicholas.

War is a product of individual choices. William believed the world would be better without certain individuals and created a list of those to be purged if the chance arose. His father, Robert, wouldn't be proud. He believed in compromise, in avoiding hostility at all costs. William wished he still did, too, but his father wasn't here, didn't see what he had, didn't live through what he had. At least that's what he told himself in the late nights when nightmares prevented any sleep, when his father visited to curse him for his misdeeds.

You said I'd learn to survive. I have for you, for Mom, for my brothers, but you wouldn't like what I've become, he thought.

"How far do you suppose we are from camp?" Charmaine gazed into the silent woods that a breeze wouldn't dare to disturb. The tree limbs stretched toward them like ghostly fingers calling to their souls, beckoning them to a world of sorrow.

"Those beasts were swift. We could be miles away, but the generals will have likely sent a search party," William replied. A party to save Nicholas more than the others.

Nicholas groaned and twitched. Charmaine held tighter, and he cut faster. A crack of thunder warned of a coming storm. The sky in the Deadlands remained solemn gray. None could predict from which direction a storm would come, or if it would miss them entirely.

"Conjure us a shelter," William ordered.

Arden's mouth twisted, warning of a cutting remark.

"We can't move further with all our injuries, and I don't think you want Nicholas waking soaked and covered in mud because you wouldn't set up shelter," William added. He didn't care if Arden enjoyed taking orders or not. If he knew what was best for him, then he would listen, and he did.

Vines breached the soil to coil around one another. By the time William finished removing Nicholas' damaged skin, a hut sheltered them. The vines rose in a dome shape, entangling themselves and their leaves. Charmaine lit the enclosure with a single flame flickering on the ground. The fire did little to warm them, but they couldn't risk more out here. None knew what may await them in the forest.

William healed what he could, biting his inner lip to stifle his annoyed groans. Every string he plucked, each gentle request he gave to his magic, was met by Nicholas' eternal fire. The tips of his fingers tingled like a sheet of paper repeatedly cut them. It was an irritating pain, but Nicholas' skin stitched little by little, preventing further bloodshed and infection.

Afterward, William pondered how to best bandage him. None of them had provisions. Arden had the cleanest jacket. He earned a handful of dry remarks for demanding the garment and tearing the fabric to shreds. When he instructed the fae to seek herbs, too, Arden had the rage of a killer in his eyes. Though he did not take a life, merely snorted and stormed off.

"Now, let us take a look at your shoulder. At least for my sake, please," Charmaine demanded once Nicholas had been bandaged and carefully laid on his uninjured side.

She hunkered beside William, peeling back the uniform to expose a gash from the front of his shoulder to the back. He stifled a yelp when Charmaine cleaned the wound. Now that the adrenaline died off, the pain emerged. His hand hovered over the wound. The gash stitched itself together. That's when William felt the tug, the warning of magic telling him to stop. He rolled his aching shoulder, knowing he would need rest before he healed anything else.

"I did not want to say so earlier, but I am fairly certain Arden used me as bait," Charmaine whispered. Her gaze shifted to the low opening of the hut. "The monster that grabbed us followed yours. When you fell, ours dropped, too. I jumped into a grove of trees that softened the fall, but I didn't see Arden anywhere, not until the beast bit me."

Charmaine glanced at her leg, where the beast caught her in its jaws. When they met earlier, five puncture wounds ran from her ankle to her knee. William sealed the wounds, but a gruesome bruise remained.

"When I thought the beast would kill me, Arden appeared. He dealt a head injury that startled it enough to fly off. Then we heard another monster howling and Arden went running," she finished.

"That isn't surprising. They're fae. We can't trust them. We may rely on each other to get out of here, but always expect the worst." When William said that, he didn't expect the worst to arrive so quickly, and as a dozen spions rather than murderous fae.

First came their familiar hissing sounds and the skittering of their legs through the pines. Charmaine and William leapt out of the hut. She thrust her revolver into his grasp. The fireballs forming in her palm would do more than well against spions.

The spions vaulted from branches and scuffled over the forest floor. Their webs sprang forth, landing in the space he previously occupied. He pivoted, catching the attention of one six-eyed fiend. The spion reared on its hind legs, stinger oozing poison and saliva slick on its fangs. Two more spions appeared at his side. In front of him, Charmaine roasted three with a wave of fire. The survivors shrieked and climbed the evergreens.

"Keep your eyes up!" He dashed for the spion in front of him. The spion sprang, as expected. They were lethal, not smart, and this would save on bullets.

Falling to his knees, he slid across the forest floor, blade up. The knife caught the spion's underbelly, its weakest point, and sliced clean through. The spion fell, legs still twitching. He jumped to avoid the webbing of the other two. The silk caught the tip of his boot. He wouldn't get that free, so he yanked his foot out. A stinger jabbed the empty boot.

With two on him, he pointed the revolver in the face of one and fired at the eyes. Their armor was unnaturally thick and sometimes required dozens of bullets to break through. Their eyes were the safest bet for a frontal assault. One shot and the spion fell. A pincher snapped at his wrist. William spun and dropped to a knee where he jabbed the revolver against its belly and fired.

Wailing, the spion hastily retreated. Another took its place, the stinger lurching forward. William felt the air graze by his cheek, mere millimeters from the poison. He sliced at the stinger. The blade didn't cut through armor, but the spion skipped backward from potential danger. Though Charmaine boiled a dozen, now scattered around the campsite, a dozen more sprang from the trees.

"Where are they coming from?" William shouted.

"We must be near a nest." Charmaine cupped her hands to her mouth and released a tower of flames, cutting through six more. Sweat trickled on her brow. They were exhausted. If they didn't end this soon, her magic would warn of catastrophe.

"Maybe that's why the damn fae is taking so long. He got himself trapped in a web." William would have laughed if he wasn't busy gutting another spion.

As if summoned, Arden sprinted into the campsite. A murderous wrath of vines and roots flared from his form, lashing out at nearby spions and slicing them to ribbons. His obstinate grin spoke of destruction. William ordered Charmaine to duck in time for Arden to spin the roots into a thin line, sharp as a blade, and sent them forward. The makeshift sickle sliced through most of the beasts. Two spions sprinted toward the forest. Lurching to her feet, Charmaine summoned a massive fire and swept the flames along. The fire hit their marks, cooking the spions instantaneously.

Charmaine spun on Arden, a fire encased hand pointing accusingly at him. "You could have killed us!"

"But I didn't." Arden spun daintily on his heel. "In fact, I saved us all. You're welcome."

"Where have you been?" William asked, gesturing for Charmaine to burn the silk from his stuck boot.

"Collecting herbs, as you wanted." Arden shoved a hand into his pocket to reveal a small collection of sage. "I couldn't find food, although we have enough of that now."

And none were happier for it, even Arden grimaced. Spion legs could be cooked, though they chewed like melted wax and tasted bitter no matter what one added to them. With their injuries, and not knowing how far to travel, awful food was better than no food.

"Then I heard the buggers," Arden continued. "First one or two, then more. I wasn't certain they were heading this way, but I turned back, heard gunfire, and here we are."

"You didn't come across a nest?" asked Charmaine. William held himself steady on her arm as he slipped his freezing foot back into its boot.

"No, not any sign of one either. No webbing or animal carcasses," Arden replied.

"Then what are they all doing here? I don't believe in coincidences, so they didn't happen upon us," William said, gazing about the forest. With the shade of the evergreens and oncoming night, shadows suffocated the woods and the threats waiting among them.

None truly knew what awaited them here. Once, the Deadlands had been farming villages known for their abundance of wool and grain. Then Fearworn had been chased out of Faerie and found his home here. The villagers weren't prepared. They had no idea what was happening until Fearworn raised the mountains and called forth storms to make a once fertile land desolate. So few escaped and their accounts varied that no information on the Deadlands was considered accurate.

"They could have heard that ruckus earlier with the beast." Arden waved a dismissive hand. "What does it matter? You said we can't risk moving. We'll cook these legs up. The fire mage and I can maintain a flame. One of us will always keep watch. That's the most we can do."

That was all well and good except another attack came by the following afternoon; two debraks rushed through the forest directly for them. William did not miss the horror in Arden's voice when one beast slammed their fist through the hut. Nicholas laid beneath the rubble, dirty and suffering from a fever, but unharmed.

By evening on the second day, fifty ratwings descended from the sky. The bastards reminded William of the monsters that carried them from the encampment, the leathered wings and long muzzles. Although, ratwings were about the size of a house cat with the body of a rat and the teeth of a shark. One took a nasty chunk out of Arden's arm. Another ripped the tip of Charmaine's ear off, and William damn near lost two fingers.

"We can't risk staying here any longer. These beasts keep coming. I've used all the sage on Nicholas, and it isn't safe for us to search for more.

We must be near one of Fearworn's cursed shimmers or you aren't telling us something." William pointed an accusing finger at Arden.

The fae pressed a hand to his chest, feigning offense. "I beg your pardon, but I have been of tremendous help, and you refuse to treat me with an ounce of kindness. Besides, moving Nicholas would be a poor decision with his fever."

"The fever broke this morning," William argued and took another gander at the sleeping fae.

Their healing capabilities were beyond his comprehension. Two days ago, Nicholas was on the brink of death. Any mortal would have died instantly. Now, he had little more than a bruise along his torso. The shade would have woken already, if not for the unusual fever.

William often dabbed the sweat from his skin, hating how, like this, Nicholas was more than tolerable. Fae were blessed with far too much. Wickedly handsome, a set of crimson lips that feigned sweetness, Nicholas Darkmoon had an aura of otherworldly beauty, ethereal enough to make one question if he were real. Of course, the fae always ruined his dastardly handsome face by opening his cursed mouth. Perhaps a shit personality was the price one paid for beauty.

"And yet he continues to sleep. Perhaps I should be suspicious of you." Arden's eyes flashed a more brilliant red. "Has the human taken this chance to seek revenge? Have you done something to keep him sleeping?"

"Don't be ridiculous. I wouldn't kill him with witnesses around."

Charmaine guffawed, and the flame in the hut flickered. "Can the two of you go one day without arguing? I beg of you. You're getting on my last nerve."

"And what will you do then?" asked Arden. "Throw a fireball at me?"

Charmaine took a loud crunching bite of a spion leg that made Arden grimace. He flinched with every loud crunch of her teeth and gagged when she chewed with her mouth open.

Arden ignored her and asked, "If you haven't poisoned him, why hasn't Nicholas awoken yet?"

"With that tone, I'd dare to say you care for him," William replied mockingly.

"Care is not a word within my vernacular. Nicholas must survive and thrive because he is one of the few who can defeat Fearworn."

"I will defeat him," a groggy voice spoke. Nicholas' eyes fluttered open. The once vibrant rose color dulled to an ashy pink hue, and his skin had a sickly sheen.

Arden assisted Nicholas into a seated position. He leaned against the wall of the hut, pinched eyes peering about.

"What happened?" he asked.

Arden knocked one of the water buckets against Nicholas' thigh. He dunked a cupped hand in to drink.

"You almost died against one of Fearworn's beasts," Arden explained.

"You likely would have died had Albie and I not tended to your wounds," William added. "And we've been under constant attack from monsters who seem exceptionally keen on killing you."

Nicholas cleared his throat. His voice held a deep huskiness from his sleep. "Of course, Fearworn wishes me dead."

"Yes, but only grumps have intelligence. The others are controlled by a shadowed disciple's will, so spions, debraks, and ratwings continuously falling upon us? That isn't a coincidence. They know we're here, somehow, so I suggest we move on."

"Moving on won't do much good."

"What do you mean by that?" Charmaine asked.

Arden leaned against Nicholas to whisper in his ear, a desperate hand clutching his bicep. If the bastard thought anything of Arden's warnings, he revealed nothing. The shade kept his gaze on William, lips parted to show the pointed canines behind.

"Answer my riddle correctly and I'll tell you why the monsters are appearing." Nicholas smirked. Even the previously miffed Arden got a sparkle in his eye from the mention of a riddle.

"Now is not the time for games," William argued.

"This is no game. It is a riddle. What learns but cannot read, is moved but also confined, and all of us hide?" The gaze Nicholas shared belonged to that of a child discovering starlight for the first time. The excitement grew every second that passed without an answer, with the possibility of having stumped William.

"The mind," he replied, rolling his eyes when Nicholas clapped.

"Oh, delightful. That was easy, here's another—"

"You said you would tell us about the monsters if I answered correctly."

Nicholas' shoulders deflated and lips pursed into a pout that William looked away from unless he admitted something regretful.

"You spoil my fun, but fine, attacking Lockehold wasn't merely about taking the stronghold. My kin have always kept watch over the Deadlands. They heard of a shadowed disciple among Fearworn's ranks called The Creator. Fearworn supposedly conjured ideas of monsters and this Creator assisted in stitching them together. That same Creator traveled to another scar outside of the Deadlands and was returning, thus passing through Lockehold. None of us wanted to miss the opportunity, so we laid siege, and I burned that Creator to ash. Now," Nicholas plucked a leather-bound book from the interior of the jacket Charmaine gave him during his fever. She and William shared confused looks about how the book got there. Damn fae tricks.

"I have Fearworn's book of monsters that has a mighty aura. Not one a human would notice, but shadowed disciples and monsters might," Nicholas declared.

"Book of monsters." Charmaine pressed a hand to her bruised leg. "So those beasts that grabbed us from camp?"

"Likely written about in these pages, although I've barely begun the translations. From what I've read, Fearworn has summoned new beasts from the scars, but nothing of the magnitude that we saw. He's creating a fucked-up puzzle constructed of monster parts and testing their capabilities" Nicholas had such an intense intrigue in his eyes that one could drown. "How thrilling."

"This is far from thrilling," William snarled. "If he succeeds in creating an army of new beasts, we'll lose so much of what we've achieved. This war may continue another decade and there is no telling who the winner will be."

"Exactly. Thrilling." Pressing a hand to the wall, Nicholas rose on unsteady feet. "Though it burns me to admit, I owe you a life debt, William Vandervult."

"I want nothing from you."

"Regardless, you are owed." Nicholas caught William's gaze. He believed, for a moment, that Nicholas would divulge how he would have taken his life had Arden not arrived. Instead, the fae continued, "I will repay my debt when the time arises. Now, where is the monster's corpse? I must examine it."

"Have you gone truly mad?" William barked, incapable of comprehending the fae's stupidity. "We are under constant attack because of that book. The other beast is out there, and you want to return to the rotting corpse?"

"Yes. It's invaluable. The beast had to be of Fearworn's creation. It may help me understand more of the journal and what both our armies may be up against in the future. This is worth the risk." Nicholas tossed Charmaine's jacket onto her lap. He exited the hut with remnants of his shirt clinging to his wide shoulders and Arden in tow.

"This is an utterly poor decision," Charmaine muttered.

"Fae are known for them," said William, as they begrudgingly followed anyway.

6

William

A THICK FOG HUNG over the forest, unnatural and creeping further up the trees. The snow never ceased, reaching to William's knees and biting through his nerves. They wouldn't risk Charmaine's flames, not in the open where something may see them. They came upon the monster's corpse laying broken among shards of evergreen. Paw prints led to and from the heap of meat. Creatures feasted upon the carcass over the days. Once white snowflakes melted into red pools. Teeth shredded and devoured much of the beast's gut. Rib bones peaked through a leather hide. The tail had been ripped off entirely, strewn about the area in pieces, and a familiar stench encircled the corpse.

"Sulfur," William noted under his breath. He smelled it as they marched through the woods. That gave him a nagging suspicion that the scent didn't come from the Deadlands, but from the beasts themselves. They could have circled the encampment, waiting for an appropriate time to strike.

Charmaine slipped away, showing interest in the monster. He kept a watchful eye on her and the two fae circling the carcass. Nicholas approached the creature, eyes alight in a vastly uncomfortable manner.

"Fearworn saw use in the ratwings." Nicholas observed one of the wings so thin it was nearly transparent. Two claws sharpened to razors decorated the ends of each appendage. He pinched one claw between his fingers as if he suspected it secreted poisons like the stinger. They did not, and he dropped them.

"Creating a flock of flying beasts to dive on an unsuspecting army is a tactic he would use," Nicholas added. "Certainly would do more damage than even a hundred ratwings."

"But why did this one shoot acid and not the other? The beast had every opportunity to fire upon me, or the mortal." Arden inquired from somewhere behind the corpse.

Neither were surprised that Arden didn't recall her name. She made an offensive gesture behind his back.

"I suspect these are monsters in the work, not quite perfected." Nicholas lifted a hind leg that looked far too big for one of his size to hold. Fae had unnatural physical abilities, capable of wielding substantial weight as if it were nothing. Nicholas leaned closer, inspecting the area.

Grimacing, William muttered, "Why are you staring at the monster's groin?"

"Because it doesn't seem to have genitalia."

That caught his attention even if he loathed to admit it. William shuffled forward. The beast had a smooth backside, save for a rectal area. Nicholas dropped the leg and his nails grew into sharp spears.

"You may want to step back. This will get messy," Nicholas warned.

"Guts do not bother me."

"What does?"

"Nothing I will ever share with you."

Snickering, Nicholas cut further into the beast's abdomen. The stench grew. More innards and blood oozed onto the forest floor. After a moment of squishy inspection accompanied by soft murmuring, Nicholas retreated.

"I don't see reproductive organs either, which I doubt Fearworn wants. He needs beasts to multiply on their own to grow an army," he declared while waving his arm. The filth splattered on the ground and evaporated from his arm in a wave of bubbling heat.

Charmaine peeked over the head of the creature. "Are we certain he created this one and did not pull it through the shimmer?"

A century ago, the world suffered terrifying weather, droughts, deadly storms, and spontaneous volcanic eruptions. Then the shimmers appeared. Mages declared the weather had resulted from Terra and Faerie realms colliding, like two glass globes scorching from the kiln knocking against each other. Rather than separating, they clung, and the broken bits let the worlds seep into each other.

Fearworn learned how to reach into another world through small shimmers at first. Monsters slipped through, equally small and not worthy of worry. But as Fearworn's power grew, so did the shimmers. Soon, monsters such as spions, debraks, ratwings, and grumps—technically called gitans, but their grumpy faces had mortal soldiers referring to them as grumps—made it into both Terra and Faerie. It would not be odd for Fearworn to have discovered more beasts. In fact, it would be stranger if he didn't. If the monster's realms were even half the size of Terra and Faerie, there had to be more species, potentially worse ones.

No one had ever gone to this dark plane Fearworn opened, at least no one survived to the tell the tale. The mortal kingdoms forbade anyone from mimicking Fearworn. No one knew what other realms were out there, what opening a shimmer to them could do, so the possibilities remained unknown, and William hoped it stayed that way.

"I seriously doubt this beast came from a scar." Nicholas climbed a hind leg to strut along the monster's crooked spine. "This beast is not well. With such a mangled spine, it probably wouldn't have survived much longer either. The wings are mismatched, too. Do you recall the look of yours?"

Arden pondered a moment, giving Charmaine a chance to reply. "It had two legs instead of four and struggled to walk. I don't recall a stinger on its tail, either, which may explain why it didn't fire on us."

"Both misfits, both likely initial creations and thus expendable for him," Nicholas claimed, then slipped the book from his tattered shirt.

William wished the fae would cover himself to not entice further unwanted staring. But the cold didn't even cause goosebumps to break across his flawless skin, so William was stuck reminding himself that Nicholas was a rotten bastard, nothing worth admiring. If only his eyes listened and would cease straying toward Nicholas' chest and the black hair descending from his navel.

That's how fae brushed past a mortal's fears. Though tales of fae were known far and wide, each more gruesome than the last, mortals continued falling for their trickery. Deceit had been woven into their very essence, into every hair and breath. Mortals looked upon them enviously and fell for their charms regardless of the warnings fed to them from childhood.

Matilda told William a few, one of a woman yearning for love. She promised the fae under her floorboards that she would weave the most beautiful blanket for their family to sleep in together in exchange for a man to love her. The fae agreed. She spent sixty days and nights constructing their blanket. On the sixty first day, she woke to the blanket gone and a man knocking at her door. He was of low noble birth but had enough to keep them secure. She had her love, but as the days went by, the man became possessive. She couldn't leave without him latching onto her person. He grew jealous of anyone she spoke to, claiming he loved her so fiercely he couldn't accept she had any others in her life, for any reason. By the end of the year, she so feared his love she risked running away in the dead of night. But her husband caught her fleeing and said he would rather die than lose her. The next morning, the staff found them hanging in the foyer together, the screeching of the ropes unable to cover the laughter in the floorboards.

Fae always delivered more than any bargained for.

Nicholas leapt off the beast to flip through the pages of Fearworns' journal, glancing continuously between the two. A frenzied glint flooded his eyes. "I have not stumbled across their kind in the book yet, but I am sure they're here."

"You truly are excited by all this," William grumbled, unsettled by the memory of his mother's story. He never discovered if the tale had been a myth or the truth, but after the time spent around fae, he believed the tale couldn't be entirely false.

"Are you not?" Nicholas shot him a perplexed look. "Your heart races."

"We're in unknown territory waiting for monsters to attack."

"Which you handled fine until now, so I don't see them as capable of frightening you."

"Your belief in me isn't the least bit flattering."

Nicholas chuckled. "Think what you must, but I will not deny that this is the most fun I've had in my short life."

"I'm continuously baffled by the humor fae find in the face of pure evil. Do you not appreciate life because you're needlessly gifted so much of it?"

"You are always so touchy." Nicholas slammed the book shut to hide beneath his clothes. He breached William's personal space, hands on his hips, and voice a whisper, "I sense you do not have many fond memories of fae."

William recalled a horror that visited him on the worst nights. A place of heat and smoke, the echoing of screams, chittering of spions, and fae laughter, conniving and cruel as the damned. The noise ripped at his eardrums, like needles piercing the tender flesh. He remembered running, a moment where he spoke to the Holy Soul after many years, begging for the moment to not be real, but deep down, he knew begging was pointless. Gods were not real, and neither was mercy. The chance of a sweet future withered away in front of his tearful eyes.

He learned to hide all of that behind a mask of apathy and a brisk voice. "Your senses are correct. I do not have fond memories of fae, especially considering one would have let me fall to my death the other day. Another used my friend as bait, and I've been on the field enough to witness the joy fae get out of torture."

"What's wrong with a little torture?" Nicholas laughed and might have honestly expected William to answer. When he didn't, Nicholas circled him like a hawk stalking prey. "Fine, humor me. What do you like to do?"

William wasn't so certain anymore. Normalcy hadn't been a part of his life for many years, but he recalled what he used to favor as a boy, safe and loved in a tender home. He hoped to keep those interests, hoped to see and feel them one day, that he could be that kind and oblivious boy again, innocent and naive.

"I like to tend to the garden, knit at my mother's side, read a good book, and take long afternoon naps after a warm cup of tea," he replied.

"How unexpectedly tame. What of bloodshed? Of the adrenaline on a battlefield? Of liquor during a grand celebration?" Nicholas hesitated at his back. His breath tickled the shell of William's ear as his voice shifted into a low purr, "What of a good fucking?"

William caught the wild glint in Nicholas' roseate eyes. The promise of danger and taunting destruction.

"I do not thrive in the face of death because I am so bored with my pathetic life, though I do enjoy a good fucking. I didn't think to mention it, as you wouldn't know what that is," William replied.

"A bold assumption I should be given the opportunity to disprove."

"So you can tell everyone afterward that I'm a traitor and laugh as they hang me? How dull do you think I am?"

Nicholas laughed. "Oh, I find you unbearably pedestrian."

"The simple mind of a child would think that way."

"Maybe you should act more like a child. Seek fun outside of testing my patience." Though Nicholas growled, amusement strangled his tone, and his attention fell across William in a slow and methodical manner.

"I am not in any position to be childish, unlike a certain coddled prince," William replied, disliking the attention entirely, and yet, he couldn't stop. He wanted to goad Nicholas further, push him to the edge, see what would make him stumble.

"Prince? Fae don't have monarchies, though I am flattered by such a lovely title," Nicholas mocked.

"I am well aware, and yet your kin treat you with a safe distance that others do for our royalty, which is by no means flattering. Quite a few of our royals have met an unpleasant demise, beheaded or worse by their own people." William's gaze swept over the beast to Arden. The fae prodded at the stinger with his foot, unaware of the attention. Then William's gaze landed on Nicholas, who strengthened at his next accusations. "You're prince-like, pretentious, juvenile, moronic, and infuriating."

"Have you met many princes to come to these conclusions?"

"I know enough to make an educated guess."

"You're quite insufferable yourself." Nicholas brushed his knuckles along William's cheek, gentle, unlike his low voice. "Every moment I yearn to hear your screams."

"My screams are one of many things you will never have."

The gleam in Nicholas' eyes stated he was about to test that theory when the forest rustled. In the stillness of the Deadlands, any noise caught their attention. The sound of crunching branches and a low growl spoke of violence.

"We should leave," William said, breaking away from Nicholas. He hurried to Charmaine, where he grabbed her arm to make haste toward the forest.

To their surprise, Nicholas and Arden followed. A couple of steps between the trees and a howl reverberated through the foggy terrain. Certainly not any wolf, that noise belonged to a much larger creature. Charmaine's eyes met his. Fear embedded itself within her wide pupils. The howl sounded too near and unfamiliar. It could be the surviving beast that caught them or another, a bigger one that Fearworn had yet to reveal. William had no interest in meeting the creature.

"Can we risk returning to camp?" Charmaine muttered, keeping a close eye on the forest and what may hide within.

"Why would we?" Arden bit.

"Food, idiot," William replied. "We have enough dried spion legs to last a couple of days."

"We're likely to run into more."

Charmaine shivered. "That is not a good thing."

"Keep quiet," Nicholas ordered. The group strained to hear thudding steps growing closer. "Returning to camp is an unnecessary risk. We move on. Now."

William clicked his tongue. Something about Nicholas gave him an attitude. "Is the big bad shade frightened of a few monsters?"

"We now know Fearworn has beasts we've never seen. There is no telling if he has more, how many, or what they are capable of. Yes, even I can be overrun by enough teeth and fangs," he replied.

Nicholas snuck through the trees, ducking under low branches and keeping to the shadows. The others followed, with Arden taking up the rear. Fae steps rarely made noise. They didn't now. William and Charmaine did their best, but nothing truly prevented the snow from crunching beneath their boots.

The snarling lessened the longer they trekked. None uttered a word, though William and Charmaine's breathing grew ragged, and steps slowed as the day slogged on. After the fog dispersed and the sun slipped toward the horizon, the shape of a building emerged, followed by another. William tapped Nicholas on the shoulder. The fae gave him a cursed look, then followed where he pointed. Nicholas took a careful step forward and another. Closing in, a town materialized, or rather what was left of one.

Young trees sprouted from the grove, shorter than those encircling the rubble. Snow buried the decrepit bricked facade, covering portions entirely. The houses decayed, overgrown by withered vines and roots, each leaning at odd angles, their foundations threatening to give out. Roofs collapsed, doorways caved apart, and walls crumbled. Steeples for three cathedrals struggled to touch the sky. A vast road led to the center of a town where a fountain froze over. Not a single soul lived there, monster or otherwise.

"We can camp here tonight," Nicholas said.

"Is that a good idea?" Charmaine's teeth chattered. "This place is abandoned for a reason."

"Yes, because shadowed disciples inhabited these lands. The people either fled or died decades ago." Nicholas nodded to Arden. "Let's search the buildings and find one suitable for a night's rest."

The fae moved without considering the thoughts of others. Charmaine had a face of displeasure equal to the sensation prodding William's chest. A foreboding aura encapsulated the village, warning trespassers, promising to become their grave. He wasn't sure if that sensation was true or it felt that way because he knew, once, this village had been lively. People lived here, like him and Charmaine, happy and oblivious to the misfortune and chaos Fearworn would bring upon them.

"I would like a roof and preferably four walls tonight. We could risk a fire, beat back this cold," he finally said, huddled against Charmaine's side. The previous attacks tattered their attire, and with the sun setting, the chill worsened. He wasn't interested in losing any of his extremities to frostbite.

Charmaine huffed. "I would too, but I still find this to be an atrocious idea."

Regardless, they entered the town together.

7

Nicholas

As if built to house the dead, the abandoned town sat desolate, eerie, and silent. The Dread Peaks spotted the skyline, reminding all the poor souls they were trapped. The townsfolk understood a gruesome fate awaited them the moment Fearworn raised those mountains. That was why Arden and Nicholas stumbled through a dozen homes containing aged remains. Bones lay beneath withered nooses or families huddled together in corners. The ones who didn't see an escape made their own.

Nicholas shuffled about wardrobes in search of attire. While the cold of Terra held nothing against the winters in Faerie, he had no interest in returning to the army looking like shredded paper. He had a reputation to uphold, strikingly good looks requiring equally beguiling clothes. Though none of the villagers had more than dated moth bitten robes. He settled on a dusty maroon blouse. Bugs and rodents gnawed at the sleeves, but he rolled them up to his elbows. A loose ribbon along the neckline of another shirt worked well to tie his mussy hair into a short ponytail.

"We should abandon them," Arden said. "The mortals are worthless to us now. We can find the army on our own. If they die on their way back, that's on them."

"We would be quicker on our feet without them," he muttered, imagining the rage burning within William's frostbitten eyes.

"And we'd be without their annoyance." Arden ambled behind Nicholas to grasp his waist. "You seek revenge against the medic. This is revenge. We leave them here to rot and be on our way."

"Thinking of them frightened and moments away from death does bring me tremendous joy." Though he would be remiss not to witness William's demise in person. The mere mention of his name fanned a spark that wouldn't disperse from the edge of his mind. A place William infiltrated and made his own with a few irritating conversations. Frowning, he hated admitting, "But if we run into more of Fearworn's creatures, or the bastard himself, a healer would be helpful."

"Mortals are hardly healers without their precious herbs and potions, neither of which he has on hand. The Sight," Arden snorted. "Can you believe they call their magic that? And yet they see so little. It's practically worthless and the longer we're out here, the more likely there is of an attack. We leave them and we return to camp sooner."

"You find them so intolerable to risk that?"

"Do you not?"

They could be an annoyance, but William was an attractive one. Nicholas found the miraculous view worth the disturbance. However, he did have a book to decipher, which he could not do here, and Laurent would have his limbs snapped one by one if he lost the book.

"So be it," he agreed, while rubbing a hand against Arden's arm. "We'll abandon them, but we should find a home to rest in for a few hours. My wounds are healed, but I remain weary. We'll leave them to their fate before dawn."

With a plan set, the fae continued their search for a suitable home. A house near the center of town held up the best. The roof hadn't caved in and the door not only shut but also locked properly. Not a ward against colossal beasts, but could prevent unwanted small critters or recently hatched spions from entering. Though small, they were born with many siblings and could kill with a few jabs of a poisoned stinger.

Arden handled the smashed windows, blocking both with multiple layers of vines. Charmaine and William found firewood and Charmaine lit the hearth. The flames eased the crispness from the room. Arden and Nicholas retrieved ice from the fountain. He sat the buckets in the backroom, what used to be a washroom.

"The mortals can wash up first," Arden declared. "I can no longer stand the stench."

"Are you certain the stench isn't your own?" William replied, earning a twisted snarl from Arden. Nicholas bit back a laugh. He wouldn't want the medic to think himself funny.

William and Charmaine swept to the backroom where she heated the ice into steaming water. Arden laid on the remains of a bed in the corner. The legs had shattered, and the frame rotted, but a dingy mattress stuffed by hay survived. Nicholas was about to join him when movement caught his eye. The washroom door didn't close properly. The hinges squeaked as it opened halfway. Steam encircled William, who sat his dirtied shirt on an old cabinet.

Nicholas ran lustful eyes over William's delectable form, the kind he'd love to get his greedy hands on. William stood with his front facing the door. His calloused hand ran a wet rag over his powerful shoulders. Water followed the curves of scarred a chest, over a pink nipple Nicholas had the abrupt urge to capture between his teeth. Further and further, the water crept down his abdomen to disappear within the golden curls above the hem of his pants. Pants Nicholas yearned to slip off those pale thighs, to feel every muscle twitch and shiver beneath his feverish touch. That would be interesting; a way to see something other than exasperation or apathy in William's eyes, to make him desire for that which he hated and relish in his turmoil.

Then William caught his predatory gaze. Nicholas smirked, and the medic kicked the door shut. Pity. He certainly was the type Nicholas wanted beneath his sheets. The medic's foul mouth would make for a much better use there.

A couple moments passed before Charmaine and William emerged, hair damp and skin cleared of most dirt. A heavy musk hung over them, something this land wouldn't let them be free of. While Charmaine announced the fae could wash up, William approached Nicholas to spit, "I know fae lack most of public decorum, but do they not understand privacy either?"

"What's wrong?" Nicholas's eyes passed over William's taut form. "Worried I may have been disappointed by what I saw?"

"Worried you liked what you saw."

"Are you truly so confident about making such bold assumptions?"

"If you didn't, then say so." William waited. Nicholas couldn't lie. No fae could, so he didn't. "Keep your eyes to yourself, bastard." Then he brushed by, ensuring to slam his shoulder into Nicholas'.

The shade bit back a snarl and hated himself for allowing his eyes to stray to William's backside. Yet another potential gem obscured by unappealing clothes.

Nicholas strolled after Arden into the washroom. Afterward, Charmaine agreed to take the first watch. Arden would follow, then William, then Nicholas, although the fae planned to depart before all of that.

Nicholas slept on the remnants of the bed, waiting for Arden to wake him. Quiet mumbles stirred the sleeping shade some time later. He woke to a dim fire. Arden lounged in one of the surviving chairs. William sat in the far-left corner of the house, his back leaning against the stonework. Charmaine slept on the floor next to the hearth.

"Did we not agree for one to keep watch? We all need our sleep," said Nicholas.

William glared, probably because Nicholas didn't bother whispering and the bed creaked with his movements. He slipped off and stretched. Charmaine stirred, but didn't wake. That didn't lessen William's annoyed attention. Nicholas' lips quivered into a smile, always proud to irritate most, but especially William.

"We've been under constant attack. I figured it would be best for all of us if two kept watch," the medic replied.

"Because of the monsters or us?" He gestured toward himself, then Arden. "Frightened one of the fae found a loophole in the treaty and would cut your throat in your sleep?"

"No, although I had a strange thought that two cowardly bastards may abandon Albie and I in the perilous woods with no provisions and monsters on our tail. Certainly that wouldn't have happened, would it?" William's eyes dared either of the fae to speak.

Nicholas dropped onto the floor beside him. William tensed when their arms brushed. He did it on purpose to get William's reaction. They always riled Nicholas up in one way or the other and he found himself incapable of resisting the pull, something almost hypnotic called him to William.

"Isn't that what you wanted, for us to separate?" Nicholas argued.

"I wish, but Albie was right. Four of us are better than two, even with that cursed book, although you may not think the same."

"You're annoyingly attentive," he said. His eyes admired the lines of William's firm jaw and the ample curves of his neck that would look wonderful marked by Nicholas' lips.

"I've learned to expect the worst, particularly from those like you."

"We could still leave. Neither of you can keep up with us at our swiftest," Nicholas warned.

"If you're intent on being foolish, then do so, but don't come crawling back when you meet trouble."

The tense air between them bristled and shifted. Nicholas didn't look away, as if the two shared an unspoken battle that whoever broke eye contact first lost. He hated losing, especially if it was against William. The mortal irked him in every way, but he didn't want the evening to end. He wished to sit here, testing how far he can push. See if William would dare to raise that revolver at him again, like he wanted to the other day. See what other reactions he could provoke that William never expected to show, that was a victory in his mind.

Nicholas waved a dismissive hand at Arden. "Take your rest. We are not leaving this evening."

The creaking of the floorboards then the bed informed him Arden had obeyed. William kept his undivided attention. Jade eyes reflected the glistening flames, but Nicholas had never seen a look so unbearably bitter and bleak.

"There's a coldness to your eyes, William. Has anyone ever told you that?" He brushed a stray hair from William's brow. He snickered when the tip of a knife pressed against his neck. Iron, the most efficient way to kill fae. His skin blistered beneath the blade.

"You are becoming far too familiar for my taste. Move aside," William warned.

"But I like this." Nicholas pressed forward, uncaring of the blade sizzling against the thin skin of his neck. William remained still, not giving him so much as a twitch. Eyes as cold as before, in the forest where Nicholas saw Death for a brief moment. "You don't tense easily," he whispered.

"Shall I congratulate you on stating the obvious?"

Nicholas leaned back. William let the knife rest against his leg. His knuckles remained bone white along the handle, prepared to strike. Nicholas wished he would. He wanted to see what William would do, what they could do together.

"Tell me, what would make the little wolf tense?" he asked.

"A cup of bad tea." William's blatant disregard and distant demeanor made Nicholas want to break him more. The game had been set, and he thirsted for the sweet taste of triumph.

"You are no fun, won't share anything with me. At least keep me entertained. I sense neither of us will get any more sleep this evening."

"You seem more than entertained right now."

Nicholas snapped his fingers. "Let us have a game of riddles. I will make the first simple."

William's defiant disapproval was ignored.

"We do not wish to meet, but always will. What am I?" Nicholas kept his excited eyes on William, momentarily confused by the sudden interest.

"Death," he said confidently. "And you stole that from Martha Middle's Book of Riddles."

Nicholas shouldn't have been surprised. The information Arden retrieved proved William came from what humans called a refined upbringing. He understood some families had better education than others. Fae knew of no such things. Knowledge could be found by those who sought it. A hag residing on the edges of Darkmoon built a library within the forests said to have a copy of every text in existence. Nicholas knew of no one other than her to have read every piece, perhaps because some ventured into the woods and were never found. The hag always laughed and claimed they must have lost themselves in a good book, but Nicholas always believed she trapped them so she could cook them up for a meal.

"You have read her works, then?" Nicholas hummed. "I quite enjoy her fables, too. Impressive for a mortal."

William gave the first sign of life outside his indifference by feigning a gag of disgust. "I despise that we have anything in common."

"What a joy to hear because I imagine we have quite a lot in common, son of Lord Robert and Lady Matilda Vandervult."

Nicholas found it, a knick in the armor, albeit small. William's eyes shut, suppressing an emotion, then opened, showing nothing, and his voice remained level when he asked, "Am I meant to be flattered by your invasive intrigue?"

"Perhaps. I like to know what I'm up against, and I will admit that you are intriguing."

"Hearing that from you is rather insulting."

"How much have you spoken with them, your parents and brothers?"

"How much do you speak with yours? I hear fae don't hold family relations to high esteem, that they do the bare minimum and are, more often than not, cruel and malicious." William countered, not allowing Nicholas to dig deeper. He was skilled at turning a conversation.

"Compared to that of human expectations, certainly not. We do not require coddling."

His words held a semblance of truth, otherwise he couldn't say them. Fae and mortals differed in many ways, their family expectations being one of them. Nicholas didn't know a family like humans did; the ones who spent a day dedicated to celebrating their birth, joining around a dinner table for good food and mirth on a religious holiday, or missing a sibling because they hadn't seen one another for a few days. However, fae had their traditions varying from creature to creature.

Sirens, for example, would sing for seven days and nights when a loved one died. Their voices, usually eerie, became so sorrowful nature wilted at the riverbanks, as if to mourn with them. They laid their dead on lily pads and surround them with keepsakes, precious stones found on the bottom of the riverbed or trinkets lost by swimmers.

Redcaps, while vicious and violent, were even worse if any threatened their young. It didn't matter who the child belonged to. If any dared attack a young, the Redcaps moved as one. They protected their own with a ferocity like no other.

Nicholas wasn't so certain what traditions his family had other than disdain and avoidance. They had their revels, like any other, but they were nothing more than loud parties where they drank themselves into oblivion. He dared to consider for a moment what it would be like to celebrate, as humans did, to wake one morning to them celebrating his birth rather than cursing his existence.

Nicholas dispersed such ridiculous thoughts and focused instead on the task at hand, one he better understood. "Tell me how such a fragile child who spent so many days in the infirmary became," he waved a hand toward William. "Like this?"

"Do specify."

"A walking sexual frustration."

His hopes of a blush were dashed when William responded nonchalantly, "Puberty." Then the mortal shared a wry grin. "Since you adore games, why don't we play a new one? Let's see who can remain quiet the longest."

He faked a yawn. "Even your idea of a game is boring. What if I share information as well?"

"Not worth it, as I am not interested in you."

"You try so hard to wound me."

"I wish for nothing more."

Those words were another string for Nicholas to grab. He settled closer. He did not miss the darkening of Wililam's eyes, the way a muscle feathered in his jaw. He relished in it, in fact. The fire at their back was nothing in the face of their intensity.

"Must make you regret even more not taking your chance back there, in the woods." Nicholas set a hand against William's muscled thigh. Still not a flinch. He wanted William to tense, to twitch, to shudder and snap under any pressure.

William feigned innocence. "What regret do you speak of?"

"A moment where you could have been rid of me with the last bullet of yours, although Arden and your fiery friend would have grown suspicious of the hole in my head."

The look returned, a bitter dullness to William's otherwise enchanting eyes. As if Death reaped the color and usurped body and mind.

"There it is. That look." Nicholas inched closer. William's side pressed firmly against his chest. They shared the air they breathed. The fae's fingers spread out across a brawny thigh he wished was uncovered, that he wished trembled or showed any sign of discomfort or yearning.

"If by look you mean that of irritation, then yes. I've always shown that to you." William raised the knife in warning.

"The lies humans weave are so tedious. You know of the look, of the chill inside you. You have the eyes of a beast, like me."

William's tempting lips, plump pink and begging to be ravished, parted in a silent breath. "What are you implying?"

"I am implying you are a dangerous man, William Vandervult, and I am curious how many know it." Nicholas' hand lifted further.

"Move once more and I will relieve you of your fingers."

"Are medics meant to be so quick to violence? Though I suppose you would excel at a mysterious dismemberment, ailment, or death here or there."

"If you believe that, then you should play nice, although for you, that may be impossible. Few people tell you no, don't they?" William's eyes shifted over Arden's sleeping form, then back to Nicholas. "As a shade, your kin show you a form of fearful respect, and I hear your father lords over Darkmoon. You're accustomed to spoils."

"That's right. I am as rotten as rotten can be. I'll do anything to get what I want."

"But you want me dead and I'm still here."

"There are several things I want from you." Nicholas would have eagerly shared the list, even the desire to relieve William of his clothes for an evening of carnal lust if only for a chance to break the stoic facade, but suddenly, William stood.

"Did you hear that?" he asked.

"I heard nothing," said Nicholas.

William clutched his blade tighter. "There's something outside."

8

Charmaine

Charmaine woke up to Arden leaping out of bed. She stumbled onto her feet, disoriented. William's attention stayed on the door. Nicholas stood adjacent to him.

"There's something outside," William said. "I know I heard—"

The roof collapsed in an explosion of dust, snow, and growls. A beam caught her in the stomach. She hit the floor, sputtering for air. Through the dust, a sinewy torso of a serpent-like abomination slithered inside. Yellow eyes flashed, fixated on a figure in the mist—Arden, based on the abrupt movement and flash of a blade slicing at the creature. Then William cursed, and another crash reverberated through the house.

Bewilderment and fear clouded her senses, weighed her like an anchor at sea. Charmaine struggled against the weight pinning her to the floor. A portion of the wall caved in. Another of the snake-like beasts lurched inside, a long-scaled body standing on six muscled and clawed feet. They weren't the flying beasts that grabbed them. These were yet another new monster intent on ripping them to shreds.

The one Arden battled against caught his arm in its jaws. The abomination slipped from the destroyed roof, with the fae kicking in its grasp.

Nicholas, donning an expression of calm certainty, surged after them, his figure encased by rose light. This left them to fend for themselves.

"Fuck!" Charmaine pressed her feet to the floor, using her waist to lift the beam. The beam shifted, then forced her down.

William slid left and right to avoid a deadly snout riddled with too many teeth. Unlike the last, these beasts were scaled blacker than ink and their spine lined by thick spikes that could pierce flesh. The abomination's long body shattered the east wall. Charmaine raised her hands to shield herself from the falling debris, wondering if this was it, if they would die here. She, buried under the house, and William pierced by vicious fangs.

The snake lunged at William. He pivoted, but not fast enough. The weight of the beast sent him hurtling into the remaining wall. His head hit the bricks. He plummeted, cursing when the monster trapped his leg between its teeth. William grabbed the beast's snout. The monster's jaw went lax to release his leg, but the creature slammed its forehead into his chest.

Panic surged, pierced Charmaine's chest more painfully than a blade. Truth be told, the day she received her enlistment letter, she found herself believing she would die young. She would rest in a plot before she had a chance to truly live. She wasn't confident she'd survive out here, especially without William. He was all hard corners, sharpened points warding off evil, and she was too soft, welcoming any misfortune.

Looking back, she spotted the fire sputtering in the hearth. The Sight revealed the strings of fire, orange tinted lines raging around the flames. They refracted the light, bewitching any who gazed upon them. She called for the fire and pleaded for their help. The strings listened, they caught around her fingers. She commanded a wave of fire at the beast. Yowling, it released William and retreated. The fire had done little more than encourage its wrath.

Snapping wide jaws, the snake gave Charmaine a look that curdled the blood in her veins. Its yellow gaze shifted to William, as if it had enough intelligence to understand Charmaine was trapped and it could come back for her later. If that were the case, they were in even bigger trouble. The grumps were the only beasts capable of thought without a shadowed disciple's control. If a monster as large as this could think of its own free will, they could bring about even worse destruction.

The monster's muscular hind legs prepared to jump. Panic and fear should have surged within her, but instead, an unfamiliar rage roared. Something unbridled, hotter than the fire at her fingertips, vicious as a sickened and cornered dog.

Charmaine wouldn't die out here. She wanted to go home. She wouldn't lose the first friend she ever truly had. Two months hadn't passed since she told her mother she identified as a woman before the draft dragged her away as a son, as a reminder. No matter what, she would return home to live the life she always wanted, that—damn it all—she deserved!

Setting her hands against the beam, she shoved the wood off with a scream. The beam rolled across the floor. Charmaine summoned the fire around her, catching every string and letting the festering rage eat at her skin and mind, then shot all of it in a violent blast. The beast caught fire. Rearing on its four back legs, it shrieked in agony.

Charmaine sent another fireball and another. The beast stumbled into the remains of the village. With every step the monster took to advance, Charmaine countered with another fireball. She felt the tug, magic's warning that she was pushing too far. Before, she always stopped, but here she kept going, as if her thoughts weren't her own. This force poured from her, demanded to attack, to survive at any cost.

Then the beast fell to the snow, hissing and withered, scales shattered and the skin blistered beneath. Dead. She stood over the corpse heaving, burnt fingers twitching and the rage still sizzling. Her arms ached and blisters formed along her hands.

"Charmaine," William called.

Hearing her name—her true name—settled the anger to a dull throb in the back of her mind. Hissing from the sudden pain, she hurried to the remnants of the house. William leaned against the exterior wall. Blood seeped through his torn uniform around his leg. Charmaine's shaking hands peeled back the cloth.

"I count at least six puncture wounds," she said.

She eased William inside. He took a seat in the surviving chair and said, "Your hands."

"Your leg first, you fool." She kept her hands close to her chest, letting him know she wouldn't move until he took care of himself. William had always been like that, watching out for others. Those he deemed worthy of it, at least.

Reluctantly, he settled a hand over his leg. The blood slowed, then ceased all together. The wound didn't heal as easily as the others. After healing everyone over these days, lack of proper food, water, and rest, exhaustion settled beneath his eyes and along his slumped shoulders. That didn't bode well for them.

"Your hands," he demanded. "I cannot fully heal both of us, but we need to be able to fight after this."

Sighing, she obeyed. William healed most of the blisters. His magic felt different than hers. Fire was hot, even in her hands, reminding her of what she commanded and how easily she could destroy. William's was the opposite, smooth and cool as river water. The magic poured through her, smoothing out pain like wrinkles in a blanket.

William fell against the wall, exhausted. "This could have been far worse," he said. "Adrenaline is no joke, particularly yours. Remind me never to piss you off."

Laughing, she caught him in a hug. William's warmth always eased her. The torment of training ended because of him. Charmaine hadn't lived her life as a woman prior to the draft either, but among frightened and lonely teenage boys, wrath was rampant. They took that anger out on those they deemed different, and Charmaine stood out no matter how she tried not to. They saw her as too soft, too kind, too effeminate and strange, so the torment became a daily occurrence. Beatings and cruel remarks all stopped because a surprisingly small boy a full year younger than her started a fight.

"When they hit you, make them regret it," William always told her.

Charmaine thought he meant to hit them back even if it was a losing battle, but over the next week, the boys that taunted her suffered mysterious illnesses. William never admitted to anything, but Charmaine understood. People like them, those who stood out among the terrified youth, would meet horrendous fates if they didn't incite terror in return.

She never questioned nor demeaned William for his actions. Never berated him for striking another name off his list, no matter how frightening because, deep down, she wanted them to hurt too. No one else would defend her, and none of the abusers would see themselves punished. She didn't like dwelling on that truth and didn't want to ask herself when those thoughts emerged or if they would ever go away.

Once Charmaine released him, William asked, "Where did those pointy eared assholes go?"

"I hear nothing. Either the beast is dead," she mumbled.

"Or it killed them." William smirked.

"Don't smile while saying that. It isn't proper."

"None of this is proper, and if I find a little joy in their demise, what's so wrong with that? They'd dance in our blood if they found us dead."

He stood with her help, and the two limped out of the house.

Charmaine never fought too hard against William's distaste toward fae. She wasn't so fond of them, either. Fae always gave her a sense of deep discomfort. The first few years of war passed without issue. Fae and human armies hadn't completely integrated yet. They worked together by sharing intel and separating tasks, thus staying mostly apart. But the closer the military came to the Dread Peaks, the more the armies intertwined. Seeing fae on the daily was normal, which meant she saw their constant mistreatment.

However, working together has always been better than working apart. The war was proof of that. Together, humans and fae did more in the last five years than decades apart. Many didn't want to admit that. Sometimes, neither did she, but she wanted to go home. Not the home where she was raised, of course. Her father never welcomed her, no matter who she feigned to be. She tried relentlessly to be the son he wanted, examined his every move to copy what a "man" should be. She kept her voice low and gravely, cut her hair short, wore bland colors, and pretended not to care about flowers, fashion, or jewelry. Every step she took was like walking blind through a minefield, but rather than avoiding blasts, she avoided the truth. Always waiting for that single moment where the truth showed through, where she would mess up and her lies would explode.

Late at night, she cried and ran her nails over her skin that never set right. She hated the way she looked, how every mirror reflected a stranger she loathed more and more each day. As time went on, she avoided reflective surfaces entirely. Not a difficult task, but occasionally, she went into town and caught sight of herself. She stared and hated and cursed and imagined digging her fingers beneath her skin to shed herself of this false suit like it would reveal the woman beneath. That's the life her father wanted for her.

Her mother, though? Bessie knew, somehow. She sensed the difference and wished to nurture it. Once, Charmaine bought her mother a make up set from town. Had taken her almost six months to save up for it. Bessie cried, thanked her, then that night while her father slept, Bessie came into her room and offered to put some on her. They would take it off before her father saw, but in those moments, Charmaine had never felt so right, so peaceful. Bessie told her about makeup and all the ways she could do Charmaine's hair one day, if she wanted. By the Holy Soul, she wanted nothing more.

Charmaine never looked at her reflection after the makeup had been done, too terrified that she still wouldn't like what she saw. However, she felt right, like someone realized she was the wrong puzzle piece and finally found her place in the correct picture.

After serving all these years, Charmaine would find her mother and herself a place to make their own, a proper home. No longer would she wear a fake persona for a bastard father or the military forced upon her. She and her mother would buy new gowns from the market and giggle over fresh pastries in the city. They'd have a life better than before. Maybe they could open a shop and live out their days far happier than they had ever been. If fighting with fae meant the start of a better life, then she would cope with them.

"Should we wait here for them to return?" Charmaine asked.

"We'll search around the village first. They might have gone through with leaving us," he answered.

Charmaine bit the inside of her cheek. William mentioned it earlier in the washroom. They agreed she would suggest taking the first watch, then wake William next. That way, he got some sleep, but he'd stay awake to ensure the fae didn't run off. Though she considered the possibility, she had hoped it to be a lie. Everyone's inability to work together pissed her off, but she was especially irritable in their current dilemma.

They searched the side of the house first for tracks. A path of blood, debris, and footprints led them a little way into the woods. Trees had been ripped from the roots. Scorch marks scarred the earth. Melted snow made the terrain muddy, then through the broken trees, they found Nicholas and Arden investigating the corpse of the downed monster.

Nicholas had the book out again as if he were nothing more than a botanist on an evening stroll collecting specimens on a boring day.

"They survived. Your resilience is becoming impressive," he said mockingly.

"No thanks to either of you," said William. "You could have returned after slaying the beast."

"We could have."

The look William passed her said enough; he wanted to kill that damn fae. Charmaine couldn't blame him. Neither of the fae were delightful company.

"What have you learned from the beast?" Charmaine pressed a hand to William's back, guiding him to a nearby boulder. He attempted to argue that he was fine, but one stern look from her had him sitting.

"They do not appear to be one of Fearworn's creations." Nicholas snapped the book shut to slip into his blouse. "None of the anatomical drawings match."

Charmaine and William shared concerned looks. She passed the monster another glance, taking in the body that, when standing on its legs, made a towering debrak seem small. The creatures were frightful, intimidating, and from what they experienced, powerful. Fearworn didn't need any more creatures on his side, but alas, the world taunted them. She felt like peace had been dangled before her then snatched away.

"If it is not a creation, then he has summoned another beast from the dark plane," William said.

"And for it to be one of that size, he has opened a shimmer bigger than we have seen." Charmaine shivered. "There could be even more new monsters in his ranks."

"The size of a monster doesn't necessarily mean the scar must be bigger, however, we could guess he has opened another that has brought these creatures. Perhaps more new monsters will follow, thus he will have more to experiment with and on." Nicholas' gleeful smile didn't go unnoticed. Neither did Arden's.

Charmaine suppressed the urge to shout at them. An unusual thought for her. She never liked raising her voice. Her father always raised his voice, even for minor issues. She sought to never follow in his footsteps, to speak in kindness and respect, but the fae were testing her patience.

"We should keep moving. Fearworn must have sent these monsters. He knows we're alone out here and he wants his book." Nicholas tapped his chest. "We must return to the encampment before we come face to face with Fearworn himself."

"Book or not, that is unlikely," William argued lowly. "Fearworn has rarely shown himself. It's how he has done all this for so long."

"Yes, but once he realizes sending monsters after us isn't working, he may come for us himself."

Charmaine hated the prospect. All heard stories of Fearworn, nightmare tales, more like it. Bessie told her bedtime stories about him, and those like him, how they prowled the forests in search of innocence to snuff out. As an adult, she understood it was their parent's twisted way of keeping them safe, making them fear the darkness and unknown as to not wander off. However, they weren't entirely lies either. Fearworn truly was the monster everyone feared, and she never wished to see him face to face. His presence meant death.

Nicholas and Arden stepped past them, heading into the woods.

"Where are you going?" she called.

"We can't afford to dawdle," said Arden.

"But William is exhausted. We all are."

Nicholas pivoted, a teasing glint to his eyes. "Shall I carry you then, darling?"

William made a rude gesture, resulting in the fae snickering.

"Keep up, little mortals." Nicholas waved for them to follow. "You wouldn't want to be left behind in the deep, dark woods."

The shadows devoured Arden and Nicholas' silhouette, leaving William and Charmaine among the debris and dead. She cast the creature another perturbed glance, overwhelmed by the power still visible in its lifeless body. Firm muscles that could tear apart caravans, razor-sharp teeth to gnaw bones, and a tough hide that sabers would do little against, that bullets may struggle to stop.

"How do they know where to go?" she mumbled.

Rising, William ambled after their rude forced partners with her in tow.

"There's no telling with them. We could be going in circles," he snapped.

"As unpleasant as this all is, I will try to view this as useful, since we can bring all this new information to the generals. They must hear of this. They must prepare." She said that more to make herself feel better than another.

William probably guessed that and nodded. "You are right. At least we know this now rather than later."

9

WILLIAM

THE GROUP GAZED AT a cavernous gorge stretching far and wide. Trees dared not tread closer, creating a wide berth for the deep wound. Nicholas stood along the edge where brittle rock fumbled into the abyss from the brush of wind. The fae peered into the shadows with little care. William wouldn't dare. Even from where he and Charmaine huddled beneath the trees, he heard it; whispers, voices in the gloom, hundreds or thousands speaking at once, urging him closer.

"This would explain not being discovered by any of our scouts yet," William muttered.

Charmaine stepped forward. He clutched her shoulder. "You're hurting me," she growled.

"Sorry. Don't look upon it."

"I don't know if that helps."

"I can't fathom what is down there," said Arden from where he also peeked over the lip.

"Nothing good, and everything fun." Nicholas skipped along the edge. "No doubt a creation of Fearworn or his shadowed disciples for reasons I would love to learn."

He retreated with two hopped steps. His gaze scanned the horizon. Arden walked in the opposite direction. Arden's voice carried over the falling snow moments later. "I don't see the end of it this way!"

"Neither do I," Nicholas responded. He faced the gorge, one hand under his chin. The cavern spanned fifty feet wide. "We'll go across. A bridge is easy enough to build."

William didn't want to cross the gorge, but over would be quicker than around. He wanted away from this place, far from the gloom transforming the snow into oiled sludge.

Nicholas stood close to the fall, hands outstretched. The forest responded. Roots tangled together, stretching over the gorge. Unlike mages and other fae, Nicholas commanded an arsenal of elements and abilities. Nicholas' power was unnatural, yet helpful, tainted, yet beautiful, captivating and perplexing. But then that beauty shuttered.

The rose light under Nicholas' skin brightened. The roots hovering over the gorge struggled. They contorted up and out and down. He swung his arm to command the forest, attempting to steady the structure with new roots, but they became a mess of entanglement. The gloom of the gorge shifted upward with shadowed hands. Nicholas retreated, bewildered by the roots disappearing into obscurity. The roots along the mouth of the cavern broke, the shadows fell, and the bridge disappeared below.

"Fascinating," Nicholas muttered, intrigued.

"Walking it is," said William.

He nudged Charmaine to the right, and they walked on. Nicholas and Arden followed, whispering to one another. Childish glee flickered in their eyes; attention pointed toward the gorge that kept their attention for a while.

The four of them remained within the trees, keeping the gorge along their left flank. Though at some point, Nicholas broke off from the group, claiming he'd search for food. William didn't believe that, but

Nicholas' momentary irritation made ignoring the whispers from the gorge easier. With his absence, William and Charmaine spoke to one another about random events to placate the voices ringing in their skulls. She told him a story about her childhood where her cat went missing. She and her mother searched all day. They never told her father. He wasn't a kind man and not interested in pets in the least. Turns out the little rascal was sleeping in her closet and came out for dinner that evening as if none of their panic had transpired. King, she called him, because he was haughtier than one.

William spoke of himself and his brothers building a massive snow fort in their yard after a terrible blizzard. They were snowed in, but the boys loved every moment. They spent the whole day outside and came down with a cold the next morning. These memories kept them from stumbling toward the gorge that would swallow them in a breath if they let it.

Then Nicholas appeared out of nowhere, practically dancing around them when he asked, "Is this not utterly fascinating?"

"Don't surprise us like that," Charmaine barked. Even her irritation had risen after the prolonged trek. "And where is the food?"

"I found none. The Deadlands are as decrepit as their namesake yet filled with mystery. This gorge, the monsters, and moving trees in the forest."

"Could you do us a single favor and make sense for once?"

"I am speaking sense. There were living trees. A grove of them tried to smother me with their roots. Once I got free, they shuffled off in the other direction. They reminded me of a time during my childhood when I became lost in the Forest of Whispers. An intriguing place in Faerie, known for random disappearances. For months at a time, the forest welcomes all under the apple trees and within the fields of wheat. Then one day the forest wakes up, overtaken by an eerie fog and decay. Nothing lives," Nicholas explained.

William groaned. "You walked right into it, didn't you?"

"Of course, I was intrigued! None know how the Forest of Whispers works, when the change will come, or how the trees determine what souls to take or return."

"I will regret asking this," said Charmaine. "But how did you survive?"

"A combination of tree bark, roots, bugs, and decaying apples for three long months," Nicholas declared far too proudly for someone spouting a story of stupidity. "But when the forest shifted, and I saw vibrant apples on the limbs once more, I escaped and learned I had been gone for only two days."

Charmaine and William shared confused glances that coaxed laughter from their fae companions.

"Time is a fickle thing in Faerie," Arden said, nodding as if he had a tale or two to tell of time.

"I do miss our lands," Nicholas sighed, exaggerated and dreamy. "Faerie lives and breathes, unlike your barren wasteland. Day after day, you see the same thing, but in Faerie you may fall asleep in a field of green and awaken along a sandy beach. You never know what tomorrow holds."

"Yes, how riveting to be in unknown lands." William glanced about at the unknown lands he wanted to run away from. "How about we refrain from going anywhere alone from now on? We don't need anyone being devoured by a tree."

"Oh, but it has made me wonder what it would be like to be devoured by a tree." Nicholas danced around them, boyish as boyish can be. "Do they have stomachs? Would I be digested, buried, spat out as old bark, or become a tree myself? Would I know I was a tree and miss my fingers and toes?"

"Are you incapable of taking any situation seriously?" William snapped. "We're exhausted, cold, and hungry, and here you are skipping."

"Skipping doesn't equate to treating the situation flippantly. I went out in search of food. There's simply nothing here."

"We'd still have those spion legs if you weren't insistent on viewing a carcass."

"That carcass was invaluable. We have information to give our military." Nicholas walked backward in front of them, smirking. William hated how he found the expression charming. "You are exceedingly crabby today."

"Because we're fucking hungry," Charmaine snarled. "William and I must eat. You may survive weeks without food, but we cannot."

Nicholas shrugged. "It's not my fault mortals are so frail."

"I'm consistently reminded of how regretful I am to have prevented you from abandoning us," William said. A headache formed in his temples.

"You wouldn't last a day without us."

"Remind me who saved your ass against that first beast and healed you." Though neither of them needed to think about how William would have killed him if the others hadn't arrived.

Nicholas held up a single finger and swung it from side to side. "Keep this up and I won't share what I found."

"You said you didn't find food."

"I didn't."

"If it isn't food, we do not care."

"Oh, I think you will." Nicholas scurried toward the forest, gesturing for them to follow. Arden did so without question. Charmaine and William hesitated. This was backtracking and there was no telling how far Nicholas wanted them to backtrack for whatever he found. Charmaine and William shared a discomforted sigh, then shuffled through the shaded woods.

Nicholas kept a slow pace, for once. They walked for a short time, then William caught sight of steam filtering through the pines. When those trees parted, they stood along the shore of water; a hot spring. The foggy blue water trickled down from layers of rocks into a large pond surrounded by lush plant life, the first any of them had seen. Little ferns sprouted between rocks. Moss curved over their surface and a patch of grass dared to grow at the bottom of the rockface.

"This is quite wonderful," Charmaine whispered, taking a deep breath. The moment William did, too, a sense of ease washed over him. Walking away from the gorge did wonders, and the hot spring promised much more. Even the rocks beneath their feet warmed him through the soles of his ruined boots.

"We'll take tu—" Nicholas' gleeful shout and a splash interrupted William.

The tepid water splattered against them. Charmaine laughed. William stood there, grimacing when Nicholas' head broke the surface. He slicked back his mane of midnight hair, showing off a toothy grin that would convince many to make questionable decisions, to decide a night of debauchery would be worth whatever happened come morning.

"Come along. We're all disgusting. At least we won't stink each other to death," Nicholas proclaimed, laughing when Arden jumped in, nude.

William's gaze swept to their left, discovering Nicholas' clothes lay forgotten, too. When Nicholas stood, the water reached above his narrow hips. William ignored his quick breath of disappointment.

"I'd rather take turns," he grumbled, forcing disinterest in his voice.

"Aw, are the mortals nervous? Shy?" Arden snickered, then lowered, so the water reached his chin. "Fear not. All mortals are lacking in some form or the other. You will be no different."

"Your poor attempts at comfort are unnecessary," Charmaine muttered, looking down.

Charmaine told William once that every time she undressed, she tried not to look at herself. The body she had didn't feel right. Military uniforms didn't help with that. The most William could do to ease her was helping her shave, so she wasn't forced to face her reflection. Both needed a shave. William's facial hair had a mind of its own, sprouting in patches unlike his father, who wore a beard from the age of sixteen—so he claimed.

Charmaine flexed her fingers and whispered, "I would love a bath, a hot one, and for all we know, these two will curse the water to freeze while they're out and we're in there. Better to share the bath now."

With that, Charmaine undressed. She fell into the water, releasing a relaxed sigh that William envied. He wanted to bathe. He rarely cared about being naked around strangers. The military made sure of that, but he thought of the many scars along his back. He had plenty more but those; they were different. And Nicholas kept a firm stare on him, taunting without words, mere moments from making a curt remark.

"Come on, get in." Charmaine tugged at the hem of his pant leg. "You'll feel better. I already do."

If William remained out of the water, Nicholas would prod at him with eyes and words. At least in the hot spring, he'd be soothed. Releasing a reluctant sigh, he undressed, not missing Nicholas' attention, the same kind he gave back in the village, one of an insatiable appetite. He would have liked the attention, the desire in those roseate eyes, the way Nicholas licked his lips, if the fae wasn't an abhorrent jackass, of course.

Sinking into the water, the hot spring eased the tension from William's muscles. As if he had been breathing in smoke for years and this is the first time he tasted genuine air. He lounged along the lip, arms outstretched, and body submerged to his neck.

Even when the troops passed cities, they didn't bathe like this. The last hot bath of pure comfort happened before recruitment, at home. He tried to recall the scent of lilac from the petals drifting atop the water, then thought of shampoo in his hair, soap in his hands, stepping out cleaned and refreshed. His clothes waiting by the door, a soft bed in the room beyond, snacks in the pantry, and his family laughing at the dinner table. Those memories felt so far away, another lifetime for another person.

Once he enlisted, the men had to take mostly cold showers among one another, never a moment of privacy, though he didn't have privacy here either. The hair on the back of his neck stood, sensing Nicholas' gaze. He caught those greedy eyes seizing him. He hated how the attention made his heart skip and a beat of pleasure plunge to his waist to nestle like a treacherous snake.

"This would be perfect if we had a delectable steak and a good brandy," Charmaine hummed. She leaned out of the hot spring to grab the knife from her belt, apparently thinking the same William had earlier. She gestured for him to step closer, and he held up his chin.

"Brandy?" William chuckled. "Have you ever tried such a thing?"

Charmaine's tongue stuck out the side of her mouth while she rid William of his worthless stubble as best she could. "No, but I hear it's fancy, and this feels fancy, which sounds unbearably sad spoken out loud."

"It does, but what I find sadder is I don't know if I remember what steak tastes like."

Charmaine groaned, and based on her pursed lips, she didn't remember, either.

"Your owners don't feed you so well, do they?" Arden asked across the spring, where he ran thin fingers through his hair.

Finished, Charmaine ran the knife through the water. "Owners?"

"The kings that own you."

"They don't own us."

"Perhaps not on paper, but you are owned. They ordered you here, did they not?"

"And what of you?" William countered while working on Charmaine. "Did your fae lords not send you?"

The bridge of Arden's nose wrinkled. "Of course not. I volunteered."

"Most fae volunteered," Nicholas explained. "If there is one compliment I can give mortals, it is their destructive and rapacious capacity for war. An invention no fae had thought of. Mortals know cruelty in ways we never fathomed, and most of us wanted a piece."

Neither Charmaine nor William spoke against Nicholas' claim, because there was nothing to argue. Humans spoke of war like fairytales with epic heroes and happy endings. Those who knew of war and violence didn't wish to speak of the matter at all. No one longed for peace more than a war-torn soul, and no one wanted war like one who had never experienced hardship.

"If you did not fight as one before, how did Faerie battle against Fearworn?" Charmaine asked. "He is from Faerie, after all."

"We fought him on our own," Arden answered flatly. "We fend for ourselves."

"But Fearworn got out of control. Many fae pledged an oath to him in exchange for leeching off his power, and with all of them at his back, he nearly ruined Faerie," said William darkly. "To think, if you fought together, maybe we wouldn't be here."

"What a pity that would have been. My first battle here was glorious. The rush."

"The utter chaos," Nicholas whispered, as if reliving his fondest memories. Then his eyes swept over William, a taunting grin staining his expression. "There is very little that compares to a perfect slaughter."

Charmaine gagged before splashing her shaven face with more water. "I shouldn't have asked anything."

"That encourages me to share more," Arden declared, and Charmaine sank when the fae spoke of his battles in order of his least favorite to most adored with extreme detail.

William set the knife aside and stopped listening. Even if he were interested, it was hard to concentrate when one particular pointy-eared dreg kept staring. Nicholas didn't bother hiding his interest. The hunger didn't sleep, choosing to howl within his monstrous eyes.

Rather than lounge there under the intensity of his attention, William swam toward the rock face. The hot spring drifted into a cavern lit by peculiar rocks embedded in the ceiling. They released a low green glow. He hovered a hand near one, testing if they were rocks or a variety of bug that, knowing the Deadlands, would come to life and devour him. He pressed a finger to the stone, surprised by their warmth.

The water rippled behind him. He passed a cursory stare over his shoulder. Nicholas stepped into the dim light. William hoped the fae would have remained behind to embellish Arden's story or relish in Charmaine's disgusted expressions. Apparently, William was of more interest than even he surmised. A warped thrill echoed through his limbs at the thought.

He refused to let his eyes stay on Nicholas for longer than a moment. The fae would enjoy the attention too much. He would rather not admit to anyone, especially himself, about how much he enjoyed the view. Out here, it was rare to enjoy anything. Blood and festered wounds kept his eyes company more days than not. He grew weak to temptation, to seeing something else, something beautiful and enchanting, albeit vicious and deadly.

"Am I not allowed a moment of peace?" William asked, holding his breath when Nicholas set a long nail against his back.

"These scars." Nicholas pressed a finger against his skin and followed one scar from his shoulder to mid back. "Who did this to you?"

"Not who, what. Years of war have left me scarred."

"Fae cannot lie, so we find it most frustrating when others do."

"I am not lying."

"You aren't telling the full truth."

William caught water in his cupped hands to run over his cooled skin. The steam of the hot spring battled against the winter air, though not enough to prevent his body from breaking out with goosebumps. That was what he would tell Nicholas if he dared to suspect otherwise. Wouldn't want him knowing that the gentle touch of his finger tracing every mark made William feel anything other than disgust.

"I see no reason to tell you," William said.

"We're travel companions," Nicholas countered with a smidge of humor in his voice.

"Not good or trustworthy ones."

"We could be better if we got to know each other." Nicholas' greedy hand settled on William's waist, holding tight enough to bruise.

"I doubt talking is the way you want to get to know me. Actually, I imagine you want to get to know the insides of my intestines."

"That has always been on the list, although I admit it may no longer be at the top."

"Oh, then what is?"

"You're observant enough to guess." Nicholas' heated breath tickled the nape of his neck.

William almost leaned into him, cursing himself for thinking with the wrong head. As troublesome as the last couple days have been, as rattled as he became over the years, laying with a fae, no matter how ethereal, would solve nothing.

Nicholas had beauty and strength that would likely lead to a more than satisfying encounter, but he also had a sharp tongue, violent and corrosive, destructive and daunting. He promised danger. And yet, Nicholas' fervor chilled the spring. His fire was unrivaled, seeping into William's bones that ached for the forbidden. For a rush of something new and treacherous. For a moment of overwhelming bliss where the world faded away and only pleasure remained. To grow numb and forget, to pretend the world outside didn't exist, that nothing bad had ever happened.

"Your file revealed you were in the infirmary often during your first year, although there was little information on your injuries," Nicholas continued, thus making William's teeth grind. "And these scars, in particular, are not new."

"My recruitment years were not kind to me," he admitted. The lock welded tight at the back of his mind prevented the horrors from unleashing, but sometimes in the night, one or two slipped through the seams. They tried to do so now.

"I'm shocked you let anyone lay their hands on you."

"I was a boy then. He hadn't learned to survive yet."

"But he knows now. He's exceedingly good at it, in fact." Nicholas swept an arm around him, lower on his waist than before. The fae's fingers spread over his thigh, a thumb caressing the skin. The other hand dipped into the water to run it up William's arm, slow and careful, continuing to test his quivering boundaries.

"Flattery won't get you anywhere," William declared.

"And where am I trying to get?"

"Between my legs, I imagine."

Nicholas chuckled. His lips pressed a possessive kiss to William's shoulder. "What *will* get me between your legs?"

A curse of stupidity. Curiosity. Boredom. Self-loathing. War eating away every piece of sense William could ever have. A combination of it all.

But when he glanced over his shoulder and glimpsed those pointed fangs, the long-tipped ears, and unnatural eyes, a raging ire swept over him. The one that always came when he least expected it. That forever boiled along the edge of his mind, waiting for that moment to erupt. It did so now, first resentment at Nicholas, then at himself for daring to crave a moment. He loathed fae. Far more than monsters and war and kings and make believe deities. Fae ruined the one light he found among the shadows. Hugh could have been his everything, and they stole that.

Setting his hands on Nicholas' arms, William shoved him away, needing to escape, to find a rock and beat some sense into himself. Charmaine was right. He needed rest. He needed to get away.

He surged around Nicholas. A hand snatched his bicep, but whatever Nicholas had to say evaporated when William snarled, vicious as a wounded animal, "Do you wish to know where the men who touched me last without my consent are?"

Nicholas' hold loosened. "Where?"

"Buried." He saw blood in the water spilling from his hands, fire and ash, buildings crumbling beneath monstrous hands, and terror peering back at him. His heart raced, and he refused to accept why.

"Did you put them there?"

"They died in battle. A terrible tragedy."

"You didn't answer my question." When William said nothing, Nicholas laughed. "What a wicked little thing you are."

William ripped his arm free and stormed out of the cave. The comfort of the hot spring vanished in the face of Hugh's memory. His soothing eyes, loud laughter, and his honesty, *"I have neither titles nor money, but I will give you my heart, William Vandervult. From this day until my last day, I am yours."*

He seized a strangled breath, struggling to bury those memories in the vault of his mind where they belonged. Wounds like that didn't heal. They scarred and bled the moment anyone prodded at them. Nicholas hadn't meant to scratch. How could he have known? But it bothered William, nonetheless.

He fell into the water, hoping submerging himself in true warmth would beat back the cold. It did not. When he resurfaced, he glimpsed Charmaine and Arden near the mouth of the hot spring, speaking animatedly to one another. A strange scene that worried him until Charmaine pivoted, holding an animal carcass.

"Look what we caught in the water," she exclaimed. "Food! Potentially?"

"You are welcome to try," said Arden.

"I caught the first one," Charmaine argued and shoved an eel-like creature in Arden's hands. "You try it."

William shuffled over to them, ignoring the slosh of water at his back and the fae who caused it. Four creatures lay along the edge, each as long as his arm. They had a fair amount of meat, based on Arden cutting one open.

After cooking the creature, Arden gave it a bite and determined the eel-things to be edible. Dressed and cleaned, they sat around a fire and filled their stomachs. That should have made William feel better, but then he caught Nicholas' attention. Those eyes remained on him. He ensured not to speak to Nicholas for the rest of the evening.

10

Nicholas

Nicholas stared at William's back. The vexatious medic avoided conversation since the affair in the hot spring last night. Moments Nicholas couldn't get off his mind, William's heat, his shivering skin, the damn scent of disinfectant that followed him here. The man stirred a ravenous craving within Nicholas that nothing could snuff out, further coaxed by his prolonged lull. Even when Nicholas spoke of vicious fun, recounting tales of horror, William found solace in his reticence. He didn't offer the fae a glimpse. Nicholas wanted those eyes upon him always. It was utterly sickening.

"Are you certain you know where you are going?" Charmaine asked from where she clutched William's side.

The two were almost inseparable. Nicholas knew the humans huddled to share body heat, but his irritation didn't fade. He wanted his hands on William instead. Clutching those powerful arms, sliding nimble fingers along the scars of his back, and clutching his strong waist.

Nicholas' fingers flexed, recalling the intoxicating sensation that drove him wild. Evoking reactions from William similar to the other day, a moment of panic or fury set upon normally calm features, that was the fun of the game. He wanted to win.

"Did you not hear our stories the other evening?" Arden replied from where he led the group. "Faerie changes constantly. How do you suppose we survive in lands like that?"

"Answer the damn question." Charmaine earned a raised brow from William. The two were fed and remained crabby. That appeared to be a normal state for humans. They reminded Nicholas of pixies, irritated by any who dared encroach upon their land, which was anything in their sights. They loved cursing one to continuously stub their fingers and toes or get an eyelash stuck in their eye. Nothing that caused too much harm but could make for maddeningly unpleasant days.

"We do not seek locations. We seek items or people," Nicholas explained.

"Our magic is within us, all around us. We command it to our whims. Fae do not have this Sight that you speak of, these strings that you pluck to do what you want. We simply feel it, in here." Arden laid a hand on his chest. "And this feeling is more than power that we throw around. It is a call to home, to safety, to a person or an item that we seek. It is easy out here where there is little else to smell other than sulfur."

And musk, Nicholas thought. Even after their bath, the aroma lingered. The Deadlands liked to mark its territory.

"Among one of your cities would be more difficult," Arden continued. "There's too much noise, too many people, and too much happening. It's confusing."

"If that is true, why can't any of you find Fearworn?" Charmaine asked. "Can't you *feel* your way toward him?"

"Do you honestly believe Fearworn doesn't have the power to cover that? He's invisible, practically a ghost."

Charmaine spoke momentarily with William, then meandered forward to join Arden. "Can you sense how far we are from the army?" she asked.

"Tonight may be our last evening alone in the woods," Arden replied, and the two fell into further discussions. Mostly Charmaine asking about specifics on how fae track. This gave Nicholas a chance to speak with William alone.

William didn't give him the attention he craved when he settled beside him. William's wan expression remained as such since the hot springs. Nicholas struck a chord, unintentionally. An unusual situation because he typically struck chords on purpose. He wanted to agitate William, but he wanted the medic to fight, not crumble into this shell, a place of quiescence and disinterest that stole the fight from his eyes. Nicholas could not lie. William was interesting. Defiant. Vexing. And hiding more than he let on.

"Do you wish to know where the men who touched me last without my consent are?" William let that slip. He regretted it. Nicholas didn't. He kept prodding that armor, watching the cracks swell along the seams. Every knick brought him closer to victory, to flames growing hotter, and he wanted them to burn together.

"Why not take this chance to leave?" Nicholas asked. William accelerated. Nicholas matched his pace. "You spoke of mortals drafting their military. You did not join of your own volition. Why not take this opportunity to escape? Have your friend lie that you died during the attack and go home."

He received it; attention. A glimpse from the corner of William's eyes.

"This will be a repeat of the village. I will continue speaking, regardless of you ignoring me," Nicholas continued. "Your family must miss you. You can see them again."

"You understand nothing," William replied. A flush crept along his neck to his cheeks. "What happens when the generals ask you and Arden what became of me? The military will learn the truth, and I will be labeled a deserter."

"And that is bad?"

"Yes. Fae have their oaths, so do humans. I'll be hunted down and hanged for abandoning the kingdom, for going against that damn treaty. Deserting will be the reason I never see my family again."

"Then don't see them. Run. Live wherever you please."

William scoffed. "Like I said, you understand nothing."

"Then explain it to me."

"Why?" William ran a hand through his short blonde hair. "Why are you bothering me?"

"I told you, you're interesting."

"I wish I wasn't. I wish you'd find another way to placate your boredom."

"How unfortunate for you that you are stuck with me."

They fell into silence, not what Nicholas wanted. Fae were easier to converse with. They always wanted to, always waiting for a moment to strike. Fae liked the game, the pressure, and the rush of causing discomfort. Humans did not share such beliefs, which was a huge reason they were normally so boring. They cowered too quickly or got caught in webs of lies due to their ignorance. They didn't dodge as well as William did.

"You care about them, your family?" Nicholas asked, uncertain now if he genuinely wanted an answer or was continuing to pester his prey.

"Of course. They're family." William cast a pitiful stare his way. "Right. You don't care about yours."

"Of course not. My siblings have attempted to murder me frequently."

William stopped, then pinched his lips together. "I should have expected as such, but why?"

"Plenty of reasons, I imagine, more than they have likely ever shared with me. Blair, my eldest sister, sees shades as a curse. She believes all should be slaughtered the moment they are revealed. Being her brother makes no difference. My brothers, however, wish to take my place. I am the right hand to my father, who they rightfully assumed to be more difficult to kill. With me out of the way, they at least have a chance at more power and authority."

"It is strange to hear you admit someone is stronger than you," said William, pleased by the information based on the cruel tilt of his mouth.

"Strength comes in many forms. In terms of raw power, I have more than my father, but he is knowledgeable in ways I may never know. He has struck deals with more creatures than I can fathom, and because of that, he is never anything less than prepared."

With furrowed brows, William started walking again. Nicholas kept to his side.

"Why would your siblings want to kill their own father?" William inquired.

"To become Lord of Darkmoon. That is how titles are passed. Whoever kills the previous lord takes their place and thus comes into more power, fed to them through the land itself, so long as they take care of it. In fact, that's how one of my older brothers was named," he explained. William's perplexed expression stated Nicholas needed to elaborate. "Solomon, named after the previous Lord of Darkmoon many eons ago, long before any of us."

William grimaced like a child tasting sour candy for the first time. "Are all of you named after someone your parents killed?"

"Exactly." Nicholas clapped. "Oh, humans have such boring reasons for naming their children after an ancestor or frivolous meanings. My father disemboweled a Nicholas foolish enough to make a deal with him during the initial years of the Collision and thus that name passed on to me."

William didn't appear to find the tale as interesting as Nicholas. As a child, he asked his father to tell him the story of how he got his name many times. Though Laurent didn't always share, the moments when he did were a joy. Back then, he viewed his father as the best trickster the realms had ever known and envied such talents. By now, he despised them. Laurent used everyone and everything to his advantage, for whatever purposes he pleased, even his children.

"I cannot comprehend the strange ways fae think," William muttered. "Naming their children after those they killed is odd."

"As if humans are not any more odd," Nicholas argued.

"And what do we do that you consider odd?"

"I have an endless list, but for starters, you claim us cruel and yet live in a world where you deny others the very world around you. Food grows on your trees and in your fields, but there are those claiming those trees to be theirs, so others cannot eat the fruit. Houses sit empty, unused, but people sleep in the cold and stifling heat. This does not happen in Faerie. You eat the food you find. You live in the empty houses or build your own. My father may lord over Darkmoon, but any fae may build a home and call it their own, so yes, I find mortals odd."

William's gaze darkened. "I won't deny that I find it odd, too."

"Another thing we have in common."

"Don't remind me."

"And then there are the medics trained to heal, but they take lives instead." Nicholas smirked when William cracked his neck to the side. "Do you find that peculiar as well?"

"Speak your mind honestly, you rat bastard," William growled.

"You complain of fae killing others, yet you've killed humans before, haven't you?"

"A bold claim."

"That you can easily lie against, but you let it slip." Nicholas leaned in. He caught the scent of pine and snow, the essence of winter itself settled on William's skin. He wore the frigidity like armor, burrowed deep into the consuming jade of his eyes. "The men who hurt you, you slayed them yourself, didn't you?"

William maintained an emotionless expression best, better than any could ever hope. A blistering storm that Nicholas wanted nothing more than to challenge, to break.

"Were they the only ones? Come now," Nicholas purred. "No one is listening."

"Why do you want to know?" William stopped only to grasp the neckline of Nicholas' blouse. He gripped so tightly the lining nearly choked a breath from the fae. "Hoping to tell the generals that I am a murderer, so they can arrest me?"

"No, I merely love getting a reaction out of you."

A shroud fell across William's face. He shoved Nicholas aside. "Find someone else to get a reaction out of."

Then William hurried after Arden and Charmaine. The two had gotten further ahead than either realized. Nicholas held out his hands and spun in a dozen circles. "There is no else here as fun as you."

"Then spare me until we return to camp where you can find another there."

"I doubt there is anyone in this world as entertaining as you, my wicked."

William turned to him. His brow wrinkled like an old hag's leathered neck. "*Your* wicked?"

Nicholas repeated the words in a husky whisper, "*My* wicked."

"I think the fuck not."

Nicholas cackled. He skipped ahead of William, walking backwards so they were eye to eye. "What ever is the matter? The pet name is rather fitting for you, don't you agree?"

"I don't want a pet name from you."

"But I like it and you don't, which gives me more reason to use it."

"You are fucking insufferable," William spat and that fed the hunger gnawing on Nicholas' bones.

He had William's undivided attention and relished in the prospect, but he hadn't the opportunity to conjure another response. A pressure like he had never felt carried over the wind. The trees creaked and cracked, bending at odd angles against the gale. Sulfur and musk stole the senses. Nicholas recognized the feeling, this sense of power invading the air.

Nicholas released a slow, excited exhale. "He's here."

A shroud encroached upon them, burying the forest in shadows. Lightning shrieked through the mist, aggressive and blinding. Out of that grim, a fae approached, tall and long-limbed with eyes of vicious violet. He held out a hand, nails sharpened into daggers. His voice, smoother than silk, chilled the air. "You have something that belongs to me."

Calix Fearworn found them.

11

William

Parents wove tales of Calix Fearworn, every depiction more fearsome than the last. So few souls saw him that every story painted him differently. He was taller than a house, with horns of midnight black and eyes of pale flames. He walked on crooked legs in a mangled form, skin a grotesque green and eyes milky white. Some claimed Fearworn had no physical body, that night itself constructed his form, a living essence of shadows.

They were wrong.

Calix Fearworn was stunning in every sense of the word, a figure of holy beauty and typical fae perfection. His thinly muscular form lay beneath countless draped fabrics, sparkling silver that caught the violet hue of his cat-like eyes. That violet stretched across his iris, save for a single glint of fuchsia within. His white hair would have trailed behind him if it weren't up in a high ponytail, revealing the sharp lines of his bleached complexion. The light caught along his cheekbones, creating a sterling sheen, as if the sun desired nothing more than to accentuate his aura.

Six shadowed disciples stepped clear of the miasma seeping from Fearworn's form. They were the tales parents wove with eyes the deepest black, as if nothing lay beyond but an empty void. The miasma lived within them, a deep purple that snaked through their bodies and showed through their leathered skin. Crooked nails thick as blades crept out of the tip of their rotted fingers and pointed teeth barely fit in their too wide mouths. Without lips, their saliva coated their fangs and stained their chins in black with a faint purple hue.

Fearworn approached. His face remained placate, uncaring even. He stood with grace, hands carefully positioned atop one another at the base of his stomach. His head cocked like a curious deer in the meadow, and yet didn't sit right, as if his neck sprouted at the wrong angle.

"You are the one who killed my Creator," he said placidly, referring to the shadowed disciple Nicholas stole the book from at Lockehold.

"I am." Nicholas donned his infamous wayward grin. "And you are the fallen shade, Calix Fearworn. I have been hopeful for an audience, but this isn't what I had in mind."

"What you had in mind was a battle on your terms, though even that would not be enough for you to best me."

Fearworn swept a hand toward the miasma. Four beasts lurched out. Three were the muscled snake monsters from the village and the other must have been the perfected version of the flying beasts. A fraction bigger, with wings set right along its leathered hide and acid dripping from its fangs, scorching the earth beneath its clawed feet.

"If you are so confident, why bring an arsenal to battle against us?" Nicholas earned glares from his companions, even Arden.

Now was not the time to agitate the bastard they had been chasing for decades. They were outnumbered and, as Nicholas admitted, even the powerful shade could be taken down by too many fangs. William had nothing more than a knife to battle with. In the face of Fearworn's power, he was inconsequential. He hadn't felt so helpless since his training days. Worth less than a bug crushed beneath an unknowing heel.

"I want my book, and I will get it," Fearworn replied simply.

The monsters leapt. The air abandoned William's lungs when Nicholas tackled him out of the way. Surprising, seemingly to both of them, as the fae offered a wide-eyed stare prior to lunging onto his feet. William scurried up, too, clutching a blade far too small in the face of these beasts.

The monster with wings and three shadowed disciples descended upon them. Arden and Charmaine battled against the rest. Fearworn watched from a distance with calculative attention. The beasts hissed acid rain. Nicholas dodged. As did William, darting behind a nearby tree that came to life. The limbs snaked around him. He slipped from their grasp.

A shadowed disciple crept through the forest. His fingers cracked like a marionette on strings, forcing the forest to obey his whims. Shadowed disciples were nasty beings pushing themselves too far, some mortal and some fae, though no one could distinguish them once they got this bad. They commanded Fearworn's beasts and the elements, and it left them rotting like a corpse. William knew little of them other than they were vicious, powerful, and died young, sickly and corrupt to the core.

Branches snapped at William, scratching and beating him. A puddle of acid sizzled a step away. Grabbing a branch, he broke it free and dragged the branch through the acid. With a wild swing, he flung the acid. The disciple shrieked when the rain came upon him, eating through his features.

William sprinted forward. He stabbed the branch into the disciple's abdomen. Acid ate through the disciple's clothes and tore at the skin beneath. He released the branch when the shadowed disciple grabbed it. The branch came to life, thorns breaking forth that would have shredded his hands.

Clutching his blade, he went for the disciple's neck. The disciple surged backwards, dropping the branch and holding a hand over his burning stomach. The black of the disciples' eyes spread through his skin. His mouth lurched open, far too wide, stretching the skin and revealing a grotesque purple forked tongue.

William ran before the man shrieked; a sound so high pitched he whimpered beneath the pain. The forest erupted, trees quaking, roots bursting forth, and thorns sprouting from nowhere. He couldn't outrun the destruction, but he could use another to his advantage.

He dashed in Nicholas' direction. His power flashed through the forest, brilliant coral light and flames. One of the flying monsters battled against him, jabbing a wild stinger and lunging with vicious teeth. Nicholas must have heard the living forest because he looked over. Waving his hand, he ripped a tree from the ground to smack the monster across the head. It spewed a sea of acid, almost hitting William, but burning apart the forest at his back instead. He skid to a halt behind Nicholas.

"Trying to get me killed?" Nicholas snarled.

"Trying to spare myself," he replied. "Where are the other disciples?"

Nicholas didn't need to answer. William glimpsed the two lying mangled on the forest floor, limbs broken and clawed beyond recognition.

The miasma crept in, leaving a vile taste in the back of William's throat. Even the monster retreated. Fearworn approached with the shadowed disciple William injured. Fearworn raised his hand. A pulse rippled through the forest, flattening trees and sending them to their stomachs.

He couldn't breathe, struggling against the phantom pressure crushing him. A wild shout of anger and power burst forth from Nicholas. The pressure upon them lifted. Heaving, William rolled away. Nicholas' fuchsia light brightened. The strings around his form seized, becoming too difficult to gaze upon. That light coalesced into the form of a hissing snake. The head snapped forward. Fearworn swiped at the snake like it was nothing more than a bug. The light dispersed.

Fearworn set aflame. Violet light smothered him, towering into the sky. His eyes widened, monstrous voids that cracked the skin. The smooth voice existed no longer, replaced by a gravelly growl. "I tire of these games. Give. Me. My Book!"

He flicked his fingers. Nicholas stumbled, pulled closer by an unseen string. Another flick, and the book appeared beneath his shirt. He clutched at it, wrangling the invisible power. A snap at their back garnered William's attention. The beast inched forward. Its stinger raised high, pointed at Nicholas' back. William threw his knife. The blade embedded itself into the creature's tail.

Nicholas lost his concentration from the noise and the tome slipped from his hands. Fearworn caught the book. His power softened and a crooked smile spread across his face, child-like. He forgot about everything else, running a gentle hand over the cover and flipping through the pages.

William dared to pity the man, an unfortunate soul cursed at birth, if the tales of shades were true. He wondered who Fearworn had been before this and who he could have been without his obsessions.

Nicholas leapt. The shadowed disciple called forth roots that ripped across his arm, but it was too late. He was at Fearworn's throat, one hand of fire raised and another bristling with the light of a storm.

William lost sight of them after the beast lunged for him. He ran for the trees. A battle echoed behind him. Blasts of powers, Fearworn's growling voice threatening destruction, and the beast's lumbering steps. He listened for the monster's deep breath. He swerved to the right, avoiding a spray of acid. His gaze swept through the forest, desperate for an escape. Then Nicholas appeared above the beast with fuchsia light at his back spread as wings. A sphere of energy pulsated in his palm. The beast dodged, though the sphere singed its side. Nicholas fell beside William.

"Run," he demanded and held William's wrist hard enough to bruise. They bolted. Blood stained Nicholas' lips and chin.

"That blood," William said, panicked and worried, though he loathed to admit it.

"It is not mine." Nicholas wiped the blood away with the back of his arm and spat into the snow.

Behind them, the miasma strengthened. The fog devoured the trees, and the winged beast lurched out of it. William and Nicholas ran toward a thick grove of trees where they had to move sideways to slip through. Bark snagged on their clothes. Branches scratched their skin. A shadow passed overhead. The monster shrieked above. William looked up. His foot caught on a rock and he fell. His body rolled down a hill, grunting and groaning. He skidded to a halt at the bottom, panting and head spinning.

"Don't die on me now, my wicked," Nicholas demanded while sprinting down the hill. His harsh touch yanked William to his feet. "I haven't had all my fun with you yet."

"That makes me wish for death." His delirious eyes swept over their surroundings. He fell into a valley. The treetops formed a protective canopy. He glimpsed a cove along the hillside. "There," he whispered, limping forward. Upon closer inspection, the cove was more of a thin strip in the rock, shadowed by the canopy and hillside. "We can hide here. Use your magic to push snow in front of us. The beast won't notice."

"I can fight the beast. We kill it and keep moving," Nicholas argued.

They heard the monster passing by and the forest creaking, perhaps by the surviving shadowed disciples' will.

"We can't outrun Fearworn, especially with those beasts under his command," William argued, while pressing both hands to his throbbing head. His exhaustion hadn't settled, but he could at least heal himself of this concussion.

"The beast will see our tracks."

"I am certain your little fae tricks can cover them." He grabbed Nicholas' arm and yanked. "Fearworn got what he wanted. He will lose interest soon enough and take those damned wretches with him. We hide, unless you want to lose against Fearworn again once he catches up. Only this time, the loss will be permanent."

"I didn't," Nicholas bit back the lie he could not tell. Growling, he dragged his feet to the cove. The trees creaked, signs of the beast growing near.

"Nicholas," William hissed. "Now."

The fae gave a disgruntled huff and slid beneath the rock face. William followed, noting the disappearance of their tracks leading into the cove. Nicholas waved his fingers. Snow piled in front of them, leaving a slim opening for light to trickle in. The cove was barely big enough for them to lie atop one another. Chest to chest. Hips to hips. A heat that could melt a glacier into a lake. But the fae didn't take this opportunity to be a torment, and that spoke far more than the racing heart William felt against his chest.

Nicholas' eyes rolled, incapable of focusing. Sweat trickled from his brow. A hand clawed at the cove, nails shredding the rocks. His breaths came out sporadically, too much, then too little. Gripping Nicholas' hand, William tore it from the rock-face otherwise the monster would hear. He pressed two fingers to the shade's erratic pulse. Nicholas snarled, though as William tugged on the strings of his heart, he settled. His eyes fell half-mast and breathing evened out.

The earth shook. The monster shuffled through the snow outside.

Nicholas set a hand against William's waist. He ignored the touch of cool fingers rubbing the skin beneath his tattered clothes. For once, the fae didn't toy with him. This was to comfort himself. He clung to William, desperate and terrified. His eyes couldn't hide that truth, wide, unyielding, frightened, and focused entirely on William. As if focusing on anything else would make him lose himself entirely.

William didn't hate the attention as much as he should have.

Heavy steps came closer. They held their breaths. Nicholas' grip tightened. Though his nails cut William's skin, he said nothing. He pressed forward. Their foreheads touched. Nicholas' trembling hand interlocked their fingers, squeezing like his life depended on it.

The monster's hot breath fanned through the cove, then the creature veered away.

Nicholas' breathing slowed, but he kept them close, practically entangling their legs and brushing his cheek against William's. It was almost sweet, almost breathtaking. As were his eyes, that stifling roseate light invading every crevice of William's mind to illuminate the most lewd and frightful thoughts. He hated imagining how Nicholas would react if he kissed him, if he took those vile lips and made them bleed, made them moan and gasp.

Fuck, what is wrong with me? He thought.

The monster flew off. The trees creaked under the power of its wings. Neither dared to move for a horrible moment where it took far too much of William's willpower not to lean in, to destroy the space between them.

Then Nicholas pushed William toward the exit. The snow tumbled away. Nicholas crawled out of the cove, panting and running snow over his face. He shoved some into his mouth as if it'd wake him from a stupor and ran it through his hair.

"The great Nicholas Darkmoon is claustrophobic. I did not expect that," William remarked. He was somewhat relieved to catch Nicholas' pointed stare. That was more like him, more like them. Bickering would help him forget that dreadful thought of a kiss, of how his heart continued racing from Nicholas' touch rather than their near-death experience.

"I will not let you spoil my good mood," Nicholas said between swallowing more snow, then running his hands up and down his arms.

"Good mood? Albie and Arden are missing. Fearworn sent us running with our tails between our legs. Most importantly, we lost the book."

"Oh, but I got something much better." Chuckling, Nicholas stood. His voice and expression feigned humor well enough, but his body betrayed him. The hands clutched at his side continued to tremble. "Shall I share a secret with you, William Vandervult?"

William stood and dusted himself off. "Will I regret this secret?"

"Most likely, for if you tell another soul, it won't only be my wrath you incur, but that of my father. Believe it or not, he is far worse than me."

William could not imagine that. Nicholas proved to be irritable and violent with little provocation. Laurent must be a force few could withstand. However, the way Nicholas admired him piqued his interest enough to ask, "What is this secret?"

"Fae do not have monarchs. They have lords over wild Faerie lands, but no lord owns their land. Faerie lands have power, each different from the last."

"Is that where fae magic comes from, why some can call upon certain elements but not others? And why even fae fear those like you?"

Nicholas nodded. "In a way, yes. The older a fae gets, the stronger they become, but ultimately our abilities stem from our homelands. Shades, like me and Fearworn, call upon more power than our kin can comprehend and that scares them. However, only the lords and their direct lineage can tap into something special, something unique from their homes. Maybe because we are the protectors of our land. Maybe because Faerie likes to play games, too. None of us are for certain, but Darkmoon has a saying that all know in Faerie; do not bleed upon Darkmoon soil, for you will never leave."

"Is that some form of curse?" William asked. "Your blood binds you forever to the lands."

"You can physically leave, but Darkmoon knows you, has a part of you, and will always find you."

"This helps us, how?"

"I am of Darkmoon, as much a part of the land as the roots of its trees." Nicholas shut his eyes. When next they opened, they were striking violet; Fearworn's eyes. Though only Nicholas could pull off such a vicious grin.

"That blood from before," William muttered, momentarily breathless at the implications. "Fearworn's?"

"Precisely. So far from Faerie, the power of Darkmoon is weakened, but enough. Enough for me to hear and sometimes see through Fearworn's eyes, same as I did with his creator, and Fearworn will never be the wiser. Now," Nicholas cackled, elated beyond words. "I can track this bastard for the rest of his damn life."

That was the first time William had felt it in years; hope. A hope so stifling he joined Nicholas in his laughter. The fae's shock rendered him silent while William sounded erratic, pressing a hand to the back of his smiling lips that wouldn't cease no matter how much he willed them to.

The always hidden Calix Fearworn got caught by the one fae he shouldn't have. Out of everyone, Nicholas got his hands on him, teeth more accurately, and those teeth would never let go. The puppeteer's string could be severed and the world set free. The war could end. William could go home, leave these last five years behind and rework himself into a new man, a better one.

His laughter spilled over so loudly his throat and sides ached. Tears rimmed his eyes, a mixture of joy and fear. Returning home was all he ever wanted, and yet, the mirth couldn't outweigh a mounting fear. What would his family think of the man he became? Would they hate him as much as he hated himself? Could he be someone else, someone new and whole?

"I never heard you laugh. I was thinking you were incapable of it," Nicholas said.

"You never stopped to think it was because you did nothing worthy of a laugh," William countered between labored breaths.

"Of course not. I'm a thrill to be around."

William's laughter continued. He couldn't stop even when Nicholas captured his neck and waist. A rough hold where his nails pinched the skin of William's nape and for good reason, he'd have pulled away otherwise. At least he told himself he'd pull away if he could when Nicholas kissed him.

It was everything. A rush. A danger. A curse.

Shivering pleasure corrupted his senses as Nicholas clung to him like a last breath. The collision of their lips was by no means gentle. Nothing with Nicholas ever was. His pressure was overpowering, his wanting engraved into teeth that bit at William's lips. His tongue sought havoc, to muddle William's mind. It worked. He thought of nothing. A moment suspended in bliss, in the touch of Nicholas' greedy hands upon his yearning skin and their bodies becoming one.

The heat of the hot spring paled to this. Nothing could mimic how good Nicholas' wicked mouth felt pressed against his, or the pleasure of hearing the soft growl emanating from the back of his throat when William dared to retreat. Nicholas was greedy even for his air, trying to kiss until all faded to black.

"Now is not the time for this," he muttered against Nicholas' mouth, although he knew he should have said more. That this was wrong. He didn't want it. But they were grand lies he couldn't pretend to believe. As their lips brushed between panted breaths, all he could think about was kissing the bastard until they became sick of each other, until he knew Nicholas' lips better than any, until he could recognize his breath.

"Now is the best time." Nicholas' lips cascaded to William's neck, zealous to mark him. "Consider that a celebratory kiss and those to come a chance taken in case those beasts return to tear us to shreds. I want a taste of you before that may happen."

"Why?"

"Because you are disobedient." Nicholas pressed their foreheads together, so their gasps mingled in puffs of white. "You are a haunted soul, wild, dark, and dangerous. I dislike you entirely, but it is a strange dislike, one I crave."

"One you crave to crush." He pressed his hands to Nicholas' shoulder and pushed. "I will not let you fool me."

"Fool you?" Nicholas' fingers danced over his erratic pulse. "You are fooling yourself. What I may or may not do doesn't frighten you. What frightens you is that you like this as much as I do, my wicked. The danger. The rush."

William bit the inside of his cheek, tasting copper.

"A warm cup of tea and books, you said?" Nicholas chuckled coldly. "You were a child, but not anymore. Now, you're a dangerous man seeking to be something you aren't, to be tame when you are wild."

William should have formed a witty remark, should have fought back, but Nicholas spoke the truth, and he hated it. The truth terrified him. In the short time they've known each other, Nicholas peeled back layer after layer through sheer force of will. His constant annoyances, the prodding, the way he observed William like a specimen caught by a scientist with too much to prove, it all led to Nicholas mapping out the darkest recesses of William's soul and he couldn't shut the fae out.

"William!" Charmaine's voice cut through the haze. He conjured the power to shove Nicholas aside.

"We're here," he said.

Charmaine appeared along the edge of the hillside, covered in forest debris and blood. A long gash tore through her twitching left arm and her right eye swelled shut.

"Most of the blood isn't mine," she said before William conjured a word. "Arden needs you. Right now."

A hand caught William's waist. Nicholas leapt up the hillside, landing beside Charmaine. His hand lingered a moment longer than it should have. Charmaine didn't notice, already rushing in the other direction. William hurried forward, intent on ignoring the lustful eyes at his back and the cursed moment shared.

12

Nicholas

William and Charmaine stalked ahead. Nicholas trailed their steps. William's shoulders remained rigid after their kiss, since he hesitated and Nicholas perceived worry and realization in those typically stoic eyes. Pride swelled, an insurmountable yearning. Riling William up proved as fun as predicted. He was never anything less than surprising. That's what drove Nicholas toward him. A curious viper investigating the hawk's nest, knowing he could strike but would face razored claws.

"Won't you let me look at you?" William asked while inspecting the herbs Charmaine found during her earlier search for them.

"Save your strength," she replied. "Arden and I downed those three beasts and one disciple, but it was rough. They could have killed us, should have, and I don't know why they didn't."

"Because Fearworn got what he wanted."

"He has the book?" Charmaine spun on Nicholas. "You let him steal the book? We went through all this for nothing?!"

"Not for nothing," Nicholas replied nonchalantly.

"Are you going to elaborate?"

"No."

Charmaine snarled. William pressed a hand to her shoulder. She cursed Nicholas under her breath, then continued toward a pillar of smoke rising from the forest. Nicholas didn't follow. Fearworn could be anywhere. The last thing he wanted was to be in range of all of Fearworn's targets.

Shutting his eyes, Darkmoon's power trickled through him like dipping one's fingers into icy waters. So far from home, it took a moment longer for the chill to slip into his mind. When his eyes opened, a blurry sight greeted him. In Faerie, he'd see clearly. In Terra, he struggled to realize Fearworn was in the sky. Clouds dispersed as his miasma seeped around him, the one that wrought Nicholas with excitement and fear.

He doubted he could beat Fearworn alone. His kin would have to be at his back, which wasn't an encouraging thought. The moment Fearworn approached, Nicholas understood what he could become. A lost shade didn't constrain power. The power fed on them, ate away at their mind and body. Fearworn held a regal posture, but his blood left a foul taste in Nicholas' mouth. The bastard was more a corpse moving on wrath and twisted curiosity. Who he was before no longer remained.

Nothing frightened Nicholas more than losing himself entirely to a power he never asked for. Falling to a beast he couldn't fight against, not knowing what or who he would become. Being without control, lost in despair, falling forever, or disappearing entirely. It was terrifying, and potentially his future, one he didn't ask for, one that he was simply born to and told all his life that he walked a destined path of horror and despair. It was unfair, he knew that to be a childish thought but it was true. Why was he cursed? Why couldn't he escape fate?

Fearworn didn't appear to be circling them, so Nicholas let the sight slip away. When he opened his eyes, he continued forward to gaze upon Arden's mangled body leaning against the trunk of a ruined tree. His right leg clung to his form and acid had deteriorated his left arm. If Nicholas had to guess, a dozen bones were broken, too. The worst of the injuries was a branch piercing his chest. The beasts and a disciple laid dead nearby. Charmaine took one monster out, the smoke came from its sizzling flesh. The others laid in a pool of blood, bodies broken beyond recognition and wrangled by the forest, Arden's doing.

Nicholas chuckled. "You've seen better days."

"Those damned shadowed disciples were more than expected." Arden coughed. Blood trickled from his mouth. He growled when Charmaine set the bone back correctly in his shoulder.

"Are you not going to help your friend?" she snapped. "He's dying."

"He'll live. We are far more resilient than your lot." Nicholas yanked the branch out of Arden's chest. Blood gushed, and Arden released a drawn-out groan.

"If you aren't going to help, then fuck off," William warned. He pressed both hands over Arden's wound that slowly stitched itself together.

"So unappreciative." Nicholas dropped to the ground, legs crossed. "I am about to be more than helpful by tracking that bastard."

"Track?" Arden repeated, voice weakened and low. "Fearworn? How?"

"A secret for me to know and you to never find out." Nicholas let Darkmoon's power overtake him. He ignored the voices, Charmaine and William arguing over how to tend to Arden, some whines from Arden, then nothing.

Nicholas' blurred vision cleared to reveal the world beneath Fearworn. The evergreen forest of the Deadlands was the only thriving thing for they stretched on and on. There were few discernable marks on the land. The gorge they passed, a pond Fearworn swept over, then another ruined village twice the size of the last. Potentially what was once the capital based on the massive center building, though now nothing more than crumbled remains. Then Fearworn plummeted. The clouds dispersed to expose a mysterious form masked behind chunks of broken mountain range. Similar to Lockehold, the citadel sat along the edge of a high rock line, carved into gray stone.

Nicholas hissed William and Charmaine's worried words infiltrated his mind. He ignored them, willing Fearworn's vision to return. In Darkmoon, he could have sat like this uninterrupted for hours. Terra proved complicated and disappointing as ever.

Fearworn stood along a ledge, overlooking the work below. A scar glistening with foreboding light cut through the sky. The scar wavered, like looking through foggy glass from the first winter chill. Monsters crowded the portal, species of which Nicholas had never seen. Their numbers were too great, far more than what the military brought. If Fearworn unleashed these beasts before Nicholas returned, it'd be a slaughter, and he'd be remiss not to be a part of it.

"Can Arden be moved?" he asked, setting aside Fearworn's sight. A green paste stained Arden's chest where the wound lessened in size and his right leg sat correctly on his person.

"Normally, I advise against it, but we must get away from this carcass. Fearworn might return or his beasts will land for a snack," William replied. Sweat coated his brow and hands shook from all the energy spent on healing. He wouldn't meet Nicholas' eyes, either.

"Fearworn's army is far worse than predicted," Nicholas declared. "For him to attack, I think it is safe to surmise that our scouts are closing in on our location. He got to us before they could. We must find them and inform the generals."

"How do you know about his army?" Charmaine asked, brows furrowed.

"I saw it." He knelt in front of Arden. "Put this one on my back and let's get moving."

"How did you see it?"

"We need to move. Now," he said.

Arden stifled his anguished groans as the others shifted him onto Nicholas' back. He clung to Arden's bloody legs and trekked on. They moved with haste and remained vigilant. Charmaine and William circled like hounds, intent on preventing another attack. As the sun set, Nicholas spotted a perfect location to make camp, a line of carriages wrecked along the side of what once must have been a road. Their wheels were shattered and tarps torn, but much of the exterior structure remained. Charmaine and William eased Arden into a carriage that set flat on the ground, the wheels long since rotted away. A few flicks of Nicholas' hands and roots encased the carriage, then a pile of snow, so they appeared as nothing more than a mound in the forest. Even the dim firelight Charmaine created within didn't melt the snow, allowing them to remain warm, sheltered, and hidden.

"I'll take the first watch," Nicholas offered.

"I don't trust your kindness," Charmaine muttered. Sleep laced her voice.

"This is self-preservation. Either of you may fall asleep and we'll be devoured by spion offspring."

Although William rolled his eyes, he settled beside Charmaine for a rest that never truly came. The man shifted and turned long after Charmaine's breaths changed to soft snores and stars lit the sky, though the gray skies of the Deadlands paled their light. They existed as no more than specks, incapable of sharing their ethereal light with the world.

Nicholas contemplated spying on Fearworn, but decided against it. There were monsters out here keen on tearing out their throats. He remained alert, gaze shifting through the bleak woods. He pondered all that lived in the dark, monsters taken from their homes and brought to fight, not much different than him.

A few hours passed. The carriage creaked. William stepped past Nicholas into the cool air, crossing his arms and rubbing his hands along his biceps. "We can switch," William said.

"You haven't slept," Nicholas argued, his eyes incapable of straying from the embodiment of desire standing beside him. He hated the air that damned man breathed, and yet, he wanted to taste every breath on his tongue.

"I slept some."

"Barely." William's back went rigid when Nicholas asked, "Since you are awake, are we going to speak on important matters?"

"What important matters?"

"Our kiss, how we want each other."

"What I want is for your lips to seal forever."

"I am sure there are ways to change your mind." He approached William, smirking at the familiar cold eyes he was exceptional at sharing. "There is nothing wrong with lust, with a little shared adventure in the twilight hours."

"There is when that adventure is a trick for a spoiled fae brat intent on causing havoc." William lurched around the remnants of another carriage, one leaning against the hillside, knowing Nicholas would follow. "I know what you want. I know this is a game for you. A test of your deceptions to see what you can get me to agree to. How is this a winning scenario for me in any form?"

"What if I make an oath not to reveal what transpires tonight to any soul, living or dead?" Nicholas suggested.

William curled his nose. He suspected William wanted to ask if he could speak to the dead. The answer was yes. There were plenty of places in Faerie where the dead walked.

"Why are you so insistent? Speak honestly," William demanded.

"I already have." He caught William by the chin, bringing them eye to eye. "You know I cannot lie. I also like the danger, the rush. I will not speak to any soul, living or dead, about what transpires between us tonight, or any other."

"You speak as if there will be a tonight or any other."

"I am speaking about what I hope will come to fruition. For you, I would even beg if it means I can spend a single evening between your legs."

William grew quiet. Time lingered, stretched, unfurled before them beneath a dreary sky.

"Then beg," William ordered.

If he believed that to be a twisted lie, Nicholas surprised him by dropping to his knees. William's breath caught. His skin blazed beneath the shade's curious fingers, brushing past the ruins of his uniform.

"Let me take you," Nicholas said, pressing a harsh kiss to the skin of William's stomach. He sucked in a breath that didn't stop the fae's keen lips from mapping his skin. "Give me an evening and I'll ensure you will not forget it, that it will be me you dream of when any other fucks you."

"That's a mighty promise to make, even for you."

"You should have learned by now that I love a challenge and I am not one to disappoint, even more so because I want you." His teeth tore into William's trembling hip. He soothed the wound with his tongue, relishing in the shivers his mouth provoked. "If your mortal gods are real, then I do not doubt they set you in my path purely to torment me. I've never wanted one as I have wanted you. Please. Let me have a taste of you, my wicked."

William's lips stilled, eyes mysterious beneath the shaded trees, then he unbuckled his belt. Nicholas tugged those wretched trousers off to get what he desired. He devoured the skin presented to him, enjoying the catch in William's breath.

He didn't hesitate to pleasure his partner tonight. William would put an end to this if things didn't go his way and he may burn this forest to the ground if that happened. His hand worked William's base as he marked all that he could. Leaving harsh kisses along William's hip and thigh until his mouth slipped over a rosy arousal. William rewarded Nicholas with a low moan. Sounds he couldn't imagine William making and adoring that they came out now, desperate for more. His pace had William slipping his fingers into Nicholas' hair. The sound of their lies set Nicholas' chest ablaze. William would hate for the others to wake and find him like this, coming undone by the mouth of a fae he hated. He was tempted to make that happen, to unravel William so completely that his cries woke all that slumbered, but dare he say he would be jealous, that he would hate any other to hear William like this.

William nearly ripped out his hair when he dared to depart. Goosebumps broke out across the medic's skin, though that didn't cease the frantic rolling of his hips into Nicholas' palm. Those reserved eyes darkened, set above pink tinted cheeks.

"Your beauty is best like this, desiring me," he purred against William's trembling thighs.

One of his clawed hands ran along William's body, tugging up a useless shirt. He stood slowly, taking his time to savor the skin presented to him. His tongue ran over the pink nipple that caught his eye days back, relishing in the taste of William's sweat. He was a glorious indulgence.

"And your mouth is best like this. Dare I say that you're almost tolerable," William replied, sounding far too composed for his liking.

"Your moans tell me I am more than tolerable."

Nicholas' teeth sank into the dreg's chest and his hand pumped William faster. William's moans grew from the ravenous attention of the shade's lips over his chest. That was what he wanted, to wreck that typically calm disposition, to make William his in a way that couldn't be denied, that would stay with them always.

He marked William's shoulder and up his neck to take his lips in a hungry kiss. He tasted forbidden, ominous, and dangerously sweet. Then of copper when Nicholas tore into a bottom lip. William returned the favor, nails piercing his neck while the other hand slipped beneath Nicholas' trousers. The first touch of calloused hands on his cock had

Nicholas reeling. Their eyes met, and Nicholas found his hungry reflection in William's lustful eyes.

"I can't wait for you to cry out my name," Nicholas said.

William smirked, dauntless even with his cheeks flushed. "Are you so confident that it will be your name? What if I'm thinking of another?"

"Dare to call out for another and I will find them and slit their throat."

"Aren't you a romantic?" William grunted when Nicholas abruptly turned him. He returned to his knees and William panted against a curious tongue fervently pleasuring his backside.

He wanted William to beg and scream, but the fire hissed and Charmaine released a quiet cough as a remembrance of their lies. Of how the others would find them should they wake, though that wouldn't stop him from curling his tongue and relishing in the shivers wracking William's frame.

William bucked against Nicholas' mouth. He reached around William to take hold of his cock. The medic's breath stuttered, legs trembling and hips rocking violently against the double stimulation. He relished in every sound William made, but when he rose and his pants fell around his ankles, William turned.

He caught Nicholas in a rough kiss, then grabbed the fae's arm to shove him toward the nearby carriage. His back met the creaking floor and William straddled him. Their bodies collided in a wave of ecstasy. He groaned when William rode him hard and fast, never relenting as the carriage creaked beneath the frenzied jerks of his body.

Nicholas wanted to break him. To take him to the point of unrivaled pleasure and bask in the moment where the smug dreg couldn't do more than moan; all the while knowing the one about to make him finish was that annoying fae he despised so much.

He ran a hand up William's body to slip around his neck. William grunted from the rough yank down for a kiss, messy and erotic and rough. Their thrusts slowed until Nicholas growled against William's ears, "I want to tear you apart."

William chuckled. "As if you could."

Nicholas slammed forward, relishing in William's fingers curling against his chest. He couldn't stop their sex even if Fearworn's beasts were upon them. Too lost to the heat suffocating his arousal, burning him from the inside out, too overtaken by William's stifled groans and the sight of him riding Nicholas like he was made for this purpose.

When they met, he wanted to break the bastard. He never knew he wanted it like this, enraptured by William's beauty, the paleness of his skin, the taste of his sweat, the warmth of his backside, and the melody of his voice. Though Nicholas didn't receive the screams he desired, that excited him more, a challenge that the mortal would no doubt make exceedingly difficult. William took him to a high he never wanted to leave, and yet couldn't wait for the fall.

William's hips thrashed, devious as his words. Nicholas' nails tore crescent shapes into his backside, bucking when he dared to still. "Why'd you stop?" William groaned.

"I don't want this to end yet. Consider this punishment for making me wait," he replied.

William kissed his neck, finally sounding breathless. "Isn't tolerating you punishment enough?"

"I believe I'm more than making up for my previous transgressions."

"You're forgetting how insufferable you are," William moaned when Nicholas smacked his ass. He didn't miss the shiver and smacked him again. William's eyes were alight with pleasure, lips swollen, and hair a tangled mess, illuminated by pale orange firelight.

Nicholas enjoyed the dander in his eyes, the glare threatening an end to their evening if he pushed him too far. He liked even more when those eyes clouded with lust from the abrupt thrusting of his hips and the touch of his hand smoothing over William's arousal. Exactly what William wanted as he tore into his lip to stifle the sounds of their sex.

"Come for me," Nicholas demanded, savoring the stutter in William's breath followed by an orgasm that left him shaking. William hid his face against Nicholas' shoulder and muffled his noises by catching the shade's skin between his teeth. Nicholas followed shortly, drowning in a sea of finite bliss, fingers clawing William's hips, bruising them and forgetting for a moment that this was real. Neither stopped until they were spent, breathless and shivering under the falling snow.

"This is the moment where you take it back," Nicholas whispered against the tasteful nape presented to him.

"What?" William hummed.

"That I couldn't possibly know what a good fucking is."

William laughed. He pushed himself onto his elbows and passed Nicholas a smug smirk. "I've fucked better."

"Liar." Nicholas kissed him more ravenously than ever.

13

William

When William woke, crust coated his eyes. He tried not to think of last night, of Nicholas' hands and vicious mouth exploring his body. Of those roseate eyes adoring him, reflecting his voracious hunger to remind him of the mistakes made. He especially refused to think of how he wanted more. In those moments, when lust overcomes all thought, it's easy to pretend nothing else exists. William can forget the world, every thought and worry he has ever had, and drown in a moment of ecstasy that lets him believe, even for a second, that life is good.

Then the next morning he always woke to grim reality. Shifting onto his elbows, he glared at the sleeping fae, no doubt aware of the internal dilemma he set upon William. It's what Nicholas wanted; to push him, to evoke a reaction. Sometimes the bastard said the right thing at the right time because fae were calculating and, as he expressed, William stole his interest. Rather, William gave him attitude when others didn't and the fae were strange enough to find that a desirable trait.

William crawled out of the carriage. Charmaine stalked outside, hands wringing together and eyes trance-like. The sun rose well past dawn. He couldn't recall the last time he slept in. As a child, he was allowed when ill, but otherwise his loud brothers or a soft kiss from his parents woke him. Here, danger lurked everywhere, so sleep eluded most even when they were in dire need of it.

"You can rest. I'll take the next watch," William called.

"Are you sure?" Charmaine's eyes narrowed. "There's a dark spot on your neck."

"Probably a bruise from yesterday's tussle." A tussle with a dumb fae who should have known not to leave visible marks, and he should have known better than to give in.

Charmaine took the bait or was too tired to think otherwise. "I'll take a brief rest then."

"You can rest as long as you need. Once Nicholas wakes, I'll search for herbs."

William threw Arden a glance. Although the fae slept, his wounds healed slowly. The shadowed disciples truly were a force to be reckoned with to down a fae for so long. And William had less power than he wanted to admit. The continuous days of little food and rest took its toll. His magic was too tumultuous to risk using further. He refused to die for a fae, of all things.

"We can't move with Arden like that, even if we are potentially close to the army," he added.

"Don't search for herbs alone." Charmaine meandered toward the carriage. "Wake me, so I may go with you."

William nodded, although had no intention of waking her. She needed rest and he wouldn't go far. Charmaine crawled into the space he previously occupied and shut her eyes. Shivering, he took a moment to search the surrounding area, ensuring nothing lingered nearby. Charmaine had done the same, based on her footprints. He continued the circle, allowing the walk to warm him and the aching of his muscles to keep his thoughts at bay. At least until Nicholas wriggled out of the carriage to catch up with him.

"Sleep well, my wicked?" he asked, catching William by the waist. The now far too familiar touch almost made him shiver.

He shifted out of Nicholas' clutches and marched on. "I said not to call me that."

"And I elected to ignore you." Nicholas skipped ahead of him. "Are you now electing to ignore me?"

William's eyes swept over Nicholas without his consent, still thinking of last night, of how little he truly saw in the night and how he'd much rather see it in the light. That was a thought he elected to ignore.

"I am relieved you haven't changed this morning." Nicholas licked devilish lips that tasted too sweet to belong to him. "It'd be no fun if you suddenly became bashful."

"If I play bashful, will you leave me be?"

"Try it and find out."

"It's always a game with you."

"Life is boring without games, and I think you've had more fun playing these games with me than you let on."

Shaking his head, William stepped toward the trees. Nicholas followed, though came to a stop when William held up a hand and said, "Keep watch. I'm going to search for herbs. Alone."

"But there is so much more we can do together." Nicholas took William's wrist and tugged him close. Their lips brushed. William felt Nicholas' wry grin, could practically hear the lustful thoughts churning in his mind, then shoved him aside.

"Stay here," William said.

"I don't like being ordered around."

"If you behave, I might reward you when I get back."

Nicholas hesitated to snarl, "I'm not a dog willing to listen for treats."

William walked away, snickering to himself when Nicholas didn't follow. It seemed the dog would listen for treats, even if he didn't intend to give any. On his trek, William found no herbs or food. They hadn't eaten since yesterday, having finished the last of the dried creatures from the hot spring. His stomach twisted, but he was accustomed to hunger. His thoughts strayed to more pressing matters; what transpired last night with Nicholas. A piss poor decision made by the wrong head.

He couldn't risk telling anyone lest he wanted a good beating, at the very least. Charmaine would be appalled, rightfully so. Nicholas swore not to tell, but fae had their ways. He knew that and made the mistake, anyway. Too tired, too cold, wanting to feel anything other than death lingering over his head. Indulgence made the mayhem of his life a little less foreboding. He never felt good otherwise, rarely had a glimpse of hope or joy.

"Fuck," he muttered and kicked at the snow. A piece rolled away, stopped by hitting a pair of military boots, same as his. William looked up, expecting to see Charmaine, but met a pair of accusatory brown eyes, ones he knew too well. That he knew wasn't actually there because Hugh was dead. That knowledge didn't stop his lungs from constricting when Hugh's mirage inched closer. Light cut through the trees to unveil Hugh's pained expression, one of betrayal and hate. He stood tall and strong, thick hands that flexed so the veins bulged beneath bloodied tan skin.

"You're seeing things," William whispered, but could not will his eyes to shut. When Hugh died, he visited William through horrendous nightmares. Then the dreams became so sweet he woke up in tears. Over the last month or so, Hugh's memory faded, as if William's mind was desperately trying to forget him entirely. But there he stood, as if he had never left.

"Was it so easy to forget me?" Hugh asked, every word carving a deeper wound to the scars already there.

"He isn't real." William closed his eyes. An icy breath hit his cheeks. He told himself it was the wind. When his eyes opened, the trees bent from a strong, frigid breeze and Hugh had vanished. The pain hadn't.

"When this war is over, when we are home, I would like to be with you, William. Properly." Hugh said that and William suddenly had hope because he did, too. He hoped his family would accept the cheerful farmer's son that made him believe in a happily ever after. But then reality hit, like it did now.

Charmaine shouted for William, breaking him from his stupor. He burst into a run, hand on the knife at his waist. Guilty thoughts diminished in the face of a potential battle. His heart leapt, ardent and desiring a distraction. His worries and excitement disappeared when he came upon their campsite. Over two dozen of their scouts surrounded the caravan. Nicholas stood among them speaking with Duke, the mentor that accompanied him on the night they met in the medical tent, along with an unknown military official. Not a general, but certainly higher up based on the symbols stitched to his jacket.

"I never thought I'd be so relieved to return to the army," Charmaine said under her breath.

"Me either." William joined her by the carriage, struggling to forget Hugh's ruined expression.

A group of fae passed, carrying a stretcher. Arden grunted from within the carriage. They set their kin upon the stretcher and walked off. Perfect timing, too. Oscar's boyish face peeked out of the crowd, bright eyed and gaping. He darted over to them, passing the fae a cursed look, then setting his thrilled attention upon them.

"Albie, William, you're both breathin'!" He shouted, showing that he shared Charmaine's love for hugging by wrapping her in his arms. Then he moved to William, who gently patted his back and counted the seconds to freedom.

"We was beginnin' to think you were dead." Oscar retreated, allowing two others to approach. Oscar and the other soldier carried jackets, gloves, water, and food. The nurse, Francesca, was a medical mage, the same as William. The only opportunities women had in the military were as healers paying off family debts or seeking money to support their families. The military loved to drown the desperate.

"Inspect Albie's leg first," William instructed. "I did what I could, but for some reason, the injury appears to have become infected."

"It isn't infected," Charmaine argued, but allowed Francesca to guide her to the edge of the carriage. Francesca peeled the fabric away. A bruise, too big for William's liking, marked Charmaine's leg. He healed her injury, and yet something was amiss.

While Francesca inspected the damage, Charmaine and William took the offered clothes. He rubbed his gloved hands together, relieved by the warmth of the fabric. Even salted pork carried a holy taste after days of spion legs and questionable eel-like creatures. Charmaine shoveled the food so quickly into her mouth he feared she'd choke.

He set a hand on her shoulder. "We have food now. No need to inhale it."

"Right. Sorry, I'm famished." She took a long swig of water.

"I know. Me too."

"What happened?" Oscar asked. The other soldier that brought their provisions hesitated to leave. His eyes wandered between Charmaine and William. They wanted a tale, one that would move swiftly through the ranks. Out here, gossip spread better than a virus.

"Those beasts grabbed us and flew off," said Charmaine between rabid bites. "Nicholas and William slayed one. We roamed these woods for days with monsters constantly on our tail, and then Fearworn appeared."

The soldier shut his eyes and pressed two fingers to his heart in a prayer. William resisted the urge to roll his eyes. Oscar and Francesca shared expressions of horror, expecting Charmaine's words to be a joke. When neither laughed, Oscar muttered, "How did ya survive?"

"Dumb luck," William replied.

His attention shifted from Oscar to a figure closing in on them, Duke. Behind him, Nicholas walked off with the other military official. William caught the fae's attention. Nicholas winked, then disappeared among the scouts.

"William and Albert, is it?" Duke called.

"Yes?" Charmaine muttered.

Settling at their side, Duke gave a low nod. "Lord Nicholas informed me of your assistance during this endeavor, particularly of you, William. He might have died out there without you. His father and betrothed will be pleased to hear of his safe return."

William bit his cheek. He tasted blood. The salt from the pork burned the inside of his mouth. His expression did not mirror the worry festering like an old infected wound in his gut.

"Betrothed?" Oscar asked in his stead. "Fae wed and the like? I always thought their kind were a bit too promiscuous for that."

"Faerie customs differ from ours, although some do ring similar. There are marriages among their kind and practices differ from land to land. I admit I'm not too educated on the subject." Duke spoke as if his next words were of genuine delight. "Regardless, Evera Bloodbane is her name. Her brother, Amos Bloodbane, serves alongside us, and their mother has sent many of her kin to fight. Don't be surprised if any of them pay you a visit one day. Fae always return favors."

William did not see that as a favor, but a warning.

"I'm glad to have been of service," he replied.

Frustrated would be a more appropriate term. William did not know of fae customs in terms of marriage or engagement, either. He could not fathom them having care for anyone other than themselves. He suspected Nicholas and Arden may have taken each other to bed, whether Evera consented to that arrangement or Nicholas didn't care was beyond him. Regardless, any excuse for trouble, fae took, and Nicholas bedding a mortal certainly spelled trouble.

"I am also most grateful. Lord Nicholas is of great importance not only to Faerie but also to Terra. He's our greatest hope against Fearworn.

I will ensure to inform His Royal Majesty about your deeds, as well," Duke added.

William wasn't keen on earning the king's attention. After all, he ordered children to war, including William. When he was drafted, he was confused and guilt-ridden. A voice whispered that his brothers should have gone, and his heart ached for ever wishing the cruelty of war upon them. But as he got older, wiser, he remembered his mother asking his father why the king chose William and Robert replied; *you know why.*

Robert Vandervult never had an issue standing his ground. That included telling the king he was failing his people. He hoarded wealth, cut funding to hospitals, orphanages, and homeless shelters. He founded workhouses instead, turning a blind eye to helping those in need. Robert claimed them all cruel. William wasn't a part of politics, but even he understood Robert had caused a ruckus by the strange looks they received in town and the parties the Vandervults were no longer invited to in high society. When the king started the draft, he ordered William to go. The Vandervult's punishment would be the loss of their youngest child, the one all knew was least likely to survive.

But William wouldn't dare speak of that to Duke, so he forced an amicable smile and nodded. Duke excused himself, then a scout ordered everyone to prepare to move out. Francesa wrapped Charmaine's leg.

"The bone is not broken, nor is there an infection," Francesca explained. William determined that, but suspected he may be wrong from exhaustion. Hearing the same from Francesca worried him. If nothing is wrong, the bruise should be gone.

"All I can suggest is that we monitor the wound and regularly heal it." Francesca approached William. "May I take a look at you?"

He nodded. The scouts banded together, preparing to leave. Francesca finished up, deeming him fit to travel. A moment later, the group began the trek to camp with Charmaine and William safely tucked between them.

"I've become accustomed to being around so many people that they make me feel oddly safe. Sometimes," Charmaine said, huddled by William's side. Her steps had a lightness to them he tried to mirror.

"I'm certainly relieved knowing there are others to remain vigilant rather than us," he replied.

Especially now, when his mind wouldn't cease. Evera, and her brother, Amos Bloodbane, William made note of the names, seeing as they may belong to the ones who slay him in the future. He never planned to speak of what transpired with Nicholas, not even to Charmaine, but now he had even more reason to keep silent. Last night never should have happened. He was a fool. He knew better.

"How long will it be until we reach the camp?" Charmaine asked.

"About two days," Oscar replied. "That damn gorge frightened the lot of us. Did you see it?"

William and Charmaine nodded.

"A strange magic," Francesca muttered. "A few of our scouts nearly stepped in and the fae tried to cross using magic, but it did not work. Took us an extra day to walk around it."

"No one knows what it is?" Charmaine inquired.

"Some fae debated it may be a dumpin' ground for Fearworn's creations," Oscar replied. "A place for his cursed magic to fade and die, but it has all been guesswork."

"Plausible guess work and, well, I don't want to go back to discover the truth."

"Nor do we!" Oscar crossed his arms to hug himself and shivered. "The military continued movin' during our search, too. They headed further north after comin' across a den of monsters."

"We outnumbered them," Francesca said. "There were casualties, but the generals saw it as a sign that we were moving in the right direction. Or that's what we heard through all the gossip, so we are lucky to have found you here so close to the new camp."

"I think we should head this way, too, if you came across," Oscar swallowed hard and whispered the name like a curse, "Fearworn."

"He came because Nicholas had something he wanted. That tome from Lockehold was a book of monsters," William explained. He didn't divulge how Nicholas had a way to track Fearworn. He would never mention Darkmoon, but he also didn't want to present false hope. Nicholas could track him. That didn't mean they would defeat him.

"Did he take it?" Francesca asked.

"Yes," Charmaine replied.

"Then we lost our advantage."

"I don't believe so. Nicholas claimed to have something better, though wouldn't share what. He loves his secrets."

"I am okay with secrets if it brings an end to Fearworn and this war," said Oscar.

William agreed, although was no more optimistic than usual.

14

Nicholas

Attention, Nicholas always reveled in it. He did so now, standing at the head of a round table surrounded by the human generals, fae commanders, and Duke at his back. They crowded in the high tent. Melted wax fastened the candles to the table. A grin worthy of a beast spread over Nicholas' features. The tent fell silent when he declared, "I can track Calix Fearworn."

"How?" asked Herald Price, a man unworthy of the title of general. Duke expressed once that Herald had more than earned his position. Nicholas bet on those smooth hands and shivering disposition that Herald bought his position. Mortals so loved their gold coins and those with the most merely passed them along to get what they wanted.

"In ways I will not divulge to you, or anyone," Nicholas replied. The room scoffed and cursed, arguments cultivating that he ignored. "It does not matter if I share for none other than I can track him."

He listened to Fearworn now, the clinking of metal and shrieking of a beast. Making more monsters or perfecting them, no doubt. Hearing the world around him as well as Fearworn caused an ache at the base of his neck, the prick of a spear pushing on his spine.

"He works in the northeast, a couple days travel on fae feet, although I remain unclear on what to expect. This could be his base of operations or a monster encampment, but there are many beasts. Far more than we predicted and some we do not know. If they attack now, we would not be prepared for such numbers," Nicholas explained.

"Then we send scouts first," said General Wright, a far more respectable mortal than Price. Nicholas fought alongside Wright in battle twice. Unlike many, he rode toward death alongside his men and dealt deadly blows even fae had to respect. He wore those battles on his scarred skin and through the gray peppering his braided beard.

"If the fae commanders agree, let us send at least six fae to scout the area. Once they have a better lay of the land and forces, they will return to our encampment. We'll determine what move to make afterward and the necessary troops to call in from the south," Wright finished, his voice stern and authoritarian.

"Should we risk waiting?" Morrison argued, another general, younger, albeit scarred and hunched slightly. He turned his attention to Nicholas. "You claimed their forces are too great, that if they attacked now, we would be horribly outnumbered."

Nicholas nodded and allowed the noise of Fearworn's world to fade. He couldn't manage the strain.

"Should we not remain as we are or retreat toward Lockehold to wait for further enforcement? There is no point calling troops that will end up replacing what we lost," Morrison continued.

"Retreating is a waste of valuable energy. Our men may march all day only to be attacked when the sun falls. I think it best we remain where we are," Wright countered.

"The fae commanders agree," Amos Bloodbane said among the once whispering fae. The Bloodbanes had an eeriness about them with their ashen colored skin varying from soft gray to a pale blue. Amos resembled a field of ash after purifying flames, eyes pure white without pupils, and his equally white hair buzzed. He always sounded bored when he spoke, unlike his sister. Evera always sounded on the verge of slaughtering everyone in the room. Though that may have been Nicholas' fault. Neither of them could stand each other, so the sight of the other put them into an immediately foul mood.

"Our army should remain here, waiting and conserving energy, while our scouts move forward," Amos said, speaking for the commanders at his back. "Have the soldiers prepare for an assault by setting up more permanent defenses. Once the scouts return, we can decide on whether to wait or move."

The generals murmured to one another. They wavered, arguing back and forth, until they ultimately agreed.

"Do you have anyone in mind to travel with me?" Nicholas inquired

"Once you inform our scouts of Fearworn's location, you may remain here. If Fearworn moves, you can inform the generals while our scouts follow or return with further information," Amos argued.

He had never been the type to care about Nicholas' safety, so that was Amos' mother speaking, the one who very much did care. Alvina Bloodbane had plans and she would see them through, even if it meant sending her children to do her bidding. No doubt Amos didn't mind, he always said his mother had never steered him wrong, so he saw no reason to defy her. Nicholas found that to be unbearably naive, that one day Alvina would use that steadfast loyalty against him.

"Your life cannot be risked," General Herald added. "As the only one who can track Fearworn, who refuses to share how."

"And what happens if our scouts stumble upon Fearworn alone? They won't take him down without me," Nicholas countered. "I fought him in the forest. He'll annihilate any we send after him. This must be a battle between shades."

Though he declined to inform anyone that he would need help, too. That would be dealt with when the time came.

"Lord Darkmoon would not be pleased should you do this," Duke warned in a whisper at his back. "You are a good faith delegate. You are not meant to risk your life so frequently. He was displeased to hear of your capture."

"If he cared so much, he shouldn't have sent me into a war zone," Nicholas argued, although he knew it was far more complicated than that.

Laurent cared about Nicholas' status as a shade. A weapon at his disposal to command, and he commanded this weapon to end the war. While fae loved their slaughters, none cared for working alongside mortals. It was necessary for survival. Laurent and the other High Fae in particular found The Collision Treaty to be an insult. A disgrace upon them they wanted burned to ash, and it would be upon the defeat of Calix Fearworn by the hands of a Darkmoon. Afterward, they could return to a life of making deals with foolish mortals, toying with them as fae pleased.

Yes, Laurent wanted Nicholas to kill Fearworn, but to do so "with tact and manner." Neither of which Nicholas had or was particularly interested in. He would not miss out on this fun, wouldn't miss an opportunity to set power free. He had never felt so much like himself than he has in this war, releasing all the pent-up energy that gnawed at him every damn day. This relentless energy would go up against Fearworn, who wore a strength Nicholas knew he couldn't stand against and that rarely happened, so when it did, he ran after that power to taste the thrill again. To perhaps postpone his own demise.

"So, who will scout with me?" Nicholas asked. Sighing, Amos nominated himself and listed options for the other four. Nicholas argued against bringing his sister, but knowing Amos, he would choose her out of spite. Once everyone agreed, the meeting dispersed.

Nicholas was to meet with the scouts in an hour. He headed for his tent, intending on taking a brief rest when he passed the medical bay. The army moved during their capture, taking to an empty grove where tents littered the area. William stood inside the medical tent, inspecting sick and needy bastards. Nicholas thought of the night they shared and how he wanted more. He couldn't have William today, but when he returned, he wanted that vexing medic in his bed.

He peeked inside the medical tent, where William spoke sweetly to an ailing patient. The words were unlike him, promising peace with a smile that didn't reach his eyes. They were as dispirited as ever when pouring medicine into the soldier's mouth. The nurses took over, adjusting blankets and pillows to give comfort, and passing off what needed to be washed. William noticed Nicholas. His scowl worsened.

"What do you want?" William asked. He held an armful of dirty linen and stepped toward the exit. Nurses whispered as he and Nicholas walked past.

"Am I not allowed to pay you a visit?" he replied, following William outside.

A supply tent had been pitched next door. Crates filled most of the space containing clean linen and bandages to potions and herbs. The scents mixed, death and decay, herbs and soap. They wrangled Nicholas' senses. He couldn't fathom how one could be around this vile odor all day.

William dropped the dirty linen into a pile. "You are paying a visit because you want something. Spit it out and be done with it."

"You've come to know me so well. I have a proposition to continue our evening rendezvous'."

"Continue?" William spat between clenched teeth. "How could you ask me to lie with you once, let alone more, when you are engaged? I dare not imagine fae customs in marriage, but I can guess your fiancé will not be pleased to learn of you bedding a human."

"Evera would find our physical union appalling, but not for the reasons you seem to be thinking of," Nicholas replied, confounded by

William's apparent worry. "We were engaged at ten, although we will not officially wed until after the war ends, at the least, if she survives that long."

"Survives?"

"We have tried to kill each other on a number of occasions. Got me a good beating from time to time because of it."

William gawked, then shifted his weight from one foot to the other. "And why have you tried to assassinate your fiancé?"

"Because I despise the wretched hag, and she despises me."

"You will have to elaborate further."

"You mortals care about the most trivial matters. How did you even come by this knowledge?"

"Duke thanked me for saving you and expressed that your father and fiancé would be relieved to hear we had been found."

That earned a laugh out of Nicholas, resulting in William's further confusion.

"Evera would throw a revel of unfathomable mirth should she learn of my demise," he explained, which did not deter William's gaze, sharp as steel. "You are right, a bit of context is in order; there are marriages between fae for love just as there is among your kind. However, many fae marry for agreements, also no different from your rulers, if I am recalling correctly. Our arrangement was made between our parents because of debts we owed to them. We do not have feelings for one another outside of grueling hatred. Neither of us are pleased with this deal. She has multiple partners, no doubt warming her bed at this moment, and I've certainly had my fair share, too."

William pressed his fingers to either side of his temple. Nicholas settled a hand on William's waist, enjoying the low growl emanating from the back of his throat. He found humor in William's irritation, how regardless of that irritation they were drawn to each other. William had a magnetic wanting about him, a force worth begging for.

"Asking about this, were you perhaps jealous, my wicked?" Nicholas snickered.

"Don't be ridiculous. Fae do not like oath breakers. I feared an angry fae would be on her way to disembowel me for ruining an engagement," William answered.

"You needn't worry about her. If anything, she'd appreciate having you as a distraction."

William stepped away from the embrace to grab fresh linen. "While I am glad that is settled, that doesn't change my answer. Go away."

"I am leaving," Nicholas said, smirking at William's piqued interest. "Myself and a handful of scouts are moving ahead to inspect Fearworn's location. I am not sure how long we'll be gone."

"And you came to see me before you left? How sweet." William's tone and expression did not mirror his words. He made way toward the exit, but Nicholas blocked his path.

"I can be sweet when I want something, and I want you in my bed when I return."

William glared. "I am not going to be your little pet that pleases you at night."

"What is so wrong with pleasing each other?"

"You know damn well what. One night was more than enough."

"Was it? Our evening together was incredible, wasn't it? And I wish for an evening where you can thoroughly enjoy yourself."

"And what do you mean by that?"

Nicholas gripped William's chin and leaned forward. Every word uttered made their lips brush. "I want you to scream for me."

"Did I not tell you that you will never have them?"

"Give me the opportunity to change your mind." Nicholas plucked a dried flower from a box of herbs. He twisted it between his fingers, commanding the herb to roll into a ring. William gave the item a perplexed stare when the fae offered it to him. "Should you decide you want more evenings of pleasure, wear this ring and meet me in my tent. This will never wilt and will hide you, so others won't notice, not even fae, though it doesn't work well on monsters, so don't use it in battle."

"Did this have to be a ring?" The hatred in William's voice could set a city ablaze.

"No." Nicholas slipped the ring into William's hand. "But the symbolism is amusing, wouldn't you agree?"

"I hate it."

"And I am happier for it." Nicholas retreated, a playful sneer on his face. "When I return, I hope to find you waiting."

William rolled his eyes and Nicholas left. He half expected William to chuck the ring at him, though released a proud breath when he escaped the tent unscathed.

15

Nicholas

Mages marched along the perimeter where soldiers shoveled snow to form a wall. Fae wards created out of stone resembling the shapes of gargoyles sat half buried in snow. A blessing in disguise for approaching monsters wouldn't notice the little beasts. If a threat grew close, the gargoyles woke and attacked. While not capable of protecting against an army, they worked well to notify anyone of trouble. The mortals glared or glanced at the gargoyles when they passed by, always watchful. They weren't fond of fae objects, calling them cursed and destined to turn on them. They weren't entirely wrong. Most fae offered enchanted artifacts with ill intent, but the Collision Treaty forced them to work together. The gargoyles were safe for mortal use, so long as Fearworn still breathed. If anyone happened to keep the gargoyles, well, only time would tell what those gargoyles would do.

The fae scouts waited at the edge of camp. Arden, Amos, and to Nicholas' immense displeasure, Blair, were among them, along with two other fae introduced as Brein and Elvar.

"Must she come along?" Nicholas nodded at his far too smug sister.

"Is it not a big sister's job to watch over her younger siblings?" Blair caught the end of his hair to twirl around her finger. If she could get away with it, she'd rip the hair off his head.

"You would sooner kick me into a gitan's maw than watch over me."

Blair leaned in to whisper, "Someone must keep you on your leash, otherwise you may wind up dead. While the world would be better for it, Father will get the ludicrous idea to send me after Fearworn instead."

"And you wouldn't survive against him."

"Look at you, coming to accurate conclusions. Perhaps there is some semblance of a brain in here after all." Blair knocked her fist against Nicholas' temple. "Play well and good or Father will have his way with you."

Sweat coated the back of his neck. Nicholas heaved a slow breath, willing his mind to think of anything other than darkness. Other than Laurent's glacial expression as the rocks caved in around Nicholas, bathing him in shadow.

"Are the two of you finished?" Amos called. "We should be on our way."

"Yes, yes, lead the way!" Blair spun on her heel and joined the others.

Amos shared a simple plan; head directly to Fearworn and keep out of sight. He didn't want to risk Fearworn suspecting their arrival. If he did, he might run off. While Nicholas could track him, they wanted to get as much information on his whereabouts and army as they could, then attack with the upper hand.

The scouts sprinted into the forest, more silent than a breeze. Nicholas led the way, always listening to Fearworn, ensuring he remained in place. There was no time or need to rest. They ran through the night, stopping once on the second day when Elvar hesitated within a grove of trees that looked like any other. The scouts mirrored him, looking to Elvar for an explanation.

"Do you hear something?" Amos asked.

Elvar nodded. "Over there."

He shifted through the woods, then stopped. The scouts crowded around Elvar's hunched figure. He nodded past the bushes, through the trees, to the remains of an old town. The broken buildings resembled those Nicholas took shelter in after Fearworn's beasts attacked him. Dozens of gitans patrolled the ruined town and thick webs stretched from one broken house to another. The chittering of spions was loud enough to hear from a distance and the stench made their eyes water. The town smelled of metallic blood and festering wounds.

"A small outpost." Brein grabbed the swords at her waist. "There aren't many of them. We could finish them here and now."

"That is not the plan," said Amos, a hand steadied on Brein's to prevent her from drawing her blade.

"The plan is boring," Nicholas countered, heart racing at the promise of battle. "You sound like my father."

"Lord Darkmoon is intelligent and careful. Two qualities he did not pass onto you."

Blair threw both hands over her mouth to cover her laughter. But she snorted and everyone fell silent when one of the gitan's swerved. The beast peered into the forest, deemed the noise nothing, then moved on.

Amos sighed. "There is no need to attack. We will take note of this outpost and inform the mortal generals."

"They are a group of brainless beasts Fearworn will use against us in the future. If we kill them now, we avoid a future confrontation," Nicholas argued, now starving for a fight. He hadn't set loose since Fearworn. His blood threatened to boil, to explode from the energy surging within.

Amos never argued. He spoke, clean and precise, like an executioner's blade. "Or we lose the opportunity to spy on Fearworn because a message reaches him about a group of his monsters dying near the facility. We keep moving and you will watch yourself. That is the least you can do after always throwing your power around to get what you want."

"Like you haven't done the same."

Amos' eerily white teeth had been sharpened to a point, so his smiles were never less than ominous. "As we all have, but at least the rest of us learned when it is and isn't appropriate to hold sway over others. You are reckless and immature, always acting as if you're better than the rest of us when you are the one cursed."

Elvar and Brein kept their bleak gaze on Nicholas, observing his reaction, which was little more than his lips twitching into a snarl. Blair kept a hand on her mouth, but nothing could hide her mirth. Nicholas needn't hear from her to know she agreed with every word, and had said far worse. He knew well what she thought of him, how many viewed him, how the treatment and the cruelties worsened after Fearworn attacked. Fae rightfully feared shades. All had proven to be a problem, in some form or another. Nicholas hadn't met his true power yet. He was young, not quite a threat as Fearworn, but one day, he would be, and so everyone treaded lightly. Some sought his favor, others whispered behind his back, and some, like Blair, spat in his face.

"This war must end so those damned treaties will too," Amos continued. "Our parents may have plans for you and Evera and your wretched offspring, but the rest of us will not let you risk everything because you are too erratic and need your father to control you."

Nicholas' words caught on his tongue, incapable of denying Amos' accusation. Truth be told, Laurent always had control. All his insistence and rules made Nicholas want to rebel, but there would be no true rebellion against Laurent. If he pushed too hard, Laurent didn't push back—he crushed his opponents mercilessly, his son included. Without Laurent, perhaps Nicholas would have given in by now. He may have joined Fearworn, if only to find a place where he belonged, where others would see him as more than a curse, but of something grand.

Nicholas would not let Amos have the last word. He caught Amos by the collar. Flames licked Amos' skin, making it blister as Nicholas snarled, "Do not think I will let you continuously speak down to me. Continue this and you will come to regret it."

Amos grinned. "Erratic, as I said, but also foolish and self-absorbed. I can't wait until my mother has her way with you."

Arden snatched Nicholas' hand. Another reminder of Laurent's control. The bastard wasn't here but Nicholas felt his watch. Knew he would hear of this should things go too far and there would be severe consequences.

"We move on. Now." Amos ducked beneath the tree limbs to continue their travels. Elvar and Brein were the first to follow. Blair stayed, giggling.

"Keep your mouth shut," Nicholas warned.

"Why?" Blair asked. "Don't like being reminded how little you really mean to everyone?"

"This war cannot be won without me."

"So you think, so you hope." She walked backward toward the group. "Regardless, once this war ends, you will be reminded how little everyone truly thinks of you. How we all wish to be in a world without you in it."

"She's toying with you," Arden whispered.

Nicholas' cracked his neck from side to side, resisting the urge to cut Amos and Blair in two with their backs turned. Nicholas didn't mind fighting dirty, so long as he won. So long as he didn't have to hear from either of them ever again.

"Come, we do not want to be left behind." Arden tugged Nicholas forward. He followed, unsure of who deserved his furious gaze more.

Blair never wanted Nicholas' position at Laurent's side. She didn't envy Nicholas' power, either. From the moment his power revealed itself, she had one thing on her mind; his demise. Many fae believed shades should be disposed of prior to becoming a bigger threat. They never mattered much to Nicholas, but having a sibling to believe such sentiments meant keeping his guard up. Always.

Amos, Nicholas could never truly read. He probably felt similarly to Blair, especially after what he had just said. But Amos' mother spun a treacherous web for Evera and Nicholas. Amos, like many others, tolerated Nicholas. He served a purpose. Nothing more. Their belief in him, their cheers, had always been fake. Even Arden. He saw Nicholas as a powerful ally, and the one he had to watch over. There wasn't a single soul who sought Nicholas for anything more. The thought never bothered him until now. Never made his breath catch or had him wonder what it would be like to be different, to have someone seek him out for literally any other reason.

Nicholas didn't enjoy somber thoughts. He had a job to do, so he focused on observing Fearworn. At least that would keep him distracted. Most observations resulted in little to no new information. Fearworn focused on his work, obsessing about the creation of creatures and endless possibilities of realms containing even worse. Observing the shade took enough of a toll on Nicholas. Fearworn's power mixed with his like dirt muddling clear water. That power crept through him, not a chill but a rapacious heat catching fire to his nerves. Some moments, he thought he wouldn't escape that hunger. Some moments, he didn't want to. Amos, Blair, maybe even Laurent, they could vanish with the snap of his fingers. Nicholas would reshape the world in what he desired, even if that left him utterly alone.

That scared him. Losing himself scared him because every tale of a shade ended terribly. Fae weren't known for good endings, but shades, they crumbled into nothing, into no one. Nicholas didn't want to fade away, to cease to exist in a pitiful state, to be used until he was worthless and nothing.

The fae trekked toward the lab for another day. Occasionally, they hid from monsters lurking nearby. Fearworn had a couple of stations in the forest that the fae noted. Outposts, of sorts, perhaps guiding new shadowed disciples or merely monitoring the lands. Regardless, the fae made no move to take any of them. Amos always scrutinized Nicholas, expecting him to make a move that never came. Then Blair smirked or giggled, and somehow, Nicholas resisted the urge to remove her head.

The last day, the scouts snuck around treacherous peaks, careful not to be detected by the aerial creatures circling the citadel along the mountainside. Nicholas noted most of the creatures were ratwings. Occasionally, the larger winged beast he fought appeared. Though he had informed the generals of the beast, Fearworn seemed to want to keep their creation relatively secret. Once the fae found a suitable position to view the citadel from a high cave hidden in the rock face, they observed. The citadel grew more chaotic than when Nicholas first saw it through Fearworn's eyes. The shade remained in his study since his arrival, so Nicholas never saw or heard of what transpired outside. He was as shocked as the others to witness the winged beasts lurch into the air after their arrival. The gates opened and monsters poured out in droves. They marched for the encampment, no doubt.

Elvar had a neat ability to build origami and breathe life into the paper. That's how he got messages through the Deadlands, but a flying scrap of paper would garner attention. The ratwings would tear it to shreds and shadowed disciples would realize they were being watched. The fae sat, quiet and waiting for the chaos to lessen, then they set the origami bird to flight with a warning that all knew wouldn't reach the camp in time.

What a pity, Nicholas thought. They would return to a bloodbath and have missed out on a glorious battle.

16

Charmaine

Charmaine peered into the gray skies. The color belonged to the Deadlands, a gloom promising thunderstorms but never gave way to rain. Snow, on the other hand, fell continuously. Soldiers maintained the camp by endlessly shoveling. They surrounded the encampment with causeways so thick and cold people marched on them to survey the perimeter. Charmaine had been put to work that morning. Although the sun rose hours ago, the heat never greeted them, forever trapped in the skies.

"Tuckerton, we're to switch out," Karles said on his approach. He reeked of cigar smoke. She grumbled when stepping aside.

Mages were tasked with monitoring from the embankment because they were quicker at defending than pistols that ran out of bullets. A boring task, but simple, and it allowed Charmaine time to herself. She disliked working alongside the soldiers, always paranoid about how they perceived her. If she came across too feminine or too weak, they would notice. She kept her voice low and puffed out her chest for the simplest grievance. Some days, she felt like a mirror, reflecting the world and never herself. One day, she hoped that mirror would break.

Charmaine moved through the crowded camp toward the medical bay. The camp grew in the days since the fae scouts departed. The soldiers that had taken their wounded from the battle at Lockehold returned. A couple of troops heading toward the Deadlands to join the upcoming battles arrived, too. Due to all the fresh faces and friends reuniting, the soldiers became boisterous. Charmaine hated all the noise, the clamoring, and now dodging a drunk man, who would be scolded once higher officers came by. Not that many cared. In the army, everyone became accustomed to a thorough shouting.

Through the throngs of bodies, she came upon the med bay. William spoke with a patient suffering a cold based on his red nose and loud sneezes. Being huddled together for so long meant illness spread rapidly. She counted over a dozen soldiers coughing and wheezing in the beds. Scribbling on a clipboard, William didn't see Charmaine until he walked by her.

"Off wall duty?" he asked on his way outside.

"Yeah. I have a few hours before I'm to return," she replied, following him toward the supply tent next door.

"Then you should take this time to rest." William slipped inside. Charmaine lit a flame that hovered nearby, more for heat than light.

"I'm not tired," she said, which was unusual for all of them. Even while waiting for the inevitable fight, the soldiers had chores. Hunting for more food, shoveling the walkways, securing tents, cleaning clothes and bedding, securing the wall, checking on supplies, sharpening knives, anything and everything kept them busy from dawn to dusk. Then they slept in old sleeping bags that took months to grow accustomed to. Charmaine usually passed out the moment she laid her head down, but the last couple of days she had a giddiness to her.

"I'd rather help you than get caught by another and told to do some boring or annoying task. I've got a bad enough headache already," she added while holding her hand out for the clipboard. Montgomery often tasked William with checking the medical supplies. After helping on numerous occasions, Charmaine knew what to do and William gave the clipboard to her without fuss.

"Like I said, you should rest to get rid of that headache," he repeated.

"It'll go away soon enough."

Times together were often spent chatting, but William examined the crates in silence. He was never as much of a chatterbox as her. Upon their initial meeting, their conversations lulled. William's abrasive demeanor deterred her from speaking. Over the years that reservation thawed, and William partook in conversations naturally. This felt like he reverted to their training days when horrors haunted their heads they had yet to learn how to manage.

As a teenager, Charmaine stood out among the ranks without meaning to. She refused to crush a frog under her boot or to tease the other boys if they cried after a bad training day. Her empathy put a target on her back. If there were others like her, they steered clear to survive. She would never fault them for that. The military crushed anyone who didn't conform to their ideals, or forced them to mold themselves into someone else entirely. She hated it. She hated them, all of it, the expectations and pain and suffering. If she could, she'd make them all pay ten times over.

Charmaine attempted to disperse her thoughts by asking, "Do you think they've found Fearworn?"

"The Deadlands is an extensive region, but fae are quick on their feet and Nicholas claims to know of Fearworn's location. If they haven't found him yet, I imagine they will soon," William replied.

He opened the next supply crate to count everything, remarking the numbers to Charmaine. She noted the items to ensure nothing was suspiciously missing or what needed to be ordered on the next supply run. She didn't envy the soldiers having to travel in and out of the Deadlands. The generals sent a force with them, but it never felt like enough.

"Nicholas never explained how he can track Fearworn," she said. The memory irritated her. He acted so nonchalant about the admission, like this couldn't change everything. She tapped the charcoal against the clipboard. That giddiness remained at the base of her spine, like a snake coiled to strike.

"Does that matter? If he gets his hands on the bastard, I'll be happy enough," William said.

"But what if he gets to Fearworn before we do? What if he defeats him without us?"

William cast her a confused stare, one that she shared because she wasn't sure what she meant by that. She didn't want to see Fearworn again. She especially did not want to fight him, at least, she didn't think so. Something at the back of her mind shrieked. Not in fear, but excitement. That should have scared her, but the giddiness in her chest exploded into a vicious light that warmed her to the tip of her toes. Similar to when she used the Sight, when the flames licked across her fingers and did not burn, for they belonged to her. She became the fire, bright and deadly.

"What do you mean?" William asked, hesitantly.

"Uh…" She swallowed hard. "What if he requires help? He wasn't able to fight off Fearworn alone before."

"I would say that it's doubtful Nicholas would make a move, but he's…"

"Beyond mad?"

"To put it mildly," he mumbled. "The other fae may prevent him from making an idiotic decision, and surely the generals and fae commanders told him not to make too soon a move."

"I suppose you are right. The generals must have us waiting for a time they deem acceptable to approach."

"Yes, our feeble brains are likely incapable of imagining their grand schemes," William said sardonically.

"You could pretend to be more curious."

"I am curious, but I know the two of us gossiping about it won't get us any closer to what is going on." He shut the crate and moved onto the next. When he opened the box of herbs, the scent hit Charmaine hard. Her mind rang, and she gagged.

"Is something wrong?" William passed a cursory glance between the supplies and her. "Do you smell something strange?"

"You do not?" Her eyes watered from the scent strangling her nostril. "That stench does not overwhelm you?"

"No. Everything smells like usual. The scent certainly never bothered you before."

"Perhaps this place is finally getting to me." She pinched her nose that had reacted too much of late. Most things had an unpleasant stench, save fae. They always had a sweet floral aroma, as deceiving as their words.

William hurried to finish that crate and slammed it shut. The scent lingered, but had dissipated enough that she breathed normally. He continued his path from one crate to the other, eyes distant and lips set into a permanent scowl.

"You've been quiet of late," she claimed. "These last few days, ever since we returned, you've been off, stuck in your head."

"There has been a lot to think about," he admitted. "First I was exhausted, then there's the possibility of getting closer to Fearworn. As you said, the generals tell us nothing. We haven't received mail, either. I don't like not hearing from my family or them hearing from me. I'm as worried and troubled as everyone else."

William spoke sense. Charmaine worried about not hearing from her mother. They didn't send letters frequently. Her father thought it was unnecessary, so he refused to pay for paper and stamps. They would be notified if she died in war, and he couldn't care less hearing about what happened here. But Charmaine feared her mother being alone for so long, that she didn't have anyone to ask her how she's feeling. On bad nights when the bastard drank, no one would be there to comfort Bessie, not even a letter from her child to remind her, in time, they would escape him for good.

Although she understood William's concerns, Charmaine couldn't stop herself from asking, "Is that all?"

"That's all."

She wasn't sure how she knew William lied. His voice itched her eardrums, pierced them like an aggravating whistle and she growled, "You are hiding something from me."

"I am not."

"We both have enough going on. I do not need to worry about your secrets too. You are the only person I have here."

He retreated from the crate of linens. "You are the one acting the strangest. It's nothing, really, but are you alright? You're... irritable."

"Irritable," she repeated, ready to argue, except that was exactly how she felt. Irritated by everything and she couldn't discern why. Even now, she had no reason to snap at him.

"No, I, I'm sorry. I don't know why I snapped." She forced her muscles to ease. Everything felt tight, like a worn violin string ready to snap. "I have an awful headache, probably from those herbs or something I ate."

"Or from eating too much, you have been devouring every piece of food you can find," he teased while stepping in for a hug. Charmaine always cherished the hugs William started first, since it was normally the other way around. She eased into him, releasing a pleasant sigh.

"We've both had a rough time of late. I appreciate your help, but I'll finish up here. There's hardly anything left. You need to rest," he said.

They released each other, and she stepped back. "Are you sure?"

Before he answered, a soldier entered the tent requesting supplies. The tension previously eased returned from a familiar face, one that haunted her nightmares from time to time.

"Good morning." Theodore O'Connor carried a devilish smirk that hadn't changed in four years, although his stocky nature as a teenage boy came to suit him. He stood tall and sturdy, constructed of pure muscle and hardened lines with a thick beard around his square jaw. His fists doubled in size. Charmaine couldn't forget how often those fists swung at her, how often her blood stained his cool, white skin.

Theodore's gaze swept over their uniforms, specifically the nametags. "Tuckerton and Vandervult? It has been a long time."

"You seem to know us, but I don't recall you," William said, like he truly meant it. Charmaine didn't believe William forgot the face of the boy he saved her from all those years ago. But William excelled at playing pretend. She didn't have the same pension for such skills. Her emotions showed too much. They were what got her in trouble to begin with.

"Theodore O'Connor," he replied with a smack to his broad chest. "I spent almost a year training alongside Albie. You and I didn't know each other long. I think about two or three months before I was shipped off? My troop arrived the other day with reinforcements."

William hummed. Charmaine fumed. Her fingers ached to release the flames she didn't know she could make back then. Memories of horrid days spent under the boots of angry teenagers consumed her. The disinterest of their instructors who found the beatings necessary enraged her. They always said the beatings would build character, teach Charmaine and many like her to toughen up. It didn't matter if the boys broke bone, if they locked her out of the barracks at night so she'd find a shed to sleep in to survive the cold, nothing changed. Not until a melancholy and precarious boy came along with a nasty right swing and brutal advice; *they will never stop hurting you, so you better start hurting them.*

And she did, albeit not nearly as violent as the boys had done to her. She took pleasure in revenge, and hated herself for it. Charmaine didn't want to be like them, didn't want to "toughen up," like the instructors said. What was wrong with being soft? With empathy, kindness, and compassion? Why couldn't her flames bring warmth rather than destruction? She knew the answer, but hated to think about it; *because the world was a cruel place and loved to remind her of that.*

"Don't smile at us as if we're old friends," she growled, animalistic and deep.

Theodore shot her a bemused look, the one he showed any who stood up to him during recruitment days. "Hey, I know I wasn't the nicest kid, but we all found ways to let off steam. I am sorry about all that."

"Liar!"

Fire roared in her hands, the same way it had during the first battle she had been dispatched to. A grump ran at her and she envisioned herself dead in its grasp. As the beast leapt, she screamed, then she saw them; the strings. Calling to them, fire erupted from her fingertips and the grump deteriorated into ash. She had been excited and scared, but here, in front of Theodore, she was angry. That animosity rose, hissing, spitting, venomous and deep. She saw red, flames high and bright, all-consuming.

Theodore took a lumbering step back, hands up in surrender. "Whoa there! Someone learned some new tricks, but I ain't interested in seeing them up close."

William took hold of her arm. If he spoke, his words eluded her. She couldn't hear anything other than the blood rushing through her veins, the fire crackling in the palm of her hands, and Theodore's panting. She smelled it somehow; his fear. Something sweet and inviting that encouraged her to raise a fiery hand, eager to watch the flesh melt off his bones.

"I think it's about time you learn what it feels like to be a plaything." She almost laughed, but then the war drums rang.

Charmaine's concentration on Theodore broke. Another overwhelming aroma stabbed at her, musky and sulfur-like. William ran outside, as did Theodore, and they stepped into a gloom like night, except it shouldn't be midday yet. Above them, the sky went black from the wild flapping of monstrous wings and death fell upon them.

17

William

Death returned, always hungry.

William dodged and cut, shot and stabbed. None were safe from the beasts pouring out of an umbral sky. Their strength caused gales that ripped tents from the ground. Fire spread. Flames chased those daring to hide, only to meet death in a myriad of other ways. Fangs. Claws. Poisons. Acid. The monsters carried an arsenal that mowed through the ranks.

Charmaine had been separated from William ages ago. The chaos of battle made one lose themselves. Survival kicked in. William's body moved of its own accord. He knew what to do and trusted his muscles to work, to fight, to survive, and maybe a part of him enjoyed this. He hated to linger on such thoughts, hated that Nicholas was right. The danger and the rush, he persisted in the face of death, defying her again when so many believed he wouldn't. Including himself.

A debrak, a red towering blister, spotted William through the carnage. It charged, as most did. He aimed for the eyes. The bullets blinded one eye. The beast didn't stop, yowling like the Broken Soul had taken hold. William knew not to swerve. Debraks were swifter than they appeared and they loved crushing one in their fists. He fell to his knees, rolling between the debrak's legs. The knife in his opposing hand sliced at one of the ankles. The beast shrieked and stumbled. William dug a blade into the ankle tendon, then lunged onto its back. He stabbed his second blade deep into its spine.

The debrak screamed and swatted meaty hands about. William stuck the head of his revolver by his blade and fired. Blood coated his cheeks. The debrak fell forward, twitching. After retrieving his knives, he stalked to its head to finish it with a stab to the brain.

The skittering of spions warned William of an attack. He jumped off the debrak as two spions sprang on. They were a rare breed, far older than any he had come across. The older they got, the bigger they became, and the two of them were the size of a horse. William fired at the eyes. Their pincers shielded themselves. The bullet ricocheted, and he bolted. He dashed through debris for a nearby group of soldiers, though ratwings soon overran them. Thousands of them tore the men to shreds, leaving little more than bloody bones. The spions chattered behind William. He kept a brisk pace, sliding around a ripped tent where a group of mages battled shouting grumps.

Their magic called to the spions, glimmering and distracting. They lurched toward the mages as William fell to a knee, grabbed a rifle from one of the dead, and fired from below. The bullets pierced the abdomen of one of the gruesome creatures. The spion shrieked and fell after bullets riddled its guts. The mages handled the last, but they would have to find and dispose of the shadowed disciples controlling the beasts to end this carnage.

William lost count of how long the battle lasted, of how many lives he attempted to save. The days were too murky here to guess the time. Gray clouds loomed, soon accompanied by suffocating smoke from the flames. Though the monsters lay dead or retreated, he could not call this a victory.

He shifted through the bodies, searching for who to save, when a pained shriek echoed nearby. The noise sounded like a woman, potentially one of the nurses caught in this debacle. He hurried toward the origin of the noise. Silhouettes swayed from within a surviving tent, sitting lopsided and torn. Keeping his gun high, he brushed back the flaps.

One nurse had shrieked from a monster, only those monsters were two men haphazardly zipping up their pants. The nurse sat huddled at the back of the tent, clinging to her ripped attire. A jittery hand covered her freshly bloodied lip and bruising cheek. William recognized one monster; Frederick Holtson. The second son of a merchant who loved reminding everyone of his family wealth, typically while tormenting them through words or fist. He never received punishment for his offenses because of his father's position, which is why he had been on William's list for some time. An opportunity never presented itself until now.

"Hey Doc," Frederick said with a nervous laugh, having noticed the stained white collar along William's arm, noting him as a doctor. "Listen, this may look bad, but let me explain what happened. Miss Elizabeth here found it in her heart to help the war effort by giving my friend and I a little relaxation time after such a terrible battle. She's a sweet lass and would likely be more than happy to comfort you too, isn't that right?"

Frederick wore a charming smile, a well-placed lie. Elizabeth shrank, whimpering with approval when Frederick's friend took a threatening step toward her. William's vision blackened, overwhelmed by a raging anger that lived eternally within him.

"The battle is over. We must bury our dead and save the injured. Now certainly isn't the time for any relaxation, lest you wish to court trouble," William replied in a steady voice, a perfect one, and offering his own lying grin to Frederick, then Elizabeth. "Take your leave, Miss Elizabeth. Your medical services will be required by staff and soldiers."

Elizabeth stumbled to her feet. Her crossed arms hugged her body so tightly she'd bruise herself more. Then she limped out of the tent, dead-eyed and muted.

"If this remains between us, I swear my father will reward you handsomely," Frederick said with a haughty laugh that his friend mirrored. William joined, forcing mirth as he settled a hand on Frederick's shoulder. The strings of magic knotted around his fingers, and he tugged. Frederick dropped, numbed, and silenced.

"What the?" The other man reached for his revolver, but the dolt hadn't retrieved his belt. William caught the beast's vile face and slammed him into the dirt. Rather than use a gun, William's blade slid between the man's rib bones. His palm muted the bastard's anguished cries that followed every piercing of the blade until his eyes dimmed.

Sighing, William stalked toward Frederick. The fool lay motionless on the ground, gaze shifting between the corpse and William. Frederick's palpable terror did nothing but encourage him. How many times had he shown that same look and received nothing but pain in return? Did Elizabeth not show that same horror when Frederick took what didn't belong to him? Was the blood on William's hands truly dirty if it belonged to wicked bastards?

"Don't worry, Mr. Holtson," William whispered. "This will remain between us."

Then his blade carved Frederick's chest, ensuring that any who stumbled upon the mess would believe a grump got their nasty claws on two unfortunate soldiers. William lost count of the lives he saved and those he took. Frederick was simply another name scratched out on his list. A face that would be forgotten in a few days' time and the world would be better for it.

The military never reprimanded sick souls, saw them as necessary to toughen up the ranks. Cruelty was welcome here. Their punishment would come after their death when the Broken Soul dragged them below the seas of Elysium. But William didn't believe in that nonsense. He didn't miss the conversations of his instructors laughing over beer late in the night about another fight in the yard, how the weak boys like William squealed for a moment of reprieve from the torment.

"The beating does them good," his instructors laughed. *"We need men in this war. Not boys."*

William hated how, sometimes, he thought them to be right. They taught him cruelty and cruelty kept him alive. Most of the time, he knew those bastards couldn't be more wrong. Pain did no one any good. That's probably when he stopped believing in the Souls. If men were depictions of the Holy Soul, pure, and courageous, then why were they so cruel? If women were depictions of the Broken Soul, sinister, untrustworthy, and vengeful, then why were they the ones who suffered man's ceaseless wrath?

After cleaning his blade in the snow, William searched the battlefield for those who could be saved. He lugged limp men onto his back to carry across fields of ash and blood to the surviving tents made into the new medical bay. Elizabeth worked among the chaos. William found crates containing herbs that surviving soldiers brought for the healers. He crushed the ingredients in a small pot. Inside the tent, he nodded at Elizabeth. Her nerves were not missed, hands twitching at her side as she followed William. They hid together in the shadows outside.

"Take this," he ordered, while handing her the bowl. "I had nothing for the taste, but it will ease your pain and ensure there are no surprises."

Elizabeth released a shuddered breath, then downed the liquid in a gulp. She stuck out her tongue, gagging. "Thank you for this and getting me out of there. I didn't think...I saw them huddled in that tent and thought they were injured."

"You did what you thought was right, and they took advantage of that. It happens far too frequently here."

Elizabeth wrung her hands together, every word erratic and pleading. "You will not speak of what transpired to anyone, will you? Please, Doctor, I...this job will pay off my family's debts, and once they are paid, a man far above my stature has agreed to take my hand in marriage. He is a good, kind man, but should he discover what happened, he may end our engagement."

Then he mustn't be a very good man, William thought, though he dared not utter. No one spoke about what transpired out here. Nothing would be done and many, like Elizabeth, were too frightened of what their partners or family would say. William certainly never spoke of his experiences, either. His family could never know.

"I will not tell," he promised.

Sharing a mournful smile, Elizabeth returned to her work, pretending nothing happened. William understood the look, dim eyes set upon bright features, hoping they'd counteract. Praying no one would ask what bothered you because you may not have the power to hide any longer. It made his hands shake and innards boil, but he had work to do, too.

Charmaine soon joined, along with the other fire mages. They were useful for cauterizing wounds. She and William didn't speak to each other, but seeing her set him somewhat at ease. In truth, nothing could fully settle the constant turmoil in his stomach. A knot formed the day he left home that expanded with every passing day.

Eventually, William stepped outside for fresh air. He wasn't called to another cot, so he took the chance to let freezing air fill his lungs. Then a soldier rushed by, arms arms full of food he probably stole. The soldier handed out the food to a group of bruised men while gossiping. "The fae scouts have returned. Seen them headin' for the general's tent."

"A little late, aren't they?" His friend grunted, the words slightly slurred because of his two missing front teeth and bloodied face. "Those monsters ripped through us."

"And how do we know they didn't spook them our way?" mumbled another shivering soldier. Blood stained the wrap around his head. "Probably got themselves caught, then went running and let them beasts come for us."

William wouldn't put that past fae, and yet that negative thought didn't prevent him from touching the ring in his pocket. The flower had not wilted, somehow becoming fresher, as if plucked that morning. The ring may shield him on the way to Nicholas' tent, where a ravenous touch could ease him. Could let him pass on to a blissful sleep and forget all that he saw today, forget all he remembered through the frightened eyes of an innocent woman, if only for a single evening.

You're a fool, he thought.

"Doctor Vandervult, we need you in here!" a nurse shouted, and his body moved. He focused on the flailing body beneath his hands. Listened to the patient beg and plead for the pain to end and know that, sometimes, it did end. Along with everything else.

By the time the dying passed, and the living stabilized, red painted William's hands. He washed himself clean of blood, staring at the threads twisting in the once clear water. His thoughts felt the same: dirtied and swirling chaos. Exhaustion settled, familiar in its gloom. Nothing like a long day or little sleep. This exhaustion was agony. It was the ocean beating against the cliff, chipping away until the cliff crumbled into the depths.

William fiddled with the ring while leaving the tent. Maybe it was night or midday. Who knew? It was always grim and damp and fucking miserable. By the Broken Soul, William was exhausted. Unwell, even. His teeth gnashed. His cheeks ached from biting them. Everything grew painfully tense. Sleep would not greet him tonight. He'd lay in bed remembering the worst of the past, of being miserable and in pain with no way of escaping. Nicholas could fix that. Just one more night, one evening to forget and feel good out here in all the horrors.

Sorry, Hugh. I'm tired. I just... I'm sorry, William thought, and in the shadows, slipped the ring on. His body shimmered, making his appendages translucent. Soldiers patrolled carrying torches or conjured spheres of flames. Two came toward him. William stepped into the light. One of the men would have run into him if he hadn't stepped aside.

The soldier shuddered. "Did you feel that?"

"What?" asked the other.

"I could have sworn I felt something on my neck."

The patrol continued, unaware of William's presence. The ring worked, although he stood there a moment longer, berating himself for another bad decision.

Apparently, he loved bad decisions.

Nicholas' tent had as much presence as its owner; a massive, deep green enclosure at the center of the fae quarters decorated in delicate vines and roses. The fae were quick, had their camp fixed before the mortals did. In fact, most of the mortal arrangements hadn't been salvaged. Soldiers practically slept on one another to fight back the cold.

The fae did not have guards, either. Any mortal foolish enough to enter wouldn't survive long. Fae senses made them keenly aware of intruders. Usually. None noticed William sweep by, still doing so as carefully as possible. That shouldn't have excited him, but it did. The rush returned, making his heart jump and fingers twitch. Getting caught would spell trouble, but getting away with it was exciting.

Checking no one was around, William slipped into Nicholas' tent.

"Finally. I was beginning to think you foolish enough to deny yourself a more than satisfactory evening," said Nicholas from a desk of thorns at the center of a wide tent.

William slipped the ring off to place in his pocket. "What if I were dead?"

"I cannot fathom you allowing such a thing."

"How flattering."

His gaze swept over Nicholas' bare chest, shirt forgotten on his bed. A much better bed than any mortal soldier had, that was for damn sure. Layers of furs covered the thick mattress set upon curving brush that broke from the earth. A trunk sat at the end, no different from the one William had back home. Two chairs sat at the center of the tent with a small table for food and drink. Nicholas' accommodations may be simple, but out here, they were grand.

"If this causes the least bit of trouble, it's done," William warned.

Nicholas approached, tugging at the strings of his trousers. "Define trouble."

"Don't toy with me. This is sex meant to ease us for the night, not a chance to frustrate me."

The fae snickered. His pants fell around his ankles. William's attention betrayed him, straying to every part of Nicholas he hadn't gotten a good look at before. The admiration didn't go unnoticed. Nicholas smirked against his parted lips.

"I will frustrate you, but in the best of ways, that I can promise." Then Nicholas captured him in a frustrating kiss.

18

William

William's clothes lay forgotten somewhere in the tent. A demanding fae had his attention and refused to let go.

Their naked forms tangled on the bed, all hands, teeth, and tongue exploring one another. He found himself between Nicholas' legs, hands wrapped around his cock. William sat back, savoring the view of the fae's breathless form beneath him. He liked it before, back in the caravan when Nicholas' eyes shown in the night, fuchsia light, more vibrant than a summer sun. They did the same here, flickering as flames behind his fluttering eyelids. Lust and pleasure swirled within his irises, hips rolling, and a hand reaching to return the favor.

William grunted at the first touch of Nicholas' hands on his arousal. Their shared moans echoed in the tent, making him bite his lip.

"Don't silence yourself." Nicholas sat up to brush a hand against his mouth. "None will hear of us, nor we of them. Tonight, I wish to hear only from you."

They shared a kiss, slowly pleasuring one another, letting the sensations build. Nicholas tugged him forward, so they fell onto the bed together. Then William took to Nicholas' neck, savoring the fae's pulse fluttering against his lips, then moving over his body. Further and further down William went until he caressed Nicholas' smooth thighs and nipped at the dark curls above his enticing hips.

He hated himself for wanting to taste the fae, for wishing to hear every noise of pleasure Nicholas could make. He moaned, the sound vibrating around Nicholas' arousal caught between his lips. The fae had far too much to be proud of, otherworldly perfect even as a panting mess. Clawed hands pierced the sensitive skin of his nape and twisted into his hair, encouraging him to move faster. He slowed instead.

"And you dare to call me insufferable," Nicholas growled, followed by a pleasured cry when his pace hastened.

Green eyes fell half mast, admiring his mouth's work. He was by no means shy in the bedroom, not anymore, and he liked how unkempt Nicholas became. Like this, all the fae could do was tremble and groan when William toyed with him by retreating.

Nicholas' hips thrust relentlessly into his smooth palm. He fondled Nicholas's balls with his mouth before holding the fae's hips against the bed to go down on him again. He tasted salty and sweet and dangerous. He shivered when Nicholas tugged on his hair, enjoying the flicker of pain. Then the fae cursed and pulled him away with a rather telling groan.

"Worried you would finish too soon?" he chuckled.

"Maybe. I won't deny that I like the way you use your mouth here." Nicholas used the hold he had on William's hair to toss him onto the bed. The sheets rubbed against his sensitive arousal, then Nicholas perched behind him. "That devilish mouth of yours makes me want to be rough with you," he said while pressing his tip between William's cheeks.

"Then it's good I am not here for a gentle evening." He groaned as Nicholas rocked him into the bed, fingers held tightly against his neck and teeth tearing into his back.

Lower and lower, Nicholas went until his tongue massaged William's rim. He cursed, fingers tearing at the pillow beneath him. The fae proved his tongue to be skilled in a plethora of ways, far more than tolerable here. He shook and gasped at the damn near torturous attention of Nicholas' mouth. The spiraling motions, the in and out as the shade's hands kneaded his behind, then two fingers joined to stretch and deepen the sensation. His rough penetrations left William reeling, fingers bone white against the sheets and moans muffled by the pillow captured between his teeth.

He had plenty of partners, but out here, it was mostly to ease their boredom, then pretend nothing happened when the sun rose. He didn't always get what he wanted, but some attention often felt better than none, far better than lonely nights anyway.Most didn't live up to Nicholas' insatiable desire. The way he couldn't keep his hands off William, mapping out his body and testing what had his back bowing, toes curling, or cries amplifying. He refused to give Nicholas more than a moan, though. The bastard would be far too smug otherwise, although he was clearly intent on receiving it because his zealous tongue ceased its pleasurable torment.

"If you don't let me hear you, I'll stop," Nicholas warned, daring to retreat.

"You're such an annoying jackass," he muttered, breathless and aroused.

Nicholas yanked him up onto his knees. The fae pressed his hips against William, teasing him. His hips bucked, wanting more, but Nicholas retreated with a laugh. "I do love it when you sweet talk me."

"Your idea of sweet talking has always been less than desirable."

Nicholas chuckled, then thrust forward. He couldn't stifle his moans as his body was stolen by the fae's aggressive sex. A ruthless and intense pace made better by Nicholas grasping his arms and holding them back. He hovered above the bed, thighs quaking as the fae fucked him.

The ecstasy froze and burned, settling between his trembling thighs. The sound of their sex filled the tent, skin against skin and high-pitched moans. This is what he yearned for; a mind free of worry, overtaken by amazing sex that'd let him forget. He couldn't think of anything but the smoldering lust between them. The unrivaled high that made him short of breath and desperate for completion. The pleasure building at the base of his spine, promising to drown him.

Nicholas wrapped an arm around his shoulders, forcing him to kneel upright. He caught William in a kiss. Their hips slowed, barely more than a weak roll to drag out their sex.

"Enjoying yourself, my wicked?" Nicholas purred.

"Are you so worried about your performance that you need to ask?" he groaned when the bastard dared to pull out.

"If you want to insult my performance, we could always stop."

"Oh, I wouldn't dream of it," he replied sarcastically. He would never admit how great he felt. How he almost whimpered when Nicholas grasped his arousal, mimicking the slow motions of his hips teasing so much more. They shared their breaths, then Nicholas took to his neck, nipping at the tender skin.

"Don't leave marks where others might see," he warned, cursing from Nicholas slamming inside of him and the rough slap against his backside. He almost dropped, reaching back to hold tight to Nicholas' arm as their hips hastened, returning to the speed he desired.

"Why not?" Nicholas snickered, sucking harder so he absolutely would leave a mark. "Worried your little friend may ask questions?"

Smirking, he replied, "Worried my other partners may ask questions."

Snarling, the fae shoved him back onto his hands. "When I'm through with you, you won't ever consider other partners," Nicholas growled.

He certainly didn't like the mention of that, but William did because it drove the fae's hips wild. So much so that William's arms gave out, and he fell to his elbows. Moaning for more as his vision dissipated and lungs fumbled over every breath. His hand gripped his cock, desperately trying to mirror Nicholas' movements, to push himself over the edge of sanity.

Nicholas gave him everything he wanted and more, fucking him to the point of unfathomable pleasure, body nothing more than explosive nerves in his treacherous fingertips. Then his orgasm rippled through him, sending his muscles into a spasming fit. Nicholas didn't stop until his powerful groan echoed around them and they fell to the bed.

William truly loved and hated how listless he became afterward. Damn near peaceful, even. Nicholas already knew that, or at least suspected, seeing as William showed up. But at least he said nothing of it, letting the both of them bask in the afterglow.

Too tired to leave yet, William shuffled onto his back and stalled by asking, "The monsters that attacked us. Did you see them on your mission?"

Nicholas whined. "Work in bed? Really? You're incapable of letting a good thing last."

The bed shifted from him rolling onto his side. His fingers ghosted over William's chest, first following scars here and there, then rubbing the skin above his still racing heart.

"I thought this was sex, not a way to steal information from me," Nicholas said while brushing hair from his eyes. William ignored the urge to insist he not do that. Nicholas looked better a mess.

"I like efficiency," he countered. "Might as well ask while I am here. There will be gossip spreading through the camp by morning, but I would rather hear from the source."

Humming, Nicholas kissed William's chest and up his neck. The tent smelled of sex and the heat had yet to dissipate. If anything, the spark had never died, merely simmered in expectation of the next blast.

"We came upon a citadel, slightly larger than Lockehold, but it was not for protection," Nicholas explained. Every breath scorched William's skin. "I saw through Fearworn's eyes a lab for monstrous creations. He read over his books and sought further depravity by conducting crude experiments. Even my gut dared to twist. The citadel had been built around a scar bigger than ever recorded where more monsters presided, along with that snake creature we fought."

William's breath caught. The fae shifted onto an elbow to lean over him. William maintained a calm expression while his thoughts were anything but. Fearworn had even more monsters. The hope he once had diminished. He felt foolish to believe, even for a moment, that things may change. Fearworn remained ahead of them, prepared for more battles, his monstrous force always mounting while William witnessed more death every day.

"We arrived shortly before the monsters took flight," Nicholas continued. "With their wings, we could not return before their assault, but we began the trek back when we could risk it."

"Fearworn gave no indication of the attack?"

"No. I am uncertain he makes as many calls as we once suspected. His madness is of monsters, of what he can make of them."

"Madness is often used to describe shades, particularly Fearworn, but he seemed in control of himself when he came for us," William said.

"The madness of shades is not what mortals believe it to be. It's an obsession with something or someone beyond what any can comprehend. A fallen shade will do anything to achieve their goal, risking their lives and everyone else's in the process, and among all that, their power gnaws away at them."

Nicholas allowed fuchsia light to cascade from his fingertips in thin streams, the brilliant aura memorizing. Beneath that beauty laid power so strong it rippled through William's veins, terrifying, corrosive, and wanting.

"I command the power within me. I tell it where to go, what to do, and when to calm." Nicholas closed his hand, and the light vanished. "Fearworn is not the same. Power controls him, eats at him. His heart may beat, but it is no longer his own. In his case, his obsession protects him. The monsters. The knowledge. The destruction. And many follow him because of that power, because of what he has accomplished and likely what he can give them. But, perhaps, not necessarily for his intelligence and strategy."

William hummed. "Are you doomed to follow that same path?"

A smile slipped over Nicholas' disturbingly charming features. "You must hope that I am."

"That isn't an answer."

"All shades run the risk, but there have been some before Fearworn who lived and died relatively normally."

"What is a normal death by fae standards?"

"A beheading or an iron dagger to the heart by those they did not pay enough attention to." Nicholas sounded far too serious for such an unserious answer. "Now, no more work talk."

"Alright." William pressed Nicholas aside to lean toward the edge of the bed.

"Where do you think you're going?" A hand clutched his wrist, tugging him back into the sheets where Nicholas locked their legs together. He pressed his naked form to William's, speaking against his lips, "I prefer my evening partners to stay."

"For pleasant company or another round?"

"Depends on their skills."

"And what of my skills?"

"If it were up to me, I would tie you to the bed and keep you here." Nicholas caught William in a kiss that fanned the spark between them to flame once more.

"Flattery doesn't suit you," he whispered.

"This is honest flattery. I will not trick here. I will be sweet, if that guarantees a taste."

William rolled his eyes. "Oh yes, how sweet of you to play pretend for sex. That is by no means a rude deception."

"Such whining." Nicholas marked William's shoulder and hand caressed the medic's thigh. "I prefer to hear such sounds in another form."

William couldn't stifle his laugh. Nicholas sat up, grinning. "That is twice I have earned laughter from you. It is a pleasant sound that you should share more often."

"Is this the horn dog talking sweet for another round?"

With a lecherous grin, Nicholas settled himself between William's legs. "You already know me so well."

19

Nicholas

Fearworn reeked of disease and festering decay. Observing through his eyes set Nicholas on edge. Fearworn had moments of clarity where he spoke calmly to his generals, fanatics, and monsters. Then came the hours spent over books, muttering to himself in a language Nicholas could not place. He wouldn't be surprised if the words meant nothing or Fearworn created one all his own. He had the obsessive nature to do so, scribbling away, experimenting, and ignoring the world. Fearworn wouldn't eat if his disciples didn't scurry in with plates to feed him themselves. None appeared to care, worshiping him with misty eyes that craved the power seeping from him. Literally. That miasma never dissipated. Power so great it took physical form shifted about his figure in streaks of violet like watercolor on canvas.

At times, that power streaked through Nicholas' veins, too, a rabid hunter in search of prey, exhilarated and avaricious. A jolt struck him to the core, overwhelmed by the promise of becoming undone, taken solely by all the universe offered, to let it settle over his fingertips. He could grasp hold of the world and never relent, unravel all that was and would ever be if he held tight.

"Nicholas!" a shrill voice yelled, then a yank startled his eyes open. His own eyes, at least. Fearworn's view fell away. He returned to camp, his tent specifically. Arden stood at his side, one hand clinging to his bicep. The other pointed at where he once sat. Nicholas smelt the smoke before he saw the burn marks creeping from the circle he had sat upon. Pink flames licked the floor, sputtering into nothing.

"You nearly caught the tent ablaze," Arden explained.

"Did I?" Nicholas couldn't recall. He remembered Fearworn's fast hands stitching a beast together with a shimmering thread that breathed life into the wretched beasts.

"What did you see?" Arden asked.

"Nothing important. Nothing more than what we've already learned."

Fae and mortals alike knew Fearworn had generals, but Nicholas' suspicions were proven correct days ago. Fearworn didn't give as many commands as previously predicted. His generals made plans. While that made the targets heavier upon their heads, it didn't deter from the truth; regardless of Fearworn's lack of commands, he was the driving force behind the war. Those who sought power or wished to cause havoc flocked to him, worshiped him as a god and for good reason. His power remained a risk, unfathomable and terrifying as nature itself.

Nicholas could fall to that, too. The moments of excitement when captured by Fearworn's visions were not his own. That excitement came from this energy within him, threatening to overtake him one day. Nicholas never wanted that. He didn't want to become undone, to have power but not his own because he wouldn't be himself anymore.

So often, he didn't feel like himself, anyway. He was born an extension of his father, further valued the moment he became a shade. Fae recognized the Lord of Darkmoon, and Laurent's children recognized him. They obeyed Laurent's every command because the consequences were too severe to risk. Nicholas danced to Laurent's song even on the days where he skipped a beat or two. That is all he could manage without fear of repercussions.

If he ever stopped playing along, if he fell like Fearworn, life as he knew it would be over. Nicholas would be a husk of his former self, alone, deteriorating into nothing and no one would care. Fearworn had his disciples, but what did Nicholas have? Nothing. No one.

"I do not find this consistent lurking to be of any good for you, or the rest of us." Arden's nose curled in distaste. "Had I not arrived when I did, you may have destroyed half of the camp."

Nicholas snorted. "Half? How weak do you think I am?"

"Would you prefer to destroy all of the camp?" Arden held up a hand. "Don't answer that. While I wouldn't mind the loss of these mortals, there are some of our kin I would like an evening of debauchery with prior to their demise."

"I will take note of your desires, but do not believe for a moment that they matter. Now, why did you seek me out? Hoping for another evening from me?"

Arden winked. "Always."

Normally Arden's interest gave way to excitement, but Nicholas found himself disinterested, disappointed, even. A voice whispered how Arden was at his side for his own reasons; power, pleasure, whatever deal he had with Laurent. He'd leave the moment Nicholas' eyes flashed purple.

"But I fear we don't have the time now," Arden added, to Nicholas' strange relief. "The generals and our commanders want an update."

Nicholas groaned. Acquiring Fearworn's blood may have been a breakthrough, but it had become most tedious for him. The generals treated him like a lapdog they could beckon at their leisure. He would give them a piece of his mind after he discovered why Duke entered the tent carrying a letter.

"Sir Darkmoon." Duke bowed. "A letter has arrived from your father."

"Yes, Duke, I can see that." And he was not eager to read the letter, so he nodded toward his desk. "Leave it there. I will read over it after I update our fae commanders and the generals. They have requested another audience."

Duke set the letter aside, then the three journeyed to the commander's tent, with Nicholas ensuring every step to be slow. Most of the generals were not pleased when he arrived based on their snarls. The generals weren't accustomed to being kept waiting.

"I've learned little more than what had already been shared," Nicholas explained from where he stood at the head of the table, palms pressed to the edges and body leaned forward. Generals and fae commanders lined the table, listening. "Fearworn does not have another army as formidable as what recently attacked us, although he is working on one in a new location. He continues to experiment on the beasts. Do not doubt for a moment that we won't face even more new monsters in the coming weeks. Perhaps not perfected, but certainly an annoyance."

"You have seen nothing to hint to where he is hiding?" General Wright inquired. Smoke filtered from the cigar trapped between his lips. He knocked the ashes onto the ground, accompanied by many more from the surrounding generals, inhaling the wretched stench.

Fearworn left the lab after the assault. Nicholas hadn't caught where, too preoccupied by returning to camp hoping to battle an army of monsters. He missed out on the fun, a disappointment, but there would be more battles to come. Another chance to unleash. Nicholas couldn't wait to give in, especially lately. He feared falling to the energy within otherwise, like he's always teetering on the edge of a cliff, wishing to return to the depths of the sea below.

"I have not," Nicholas replied. "Fearworn rarely leaves his room. When he does, he never goes outside. I continue to believe this lair is underground or built into a cliff side. It's certainly not a fortress of brick and mortar."

"And we have found various underground hideouts, so there's proof they have done this before," Amos said. He absentmindedly toyed with a coin that slipped between the groove of every finger. "Our scouts recently dispatched a hideout not far from here. They believe it was used to spy on us, so the scouts are continuing ahead. I believe the army should continue their march, too. We should take the lab while Fearworn isn't there and their forces have weakened. We're onto them and they know it."

"We shouldn't stretch ourselves too thin. What if Fearworn moves around us? What if more beasts took to the lab since the attack?" Herald asked.

"That is why we have reinforcements guarding the remains of Lockehold," Morrison said. "Fearworn created a haven for his beasts, but there is only one way in and one way out. His flying monstrosities may be able to escape over the mountains, but the sides and rear are surrounded by freezing waters. Even if they somehow dug out of the mountains, they'd be slow and cold. His generals wouldn't risk that, so they would have to pass by Lockehold, or move through a shimmer into Faerie."

"My kin are watching the scars on their end," said Amos. He tossed the coin and caught it. "If Fearworn tries to go through one leading to Faerie, he will meet more formidable foes than he could ever expect. As for the lab, that is a risk we should take. If we take hold of it, that is one less place Fearworn can turn to and another scar under our supervision."

"Agreed. We want to ensure Fearworn's armies are left in the open, that they have nowhere to run, so we should press on," Morrison encouraged. "We can't stop now when we are so close. You can't stop, Nicholas. We need to know every move Fearworn and his disciples make."

Nicholas nodded. The generals continued their discussion. In the end, they agreed to send half of their forces to take the lab. The other shall remain, waiting for reinforcements summoned from the south. Nicholas would be among those battling for the lab, which had his fingers twitching beneath the table.

"Your father's letter," Duke muttered behind him after the generals called an end to the meeting.

"Will be read when I damn well feel like it," Nicholas growled.

"We both know he doesn't like being kept waiting. The messenger will leave by morning."

"Then I have all night." He waved dismissively. "Leave me."

Duke didn't hesitate, although his cold eyes said enough. He hated waiting until the last minute, even if Nicholas always responded on time. He tempted trouble with his father, but never truly courted it. He knew better. Laurent had a nasty temper. Most wouldn't believe it upon meeting him because he held himself with the grace that many High Fae did. Nicholas shared his father's blood, but not his uncanny ability to appear harmless. Any who dared to think such things learned swiftly that Laurent was anything but.

In Nicholas' tent, the letter sat atop his desk like any other, but it held enough weight to make his wrist ache. He sat at the desk, clutching the scrap of paper, glaring at the stamp along the back. A full moon set into black ink with a shooting star encircling it, the symbol of Darkmoon. He slipped a nail carefully under the seal. Laurent didn't play as many games as his children, but he enchanted a letter once to bite Nicholas' nail off. The letter opened without a maiming and was as curt as ever.

> *The eyes of a corrupted shade is a dangerous place to lurk. Limit your time and use it wisely, less you risk a similar fate. I do not enjoy repeating myself, either; do not needlessly put yourself in harm's way. You have duties, a woman to marry and children to sire. Be smart.*

"Test subjects to sire," Nicholas grumbled, then caught the letter a flame. The contents barely differed from the previous letters. Laurent played a game and expected Nicholas to do the same when he lacked any interest.

After writing a halfhearted response, assuring Laurent he would be more careful, Nicholas tossed the letter at a random fae passing by his tent to give to Duke. They sprinted off while he stepped toward the encampment, intending to tumble with Arden except the thought of sex led his mind astray, to eyes colder than the air in his lungs and hair of golden silk caught between his fingers, the scent of disinfectant and a witty mouth. A night not of mediocrity, but of drowning attention. Nicholas' feet carried him to the mortal camp in search of a moody medic. Desire blossomed in his chest, unyielding in its ferocity, ravenous in its hunger.

Nicholas discovered his favorite plaything inside the supply tent. William searched through crates containing herbs and potions. Charmaine kept close, carrying a clipboard while speaking out items William searched for in the crates. Once found, he slipped a handful into a dozen leather bags and they moved onto the next. The fae hid along the exterior of the tent, listening intently. Their packing could have just begun, but Nicholas intended to wait. He had things to discuss with William. Apparently, so did Charmaine.

"You've gone missing a few nights this month." Her tone carried a hint of excitement. "Who is he?"

"He?" William repeated.

"Who is the man you are spending your evenings with? I am sure you have a few tales to tell, considering I don't see you again until nearly dawn."

"What does it matter? I've taken plenty of men to bed. There is no reason to get excited."

Nicholas stifled a growl. He never cared about one's previous partners. Arden had more than any could count and earned a plethora of near-death experiences from spurned partners. Nicholas certainly had his fair share, too, near-death experiences included, but the idea of another putting their hands on William infuriated him. Knowing others heard William enraptured by ecstasy, knew he could be so much more than apathetic, made Nicholas imagine foul scenarios.

"Of course I'm excited. You have hardly seen anyone since Hugh, I just," Charmaine abruptly cut herself off. A suffocating tension, thicker than smog, clung to the air.

"It's pointless sex, nothing more," William said with his carefully crafted deadpan tone. "There is no point in having a relationship here. It is a distraction, that's all."

Nicholas stepped aside, shielding himself further in the tent's shadow, when a vexed medical officer approached. She entered the tent without noticing the sneaking fae.

"Tuckerton, what are you doing here?" the officer asked and meandered through the tent in search of something.

"I have wall duty in an hour, sir. I wanted to help William until then," Charmaine replied.

"Well, you can help me for a moment, too. A couple of idiots got into a fight and two of our nurses are sick with a cold. Now, come along," the officer demanded and exited the tent with arms full of bandages and herbs. Charmaine swiftly followed. When she passed, a potent scent of musk hit Nicholas' nose. Stifling a sneeze, he slid into the tent.

William had his eyes on the bags but still sensed Nicholas. "What are you doing here?"

"That is an impolite way to greet someone." Nicholas grabbed William's wrist and tugged him close. "You should start with hello." William denied Nicholas attention by continuing to read over the clipboard. The fae scowled. His hand fell to William's waist. "Do you find monotonous work more interesting than me?"

"I find most things more interesting than you," William replied.

Nicholas pulled at William's shirt, dislodging the fabric from where it had been tucked into his pants. His fingers caressed small circles into William's shivering skin. "Your trembling says otherwise."

"Trembling," William mocked. The bridge of his nose wrinkled. He appeared a moment away from arguing, then fell silent when Nicholas brushed his lips over the fluttering pulse of his neck. Nicholas smiled when William leaned into the touch, one hand now clutching Nicholas' arm while his lips ravished smooth skin. He tasted of desire, taunting and addictive.

"Who is Hugh?" Nicholas asked. William tensed, causing Nicholas' curiosity to deepen.

"A dead man," William replied.

"That you had a previous relationship with?"

"Which is no concern of yours." William escaped Nicholas' vice grip. He opened another crate and grabbed a handful of items to place in the packs.

"Concern?" Nicholas repeated. "Perhaps not, but I am curious by nature, and you are constantly testing that curiosity."

"Keep that curiosity to yourself or you will come to regret it."

"Your desperation to avoid the topic tells me he was more than a bedding partner." Nicholas expected a glare. However, William flipped through the pages of his clipboard, double checking his work like the well behaved soldier he feigned to be.

"A lover, then," Nicholas said, flexing his fingers. The back of his neck heated. "How peculiar. You don't seem the type to hand over your heart."

William huffed. "Does your visit have a purpose other than annoying me?"

"Yes, but I enjoy the way your forehead creases when annoyed, so I may continue this banter for my own pleasure."

"I will point my gun at your crotch again, but this time I will shoot."

"So nasty!" Nicholas feigned a frightened shiver. "Fine, I've come to share news about Fearworn."

His eyebrow twitched at how swiftly that earned William's undivided attention. Nicholas loved the attention, but in this case, Fearworn's name got William's mind reeling, not him. It was infuriating. He had never ached for one's gaze as much as William's. He hated it. He wanted someone to look at him, just him, to see him and want him. Of course that wouldn't be William, but Nicholas ached all the same.

"What news do you have?" William asked.

"Fearworn has left the lab, though I know not where. He continues to manipulate new beasts to prepare his next army. The generals have summoned reinforcements, although we will not be at full force for at least a month."

"Surely they won't have us sit here for a month, either. We're fish in a barrel."

"Indeed, which is why we won't attack Fearworn directly. Half of our forces shall remain here waiting for reinforcements while the others take to the lab. The generals seek to destroy the monsters remaining there, claim the scar and the fortress while ensuring Fearworn has one less place to hide. I will be among those forces which sets out tomorrow."

William gave him a slow once over. "Your tone says you are leading up to something. Go on, speak it."

"Come to my bed tonight."

"Why should I exhaust myself with you when there's a chance I'll be leaving tomorrow, too?"

"Because I want you." Nicholas grabbed William's hand and brought them chest to chest. "And you want me."

Nicholas caught whatever snarky remark William had with a kiss. He couldn't get enough of the taste, of the force caught between them. William clung to his waist and stole the breath from his lungs. When they separated, it was for a mere breath before diving in for more, as if this was the first and the last moment they would share. Then Nicholas set their foreheads together, each panting for breath.

"Do you not have another unfortunate mortal to chase?" William muttered. Every word made their lips brush. Nicholas couldn't stop from kissing the fool again, from nipping playfully at his pink lips.

"There is no being upon this realm, or any other, that has my interest as much as you." He kissed along the edge of William's mouth, over his cheek, and down to his neck. He wanted to devour him, to burrow beneath William's skin and sear his bones. "I merely want the arrogant bastard who continues to toy with me. I cannot imagine there is another like him."

William scoffed. "How am I toying with you? We've spent a couple of nights together."

"A mere five."

"Oh?" William tangled his fingers in Nicholas' hair. With a yank, he forced their eyes to meet, stealing Nicholas' infamous grin and wearing it better than even he. "I always knew I was a good lay, but to have the great Nicholas Darkmoon count our time together so seriously, I must be grander than even I surmised."

William dodged the kiss Nicholas tried to give. He growled, "This is the moment where I threaten to leave because you are beginning to annoy me."

"Now you know how it feels." But William gave the fae what he wanted, another kiss he could have dragged on for much longer, but William retreated. "I will see you this evening, trouble."

Perfect timing. Footsteps grew close. Nicholas suspected Charmaine was about to return, so he kissed William again and vanished, keen for night to fall.

20

Charmaine

Montgomery had Charmaine cauterize a nasty wound a soldier received from fighting with another over trivial matters. The stories were typically all the same variety; one soldier spoke idiotically, and another responded with equal stupidity. A fist was thrown, or in this case, broken glass. The high tension forever staining the camp exploded into a mess the medical officers had to take care of. Nothing different from usual.

Once the fool left, Charmaine returned to William. He hadn't finished his task of ensuring the medical packs were prepared for healers. In the chance of an attack, and if they were able, they grabbed packs and set to the field. Perhaps he took a brief break. Regardless, Montgomery shared exciting news and Charmaine was eager to share.

"Montgomery spoke of Grand Mages from Heign's Magical Society paying the troops a visit. There are rumors they have discovered something to help with the war effort," Charmaine explained.

"Is that so?" William opened the last crate to inspect. A red tint along his neck caught her attention. Charmaine approached. A floral scent invaded her nostrils. She leaned forward to sniff.

"What are you doing?" William retreated, one eyebrow raised and lips pursed.

"You smell strange." She wracked her mind for an answer to the aroma. A scent close by, a smell that hovered over the encampment. Not quite flowers because there was nothing so gentle in these parts, but sweet and earthy, nonetheless.

"First the herbs and now me? What could possibly be wrong with your nose?"

"I don't know, it's…" The words caught in her throat as the answer finally hit her. Fae. The scent always became strongest when fae were nearby. They're floral, all of them, the sweetest scent, intoxicating. Yet another way they deeply contrast who they truly are because one smelling so sweet should never be so wicked. If that scent was here and all over William, who had gone missing multiple times through the night, then…

"The man you are seeing, is he fae?" Charmaine asked.

William shut the final crate and stuffed the clipboard under his arm. He wore apathy better than anyone, as if the expression belonged solely to him. "Why would you ask that?"

"The scent of one is all over you."

"Do you pay attention to the way they smell that much?"

She didn't reply, couldn't, because it made little sense to her, too.

William sighed. "Fae are all over the camp. This place must smell as much of them as it does us."

But he told lies. She sensed it again, this gnawing suspicion at the back of her mind accompanied by little ticks she never noticed before. His muscles tensed and the briefest intake of his breath. The headache she had all day intensified. For a moment, she thought she felt the vexation literally crawling beneath her skin.

Pressing a palm to her ringing ear, Charmaine muttered, "Why do you continue to lie to me? I do not need any more stress."

"I am not lying. Besides, who I may be sleeping with is none of your business."

"Implying there is business?"

"Charmaine," he hissed. Her true name uttered angrily through his clenched teeth made her blood boil.

"Don't call me that when you're keeping secrets, secrets that will get the both of us in trouble. Fae are bad news. You should know that better than anyone, or has this man made you forget what happened to Hugh?"

William spun on her. He slammed her against the crates. The edge of one dug into the middle of her back, paling to the heat radiating from William's feral eyes.

"You are overstepping," he warned in a voice that could put fear in the Broken Soul herself. "Do not bring him up again."

"Getting so upset makes me think I'm right." She shoved him aside to storm out of the tent. William didn't call for her. If he had, she may not have heard.

Charmaine hissed from the overwhelming noise and bodies hustling by. Soldiers changed positions, shoulders bumping into hers, and all she wanted was to push them aside. She barely contained the urge by rubbing her palms against her aching temple. Everything was too loud, too much. The light, too. *Light,* what an odd thought. She peered at the sky, bleak and gray, pondering how her eyes ached. The last few days she craved gloom, found herself more alert the blacker the sky became.

A terrible itch slithered through her. She clawed at her arm and legs. The ragged fabric of her jacket worsened the itch. She tore the attire off, eased by the frigid air gnawing at her exposed skin. Soldiers passed incredulous glances as she tugged at her shirt, dislodging the top buttons so the wintery air bit her chest. Charmaine ceased her senseless itching and made way for their poor excuse of a kitchen to appease her grumbling stomach. The damn thing had been rumbling all day. No matter what she ate, she wanted more.

Charmaine gained her rations, then sat by the fire to devour the food that did little for her hunger. Those around her licked the salt from their fingers, talked and laughed, but she could not join. All that was on her mind was food, more food, anything to eat, something juicy and red would be best. Salted pork day after day, accompanied by lackluster bread and ale, couldn't sustain her.

"Good evening," Oscar chirped. The young soldier plopped into place beside her. His curious gaze fell on William stalking over to the rations. He walked in the opposite direction of them. Charmaine grumbled under her breath when Oscar called, "William, where are you going?"

William didn't answer. His silhouette fell into place at another firepit.

Oscar regarded her in hesitant curiosity. "What was that about?"

"Don't know. Don't care," she replied.

The salted pork in Oscar's hands made her salivate. She sucked on the inside of her cheeks, willing herself not to snatch the food from his hands. She hadn't felt so much hunger since she was young when her father had a particularly bad year drinking away their coin. Her mother took any job offered. Charmaine assisted at every opportunity, tending to the neighbor's farm, working for the elderly who couldn't perform hard labor, stitching a neighbor's dress, or cleaning a house. None of the jobs paid well, so they often found themselves huddled around a bare dinner table.

"Are the two of you fightin'?" Oscar muttered between bites of his meal.

"No," she replied.

"Sounds like you're fightin'."

"Why don't you ask William about it?"

"He talks less than you, way, way less."

"Yes, he does."

His silence made keeping secrets easier. They weren't meant to keep secrets from each other when they had no one else to depend on. She thought he depended on her, but he's seeing a fae, risking his life for moronic reasons, and he hadn't told her. That hurt more than she was willing to admit. If they didn't trust each other, then they would be alone, isolated.

"My Ma always said people who talk less tend to feel more, so maybe he's feelin' a lot and needs a little break. I'm sure it's nothin' personal," Oscar said.

"Maybe," she mumbled.

"Or are you the one feelin' a lot?"

Charmaine's tooth cut through her cheek. Copper fell on her tongue. "Oscar, I don't…"

Her words fell silent. Chatter died into nothing when a man, face beaten to being unrecognizable, wandered to the rations cart. With his back turned, whispers began, talks of a traitor. Charmaine needn't hear more to know what happened, but Oscar still said, "He got caught with a fae this mornin'. I heard the beatin' outside my tent, real nasty." Then Oscar spat in the snow and grumbled, "Idiot."

The soldiers at the cart tore at the man's rations, claiming they were running low. He was lucky to get half, lucky to have survived. The man didn't bother sitting at the fires. He didn't offer anyone a glance before disappearing between the tents. That would be William's fate if anyone learned the truth, if he were lucky.

Charmaine peered toward William. His back remained turned, pretending as if nothing happened. *Fool,* she thought over and over until the aching in her head was too painful to ignore. She lurched away from the fire. The thick aroma of smoke made her nose burn, anyway.

"Spend your evening around William. He will make better company than me," she said and wandered off. Snow crunched beneath her worn boots. Torches lit the pathways of the camp. Brief flickers of light made her squint, so she kept to the shadows.

Charmaine went for the tents, where she bundled up her belongings. She had no desire to see William, so she shoved her sleeping bag in a tent a few rows over. No one paid much mind to who slept where anymore.

Captains had more important matters than ensuring soldiers slept on the correct spot of dirt. But as she laid down, a scent caught her by the nose; intoxicating, delicious, a mouth-watering aroma.

She stumbled outside. Campfires flickered in the distance, but the smell did not originate from them. Charmaine moved through camp and ascended the wall where soldiers shuddered under the snow. None paid her any mind, didn't even hear her slip up the stairs. Her steps had never been so gentle, noiseless, even after she dropped to the other side where the scent called her to the woods.

A delicious meal waited in the forest. She slunk into the shadows to find it.

"What manner of creature could have done this?"

The question broke Charmaine's slumber. A soft material tickled her nose. She swatted at it, fur of some sort from the interior of her camping bag. Charmaine made a mental note to have someone look the bag over for tears. Sneezing, she sat up. Dawn light filtered in to illuminate the silhouettes of sleeping soldiers. More were awake than usual for such an early hour. They huddled together outside in a circle.

"Don't know, but it got damn close to our tent. Too damn close," said another.

Charmaine rubbed the crust from her eyes and yawned. A strange taste lingered on her tongue. She smacked her lips and grabbed the canteen by her sleeping bag to drink.

"Most likely a fox, or whatever type of similar creature this wasteland has. It didn't bother us, but I'll mention it to the captain. Maybe the critter is lingering about the campsite looking for scraps," another soldier said.

"With all the rabbits it tore up, I'd say it doesn't need our scraps at all." One silhouette slapped another on the back. "Alright, clean this up, Ronny."

The shortest shadow, Ronny, threw his hands in the air. "Why me?"

"Because you're the youngest." The group laughed. Their silhouettes walked off, leaving Ronny to kneel and clean up the so-called mess.

Charmaine eased herself out of the sleeping bag, surprised by how little the cold affected her. Others shivered beneath their covers and teeth chattered when they awoke to shove their feet into their boots. She stood and stretched, uncaring of the cool air against her skin. In fact, it felt good. Her headache faded and her muscles never felt better. Dare she say that last night was the best sleep she had in an age, since she had a proper bed, even.

The morning horn blared by the time Charmaine dressed and set out of the tent. A light brown-skinned boy struggling to grow a patched beard muttered, exhaling puffs of white smoke, while using a shovel to scoot clumps of viscera into a pile. Remnants of the deceased rodents littered the snow, staining pristine white to pale pink and deep red. No footprints led to or from the kill, merely the remains of many meals, mostly bloodied bones and pieces the creature determined too vile to partake in. Her stomach howled ferociously and mouth watered.

Ronny snorted. "How can you be hungry after seeing a sight like this?"

"Suppose I've grown desensitized to bloodshed," she replied, though didn't believe the words.

Charmaine wretched many times over the years from working in the med bay. Even after seeing the worst of humanity, her stomach always went queasy, although she hadn't felt sick from that lately. More of a relentless hunger and that damned headache, both of which finally vanished after too many days of torment.

21

William

"Has the war between you and Albie ceased yet?"

William yanked on Oscar's ear.

"Don't take your anger out on me." Oscar shoveled snow out of the path into a wheelbarrow.

William stood outside of the med bay, arms crossed. "Don't ask invasive questions."

"It isn't invasive, it's important 'cause Albie has been a little unpleasant lately."

"You have a way with words, Oscar."

"You sure don't. You barely speak 'em." Oscar jabbed the shovel downward and leaned against the handle. "The two of you better talk this out, if not for yourself, then for the rest of us. We're gonna suffer Albie's wrath."

Yes, William had seen that. Three days ago, Charmaine stole rations from someone, snatched the food right out of his hand and walked off as if she hadn't done it. Over the week, she snapped at nurses for mundane issues, being too slow, too loud, or getting in the way. Medical wasn't busy by any means, mostly minor wounds from bored and idiotic soldiers. There was no reason to be hasty, but Charmaine buzzed with unrivaled energy.

Her actions put him on edge, although they may have had to do with their fight. They had never gotten into an argument before. The evening they fought, she wasn't in their tent and he hadn't searched for her. Especially after what happened at dinner, the ostracized soldier was a harsh reminder of William's foolish decisions. He would be in that same position if the wrong person discovered what he had done with Nicholas.

Somehow, Charmaine could tell that he spent time with Nicholas. He could have told her, should have, but Nicholas was his shame. A time he would rather not admit to another lest they judge his horrible decisions and potentially harm or kill him. He hadn't a clue how to remedy the situation. If he apologized, Charmaine would ask questions, so he had to be honest, and that terrified him.

What honesty could William give? He didn't understand this hunger, either. To put it simply, he was horny and Nicholas offered. To make it more complicated, he enjoyed the danger of it and needed it to survive out here. Charmaine may not believe that. She probably wouldn't understand. William hardly understood. Not speaking to her again terrified him more than admitting how fucked up he felt.

"How did ya manage to piss Albie off, anyway?" Oscar squinted like he could get an answer from the snow flurries. "Albie is the nicest guy I've ever met."

"How are you certain Albie didn't piss me off?"

Oscar laughed, then hiccuped at William's death glare.

"Speak your mind, Oscar," William hissed.

"I ain't sayin' a damn thing." Oscar returned to shoveling and hastily moved along the walkaway far, far from William.

Oscar was right. Charmaine did not anger easily. At this rate, they wouldn't speak for some time. William wanted his friend back. If that meant admitting his mistakes, then he had to be willing to do so. Which was much easier said than done. His stomach churned. If he had eaten breakfast, he may have thrown up from nerves.

Breathing through his nostrils, he entered the medical tent. Charmaine sat at the bedside of one of the soldiers suffering from a fever. Crowded like this in the glacial weather, viruses clung no matter what anyone did. Some nurses suffered from those same colds, resulting in Charmaine being there to make up for those who needed rest. William settled by Charmaine, hands clutched behind his back. "May I speak with you?"

Charmaine dabbed the sweat from the soldier's brow. Her right eye twitched. A vein throbbed in her temple. Irritability had plagued her since their capture, since that damned wound, the bruise. Something was amiss, but he hadn't figured out what.

"Depends on what you want to speak about," she finally replied.

"Do you still suffer from headaches?"

Her jaw moved side to side.

"Come here." He grasped her hand.

Charmaine grumbled, but allowed William to drag her to the supply tent. There was more privacy there, supposed to be, anyway. Two nurses claimed the tent for their smoke break. They jumped at the sight of Charmaine. She lectured one girl earlier, so the nurse ushered her friend outside.

"Take a seat and show me your leg," William said, gesturing to one of the crates.

"My leg?" Charmaine asked.

"Your headaches started after the attack and you said that you have been irritable lately, so let me take a look."

"Is that all you wished to speak about?"

"No, but I will speak more while looking over your leg, so sit."

With a reluctant huff, Charmaine fell into the chair. William knelt and gently tugged up her pants to expose a scar, nothing more, no sign of an infection. He pushed the fabric up to Charmaine's thigh.

"See? Nothing unusual," she said and knocked her leg up and down to prove there was no pain, either.

William pressed a hand against her balmy skin. The Sight should reveal all. The silver strings circling Charmaine's muscles same as always should put him at ease, but they didn't. They felt like lies. He ran a careful finger over the strings, begging them to reveal the truth, but their light flickered and all remained as it was.

Sighing, he tugged the pant leg down. "Did you not suffer any other injury back then or recently?"

"I haven't. You are worrying too much."

"I would argue you are not worried enough," he muttered. Charmaine's hardened stare pierced the turbulent guilt at the base of his gut. He groaned. "You were right the other day, about who I have been seeing."

"Am I also correct to assume he's the most troublesome option there is?"

He swallowed hard. "Yes."

"William," she hissed. He stood with his back to her, peering outside to ensure no one listened. "That is a horrendous idea. You could be killed. You saw that man the other night, so people are on edge and probably looking for more trouble. Why would you even consider something so nonsensical?"

"Because I..." He didn't know what to say. Feelings caught in a web of his mind, struggling to free themselves, and coming out as nothing more than a mumble, "Like you want hope for tomorrow, I want comfort. Sex gives me that, lets me forget about all of this for a few blissful moments."

"Comfort normally doesn't come from danger."

"There is little danger involved." He leaned against a crate and retrieved the ring from his pocket. Making sure they weren't being watched, he slipped the ring on. Charmaine jolted from his disappearance, then he took off the ring to put back in his pocket. "This keeps things simple."

"How..." she snorted, that frown changing to a humored smile. "Romantic?"

The two laughed and any tension previously there faded. This is what he wanted, what he needed. Both of them did. Their friendship was a small fire in the dead of night, not enough to battle against every sorrow, but always there and forever warm.

"I am sorry for lying and troubling you. I knew you would be concerned, that you would find this to be a horrible idea, and frankly, I thought it would be better if you weren't involved at all. If something happened, it would only harm me," William said.

"I don't want that. If there is trouble for you, then there is trouble for us. That is the way it is and always will be." Charmaine scratched her neck. "I shouldn't have overreacted. I'm sorry. I don't mean it as an excuse, but I truly am out of sorts of late. The other day I thought my headache was gone, but it has returned and became even worse."

"Is that all?"

"No, I have sensitivity to smells and hunger, always so hungry. If there is a medical issue that you cannot find, maybe this is a mental one. Maybe this place has truly broken me."

"It has broken all of us in one way or the other." But William doubted Charmaine's problems were mental ones. They had been through a lot. Such headaches, hunger, and irritability could be an ailment he hadn't discovered yet. Perhaps she caught a virus. William would ask around, consult Montgomery if Charmaine offered her permission. If other soldiers suffered from similar symptoms, the camp may face an outbreak.

Before William could speak further, a nurse tugged the tent flap open. Her curious eyes fell on William. She waved to someone behind her when declaring, "He is over here, sir."

The nurse stepped away, allowing the last person William ever expected to enter.

"Henry," William muttered. His brother's name felt foreign on his tongue. A lot changed in five years, for both of them. Henry, the scrawny teenager cutting himself in the mirror trying to shave what wasn't there, had grown a beard that hugged his full cheeks. Once a lanky frame stood sturdy in the entryway, carrying wide shoulders stuffed into a dirtied uniform. William didn't want to see any of his family in this damned uniform. It meant they weren't safe, that they were a target, that he may not be able to protect them, that they may discover the truth of what he became.

"You got taller." Henry chuckled with a shimmer to his autumn eyes, comforting as ever. William didn't know what to say, although he had countless things he wanted to say.

What are you doing here?

I missed you.

Why would you come here when I've tried so hard for none of you to see me like this?

I wish you came sooner.

You aren't staying, are you?

Please stay.

You have to go.

I can't lose you.

William had at least three opportunities to visit home over the years, each of which he declined out of fear. He knew the moment he stepped through those doors, smelt his mother's perfume and even the hated cigar smoke, he would never leave. Then his family would have questions. They would notice how he changed. They would ask what happened in subtle ways and he wouldn't have the heart to tell them. Wouldn't want to admit all he had been through and done, if only to avoid witnessing his mother's tears. He wanted all of them, including himself, to believe he was the same boy who left, that he could be that person again and forget all that transpired.

"You must be Henry Vandervult. I'm Albie Tuckerton, a friend of William's," Charmaine said to fill the space. She approached Henry with her hand outstretched. Henry took a firm hold and smiled, all teeth and two deep dimples in his rosy cheeks.

"A pleasure to finally put a face to the name. William has mentioned you in his letters," Henry said.

"Did he? Good things, I should hope."

"Of course. You're the friend we've all been so eager to meet. I hope once this war ends that you'd do us the honor of a visit. Our mother would be especially happy to meet you."

Charmaine gave a nervous laugh, then cleared her throat. "I have heard dinner at the Vandervult estate is something to look forward to."

Henry laughed. By the Souls, William had missed the sound. It nearly brought him to his knees.

"Maybe not in the way you think. We can get out of sorts, but I can promise you won't be bored," Henry said.

"That makes me look forward to it even more." Charmaine glanced between the brothers, hands clasped at her waist. "As honored as I am to finally meet one of the infamous older Vandervult brothers, I'll take my leave so you may catch up. Thank you for the invite, Henry. I will certainly take you up on it."

Henry clapped Charmaine on the shoulder before she left. The moment she disappeared, he caught William in a hug. William knew he made the right choice to never go home. This was already too much, encased by a love so tight he ached under the crushing weight of Henry's grasp. But he said nothing because he would rather be smothered than melancholy and aching.

Henry smelled like home. At least William thought so. He could have imagined the aroma of roses from the back garden that always filtered through the open windows. Was it spring already? Summer? Here, they only knew winter, and he had forgotten a world existed outside of ice and snow. He forgot what the garden looked like, where the flowers were and where the paths led. The information became trivial to his war rattled mind, and yet, he hated himself for dismissing the memories.

"Why wasn't I informed about this? I heard mages from Heign's Magical Society were coming, but certainly the generals knew who and would have informed me," William said while struggling to keep his voice calm.

"There were a couple of changes to our arrival and I wanted my visit to be a surprise." Henry released him and reached into the satchel he carried. "Along with these!"

Henry presented two plain books. William recognized the author when he opened the first page. The words were a blow, another piece of the past haunting him, reminding him of change he never wanted.

Henry had that sparkle in his eyes he shared when excited. "The series you loved finished. That first one is the last book, and the other is the first to a new series the same author recently started. Mother acquired the proper copies, but I thought you may want a more discreet set here."

Romance books. William ran a finger over the title page. He read the prequels late into the night. The parts he remembered made him cringe. The foolish boy he once was blushed from the male lead's suave words and kicked his feet during the first kiss. Then grew envious of the love freely shared, of the boy who believed in this nonsense and dreamed of a similar future.

"If I'm recalling correctly, you are the one who said these books are unbefitting of men, that it isn't the way of things," William countered.

"And yet that never stopped you."

"It should have. You were right." William slipped. He hadn't meant to. The words released in a breath he didn't consent to give, and now Henry caught him, the one brother that would notice instantly.

Arthur may have taken after their father in terms of politics and Richard could charm, but Henry earned his position as a mage's apprentice at a young age for a reason; observation. Always watching, always listening, always deciphering everything like a puzzle, figuratively and literally. William had a love for books while Henry loved puzzles, often buying odd ones from the market that came from across the sea. Henry spent hours, days, even weeks putting the puzzles together. When completed, he strutted through the estate with such confidence the boys teased him for it, of course. William had become one of those puzzles, and Henry didn't like giving up.

"Is this why you've been avoiding us?" Henry didn't sugarcoat his words. They sounded as hurt as William felt.

"Avoiding is a bit harsh."

"Harsh but true. Five years is a long time and I've met many in the military who served less time than you and earned visitation. At least before our troops crossed the sea. One needn't think long to decipher what you are doing, although," Henry hesitated, eyes more despaired than William had ever witnessed. "Maybe you made the right choice, no matter how much it pains me to say so."

William's knuckles whitened against the book spines. "What makes you say that?"

"Mother was in hysterics for the first six months after you left. I doubt she spoke of that in her letters."

No. Matilda's letters were always cordial, written in her elegant slanted writing and speaking of home. How terribly she missed William, and that everything would be alright, that he would survive, he would come home, then everything would be perfect, as it always should have been.

In the beginning, William slept with the letters clutched to his chest. He believed in her promises, but only now did he think she made a promise for the both of them.

"She slept in your room, and wouldn't come out for anything," Henry added. A slight tremble caught in his breath. "Father had to call upon mages to get her to eat. She cried and screamed and begged Father to speak to the king, to shut down the charities if it pleased His Majesty, or send her in your stead. Eventually, time led her to come out, but she isn't the same either, William. A part of her left with you and I don't think it will return until you do. But had you visited, I doubt she'd have managed to watch you leave again."

William couldn't imagine his mother in such a state. Even when his grandparents died, Matilda told jokes at the funeral with tears in her eyes. People laughed and spun tales that made most unsure if they cried from sorrow or joy. William was too young to understand what happened, but he understood that his mother always had an air of joy about her. She spun sorrowful moments into comfortable ones, to ease the suffering of others.

To think she didn't for so long, that she laid about in his room crying and knowing he was doing the same during recruitment. Every night he laid there wishing to be home. He begged his family to save him when the pain became too great, when his heart shattered and he was left alone with the broken pieces.

He released a strangled breath Henry didn't speak on. Instead, Henry said, "Arthur and Richard didn't speak to Father for two years, either."

William choked. "What? Why?"

"Because they were upset, all of us were. None of us wished to worry you, so they kept it together until your enlistment. Arthur and Richard believed Father should have done more, that he shouldn't have accepted the punishment. They went to King Ellis requesting one of us be sent instead. Richard was shot down instantly, of course."

"The fool has a heart condition. He cannot serve. It was a foolish thing to do," William muttered, even if he loved the thought of Richard marching into the throne room red faced and demanding. He would be the one gaudy enough to make such an attempt.

Arthur, though? He had always been the responsible one, poised, held together with the toughest mortar. His rebellion held surprise and made William love him all the more, made him miss his brothers all the more. They could be a rambunctious and tedious lot, but they were William's rambunctious and tedious lot. He'd have them no other way.

"Since the decision had been made, we were told you would be labeled a deserter if we dared to try anything," Henry explained. "I thought of joining so you'd at least have someone with you, but after Mother fell apart, I took time away from schooling. I kept to the estate to give her more company, and it helped, to an extent. She certainly wouldn't have coped with the possibility of losing two children, and now here we are."

"Here we are," William repeated. He set the books aside, then clasped his fingers tightly behind his back. They did little to ease the feelings threatening to spill over. Every wall he built cracked under Henry's attention and at the sound of his voice. "Are they... angry with me for not coming home?"

Henry snorted. "When have any of us been angry with you? It's truly unfair how the youngest sibling gets away with everything. Everyone misses you. The house isn't the same. It's too quiet and there aren't enough books on the floor to trip over. I've considered stacking a few by the corners purely for the feel of stubbing my toes."

William chuckled, and it felt real, right, normal.

"We want to be a family again and you have new family to meet," Henry said.

"So I've heard."

"Luckily, your niece looks like her mother."

William smiled, genuine and nearly painful. "Don't let Arthur hear you say that."

"Oh, that isn't my job."

"It's Richard's," they said in unison, and William hadn't realized how much he missed laughing with his brothers until now. Those chuckles faded when William whimpered a breath that he desperately tried to strangle. He wanted to savor this moment and the touch of Henry's hand clutching his shoulder. A hold of desperation, one that spoke more than words ever could.

"I have come with the Grand Mages to speak with the generals. We've been working tirelessly over the years hoping to discover anything that could be of help, and we've done it. Truly, William, we..." Henry cast a suspicious glance over William's shoulder, then tugged his brother closer. "You cannot share this with anyone, not even your friend. We have discovered a way to momentarily close shimmers."

William feared hope but anyone could hear it in his words, "I thought that was impossible."

"As I said, it is momentary, nearly ten minutes of time. I know that sounds little, but it could be enough to stop Fearworn from running, to trap him somewhere he feels safest. There is a shade among your ranks, is there not? With this, he may be able to kill Fearworn. Do you understand, William?"

He clutched Henry's wrist like a lifeline, another string of hope that felt stronger than ever. If he tugged, if he held fast, maybe the lifeline would take him home.

"I truly do believe this war is coming to an end." Henry settled their foreheads together, eyes closed and lips set into a hopeful grin. "You will come home and we will all be together again."

That's all William wished for. An end to the war, going home to pretend this never happened. But deep down, he couldn't imagine how he could be happy after all he had seen, all he had done, and all that had been done to him. William couldn't imagine a future. Children carried dreams. He had many before the war. He spent more days than he could count imagining his future as he clutched a book to his chest. Some afternoons, when he was feeling brave, that young boy envisioned himself ridiculously in love, living with a sweet and funny man on a small piece of property where they spent their days enjoying each other's company. Other days, he saw himself becoming a renowned playwright sitting in a high booth, watching his stories come to life on stage, even if he lived alone, without a lover. He went to all the parties in high society, adored by the masses for the tales he wove.

But William hadn't pictured the future for many years. The one time he dared ended with Hugh's death, which is how he always thought this war would end. Of course, he hoped. Of course, he wanted to return home, but deep down, William didn't see life after the war. He saw pain and death. He saw himself broken beyond repair, like the many men he had come across over the years. He saw the war ending and his life ending with it. Nothing more.

"Will you not be staying long, then?" William asked after Henry stepped aside.

"A week, at the most. I barely secured a position on this trip. King Ellis hasn't allowed unnecessary travels to the Krenia Kingdom for the last two years, which so happened to be when my instructors decided I had enough experience for field work." Henry rolled his eyes. "Then this opportunity arose, and my superiors were offered to bring the good news first."

"How did you manage to slip in?"

"One of the Grand Mages is a bit obsessive over cleanliness, so I spoke of how dirty it would be here until he panicked and offered me a place in his stead. We wouldn't want him to panic over here."

William smirked. "Oh yes, how noble of you."

"I would have to agree. Now, why don't you show me where the food is? I'm famished."

"I fear you will still be famished after we eat." William gestured for Henry to follow him out of the tent.

They spent the evening together sharing stories. Henry never pushed for more details, although William knew his brother filed away every word, tone, and movement. He'd unravel every thread because that's how his mind worked.

When the evening grew late, Henry took to the tent set up for him and his colleagues. William lay awake most of the night worrying, paranoid there would be an attack, that he'd find Henry's corpse among the rubble. Though he had been happy to see his brother, comforted by his mirth and stories, William wanted the week to end. Then Henry would go home. He would be safe. He would never see what William did, would never know war, and never learn what William was willing to do to survive.

22

Nicholas

Monsters laid dead at Nicholas' feet. Fire burst from shattered windows and entryways. Blood stained his arms up to the elbows. The battle for Fearworn's lab ended, won with little effort. Since Fearworn and most of his forces vacated the lab, not enough remained to guard the citadel. Now it, and the scar, belonged to them.

Nicholas stepped over corpse after corpse to approach the scar shimmering like tears of a falling star. The portal hovered at the center of the citadel, barely as thick as a quill. The air around the scar bristled with corrosive life. Violent tremors and strikes of lightning hit the ground, burning the earth black. He peered at the despondency swirling within, feeling it coalesce beneath his skin. A clawing, gnawing bite, his fingers twitched and neck cracked. That scar spoke of corruption, misshapen and condemned. He retreated, for perhaps his father made a point. Sometimes, a fae had to know when to stop meddling. This scar spoke of horrors even Nicholas didn't want.

His suspicions were proven correct when a mortal soldier dared to touch the scar. They screeched like the damned, veins set ablaze by flames. The soldier flailed, then deteriorated into ash. Nicholas had never seen that happen before, though heard stories about scars that Fearworn opened were different, violent in nature.

Blair's hands shoved against Nicholas' back with such force he tumbled toward the scar. He caught himself and swung on her. She dodged, cackling, eyes crinkled into joyous crescent moons.

"Are you not old enough to know to keep your hands to yourself?" Nicholas retreated, but Blair threw an arm around his neck.

"What's wrong? Scared you would have fallen in?" She clicked her tongue. "Ever think about trying to close one?"

"No one knows how."

"A shade opened this one. A shade should be able to close it."

"I will likely die trying."

Blair laughed. "Then that is how your end will come to be."

Nicholas shoved her hold aside. "What is that supposed to mean?"

"Don't be daft," she spat, eyebrows knitting close together. "What do you suppose will happen after this war is over? Father will want these portals closed, in Faerie, of course. They spell trouble for all of us."

"He won't risk my life. Unfortunately, I have children to sire, remember?"

"Which you and Evera will get out of the way as hastily as possible. Once you're through, Father will find the next issue for you to deal with." Blair waved her hand at the scar flickering with foreboding light. "He will send you to close these because you are nothing but his tool. With some luck, you'll slip through and never be seen again. You'll die alone or become another creature's problem across the realms."

"You needn't remind me every chance you get that you wish me to be dead."

"Is that really what bothers you?" Laughing, she walked away, knowing she was right to question him.

Nicholas scrutinized the scar, little more than a thin cut in the world, and imagined slipping through. This wouldn't be like the one he passed from Faerie to Terra. There would be pain, most likely death. Though Laurent knew that, he would send Nicholas to deal with the scars. If he died because of Laurent's plans, so be it. Laurent would mourn the loss of a weapon, but he would find another to sharpen as beautifully as he sharpened Nicholas.

You are nothing but his tool.

Nicholas stormed off. He, and everyone else, steered clear of the scar. They attended to the lab, ensuring every monster lay dead, and tossed their corpses into a ditch outside of the citadel. Soldiers cleared out rooms, preparing the space for a good night's rest. A handful of their troops would return to the rest of the military in the morning. The others would keep to the lab, ensuring no monsters returned.

That night, Nicholas didn't join the others at their fires to celebrate this supposed victory. He found a room, lit the lantern hanging from the wall, then fell upon the poor excuse of a bed. Blair's words irritated him more than they should have. No love had been lost between Nicholas and his siblings. Their love had never been on his list of wants, nor his father's. But it would be a lie to say he didn't want someone to care for a cursed shade doomed to walk a poor path. Realistically, he would succumb to his power and become a shell of who he once was. If he somehow didn't, Laurent would continue leading his life without remorse or care.

Nicholas often considered battling Laurent. Finally, putting his foot down and demanding to be respected. Then darkness settled in. He couldn't breathe recalling the days or weeks spent trapped between cavern walls, his father's footsteps echoing nearby and his dispiriting voice asking, *"Are you ready to behave?"*

Nicholas struggled. He fought. He scratched at the rock that always returned. Somehow, someway, Laurent always had the upper hand. Knowledge from eons of lives spent while Nicholas was considered little more than a flake of dust. Twenty-three years meant nothing in the life of fae. He was less than a child by comparison. Laurent was proof that it was always brains over brawn. Nicholas hadn't caught up. He wasn't sure if he ever could. He didn't understand the full extent of his power and he didn't want to find out in case it risked urging his destruction closer.

A rap sounded at the door.

"Fuck off, Blair," Nicholas growled, in no mood to play more of her games. He mentally chastised himself for that truth because what fae didn't relish in games? William's boring ways must have rubbed off on him.

"Not Blair," Arden replied. The door swung open. "Why are you here rather than outside with the rest of us?"

"I'm not in the mood."

"For alcohol and sex?" Laughing, Arden fell onto the edge of Nicholas' bad. "Were you perhaps stabbed in one of the G's?"

Nicholas cocked a brow.

"The gut or the groin, because I imagine only pain could keep you from a fun evening. The others were thinking about pranking the mortals. They're extra jumpy this evening." Arden looked ready to go into great detail about this prank until he realized Nicholas wasn't listening.

Arden nudged his leg. "Are you actually unwell?"

Nicholas spoke with more bite than intended, "There is no need to panic. I am as healthy as a shade can be. You may tell my father that yourself."

"I would not tell him a thing if I did not have to."

"Please, even if my father hadn't caught you in whatever deal was struck, he would have found some way to convince you to spy on me."

Arden thought for a moment, then shrugged. "Probably, but why does it matter?"

Arden didn't understand. Every choice he made led to consequences, good or bad, but they were his own. Nicholas, from the moment of birth, lived under the rule of his father, and when the time came, he put

Nicholas to work. Arden's life would always move in the direction he desired. Nicholas never had a chance. Sometimes, he wondered if having a mother would change that. Would she have put a stop to Laurent?

They were ridiculous questions because they didn't matter. Nicholas' mother died after a nasty deal gone wrong. Had a knack for fighting and sometimes got herself into too much trouble. Nicholas was three and couldn't remember anything about her. She couldn't protect him. Even if she were alive and cared, even if he somehow escaped Laurent, he would always stand under the looming threat of his condition. Nicholas truly was a tool of both his father and his future as a shade. No path he walked would ever belong entirely to him.

"If you are upset, I would be more than willing to ease your discomforts." Arden's hand fell on Nicholas' thigh. He caught Arden's eyes and found they were not as enchanting as they had been. They did not hold a winter storm begging to nip at his heels. His lips were not full enough and nose was not upturned enough. Something was off, the sound of his voice, even, had Nicholas shaking his head.

"No, I think you should join the others," he said, softly and broken. "I will not make for good company this evening."

Arden didn't bother him further. Nicholas wouldn't have known what to say had the fae tried. He simply didn't want Arden. He wanted another. The coolest of green eyes and hair like golden fire, and found the bed too cold without them. William slept on his side, but if he rolled onto his back, he snored. Nicholas would curl around that muscular form and settle them onto their sides until William's breathing evened out. He dared to miss it. Finding that hugging a pillow made him more irritable.

Nicholas rolled onto his side, facing the wall. He pressed his knuckles to the stone, half expecting for a reaction, then grew disappointed when there wasn't one. He hadn't realized how loud Faerie was until he stepped upon Terra land. Sludge filled lakes, silencing their voices, and timber laid upon charred ground that forgot its songs. The mountains didn't whisper through the winds. All had been so eerily still. Nicholas awoke in the night, wondering where he would wake, then see nothing changed. Sorrow settled in, a sense of missing a home he hadn't understood until then.

Faerie had its problems, annoying siblings, an angry betrothed, a distant and cruel father with troublesome expectations, but Faerie had been the only home Nicholas ever knew. Darkmoon, specifically, made him proud, and it was proud of him. The land carried him from place to place and he believed beyond any doubt that, if true trouble knocked, Darkmoon would protect him. In this case, he wanted Darkmoon to soothe him. Hill Castle, his home, knew when he was upset. It'd grow his favorite flowers on the windowsill or knit a blanket of moss to drape over his shoulders. Nothing of that sort happened here. He sat alone in the dark, awake long after the lantern burned out.

The next morning, Nicholas took off alongside half the troop returning to camp. Their journey over the course of a couple of days dragged in ways it hadn't before. When they came upon camp, he found his attention straying toward the medical bay. However, Duke had been waiting for Nicholas' arrival.

Duke badgered him with a request from the generals to hear of what transpired. Grumbling under his breath, he shuffled off to give the damn update with curt words and little attention. Amos already sent word containing the events. His information wasn't any different, nor did he learn anything more about Fearworn, but the generals had learned something.

"Grand Mages from Heign's Magical Society have stumbled upon a way to close a shimmer for about ten minutes," General Wright explained. None missed the expectation in his tone. "We must close Fearworn in and continue to take every citadel we find. When he runs to one, believing he can escape through a shimmer, we will close it off and that is where you must do your part. Once he realizes what we've done, we may not be able to pull this move again."

"In ten minutes," Nicholas chortled, recalling Fearworn and his fearsome power. But if they trapped him, if he was startled by the unexpected and surrounded by an army, that could spell his end. "Well, I suggest you get to planning our final move. Do your part and I will do mine."

He left the tent, berating himself for daring to step toward the medical bay. It would be pathetic to seek William out, so Nicholas begrudgingly went to his tent, where he collapsed on his bed instead. But William's scent lingered there, twisting like thick vines around his burning limbs. Even like this, the bastard tormented him, lingering at the end of every thought.

As if summoned, William materialized in the tent. Nicholas thought his appearance to be a trick, a mirage of his mind, but William was as real as the kiss he gave. Greedy, devouring, a dangerous want that had Nicholas' lips tingling. Fingers tore into his hair. Teeth bit at his lips. William's hips met his, reminding him of the dreams William loved to haunt.

"This isn't how I expected to be greeted," Nicholas said against William's mouth. "Did you miss me, my wicked?"

William pushed them onto the bed and tore at Nicholas' clothes. As much as he wished to be undone, William jerked and trembled. Every brush of his hand was erratic. Grabbing William's hair, Nicholas yanked him aside. His gaze carried a worrisome dullness.

"You are out of sorts," Nicholas said.

"Don't feign care. It's unnecessary in our arrangement." William caught him in another kiss, tasting of desperation. Nicholas gripped William's hips, but a discomfort weighed on his shoulders. A suspicion forced him to push William back.

"Unnecessary unless this ends with you stabbing me, and not in the way I desire," Nicholas declared in the face of William's ferocity. "What is on your mind?"

William slapped his hold aside, face contorted into indignation. "I am here for sex and if you are not going to give it, then I am leaving."

The words hurt, somehow, some way. William wasn't different from anyone else. He came for a purpose. If Nicholas didn't serve that purpose, he would leave. But he didn't want to be alone. He wanted William here, even if that meant serving a purpose. Nicholas caught William by the waist.

"Oh no, I never said that," he hummed, tugging until William fell into his lap.

"Then what are you saying?"

"You should speak your mind," he said with the same apprehension William wore.

"Why would I speak my mind to you? Berating me will further entice my anger."

"I won't deny I am the last soul to comfort anyone, but I can try. After all," Nicholas' thumb rubbed circles along William's side. "You haven't spoken of my aversion to enclosed spaces, have you?"

He could have. Nicholas' kin would find that fear humorous, a weakness one would exploit in the future. Laurent had. If Nicholas pushed too far, he found himself buried, begging, lost and incapable of thought. He couldn't let others know the truth, so he kept those fears close to his chest. But William learned and said nothing. At least he was different that way, unwilling to stoop so low.

"You will tease me," William muttered in a voice so unlike him, clipped, lacking any of his natural tenacity.

"I will not."

"You wouldn't understand."

"I may not, but I will listen."

William became the definition of discomfort, of hesitation and disbelief. His typically haughty presence faded as his shoulders caved inward and eyes lowered. Nicholas had no confidence in settling William's worries. He wasn't sure why he was so insistent in hearing them, either. There was simply something at the back of his mind wanting to hear, to know, to listen. Then William took a shuddering breath, seconds or minutes later. Nicholas hadn't counted because he got lost in William, exactly as he wanted, but in a way he didn't expect.

"My brother is here," William said simply, nothing more, and for once, Nicholas was the one in need of an explanation.

"This troubles you?" he asked.

"I don't know. I've longed to see my family. All these years, I survived by thinking of returning home. Each year that passes, I wonder if they will recognize me, if I will recognize them. Have I lost myself here entirely? I don't know, I..." William trembled so fiercely one would mistake him for having been lost in a snowstorm.

Nicholas didn't know what to say, so he waited and listened.

"I have never wished to desert so badly. I want to run home and pretend none of this ever happened. Lie to myself that I've spent the last five years with them, hearing my father telling bad jokes, my brothers bickering over the best hunting spots, and knitting with my mother after a long morning at the hospital. Who would I be had I spent these years with them rather than here?" William's fingers slipped into Nicholas' hair, a gentle hold so foreign that he froze. Neither of them were gentle, but like this, they were soft and comforting in a frightening sense.

William twirled Nicholas' hair around his fingers. His voice became softer than Nicholas had ever heard, and it had his heart palpitating, "My father loved to tell me bedtime stories. Even as I got older, he came to my room, and we'd sit together by the fireplace. Sometimes he read to me, other times he made a story up. My brothers were never as fond of tales, so that was a tradition belonging to us. I feel childish about missing it, naïve."

Nicholas held William closer. The movement broke William from his trance. He fell out of Nicholas' lap, stumbling over his own feet. Nicholas had never missed something more, had never wanted to snatch someone close and never let go. He never saw himself as possessive before having William near.

"This is pointless. I'm leaving." William went for the exit. Nicholas caught his wrist. One gentle tug and William fell into his arms.

"Do all mortals share such stories?" Nicholas whispered. "Father's telling their children bedtime stories and missing those at home. Is that common?"

Because Nicholas couldn't fathom it. He missed Darkmoon, the place, but not his father or his siblings. Quite the opposite. He enjoyed his freedom far from them. Though he wished to feel Darkmoon's heart beating beneath the sole of his bare feet and to lie in the tall grass, he could go the rest of his life without seeing those he grew up with. They shared few memories of joy together.

Laurent wove tales, bloody and vicious. Nicholas enjoyed them while understanding he could be made a part of those tales if he slipped. His siblings found him a nuisance and often tormented him, although he always replied in kind. He could not imagine a family like William spoke of, but it sounded sweeter than the best kept lie.

"I know that my family is kinder than most, softer, some would say," William replied.

"How strange."

"I suppose for you it would be."

Nicholas' hand fell on William's waist. "I believe mortals call it corporal punishment. My father wholeheartedly believes in that. Once I got up to trouble and he broke every bone in my fingers and toes."

Nicholas chuckled at the memory. William did not. His expression paled. "That is cruel," he said.

"I was a naughty child."

"That doesn't make the punishment less cruel." William ran a hand down Nicholas' arm to take the hand on his waist. He ran a gentle finger over every knuckle. "Is that why you are claustrophobic? Was it a result of punishment?"

"Oh, no, I was kidnapped as a child. It led to my engagement with Evera, in fact."

William's mouth opened and shut, teeth clicking together. "You must learn to elaborate because you make the most absurd statements."

"I find kidnapping to be rather self explanatory."

"Why were you kidnapped? What happened? And how did that lead to an engagement?"

"So curious all of a sudden." Nicholas had recounted the story frequently while drunk on faerie wine, but here, his tongue weighed heavy. Telling William felt different. This felt different, like he was opening himself up to catastrophe. William knew too much already. He accidentally learned of Nicholas' fear. Now he wanted to learn about his past.

"Will you feed that curiosity or not?"

Nicholas couldn't resist the opportunity. "I'll tell you if you answer my riddle."

"You are troublesome." William rolled his eyes. "Go on, then."

"It can break without being broken, race without running, and skip without skipping." He didn't know why he said that. It was the first to come to mind.

The answer came upon William in less than a breath, but he waited to reply, voice hardly above a whisper, "A heart."

"Always so clever, aren't you?"

"Maybe you share awful riddles."

Nicholas scoffed. "How dare you."

The charming dimples in William's cheeks made Nicholas admire him all the more.

"I answered your riddle, so tell me," William said, but the truth caught in Nicholas' throat. The more William admired him, the more Nicholas got lost in his eyes. "Well?" William hummed.

"Those like my father view shades as weapons, tools to be used," Nicholas said. "Others, such as my sister, believe the moment our eyes shine, we should be put to death. Then there are those who see shades as an opportunity. I was ten, playing in the forest, when a group of assailants captured me. My powers recently revealed themselves, so I knew little about how to make use of them. These fae were lowly forest sprites seeking power like my father's, wanting to become lords of a land. They thought a well-trained shade could accomplish that. I was held in a small, somber cell for six months. Any escape attempts were met with severe punishments. I had no reason to believe my father would come, so I was quite shocked when I was rescued. Alvina Bloodbane, Evera's mother, found me. I owed her my life. My father owed her for saving me and ridding my father's land of traitors. She asked him to engage me with her daughter, and the deal was struck."

"Your claustrophobia started after that experience?" William asked.

"The cell was hardly large enough for a child, and I stopped summoning flames after my captors' punishments." His throat went dry. He could hardly swallow, recalling the long days of hallucinations and desperation. "The night can drive one mad."

"I suppose that explains quite a lot about you." William smirked when interlocking their fingers. Nicholas offered the connection a confused stare. "What?" William muttered.

"You are holding my hand."

William let go. "Do you not want me to?"

Nicholas caught him with a vice grip. "I did not say that."

They gazed at one another. A new tension formed, one Nicholas couldn't put into words. He found that happening often of late, specifically toward William.

"Why are you holding my hand?" he whispered, somehow fearing the response.

"Because we were discussing matters that caused you emotional harm." William pursed his lips. "And I stupidly forgot you don't understand comfort."

"I do find it odd."

"Odd or different?"

Nicholas contemplated the sensation of William's rough skin, calluses on calluses pressed against his palm. He played with William's fingers, touching thumb to thumb, fingertip to fingertip. William never said a word, didn't ask why, then Nicholas held that hand, one that felt so unbearably right in his.

No, this did not feel odd at all. He liked it, the way their hands looked together. How he wanted more, to never let go. Nicholas reached out to curl his fingers in William's hair. William fell into him, letting his breath caress the skin of Nicholas' neck.

"Different," Nicholas replied, heart fluttering, as he took in William's scent, that damn disinfectant and soap, but also uniquely William.

"Is different wrong?"

"No, I do not believe it is."

They sat like that, silent, but Nicholas had never been so content, had never wanted so simple a moment to suspend into eternity.

23

William

William thought he remembered home. Henry's presence proved otherwise. The laughter of his brother and the joy his smile wrought had always been bright in memories, but paled compared to reality.

"The days will be dull without your company," Charmaine said from the chair she occupied at the back of the medical tent. Henry took the seat beside her, both staying out of William's path while he tended to a soldier suffering from food poisoning.

"Do not compliment him so openly. It will all go to his head," William teased.

"Ignore my dear baby brother." Henry leaned toward Charmaine. "Compliment away. I am worthy of them."

William rolled his eyes and covered the soldier with a blanket. He took his medicines and his droopy eyes closed. Then William joined Henry and Charmaine. He grabbed another chair so the three sat together. This had been the most at home he had felt since his inscription. He couldn't imagine losing it again, though he couldn't imagine Henry staying longer, either. It was too much of a risk. William's paranoia kept him awake most nights. The smallest sound had him imagining

Fearworn's beasts encircling the camp, preparing to strike. Henry would be taken and William would blame himself.

He repeated day and night that nothing would cause Henry harm. He would never allow it, and the generals would ensure their safety, too. No amount of convincing eased his worry. After all he had seen, it became difficult not to concoct the worst-case scenario in vivid details.

"How long will the journey home take?" Charmaine asked.

"About a month." Henry chugged a pint of wine that had been brought earlier, courtesy of the generals for one of the oh-so-important mages. "Traveling the sea takes the longest, but once this war is over, the trip will be little more than a blink to you."

Charmaine wrung her hands together. "I hope so."

"You should prepare yourself, William. Mother is unlikely to let you out of her sight once you're home."

"I can't wait," William admitted honestly.

He didn't care if one thought him to be childish. The moment he returned, all he wanted was a hug from his family and to waste the days away with his mother. They would knit like they used to and read books together in the lounge. Hopefully, the garden will be in bloom. Asiatic lilies had always been his favorite, planted in a patch along the west side of the garden. They could take a walk to see them, then have a cup of afternoon tea. Their cook, Sherry, made the best chamomile tea this realm offered. A single sip could lighten the foulest day.

William craved the mundane, the simple moments. Somehow even more so after talking to Nicholas, who learned too much, but William learned quite a bit too. More than he ever expected to hear from the fae. He wasn't certain how he felt about that. Was it wrong to have enjoyed being with him? Had he gone truly mad out here?

"It grows late. We should grab our evening rations," Charmaine suggested.

The three rose. William exited the tent first. He came face to face with the last person he wanted to meet his brother.

"Good evening." Nicholas had an impish gleam in his eyes. Charmaine and Henry closed in, chuckling about Henry spilling wine on his uniform. William's older brothers often snagged a bottle from their father's office to drink—they got William cookies from the pantry for his secrecy—and Henry could never hold his liquor. Based on his flushed cheeks, nothing had changed.

"What are you doing here?" William clutched Nicholas' wrist, intending to drag him into the shadows. A drunk Henry and curious Nicholas would not make a good combination. He didn't know what to expect of Nicholas around his brother, if the fae would behave himself or William had to fear for his brother's life and limbs.

"Do not look so panicked. I merely wish to meet your brother," Nicholas said.

"There is no need."

"There is every need. My curiosity requires it."

The tent flaps fluttered. William released the fae. Henry cleared his throat and rolled his shoulders. "Good evening, Lord Darkmoon."

Henry mentioned a shade being among the ranks. William hadn't expected him to know Nicholas by name, or to recognize him. He wanted to ask if the two had officially met, but Nicholas stepped in.

"How polite. Call me Nicholas," he replied. "I hear Heign's Magical Society has some of the best mages Terra has to offer. The Vandervult family must be blessed to have two adept mages among them."

He resisted the overwhelming urge to shove Nicholas into an obscured corner and slap him over the head. Charmaine was too, based on her wrinkled nose.

Henry gave him a curious glance. "Are you acquainted with my brother, then?"

"Indeed, I am. Were you not informed of our capture?"

"Capture?" Henry's eyes said William had a lot of explaining to do. "No, I have not heard of that."

Resisting the urge to curse, he knew better than to attempt stifling Nicholas, so he set off for the rations and let the others fall in behind him.

"Oh yes, it was quite the ordeal. I am sure you heard of our momentary acquisition of a book of monsters belonging to one of Fearworn's shadowed disciples. Fearworn was very displeased and sent beasts to reclaim it. William and Albie here got caught in the crossfire and we were taken off into the forest, where we battled to survive for many days." Nicholas' story piqued Henry's interest enough to ask further questions. Nicholas was, of course, more than happy to explain the details. Thankfully, he did not speak of the nights he and William shared, so at least he had some sense.

Charmaine walked beside William to ask, "We should put a stop to their chatter. Why is Nicholas even doing this?"

"Curiosity," William answered. "And likely to torment me."

"He won't torment Henry, will he?"

"No, he wouldn't..." The words congealed on his tongue upon realizing he truly believed that. Nicholas can be troublesome, chaotic and rude, but he and Henry weren't in danger. Not anymore. When did his thoughts change so much? And why was he relieved about that change?

Henry laughed at Nicholas' story about the trees nearly devouring him and the fae appeared enthusiastic to speak more on the matter. William's fingers flexed. He looked away, fearful of his own expression, of this growing sensation at the center of his chest, more powerful and frightening than the battlefield.

"He wouldn't, what?" Charmaine asked.

"Nothing. Nicholas is being troublesome, but we should be alright." William hurried. Soldiers surrounded one of the ration stations, and it took them a while to get their portions. Not that Henry or Nicholas minded. The two finished the harrowing tale of their capture as the four of them sat around a fire.

"I have shared a wondrous tale with you, so I find it only fair that you share a story or two with me." Nicholas' conniving grin had William debating on chucking a fiery log at his head.

"What kind of tale would you like?" Henry's words slurred because Nicholas had been kind enough to grab another bottle of wine. He didn't ask, just waltzed into their makeshift storehouse and took one. No one had the courage to say otherwise, and William didn't mind having another glass, until now.

"William here can be so dour. Would you mind sharing an embarrassing story?" Nicholas pleaded.

"Ha!" Henry slapped his thigh and threw his pint high. "I am more than happy to give a dozen of those stories."

"How marvelous." Nicholas snickered under the immense heat of William's glare.

He couldn't fathom why Nicholas wanted to know. He claimed to be curious, but they shouldn't be curious about each other. They shared a bed sometimes, nothing more. Nicholas shouldn't be listening to Henry for every detail. William shouldn't feel nervous about how Nicholas will react, if he'll find the stories humorous or think little of William. None of it mattered, that's what he kept telling himself.

"As a boy, William's interests switched day by day. For six months, he wanted to be a florist until he killed every plant in the garden. Then he wanted to be a chef, that was short lived after he burned his eyebrows off. Took months to regrow them," Henry exclaimed, his eyes glassy from intoxication. "But books, they're his first love. Any holiday, every birthday, he asked for more books. The boy had so many piled in his room that he went to grab one and he caused an avalanche. My father and I heard his dreadful shrieking from down the hall. We believed him to be injured, but when we arrived, we found his bottom half covered in books and his top helplessly trying to crawl his way out."

A flush crept up William's neck from the group's laughter, even Charmaine, but Nicholas' attention made his heart stutter. He was scared to explain this feeling, this beauty of warmth—like the first rose budding in a field of weeds.

"To this day, we find his books scattered throughout the house. He left some under tables or stashed behind a couch cushion like a rat hoarding treats."

William grumbled over the rim of his mug. "You exaggerate. I was never that bad."

"You fell asleep nearly every night with a book. Mother had to check on you to ensure you didn't drool on the pages." Henry wheezed from his laughter and took another drink.

"I didn't drool, either." William's flush deepened when Nicholas mouthed *'you snore, though.'*

"Our father mapped out all the bookstores in town, ensuring we avoided them on busy days. If we passed, William had to stop and none of us had the heart to say no. Being the youngest truly has its perks." Henry leaned over to pinch William's rosy cheek.

Henry's tale put a thoughtful expression on Nicholas' face. "Is that common? For the youngest child of a family to be treated with such affection?"

"It is certainly quite common, from what I have heard and seen."

"Strange for him to grow up to be such a boorish and crude man," Nicholas teased, furthering the group's laughter. Charmaine gave an apologetic grin when William cast her a disbelieving stare.

"I thought you would be on my side at least," he chided her.

"I normally am, but you are boorish and crude sometimes." Charmaine shoved the last of her rations in her mouth as a poor excuse to silence herself. William gave the rest of his food to her. It helped her headaches and an ache formed in his stomach, albeit, not as unpleasant as he expected.

William slumped against the chair. Nicholas devoured every tale Henry shared from nightmares that sent William running for his brother's room to the time a carriage passed on the street and the wheels threw horse manure in his face, then he vomited on a gentleman's shoes. That last story may have put a smile on his face because it had Nicholas laughing until tears filled his eyes. They made the pink hue an even more enchanting shade.

When he cast his attention toward Nicholas, who listened with rapt attention and a gleeful smile, William dared to think a day together in town would be nice. He wouldn't be opposed to taking Nicholas to all those bookshops and sit in the park listening to a band play. They could spend an evening at the opera or share treats at the bakery. Nicholas would find their town curious, the shops, the streets, perhaps the architecture too. He didn't know what Faerie was like, but he heard stories that the lands were of nature. They had no brick buildings like Terra. The city would be a whole new world, and William could show him that world.

Then maybe they could visit Faerie together. Nicholas would show him a new realm, a world he couldn't fathom. The little he knew of Faerie painted it as mystical and strange, something only the mind of a child could conjure. He never thought he would want to see the home of fae, and yet, he had the urge now.

They were alarming thoughts, troublesome as Nicholas himself. The two indulged in one another to pass the time, for William to forget, nothing more. There shouldn't be more. He repeated that through Henry's tales until the man inevitably drank too much. His brother fell off his makeshift chair, words too slurred to continue, and the last remnants of his wine spilled across the snow. All had finished their rations long ago. Others hadn't joined them at their campfire, fearful of

Nicholas. William worried his fellow soldiers would ask questions, but Henry's presence may be enough to ward off any suspicions. It would make sense for a mage from Heign to converse with Nicholas, the shade expected to end Fearworn.

Laughing, Charmaine stood. Her eyes had taken on a glassy sheen, but she had the ability to speak evenly, "I will take Henry to his tent."

"You should leave him. Let him regret all of this in the morning," he said as he prodded Henry's cheek with the tip of his boot. Grunting, Henry smacked his ankle and rolled over. William's cheeks ached because he hadn't smiled this much in years.

"Don't be so cruel. He has a long journey ahead of him." Charmaine wandered around the fire. She must have sensed William wanted to have a discussion with the bothersome fae that had the aura of a man who won far too many prizes. Charmaine wasn't too different. That grin spoke of shared amusement after listening to Henry weave childhood stories long enough that the fire was little more than sparks.

"Up we go." Charmaine lugged Henry onto his feet. He swayed, somewhere between dream land and drunken reality.

William wished both of them a goodnight. Henry tried to ruffle his hair when passing by, but his fingers barely swiped over William's head. Then the two disappeared. His heart ached and leapt at knowing Henry would leave tomorrow. This momentary joy wasn't enough. The intensity of his yearning to see his family grew exponentially. He could not fathom another day, another week, another month to a year or more without them. But he didn't want Henry here, either. His eyes shut to keep the tears at bay, then he set his firm attention upon Nicholas.

"Did you have fun?" William asked.

"The evening was an utter delight." Nicholas rose, only to take a seat at William's side. "Your brother cannot hold his liquor."

"Luckily for you."

"Very lucky." Nicholas' hand inched closer, allowing their fingers to brush. William couldn't risk this. He set his hands on his lap, breaking the connection and ignoring the fae's scowl.

"This wasn't only about curiosity, was it? Why did you spend an evening listening to childhood stories?" he asked.

"Your childhood stories. I wanted to hear them, and your brother was here. I thought he would give them up easier than you."

"Why did you want to hear them?"

Nicholas sent his attention skyward, where the gloomy clouds forever reigned. "I mentioned my father and siblings before, so you should be able to guess that I do not have such fond stories of my family. Any childhood story of mine that ends well pertains to the land."

"I believe it's only fair if you give an example, considering all you learned tonight without my consent."

"I cannot argue with that." Nicholas chuckled. "Hill Castle, that is where I was born and raised. My siblings and I knew our home well, so we couldn't hide from one another when times were rough. I escaped their cruelties by hiding in the field of sunflowers at the back of the estate. They liked me."

"The flowers did? How could you have known that?" William inquired.

"If my siblings followed me into the field, the sunflowers tripped or swatted at them. If they got close, the soil shifted, and the flowers held me. I would spend days at a time playing there. If I wasn't in the field, I went to the mountains nearby. They loved making labyrinths to test my skills."

"The mountains constantly changed their path?"

William's disbelief was clear enough that Nicholas laughed. "You do not believe me."

"How can a mountain forge a labyrinth? Someone must carve through it."

"A mountain range in Faerie is as alive as you and me, as is the sea, the trees, and the flowers. They have minds of their own and I spent my days among them because they loved a good game as much as I did."

"It's strange," William muttered. "You've making me want to see Faerie for myself."

"I do not exaggerate its beauty and charm. There truly are no words to express it. I wish for you to see it one day, for I genuinely believe you would love it as much as I do."

William started to believe he would, too. He couldn't imagine Nicholas' tales, but he wanted to see them. However, after this war ended, he and Nicholas wouldn't see each other again. The end of the war would spell the end of them. His heart lurched when it shouldn't, when it should be harder than steel.

"Well, this has been an interesting evening." William stood and willed the ache in his chest to cease. "Goodnight, trouble."

"Goodnight, my wicked," Nicholas whispered.

When he stood, the two were close. William dared to shut his eyes when Nicholas leaned in because he wanted a kiss, wanted to feel Nicholas' addictive mouth against his and run his fingers through unruly hair. Then he remembered all the dead left to rot for being stupid enough to be with fae.

"What are you doing?" William pushed Nicholas aside and retreated. His frantic gaze swept over the camp, falling on a group of soldiers laughing around a firepit. No man mentioned seeing them.

"They aren't paying attention to us," Nicholas said.

"How easy it is for you to say that. They won't slit your throat in your sleep, you fool." The insult pointed more at William than Nicholas because he had been a fool to ever accept Nicholas' invitation, let alone more.

William walked away, relieved Nicholas did not follow. He pressed a hand to the fierce beat within his chest, willing the damn organ to cease its dramatics.

24

William

After Henry and his colleagues left, the army marched like hounds on a fresh scent. Soldiers joined from the south, thousands in the span of a week. Their forces infested the Deadlands like a sea of cockroaches. The generals used the information Heign's Magical Society brought to prepare for a final battle, hopefully.

The troops eventually came upon Fearworn's lab, taken over a week ago. A restless aura enveloped the troops, gleeful to sleep in a room, crowded or not, but joy dwindled upon their arrival. The citadel may have had high walls of solid rock to protect against the winds, countless rooms, and a wide center perfect for fires, but a shimmer sat at that center. One of Fearworn's, one of monsters. With or without the Sight, one saw the power around the shimmer, flickering with dangerous energy.

William saw a few shimmers up close. He never went through one to Faerie. Certainly never wanted to step through that one, to the realm unknown, if anyone even could. Rumors said a soldier died touching it, so none could fathom walking through it. But he was curious, as were others peering from a distance. His curiosity soon turned to worry concerning how many soldiers would fall to shimmer sickness, though.

The first night at the lab, he sat around the firepit with a dozen others. Oscar chugged a drink, listening to the chatter all assuming one thing; the final battle was upon them. William rolled his eyes. Soldiers erupted in laughter and cheer, expecting an end to the slaughter and cold. Nicholas disappeared, too. They hadn't spoken since Henry shared those tales, where Nicholas learned even more. Somehow, the fae dug deeper, embedding himself in William's life in a way that never should have happened.

William couldn't stop thinking about Nicholas' hand clutched in his and the soft hair tickling his neck, slow and steady breaths, the sweet scent and charming eyes that could fight back the most vicious of daydreams. How they laid in bed some nights talking about nothing. They bickered and William laughed and Nicholas kissed him and it felt good, right, normal, like everything he could ever want and more.

"Drink up!" Oscar bellowed, red-faced and bright-eyed. His shoulder bumped William's and wine sloshed over the rim of his mug to dampen his pant leg. "Oh, uh, sorry, I'm..."

"Drunk," William finished for him.

"Yeah, it's wonderful." Oscar laughed and finished the last of his drink in a gulp.

"Stay mindful," William warned him. "I've spotted a few fae sneaking about looking for trouble."

One stood out in the corner of his eye, a woman with sharp teeth and pale blue skin. She caught the attention of soldiers with her otherworldly beauty. Drunk or sober, it didn't matter. Many fell for fae charms. William couldn't blame them any longer, considering what happened with Nicholas. Nevertheless, he kept his eye on the men. If they made any move to follow her away from the campfires, he would step in. He didn't want them taken advantage of, limping to medical come morning, or worse, brought in a bodybag.

"I ain't goin' near any fae," Oscar slurred and hiccuped. "No worries, no worries, but more drinks!"

The soldiers cheered and William felt Charmaine tense beside him.

"Is your headache still bothering you?" he whispered to the poor girl trying her best not to wince. She nodded. "Shall I walk you to your room?"

"No, I want to celebrate too," she argued over the rim of her mug. A familiar spark shimmered within her eyes; hope. "I pray to the Souls their assumptions are right, that the end is almost here. I won't ask what you think."

"That would be for the best."

"Has he mentioned anything?"

William knew she meant Nicholas. "No, we haven't talked in a few days. The last we spoke, he mentioned this." William gestured toward the towering citadel around them. Fires ran along the walls, torches burning bright in the suffocating gloom. His attention shifted to the man speaking with the fae woman along the outskirts of the firepits.

"You make it sound like this isn't a big deal," Charmaine said.

"I don't mean to sound pessimistic, but I rather not get my hopes up, either."

"I know." She patted William's leg. His tension eased a smidge when the man wandered away from the fae to sit with friends, but then more loud voices joined those around the firepit. A familiar face stepped forward, Theodore, the man who tormented Charmaine during her recruitment days. The flames lit his flushed features, eyes dreary and far away.

"Tuckerton!" Theodore called, arms spread high and wide. His drink spilled over his hand. He cursed, then lapped up the drink and burped. He stumbled toward one of his buddies to throw an arm around his neck. Theodore pointed toward Charmaine and said, "Do you recognize him? Albie, Albie Tuckerton, that little shrimp from recruitment!"

"Let's go," William muttered, rising, but Charmaine did not join. The fire reflected in her angry eyes fixated on Theodore and the soldiers listening to his boisterous story. "This one was the smallest of our lot, can you believe that?" Theodore cackled and dropped into the seat William once occupied to throw a hand on Charmaine's shoulder. "You've grown quite a bit. You're not still crying every night, are ya? We couldn't get this one to stop wailing, begging for mommy to come get him."

"That's enough," William warned. Theodore peered back at him. The drunk tried to look angry, but it leaned more toward constipation.

"You." Theodore pointed and stood, swaying. "You stood up for the twerp back then, too, but I heard a little something about you." Theodore leaned forward, his wretched breath burned William's nostrils. "You bedded the guys in your unit, didn't ya? Rather get fu—"

Charmaine shoved Theodore hard enough to toss him over the sitting soldiers. Oscar squeaked out a hiccup. The group jeered and cried, too drunk and excited about a potential fight to realize the unnatural power Charmaine had shown. She stormed forward. William caught her arm, perturbed by the burst of anger and strength.

"Not here," he said. Charmaine struggled against the hold dragging her from the fire. "He is drunk and you are the one who will meet trouble if you do anything. Leave him be, for now."

Charmaine ripped her arm away and stomped into the shadows. William hurried after her into the citadel. Rusting torches lined the hallways, scarcely illuminating the interior. The citadel always smelled dank, like rain and rust. Charmaine threw open an old door creaking on its rusted hinges to a makeshift sleeping area. Dozens of sleeping bags lay scattered throughout the room. None had taken to bed yet. The soldiers continued drinking merrily outside, their joy heard through the halls. The torchlight from the hall let William find a lantern situated on the floor. He lit it, holding the lantern high to inspect Charmaine's heaving figure.

"Are you feeling alright?" He kept his distance. His gut told him to and his gut rarely led him astray.

Charmaine's muscles tensed. Veins throbbed in her hands and neck. She breathed rapidly, then that breath ceased at the sound of Theodore's voice.

"Hey, hey, I meant nothing by what I said. Gotta do what you gotta do out here!" Theodore laughed, stumbling up behind William from the hallway. He caught the fool's arm in warning. Something didn't feel right, but Theodore knocked the hold aside to clap a hand on Charmaine's shoulder. "Don't be so sensitive—"

Charmaine snapped Theodore's neck. Theodore dropped. A broken bone stretched the flesh of his neck. William's hand went for his revolver. Charmaine growled low in the back of her throat, eyes pure black, wrong.

"Charmaine," he whispered, but couldn't bring himself to point the gun at her. Every step she took toward him worsened the sweat pooling along his neck. She moved like a predator, calculating and watchful.

"You're...you're out of sorts," he muttered. "Take a breath. Try to calm yourself."

She lunged and he pivoted. The handle of his gun cracked against the back of her skull. Charmaine fell forward, whimpering, then motionless. He pointed the revolver at her back. The tip of his boot knocked against her leg. She didn't move. He swallowed hard while running through every scenario. He hit her too hard, cracked her skull, and killed her. If that were the case, he wouldn't forgive himself. He was going to be sick, but then Charmaine took a deep breath and sat upright.

"William?" Groaning, she pressed a hand to the back of her head. The blackness of her eyes faded, revealing the natural brown beneath. "What happened?" Her gaze shifted between the gun and Theodore's corpse. "That wasn't...did I?" William nodded. She whimpered. "I didn't mean to! I don't know—"

Footsteps sounded in the hall. William shut the door. Theordore's corpse laid behind them. He kept a firm hold on the doorknob, in case someone attempted to enter. The footsteps became louder, louder, and his heart mirrored them. A shadow passed under the door, then they vanished, and his heart slowed.

Charmaine croaked, sounding sick. "What am I going to do? I didn't mean to. It just happened. I don't even remember doing it."

"I know."

Whatever happened wasn't her. She wasn't herself. She mentioned odd symptoms of late, ever since they were attacked by those beasts. He couldn't believe the thought crossed his mind, but Nicholas may have answers, may be able to tell if this is some fae spell because it certainly isn't a virus. He spoke to Montgomery days ago to keep an eye on things, but neither of them came across strange symptoms similar to Charmaine's. What happened to her wasn't normal.

"No one saw this. I doubt anyone remembers Theodore coming after you either, so I need you to stay here. Make sure no one comes in." He handed Charmaine the lantern and slipped the revolver into its holster.

She trembled, eyes erratic in their movements. "How?"

"Make up a story. Tell them you got sick in here, anything to keep others out. I'll be right back." He clutched her shoulders. Her bottom lip trembled when he declared, "We are going to figure this out."

Charmaine didn't look convinced. William wasn't, either, but he had to do something. He lost enough. He would not lose her. He never expected to make friends here, but he had. Charmaine fit into his life so perfectly, as if they were made to fill in each other's broken pieces. He didn't believe in fate or soul mates, but he liked to believe she and him were made to be lifelong friends.

Slipping on Nicholas' ring, William vanished. The fae occupied the opposite side of the citadel. If Nicholas wasn't outside, he likely had his own room, or so William hoped. He hurried past the firepits, relieved that none of the soldiers appeared ready to end the night yet. Fae were no different, drinking, dancing, and singing in their native tongue. His gaze swept over their silhouettes, finding Nicholas seated by Arden.

One of their kin told a joke, making the fae laugh. Arden's hand fell on Nicholas' thigh as his body lurched from joy. William flexed his fingers. His teeth gnashed. He had the urge to chuck a rock, specifically at Arden's face. He might have, if Nicholas hadn't stared right at him. William worried others could see him, but no one paid him any mind. Nicholas whispered to Arden and stood, walking around the firepits to a nearby door he left open behind him.

William skirted around the fae and entered the citadel. He met a dim hallway where Nicholas entered a room. William followed, finding Nicholas seated on a rock shelf covered in bedding. His familiar fuchsia flames flickered above them. William shut the door.

"You can see me with this ring on?" he whispered.

"Of course. It's my magic," Nicholas replied.

William removed the ring, clutching the item in his palm in case he needed to vanish. He felt foolish wanting to ask about Arden, if the two of them were spending evenings together like he expected they were before. It wasn't important, even if his gut wrenched at the thought.

"Right, well, I need your help," William muttered, the words nearly congealing on his tongue.

Nicholas tilted his head. "With what?"

"Charmaine."

"Who is that?"

William ran a hand through his hair, frustrated at himself. "Fuck, Albie. I need your help with Albie."

Nicholas puckered his lips together like a fish. "First tell me why you called him Charmaine."

"I do not have time for this. Just be quiet and listen."

"That is asking a lot of me."

"Nicholas," William snarled. The fae raised his hands defensively. "Albie has had strange symptoms since we were attacked by those beasts and tonight, he killed someone. Do not grin about this."

Nicholas covered his annoying smirk with his hand.

"But whatever happened, it was not Albie. There is more to this, a fae curse, perhaps. Will you help?" he asked.

"Have you forgotten already?" Nicholas rose and prissily dusted off his shirt. "I owe you a debt from saving me in the forest. You are lucky I am so kind to you."

"Because you would have said no otherwise?"

"Oh absolutely not, why would I miss out on such a wonderfully awful situation? You are simply lucky."

William would have complained, but there may be no other option than Nicholas.

"Follow me," he said, putting the ring on and hurrying outside.

Nicholas trailed his steps, feigning a nonchalant midnight walk. William kept to the shadows on the mortal side of the citadel. Nicholas did the same, doing his best not to gain anyone's attention. Charmaine remained alone with the corpse by the time they arrived. She bristled at the sight of Nicholas, who's curious gaze swept over the body.

"Aw, I wish I could have witnessed this," he whined.

"Do not be an insufferable jackass," William warned, reappearing in the room. "Will you help or not?"

"I said that I would, so I shall." Holding out his hand, fuchsia light cascaded over Theodore's corpse. The stone opened its gaping maw to swallow the body, vanishing deep beneath the rumbling earth, then the stones returned as if nothing transpired.

"There." Nicholas clapped. "No one will be the wiser."

Charmaine hiccuped from tears trickling down her cheeks.

"William mentioned symptoms." Nicholas tugged Charmaine to her feet. He circled her, one hand beneath his chin while the other prodded at her. "Tell me about these symptoms and when they began."

"While we were lost in the forest," she replied. "I've grown irritable since then, easily set off by the most mundane things. The smells are too strong, the noises too loud, as if my senses have heightened ridiculously. I'm hungry, too, starving all the time and I..." Her eyes widened and she gagged. "Holy Soul."

"What?" William asked.

"The rabbits, the ones found dead outside the tents the other day. It was me, wasn't it?"

Nicholas grimaced and stepped aside when Charmaine fell to her knees and vomited. William dropped to press a gentle hand on her back, soothing her as she retched.

"Speaking of strong smells." Nicholas pinched his nose. "Other than this ghastly display, I have noticed a foul odor around you since our time in the woods. I thought the scent merely came from this humdrum place, but it may be more complicated than that."

"Is this a fae spell? Something from Fearworn or the woods?" William asked.

Nicholas continued Charmaine's examination from afar. His lips pressed into a grim line, then his eyes fluttered and he laughed. "Oh, that is rather devious. The creature, the one that grabbed us from camp, do you remember it?"

"Of course I do. You nearly killed me while trying to defeat it."

"If you recall, the monster had no reproductive organs. What if that was on purpose? What if these creatures reproduce in another way?"

Charmaine hugged her torso. "Are you saying I'm...going to become like that thing?"

"Maybe. Maybe not. You are bitten and start to change, I do not find that a coincidence," Nicholas replied.

"But you were also bitten. You're not changing."

William pondered for a moment, then declared, "He came down with that awful fever. Your wounds healed, but afterward, your body reacted to something."

"I must have fought off the infection while you could not. This would coincide with what I've learned of Fearworn. He has a fondness of changing bodies into what he perceives to be perfect creations. He may have sought to create a monster that moves from one host to the other. Perhaps not a perfect match, but a beast nonetheless," Nicholas explained.

Charmaine buried her face in her hands. "So I am doomed."

"Most likely, and more may be doomed if we keep this to ourselves." William's heart dropped. "We will not tell another soul about this."

Charmaine and Nicholas shared similar looks, as if they understood each other without speaking. Charmaine took William's hand. Fear laced her words when she said, "Though it frightens me, we cannot keep this a secret, William. If Fearworn is capable of infecting me, he can infect others. There could be an outbreak."

"Or Fearworn has no idea the infection worked. He hasn't seen you and no one has shown any of your symptoms. I have been watching. We are not telling anyone when it means the generals could kill you."

"The generals may not do any of that."

"Now is not the time for hopeless optimism," William countered. His voice rose with every word making Charmaine squeeze his hand, reminding him to calm down. "Besides, let's say they let you live, they won't let you remain among our ranks. They may lock you up and rumors will spread of a peculiar soldier. Fear will spread next and the men will be rid of you themselves rather than risk trouble. We are keeping this between us."

"Maybe being... being rid of me is for the best," she whispered.

The color drained from William's face. "Don't you dare say that."

"I'm sick, William. I killed someone without even realizing it. If you hadn't hit me, I probably would have killed you. If I ever hurt you—"

"You won't," he interjected, anguished, broken, and desperate. "We will fix this, I swear."

"Are you truly willing to threaten the lives of everyone in camp?" Nicholas asked, causing William to stand and shove him.

"Don't ask that as if you wouldn't burn this camp to the ground to get what you want. I don't give a damn about this fucking war or the fucking generals and their fucking plans. Now, are you going to keep this secret or not?"

Nicholas chuckled. William would have been further irritated if the fae hadn't said, "Fearworn is the paranoid type. I imagine he has cures for his creations, his own form of protection from these beasts in case they do overpower our natural healing."

William's breath caught. He struggled to form words, wanting to hope while knowing how little it had done for him until now. "If that is true, the cure is with him. We need to find a way to prevent this from happening again until we acquire it."

"The answer seems simple enough, she reacted from anger, so don't anger her."

Charmaine cast Nicholas a curious glance.

"We're at war. Anger and irritation is everywhere," William countered.

"Getting upset at me will not change the situation. This is all the help I can give."

"I appreciate it, regardless." Charmaine rose to her feet. "At least we have a potential explanation."

"We are on Fearworn's tail," William whispered when taking her hand. "The generals have gathered more troops than we have ever seen. They believe this to be the end, so we are close. If Fearworn has an antidote, we will acquire it."

"If," Charmaine repeated in a shuddered breath. "*If* he has one and *if* I am not a rabid beast by then."

Nicholas grunted. "The both of you are so dramatic."

William was a moment away from telling the fae off when Nicholas knelt. He plucked a wad of mud off William's boot to roll in his hands. Pink light filtered between his fingertips, then he presented two perfect spheres.

"While I would love to watch you slaughter the camp, take this if you feel the abrupt urge to. It should knock you out." Nicholas pressed one sphere into Charmaine's open palm. He set the other in William's. "And if you happen to witness any borderline murderous acts from Charmaine, force this down her throat."

Charmaine stiffened. "I knew I heard you say she before."

Nicholas smirked. William yanked on the bastard's wrist, hissing, "Must you do that now?"

"I am merely curious why you mortals are so uppity about how you refer to one another. You may call fae confusing, but I find your ways moronic, at best," Nicholas replied, refusing to look anything less than proud.

Sighing, William gave Charmaine's hand a reassuring squeeze. "I'm sorry. Earlier when I rushed over, I said Charmaine."

"It's alright, so long as Nicholas won't tell anyone." Charmaine gave him a worrisome stare.

Gasping in feigned offense, Nicholas said, "Believe it or not, I like keeping secrets. They're a challenge."

"I'm sorry. He can never take a damn thing seriously," William growled and wondered how, for any moment, he could have come to enjoy Nicholas' company.

"You take things too seriously." Nicholas tapped William's nose with his finger. "Now that I have done my part, I should take my leave. I wouldn't want anyone to find us like this. Do try not to kill anyone else this evening, unless I am present. I love a good show."

Charmaine slipped the sphere into her pocket and muttered, "I truly do appreciate this."

Giving a dismissive wave, Nicholas left. Once the door shut, Charmaine nudged William and muttered, "You should probably thank him. He didn't have to help us."

"Technically, he did. He owed me a debt from when I saved him in the forest." But Nicholas said he would have helped anyway and that meant a lot, more than William could put into words. Dare he admit it, he didn't trust anyone else to have helped, to be capable of it.

"Still," she whispered. "You want to thank him."

He couldn't deny that. Charmaine settled a hand against his back and pushed him forward. William hesitated because he knew this meant another moment getting closer to Nicholas, becoming deeper intertwined. Somehow, they found themselves caught in the other's web and entirely uninterested in setting themselves free.

His feet carried him into the hall. Nicholas hadn't left yet, so William caught him by the shoulder and opened an adjacent door. No one was in the room. He guided Nicholas inside where only the light of his eyes survived the shadows.

"Thank you for helping Charmaine," William whispered, not thinking of the consequences until it was too late. Nicholas stepped closer, eyes playful, as devious as ever, but William didn't feel an ounce of fear or concern. As Nicholas interlocked their fingers, his heart dared to hiccup and he dared to love the feeling.

"You of all people should know not to thank fae. It implies we are owed," Nicholas said without any true threat.

"Maybe you are owed. You didn't only spare Charmaine, you also gave us hope that we can make this right."

"One could say I was your knight in shining armor this evening."

"I could say that, or I could reward you in another way." William caught Nicholas by the belt loops, tugging him in for a ravenous kiss. He should have gotten tired of this taste by now, but he found Nicholas more addictive after every try. Nicholas was relentless against any wall William fruitlessly built. They crumbled from a touch, the timbre of his voice, the curves of his perfect body pressed against William's, enticing a pent-up want.

"Tomorrow night, trouble?" he whispered against parted lips.

Nicholas smirked. His knuckles brushed against William's cheeks, gentle and sincere. "I am looking forward to it, my wicked."

25

Nicholas

Nicholas did not like having deep thoughts. Deep thoughts were for men like his father conjuring dastardly plans for a boring day. He preferred literally anything else, but alas, William proved forever defiant. He roamed Nicholas' mind like he had made it his permanent residence.

Yesterday, he hadn't expected William to be so determined to spare Charmaine. He understood the two were close, practically inseparable during their capture. To damn everyone if it meant sparing her? He couldn't fathom such emotions, such loyalty and care.

On the floor of Nicholas' room, Arden finished the last of the wine they stole from the mortal's rations. Nicholas took to his desk, scribbling what he saw earlier in the day from Fearworn's eyes. Arden waited to take the information to the generals, but Nicholas didn't hand over the scraps yet. Lost to his thoughts, to wondering what it would be like to be in Charmaine's place, to have someone care for him so fervently, for William to care for him in such a way.

"If I were sick, and damning the lives of everyone in this camp would save me, what would you do?" Nicholas asked.

Arden sat up straighter and laughed. "What an odd question. What brought this on?"

"Humor me."

Pursing his lips, Arden nodded. "I would damn the camp if it meant sparing you."

Nicholas bit back a smile.

"We will not win this war without you," Arden continued, and Nicholas' mood plummeted. "Most of the soldiers here are worthless, little more than cannon fodder. You are far more significant, and Lord Darkmoon would have my head if you were lost."

So you would save me out of necessity, not care? Nicholas wondered. Papers crinkled in his grip, then Arden got up to tug those papers aside. He leaned over Nicholas' desk, brows furrowed.

"Are you ill?" Arden asked.

"No, I wanted your opinion on a peculiar scenario."

"Peculiar, indeed." Arden wanted an elaboration, but Nicholas gave none because he didn't have answers for either of them.

Why should he care? Why couldn't he stop thinking about how determined William was to save Charmaine, how much he cared for her? It was silly of him to linger on this. To think of asking William what he would do if Nicholas and Charmaine's positions were reversed. Would William show that same determination? Would he care? Would he do anything to save Nicholas? And if he would, was it for the same reason as Arden's? Simply save the tool necessary to end the war so William could return home to the people he loved, leaving Nicholas behind.

He dropped the pages on his desk. The hour grew late. William promised to visit. Nicholas' eyes fell upon the bed where he imagined William's nude form waiting for him, lust caught in his brilliant jade eyes. He felt as if he were born for these moments, waiting for William, wanting him. He relished and reviled such thoughts.

"Here, take these to the generals," Nicholas said, presenting the notes to Arden.

Taking the scraps, Arden bid Nicholas a good night and scurried out of the room. Nicholas waited, fingers tapping impatiently on the desk. He squirmed, paced, fell on the bed, shuffled to the door to check the hall, then leaned against the desk, wondering why William was so late. Being late meant Nicholas had more time to think, to worry, to hate Charmaine a little for having so much of William's attention and care, to hate himself for wanting William so fervently that he couldn't think properly.

Then the doorknob rattled once, twice, and a third time. Nicholas opened the door to find William's mirage standing in the hall.

"I didn't want to come in if someone else were here," William explained, cursing when Nicholas flung him onto the bed. The shade fell on him for a smooth kiss he thought far too much about since their promised rendezvous, and he needed this attention, to feel William here with him.

"I don't even get a hello?" William whispered when Nicholas moved from that tempting mouth to an equally enchanting neck. He marked the skin, uncaring of William tugging at his hair in a futile attempt to remind him not to. Nicholas wanted William to think of him whenever he caught his reflection, when anyone asked about the mark. He would sear his memory into William's very bones if he could, and he hoped William felt the same.

"Hello," the fae said, savoring the sensation of William's chuckle echoed against his mouth. Nicholas yanked at his shirt, encouraging William to rid himself of the useless garment. Then he had his lips moving across William's tempting collar bone, before he dared to yawn.

"Yawning during a moment like this is wildly inappropriate," Nicholas grumbled, slightly flustered because this was not a common occurrence, and embarrassed for that same reason. Had William not been thinking about him all day? Was Nicholas the only one tormented?

"Do not speak to me about what's inappropriate when you are the very definition of inappropriate." But William yawned a second time. The hood of his eyes fell. Nicholas nestled himself between the medic's legs. He could lie like this all night, enraptured by William's form, and somehow it was enough to set him ablaze.

"You are tired," he declared.

"A marvelous deduction on your part."

"Who dared to exhaust you when I need your attention?"

"Need?" William mocked. A dimple pressed into his cheek from his small smile. "You're so dramatic."

"You like my dramatics."

"Do I?"

"I imagine you wouldn't tolerate me if you didn't."

William snorted and rested a hand on Nicholas' hip. Calloused fingers danced over his skin, leaving goose feathers in their wake. "There are too many idiots in the military. Two fools shot themselves today, one in the foot and the other in his left butt cheek. Do not ask me how he would not tell and I doubt either of us can conjure an idiotic enough scenario to explain it. That, along with my usual duties, has led to a tiresome day."

Chuckling, Nicholas suggested, "Shall we rest a bit? You need your energy for all that I want to do to you. I want you to be loud for me this evening."

"Is that my form of repayment for the other day?"

"Yes, I deserve praise and the sweet sound of your voice in utter ecstasy."

That enticed another chuckle prior to Nicholas catching William in a kiss, hoping it would serve as a distraction to the odd warmth spreading in his chest. He would not dare admit to liking the sound of William's laughter. Speaking that aloud would be dangerous. It would be real, and the admittance would be like poison upon his tongue, damning him.

William's fingers caught in his hair, tugging the tie loose. Then Nicholas fell away, laying beside the medic, who's eyes closed. Like this, William looked soft and serene, so easily breakable. Nicholas learned better. The moment those eyes opened, he met unrelenting steel, an immovable force that no magic of this world or any other could stand against.

"You don't seem the type to choose the path of medicine voluntarily," Nicholas said.

William hummed. "Didn't you sneak papers on me? Montgomery discovered I had the Sight and set me toward the medical field."

"So, you didn't choose it, it chose you, but why stay?"

"Survival."

"I thought I was the vague one." His foot nudged William's leg, then his finger traced a scar along William's stomach. He had plenty of them. Nicholas kissed them. He felt and heard William take a breath, skin shuddering beneath his lips. William twirled Nicholas' hair around his finger, letting the fae press one chaste kiss after the other until he reached William's lips. He tasted too sweet to be real.

When Nicholas retreated, William whispered, "Do you recall how I mentioned that my training days were rough?"

"How could I forget? You were naked."

"You're so unserious," William chided him, but he sounded amused.

"Unlike a certain someone, I like to have fun, but I will sustain from jokes as I sense you have serious matters to discuss."

William's fingers tapped against the back of Nicholas' neck.

"Are you frightened I may tease you?" he asked.

"No, I worry you may share what isn't yours to tell. That you will use this against me in some form." William hesitated, perhaps having more to say, but settling on that.

"I may take nothing seriously, but you are paranoid, albeit for good reasons. I am a rotten bastard."

"I am so relieved that you know that."

"Come now, tell me a story. You know I love them." Nicholas curled against his side. He settled a hand over William's on his chest to interlock their fingers. He couldn't stop himself from seeking William's touch, yearning to feel those calloused hands and listen to his serene voice.

Silence fell over them for a long moment, then William explained, "Many young boys were recruited and they had to release that anger, fear, and confusion on someone. In our group of recruits, that someone was me because I was an easy target. Our sergeants did nothing. They viewed this as necessary, a way to toughen the weak ones. The boys sent me bloody to the infirmary more times than I could count."

William released a shuddering breath of rage and frustration. Nicholas held his hand tighter, realizing the burn hissing through his blood was a rage for any who dared put their hands on William, who dared to upset and harm him so. If Nicholas got his hands on them, they would regret the poor decisions they made all those years ago. He'd hurt them, and that wouldn't be strange. What was strange was that Nicholas wanted to make someone feel better, that he sought revenge for someone other than himself.

"That's how Montgomery found me, how she sensed I had the Sight, always working to protect me from the beatings when I hadn't realized it. Being able to heal gave me a purpose, made me capable of caring for myself, made me realize I had power. Now, none would dare cause me harm when I may be the one deciding if they survive the next wound. So, you are right, I chose this path because it was the only route to take if I wanted to survive." William shifted onto his side to face Nicholas. Their hands remained locked between them. "What about you? You mentioned once that you would have gone to war even if your father hadn't ordered it. Why? And don't say for fun, there is more to it than that."

"Is there?" Nicholas countered. "Do you think I'm hiding a sad little secret?"

"I am certain you have many sad, not so little secrets, otherwise you wouldn't be such a pompous asshole."

Nicholas locked his foot around William's ankle and muttered, "War seemed a good place to release all this energy. The power I have is turbulent, ever changing, and what better way to be rid of it than here?"

"Are you scared of it, your power?"

By all the realms, yes, he was terrified.

Nicholas read and heard of many stories about shades fading away, becoming someone else, someone they would never recognize. Although they breathed, although they walked the same lands they had known since birth, somehow, they were forgotten and misplaced. That had always been a possible end for him. One he didn't want. Fearworn lost himself, and no one knew who he was before. Perhaps he had always been a scientist, experimenting and searching for answers. Perhaps he had a family, one he destroyed. No one knew.

Peering through Fearworn's eyes reminded Nicholas that he could be next. He could follow in Fearworn's footsteps. He could forget all he had ever been and all he had ever known. He'd be a corpse, nothing but a potent power yearning to unleash. The world would set him on a path no different from Laurent. No matter what Nicholas did, he had so little control over his future. He had no say in who he would truly become.

"Yes," he answered in a whispered breath. "I do not want to end up like Fearworn. When I die, I want to die as Nicholas Darkmoon, not a shell of who he used to be."

"To ensure that happens, you could always hitch an early ride with death." William's joking tone made him laugh.

"I believe you would miss me if that were to happen."

"I might miss the sex, but not you."

"It is unfair that you can lie." And even more unfair when William smiled. It made Nicholas' heart stutter. "Be honest," he hoped he didn't sound pleading. "Would you miss me if I were gone? Would you mourn me if I followed in Fearworn's footsteps, if I wasn't me anymore?"

They stared at each other for a long moment, and in that moment, William's eyes darkened. His expression was ruination. Then he sat up, separating them.

"Do not ask me to answer that. It is tough enough being here," William said.

"Why?"

"You know damn well why."

"I don't think I do." Nicholas pushed forward. He had to know, needed to hear this truth more than anything else, and he couldn't explain why. "If you must lie, let me hear it. A lie from you will still sound sweet."

William would not look at him when all he wanted was William's attention. He had never craved for anything more and that wanting frightened him.

"I would miss you, annoyances and all." But when William looked back, his eyes were a wasteland, tremendously reserved. "I hate it, thinking this way, and being here with you. I hate fae. You're nasty, greedy, and insatiable bastards seeking the worst of everything and destroying anything good, like Hugh. He was good, great, even."

"Your lover?" Nicholas loathed the word on his tongue, that it dared to belong to another.

"Yes, although I didn't truly accept it at the time. He was meant to be a good time between the bad, but by the Holy Soul, he was so much more. He was the prince charming I read about, the man I always wanted. Hugh didn't feign disinterest once the deed was done, and he wanted us to be together after the war. He promised to love me until the end of days, and I dared to believe him out here in this fucking shithole. Then one like you ruined everything." The temper in William's eyes could burn this world to ash.

"Speak their name and I will get rid of them for you," Nicholas said, even if he was jealous of a dead man, of what he had been and promised to William.

William laughed. "Would you really do that for me?"

"Yes." Nicholas didn't understand why, but he would hurt anyone if William asked it of him. He would hurt them even if William didn't ask. If they laid a hand upon his wicked, that would spell their end.

"You are surprisingly good at romancing someone, aren't you? But there is no need to speak their name. I handled them."

Nicholas sought William's hand, like he had done nights ago after they spoke of his fears. Comfort, William called it, after speaking of terror. He did not pull away, so Nicholas tugged him closer, closer, until he held William tight. William eased into his arms to settle his forehead against the fae's chest.

"It was a battle like any other. Spions and shadowed disciples invaded a local town. We were sent in to rescue anyone we could and be rid of the beasts," William mumbled.

Nicholas wondered why William spoke more of what troubled him. The more William spoke, the more he asked himself if William told anyone this. Even Charmaine, every detail, spit between clenched teeth, the raw fury and muffled tears as he trembled in Nicholas' grasp.

"Many of the nests the spions spun were tough and overrun. There were thousands of the beasts spawning out of nowhere. I lost sight of Hugh, so I ignored my duties. I searched for him and I heard this awful wailing, begging, and knew it was him. I ran and there he was, carried by a fae who tossed him out like trash. His leg was already broken, perfect bait for a spion nest. I ran for him, but it was a mess, bodies everywhere, webbing. I got stuck. Spions smelled the blood. Although he knew to be quiet, they already heard him. Nearby, that damn fae waited for the monsters to tear Hugh apart. Then the fae lit up their defenseless nest and all of them in a flash, and Hugh with them. I didn't have a body to bury. Now, here I am with you. How fucking vile is that?" William cried, and every tear made Nicholas' chest ache more.

Nicholas never expected to be speechless while William wept. He held tighter because he did not know what else to do. No one cried around him unless he caused those tears. No one clung to him as if he were what kept them from drowning. He hated every passing second where he could not fix all of William's problems.

"I've never had such feelings," Nicholas murmured honestly, not knowing what more to say.

"What? Love?" William looked up, eyes rimmed in red. He squinted cutely when Nicholas' thumb brushed the stray tears away. "Not once? For family, friends, a partner?"

"If someone ruined my hair, I would be very upset."

"That is sad, Nicholas. It's a beautiful thing, being in love."

"But it has brought you so much pain, hasn't it?"

"Losing Hugh brought pain, but loving him was the best feeling in the world."

Nicholas couldn't fathom such intensity. "Tell me more," he said. "About Hugh and the prince charmings you read about and what it supposedly is like being in love. Feed my curiosity. I will consider it my reward for yesterday instead."

"Really?" he laughed, somber and broken.

"Really. I want to know."

William spoke of butterflies in his stomach and warmth in his cheeks and wanting to see someone every moment of every day. He talked about missing someone even when they departed moments ago, of wanting to learn every detail, of memorizing a soul that they could recognize from a single breath. Nicholas listened, finding every word to be painfully naïve, and yet he wanted all of that. He didn't know why. Because it sounded incredible and maybe, after William fell asleep in his arms, he wondered if the tickling sensation in his stomach were the butterflies William spoke of. If they were, he liked them very much.

26

William

Sleep often ended by the shouting of a sergeant, the scuffling of feet, or the fright of a nightmare. That morning, William's eyes opened of their own accord. Overtaken by bliss, he swore he saw home, his bedroom where the sun cut in through the open window and books towered precariously on the bedside table. Then he blinked and found himself enveloped by fuchsia light emanating from hovering flames in Nicholas' room. The sheets coiled around his legs. He sat up, perturbed by the empty bed, then discovering the owner seated at his desk.

"And here I thought you to be an early riser," Nicholas teased over a steaming mug. "You often departed prior to sunrise during our previous engagements."

"You should have woken me up." William cleared his throat. Staying over wasn't meant to happen. Nicholas had been right, William always left as early as he could, but for the first time, he slept as if he didn't have a care in the world. "I have work to attend to."

"I was trying to be sweet by letting you get the sleep you so sorely needed."

"Don't feign sweetness. It's unsettling."

Nicholas cut across the room at record speed. He clutched William's ankles and yanked him toward the edge of the bed, where the fae settled between his legs. He leaned forward, pressing their bodies firmly together. William melted against him, little more than putty for Nicholas to command.

"So be it. If you wish me to be rough with you, then I will be," Nicholas said teasingly.

"Can you not wait until tonight? I have patients to attend to and sergeants dislike late medics." But he didn't want to leave, either. William wanted to stay here, trapped by Nicholas in anyway he desired.

"Your sergeant may find themselves a little forgetful this morning." Nicholas devoured his neck, all greedy marks growing more passionate. "They will forget all about your late nature, or perhaps I'll make them forget you didn't show up at all."

"You wish to keep me here all day? How voracious is your appetite?"

"You're about to find out."

He lost himself to Nicholas' touch, the fae's ravenous mouth claiming him and his hands shoving their way past the barrier of his shirt. Clawed fingers ran up his shivering skin. Their hips danced together as if they had never separated. He couldn't comprehend how the pleasure escalated, how every evening he wanted more. No touch could quench his thirst, but the pleasure between them came to an abrupt end when the door swung open, and a stranger entered. Nicholas' expression fell, twisting into a moment of terror.

The fae separated himself expeditiously, standing tall and straight. Nicholas clutched at his loose pants, keeping them around his hips. "Father, what are you doing here?"

Lord Laurent Darkmoon carried the arctic winds themselves through the mere brush of his gaze to his calculated movements. Every step he took sent a wave of fear through William's veins. Laurent didn't have the carefree expression of his son, even if they shared the same ebony hair and oval shape of their eyes. Laurent's, however, were gray as fresh storm clouds and his hair fell in waves over his thin shoulders. Thick gray horns sprouted from his scalp, twirling at a low angle behind his head.

"Get rid of your plaything, Nicholas," Laurent demanded in a voice that cut.

"Leave," Nicholas ordered without offering William a glance, although he suspected that was for the best. If the typically joking fae spoke so urgently, then Laurent had done worse than Nicholas ever shared.

William's hands clenched into fists. He couldn't explain the anger or sorrow when Nicholas cast him a pleading stare. The strangest urge overtook him, one where he wished to reach out, to take Nicholas' hand and comb his fingers through that wild hair, asking him what had gone wrong and what he could do to make it better. The feelings swelled, whipping up a storm that shouldn't exist, that he had to set aside because this was madness.

He hurried out of the room. The door clicked shut. He buckled his belt and threw on his shirt. Others were already in the hall. Inquisitive eyes took notice of him. The ring. Damn it all. William sought the item to find nothing. The ring must have slipped out of his pocket, and it didn't matter if he took a risk of returning to Nicholas' room because it was too late. Behind him, a few doors down, an officer spoke to a fae and the two mortal soldiers shadowing him saw William. The men whispered to one another, eyes shifting between Nicholas' door and William.

"Fuck," he grunted, turning up the collar of his jacket in hopes that it may obscure his face. That they may not have got the best look at him, or they may suspect he was on an errand, too. He rushed through the halls, head low to avoid being seen by another. Outside, soldiers patrolled the causeways. William slinked through the shadows, quiet, careful, and double checking over his shoulder that no one followed.

The med bay had been set up in one of the largest rooms of the citadel, what potentially may have been a dining room for Fearworn's shadowed disciples. Cots filled the area. Some invaded the adjacent rooms, creating a hall of shuffling nurses and the thick aroma of soap and alcohol.

"You're late, Vandervult!" Montgomery hollered after his arrival.

"Sorry, sir. Won't happen again," he replied.

"You will run the perimeter tonight. Twice."

"Yes, sir." William threw aside his jacket and washed his hands in a nearby basin. Montgomery muttered under her breath. His first offense was still an offense. Had anyone else been late, they would have gotten much worse.

Toiling among the sick and weary, William maintained a watchful eye for the soldiers who spotted him. He rolled over idea after idea, desperate to find an excuse if anyone came knocking. They were unlikely to believe any lie he weaved, but he had to try. Every shadow passing the doorway, any soldier who entered spelled potential trouble, and, eventually, trouble found him.

A quick glance into the room and William saw him; one soldier inspected the cots. He cursed the military for ensuring his uniform would stand out. No one missed the white armband of his jacket signaling him a medical officer. The men knew where to look for the traitor. One of them beckoned William over with his fingers. He finished administering medicine to his patient and stepped into the hall.

Settling his hands behind his back, he forced an amicable smile. "If either of you is ill, there are cots available."

"Don't play coy. You know why we are here," the man replied. The tag on his uniform dubbed him York and the other man Bobbett. York yanked William toward the adjacent room. Medical supplies lined the facade. A single torch clung to the wall on rusted hinges.

The two men shut the door, then surrounded him. Bobbett stood a head taller, wide as a carriage with fists thick as boulders. York may have been shorter, but he wore years of being a soldier through firm muscles and a scarred expression. Both had their hair shaved to the scalp and wild eyes.

"What were you doing sneaking out of the shade's room so early this morning?" Bobbett asked through clenched teeth.

"I was not sneaking. We had business to speak of concerning the time we were lost," William explained carefully. "I was injured by Fearworn's monsters and have suffered strange symptoms since, headaches and irritability mostly. The shade occasionally requests an audience to see if I suffered any strange ailments from the beasts sent after us."

Gossip spread swiftly through the ranks. They had little else to do, so he suspected the men were made aware of soldiers having gone missing alongside two fae a while back. However, that didn't mean either would believe the rest of his story.

"There are many traitors in our ranks. Great liars they'd have to be, to us and themselves, to actually share a bed with fae. Are you a traitor?" York asked, and Bobbett inched closer. His shadow swallowed William.

"Does my response matter? Sounds like both of you have made up your minds," he replied.

"We just know when someone is spewing shit," Bobbett countered, then his fist buried itself in William's gut. A brick would have been softer. He nearly fell to his knees. Had he eaten breakfast, it would have been on their shoes.

The men dug their fingers into William's shoulders, one on either side, and yanked him into a standing position. Their sharpened eyes promised violence, as did the low tone of York's voice, "You best keep your eyes peeled, traitor."

"Get your hands off him," Charmaine's stern voice had York and Bobbett retreating. She stood in the open doorway, eyes dimmer than William was comfortable with. He slipped a hand into his pocket, relieved to find the medicine Nicholas shared. At least that hadn't been lost.

"What are the two of you doing disrespecting one of our medical officers?" Charmaine's voice dropped another octave, low enough to growl. William took a slow step toward her.

"There was no disrespect." York smiled until his eyes crinkled. "We were having a chat, nothing more."

"Nothing is wrong," William added. He settled a hand on her arm. "We were chatting, like he said."

"It didn't look like a chat." Her muscles tensed, like wires pulled tight enough to snap. Her attention switched sporadically between Bobbett and York.

"Everything is fine," he whispered and presented the sphere. "Take this, if you need it."

Charmaine's fingers twitched when York stepped around them toward the door.

"Sorry to bother you. My friend and I are leaving," York said.

Bobbett wore a taunting smirk. "But we will be seeing you later."

"Why?" she asked. "Your chat is finished, isn't it?"

"Albie," William warned and tried to steer her away. If he slipped the medicine into her mouth, they could get out of this without another incident. With the door open, others will hear the ruckus if Charmaine got her hands on either of the men. If others somehow didn't notice the ruckus, William wasn't certain he could go to Nicholas for help, not with Laurent there.

"If you truly wish to know," Bobbett laughed, and York gave him a warning glance that the bigger man ignored. He pointed a meaty finger at William. "That so-called friend of yours is a traitor. Caught him sneaking out of the wretched shade's room early this morning. Fae cannot be trusted, and those foolish enough to lie with them are even worse, if you ask me." Bobbet ran his thumb slowly across his neck, mimicking the cut of a blade. "He'll get what he deserves when the time comes."

Charmaine slammed into Bobbett. They fell into the hall, cursing, then screaming. Blood followed the seams of the rocky floor as Charmaine's thumbs tore through Bobbett's eyes. York shouted. William grabbed Yorks' wrist before he got to his revolver.

"Fuck off!" York hollered between the loud crunching of bones.

Charmaine hit Bobbett with such force that she needn't hit him again, but she did, over and over, his body motionless beneath her heaving form. She staggered onto her feet. A gaze, blacker than night, fell upon them and her body twitched unnaturally.

"By the Holy Soul, what is wrong with you?" York shoved William aside. His revolver fired in quick succession, every bullet missing Charmaine as she dropped to all fours and leapt. Her teeth tore into his gut, piercing skin and muscles as if they were thinner than paper.

Officers and nurses sprinted out of the adjacent room. Screams followed, rushed steps of those hiding or seeking help. William fell onto Charmaine's back, the medicine crushed between his fingers. He grabbed Charmaine's chin, but the blood made her slick and she was strong. That unusual strength threw him aside with a wild toss. His back hit the wall. The medicine slipped from his fingers. Shouts rose when a group of soldiers came into the hall, firearms raised.

"Stop! Don't!" William shouted, panicked.

Guns fired. The bullets caught Charmaine's shoulder. Her shriek brought everyone to their knees. The sound rose to such a high pitch that his ears rang, and the walls shook. Violet tendrils shimmered beneath her skin. They stretched through her, up her neck and over her cheek. When their eyes met, he caught recognition and fear, but another gun fired. The bullet pierced her leg. She shrieked a second time, causing a dozen men to vomit.

"Kill him!" someone bellowed, but Charmaine was on the move. She shoved past the soldiers filling the hall, little more than pebbles in the face of her raw power.

"Damn it!" William hopped over the stunned soldiers. He followed her path of destruction through the hall. Doors had been ripped off their hinges. Soldiers laid across the floor, shoved aside or clawed if they dared to get into her path. Outside, the camp screamed and mages had their sights on her. Their magic rippled through the air, fire, lighting, wind and ice tore through the sky.

Charmaine swerved toward the citadel's causeways. She bounded over one in a single jump, then she was gone.

"Fuck!" William's fingers caught in his hair. He kicked the damned wall, toes throbbing and heart lurching into his throat. "Fuck!" he screamed until his throat was raw and he fell to his knees.

27

Nicholas

Water would be envious of Laurent's graceful movements. Artists strived to create masterpieces capable of capturing such a bitter stare set upon perfect features. Nicholas didn't share those features. He took after his mother. The paintings hanging about the castle had a stranger who wore Nicholas' face, only curvier and rounder with eyes of pale green.

Laurent caught Nicholas by the chin. He ceased pretending not to be fearful of his father's touch. Laurent didn't care about the tremble he invoked, holding tight and forcing Nicholas' head from side to side. In his peripheral vision, he spied William's ring in the bedsheets. *Damn*, he thought bitterly.

"You are spending too much time in Fearworn's mind. You do not take my warnings seriously. I am not surprised." Laurent enunciated each word as if he spoke to a toddler.

In a manner, Nicholas was, for he did not know Laurent's age. Laurent probably didn't remember, either, having lived long enough to claim he watched the first mountains form. Shades were powerful, all knew that, but High Fae who walked the lands longer than any remembered tempered seas with knowledge alone. Nicholas witnessed Laurent's power, how other fae stepped out of his path, how they revered him, and that said enough.

"If we are to win this war, then I must remain vigilant. The generals require updates, and I give them, which means I must see through Fearworn's eyes," Nicholas explained, choosing not to mention his own curiosities. He noted the frustration in Laurent's gaze, the briefest flicker of ire that could settle a swelling storm.

"Every moment is a risk, which you either cannot or refuse to grasp." Laurent laid a hand on his shoulder that promised pain. Though he closed his eyes in preparation, that pain never came. "However, Fearworn is now moments away from death, regardless of your horrendous decisions, and for that, I am a little less disappointed in you."

He released an imprisoned breath when Laurent let go. He took a seat at Nicholas' desk. Any who entered would think this room belonged to him. Laurent wore every space and moment as if it were his own, stitched entirely for him by lesser beings.

"Soon, our alliance with the mortals will end. We will return to the way our lives should have always been. We shall never stoop so low again," Laurent said.

Nicholas approached the bed to sit and plucked William's ring from the sheets. He slipped the ring into his pocket. "And how do you plan to ensure that?"

"Through you, should our work go accordingly. You will wed Evera after this mess has been cleared. The children sired will be carefully studied. Alvina is most excited about this."

"How could children ensure we will not work with mortals again?"

Laurent gave him another disappointed stare. "I suppose you wouldn't understand. I did not allow your betrothal because I had to. You think I'm incapable of escaping Alvina's traps?"

"Of course not, Father."

"She has an excellent plan with no real vision, so I am using her to my advantage. Alvina will study you, as she does anything she can get her voracious hands on. She will study the children you sire, learn if having a shade for a father affects them in any way. We may yet learn to control the power within or prevent it entirely, then there will not be another Fearworn and no unwanted alliance."

"Allowing your son and grandchildren to be test subjects to another fae lord, would that not make you look weak?" Nicholas offered, rather than stating he wanted no part in this. He made that mistake before, after Laurent agreed to his betrothal.

As a child, he cursed his father in his own throne room. Laurent did not wait to deal out pain. He ensured everyone witnessed Nicholas' torment. To ensure not only Nicholas' humiliation but also remind everyone that no one, not even his children, had any right to stand against him.

"Do not feign care," Laurent ordered, for he saw through every trick Nicholas crafted. "It is far more important that we never be tied to mortal whims in the future. We are above them and it should remain as such. Alvina will do her job well and just, as will you and Evera. Three children is nothing in the span of your lives and I cannot imagine you would ever care for such things."

Indeed. Nicholas couldn't fathom caring for children, but he didn't enjoy being ordered around. He hated the thought of another potential shade pressed under one's thumb, experimented on as if they were lesser. Nicholas was not less. He was more, more than any of them. He was the slow tide creeping in. He'd overtake them when they weren't paying attention and remind them what true power was. Or so he hoped, because no talk, no strength, nothing within him ever urged him to stand up to Laurent. He always faced the consequences and no power he threw at his father ever stuck.

He would never care for Evera, either. They were infuriated with each other the moment they learned of their parents' plans. That hatred grew and grew, even now, as Nicholas realized being with her meant less time with another, less time with William. Would he be jealous of Nicholas' union with Evera, regardless of there being no feelings between them? Would William worry about losing Nicholas' affections? Nicholas bit the inside of his cheek to stave off a grin. William's jealousy. His concern. His wanting. Oh, he would like that very much.

"What if none of our children are shades? We haven't heard of the power being passed from one to the other. This could lead nowhere," Nicholas said.

"There are plenty of tasks for you," Laurent replied, reminding Nicholas of what Blair mentioned, risking his life to close the scars. Then Laurent chuckled, unamused. "If you don't lose yourself before then."

Nicholas held tight to William's ring, promising not to lose himself. He wouldn't be like Fearworn. He would cut a path through life, one of his own choosing. One day. If only he believed that to be possible.

A wild ruckus had Laurent and Nicholas rising. They listened to the mortals bickering and rushing outside. Laurent's slow nod excused him. He sprinted out of the room. Shouting echoed from within the camp, then shots fired. He dashed for the noise, intrigued and eager for any excuse to leave Laurent behind. The scent of blood hung in the air, then a familiar musk.

Charmaine? Nicholas' stomach lurched. William and Charmaine were nearly inseparable. Had things gone wrong, had he been near...

Nicholas burst into a run, hands stifling hot with power. A crowd formed around a doorway that led to the mortal's medical bay. He shoved bodies aside to peer down the hall. Soldiers laid injured, others shouted orders about chasing one of their own.

"Catch the damn beast!" someone commanded. Mortal mages fired upon a figure. They rushed toward the wall. Nicholas followed, noticing footprints through the snow and blood. Then a shadowed silhouette leapt over the wall; Charmaine.

A gale of wind whipped past his head, a single shard of ice caught by the breeze. He recognized his father's work, but that did not stop him from his search. He kept running until he heard William's wild curse, once and a second time. Then William appeared and Nicholas took a strangled breath, beyond relieved to find him unharmed.

"Vandervult, what happened?" an officer bellowed, brushing past Nicholas to take hold of William's arm.

Nicholas' teeth gnashed, overcome with the need to tear that damn hand off if they didn't loosen that grip. Then William's swollen eyes caught him and he didn't know how he felt, similar to last night, when William cried in his arms. He hated it, hated the sight, the thought, the sound, and wanted to wipe every tear away.

William's gaze fell upon his superior. He licked his lips and, like a sealed door, stashed every emotion behind his apathetic expression. "I do not know, sir. York and Bobbett were speaking to me concerning cold symptoms, but Albie arrived and attacked them."

"Fearworn has stumbled upon something troublesome," said Laurent, approaching with the ice shard from earlier in his grasp. A trail of blood trickled from the tip and he ran it slowly over his tongue. Disgust painted his features, then his gaze swept over the wall, silently calculating. "He was one of the soldiers taken to the forest with you, I presume?"

"Yes." Nicholas said no more. William hadn't mentioned Charmaine's symptoms, nor would he. Laurent may seek to kill her. Normally, Nicholas would agree, but his attention fell upon William again. It didn't matter how the medic presented himself, Nicholas saw it now; the hint of sorrow settled in green eyes. William hurt. He hurt for Charmaine, the loss of her, and Nicholas had the urge to play the hero, to try and bring her back if it meant William would smile at him, if it meant he'd stop pretending to be alright.

"We will track the beast," Laurent said, catching the attention of the superior officer speaking to William.

He recognized Laurent, swiftly standing at attention and bowing. "Lord Darkmoon," the officer said. "I heard you were paying us a visit. Did I hear you can track our lost soldier?"

"I can. The beast will wander into Fearworn's grasp, and we will finally know the whereabouts of his hideout. Lead me to these generals of yours."

"Of course, this way, Lord Darkmoon." The officer gestured for Laurent to follow and he flicked his fingers, instructing Nicholas to accompany him. Nicholas had no desire to do so. He sought to comfort William, to hold him, to twist a lie into a promise of finding Charmaine so he wouldn't look so hurt. And maybe William wanted that, too, because he pinned Nicholas with a forlorn stare.

"Nicholas," Laurent warned. His blood ran cold. He left William, even if all he wanted was to take his hand. Nicholas caught up to his father, who spoke in a low voice, "The mortal from your room, tell me more about him."

His lips sealed shut. He didn't want Laurent to know a damn thing, but his father would learn, one way or the other. Better by his own admittance than through his screams, or worse, William's.

"William Vandervult, he is the other soldier that was taken to the woods with me. Why does he interest you?" Nicholas asked, fearful of the response.

"I am ensuring that you remember a mortal plaything is only that."

Nicholas tried to say he would never think more of William, but the lie congealed on his tongue. He swallowed the words, terrified by his incapability of speaking them. They should be the truth. His heart sputtered as he struggled to conjure a word to describe William that would set his father's mind at ease, or at least make him less interested.

"We agreed to spend our evenings together, but I will focus more on the task at hand," he said instead. "Fearworn's fall is close, and I will defeat him."

"Good."

Tension stitched itself between their reticence. Nicholas kept his attention on Laurent, curious about what would happen next, of what he may do. He maintained a distance from his family, for good reason. They weren't known for delicacy or care. His siblings were best at revels where they could drink, curse, and torment the days and nights away. But if any of them learned of William, if Laurent thought William meant more, then...

A door creaking open broke his focus. Laurent stepped into a large room. Two generals stood within. The others were on their way. They introduced themselves to the Lord of Darkmoon. When the others followed, Laurent explained he could track Charmaine the way Nicholas tracked Fearworn. Everything fell into place. Mages came with a potential way to prevent Fearworn from escaping. Charmaine could lead them directly to the bastard. The generals grew more ardent, insisting that the time to strike was now.

28

William

There was no respite in rest. Fear, anxiety, and exasperation smothered him in the night. He laid in the room full of snoring soldiers. Fabric rustled, a man coughed, another sneezed, and he stayed silent while playing out every worst-case scenario. Fearworn took Charmaine. A monstrous infection ravaged and dragged her away.

His hands fisted into the sleeping bag. His teeth pierced his bottom lip. He tasted copper among his anger, a twisting nether of fury that had him kicking his way out of the bag. Stumbling over sleeping soldiers, he wandered through the dim hall to fall into the snow outside where he rubbed the freeze against his cheeks. Snow, ice, the gray sky, all of it reminded him of another problem; Laurent.

Nicholas' father caught them. A fae knew, a powerful one at that. Nicholas feared him and that meant he should, too. In every shadow, he worried Laurent would be there, waiting. Those eyes held death, promised a bitter end. He worried he saw them unblinking in the night, waiting to steal him away like the fae tales.

What a fool he had been. He knew better than to lie with fae, and Nicholas, of all people. William liked the danger and now he faced the consequences. Yet, he wanted nothing more than to see Nicholas at this moment. Not even for sex, just for comfort, for someone to tell him Charmaine would be alright, that she'd somehow return as if nothing awful had transpired, and that had him releasing a pitiful laugh.

Damn it all, he wanted Nicholas to hold him, to run his fingers through William's hair and ask silly questions that would make him forget about what happened. They could lie in bed, snuggled beneath the covers. He would count the seconds between their silence, knowing Nicholas would conjure a question, a joke, or even a riddle, and he would be set at ease. Even if it was false. Hearing his voice, feeling Nicholas' pulse beneath his fingertips became what he yearned for, what made his heart race or settle.

"Idiot." He slammed a fist against his chest, over a traitorous heart.

"William?" Oscar called, illuminated by the torch clutched in his shivering, gloved hands. Snow crunched beneath his rushed steps. "What are you doing up so late? Are you hurt?"

"No, I... wanted some fresh air." He stood and dusted the snow off his trousers. "Are you on watch duty?"

"Yeah." Oscar's teeth chattered behind his chapped lips. "I heard about Albie. All of us had. That...I'm sorry. It's a real shame to have lost him."

"We haven't lost him for good. Fearworn wouldn't risk creating a monster that could infect him, too."

He repeated that to himself a thousand times. There had to be a way to get Charmaine back, to take her home. They had so much to do, so many stories and adventures they spun when sleep wouldn't spare them. William promised to teach her how all the ladies of high society danced. Charmaine promised to teach him to sing and play the acoustic guitar. She was meant to buy a new home with her mother where she could live as her true self. He was meant to return to his family and try to be the man he should have become. They had too much to do to stop now.

"What is that supposed to mean?" Oscar asked, sniffling. Mentioning Charmaine made his eyes water.

"That there may be..." William fell quiet. A shadow shifted nearby, then a pair of fuchsia eyes blinked in the shadows. He wished to run toward them. "A cure," he muttered.

"Wow, I ain't ever heard you be so optimistic before."

Not optimistic, desperate, William thought.

"I hope you're right. Hopefully, he's out there and we find that cure and he can come home," Oscar said while patting William's shoulder. His attention shifted between Oscar and Nicholas' figure concealed by the tents. "Well, I better get a move on or I'll be late to my post. Goodnight, William. Try to get some sleep."

"You, too. Goodnight."

The firelight faded. Nicholas' eyes brightened. He flicked his fingers, beckoning William forward. In the shadows, Nicholas caught his hand. A fae shouldn't calm his days. Nicholas' attention shouldn't ease his discomfort. His smooth fingers cradling William's neck should make his teeth grind. Instead, he melted into those arms that let him breathe, slowly, deeply, exactly what he needed.

"Are you alright?" Nicholas asked. "We weren't able to speak earlier about what happened."

"Should we be speaking now?" Fear bubbled in William's abdomen. He stepped aside, missing Nicholas' touch and the foreign comfort he gave of late. "Why are you here? Someone may see."

"My father and the generals had my attention until now. As you were not in my room, I came looking for you." Nicholas caught his fingers, toying with them until he opened his hand. Nicholas dropped the missing ring into his palm. "I found this in my room earlier. Put it on and follow me."

"Nicholas, I'm not in the mood for sex."

"We are not going to my room. Trust me." Those two words hung between them. Tempting. Risking. So different from how they started, from what they expected to come of this. Trust never should have grown between them. There was meant to be hate and lust, but trust forced it way through like dandelions in a garden.

Nicholas retreated. He moved elegantly, stopping once to urge William to follow. Hesitantly, he slipped on the ring and became Nicholas' shadow. They swerved through the encampment, Nicholas not caring who saw him. No one, especially a mortal, could stop him from doing whatever he desired, like leaving the citadel through the gates.

William stood by the cracked wall, repaired by remnants that any soldier could find in the citadel. Charmaine leapt over this wall earlier, as if it were a mere foot off the ground rather than thirty. Soldiers patrolled the embankment and manned the gate. They gave Nicholas peculiar looks, but said nothing about his passing.

Nicholas disappeared within the tree line. William wasn't so sure he should follow. He yearned to run after the fae, disappear with him, forget about all this, and that elated him, scarily, so. If they disappeared in that forest together, never to be seen again, he wasn't entirely certain he'd mind.

With a shuddering breath, he slipped outside and took to the trees. He jolted when a hand snaked around his wrist. Nicholas ran, his fuchsia light fled from him like fireflies. They flickered around them, illuminating the forest floor once eerie and now beautiful.

"Where are we going?" he grunted.

"Away from there," Nicholas replied.

William fell into a run beside him. Somehow, this felt natural, necessary. They came upon a meager clearing. Trees parted where a mound of rocks rose, clustered together. William took a seat on one, then returned the ring to his pocket, shivering under the moonlit sky.

"The moon," he whispered, awestruck. A gray overhang hid the sky since their arrival, but here, the clouds cut apart enough to reveal the soft moonlight. Nicholas fell on the stone beside him. He did not miss how their fingers brushed, how Nicholas linked their pinkies as if it weren't sweet.

"What happened earlier?" Nicholas asked.

William slid his boots from side to side, then clicked the heels. "She changed because of me. The first two soldiers who died today, they saw me leaving your room and assumed we spent the evening together. They were threatening me when Charmaine arrived. I saw her getting irritated and tried to intervene, but one man said the wrong thing and she attacked. I tried to feed her that medicine, but her strength was too great, then she was gone."

Nicholas wore a lopsided grin. "You did what you could?"

"Sometimes it is alright not to give words of comfort. You don't excel at them." William shuddered from the chill and his worries. "Your father, will he tell anyone about us?"

"Doubtful. He saw you as my plaything, and I did not dissuade him."

"I see." Bile rose in his throat. "And he took that fine?"

"My father cares little about what I do, so long as it doesn't go against his plans. He will not speak of anything."

"Is that why you came to see me? To let me know that your father approves of your plaything?" That last question came out with more bite than William meant. The words left a foul taste at the tip of his tongue. He didn't want to be Nicholas' plaything. He wanted to be more than that.

"No, the generals and my kin are worried about what happened to Charmaine. They had the same concerns we did. If Fearworn can change one, he can change others. They will push me to my limits. I will have little time to speak over the coming days, but I wanted you to know that my father is tracking her."

William lurched to his feet. "What? Now, as we speak? Where is she? We have to find her."

Nicholas caught his hand and encouraged him to sit. The fae cradled his face, speaking softly, "We will. My father tracks her as I track Fearworn. We expect she is running to him, so we will find his hideout."

"The generals will not wait long to attack. We could find her. We can save her."

Nicholas wore a solemn fear. "My wicked, she is lost."

"She isn't!" He screamed, angered by her loss but also Nicholas giving up so easily. If anyone could help, it was him, and William wanted, no, he needed that help. Nicholas clung to his neck, easing William into his arms. He struggled against the hold, fingers tearing into the shade's arm. "You said there could be a cure. You said we will look for it."

"We may not have the time. You are right, the generals will not wait. This is our greatest opportunity. Scouts are following her trail. They are scoping out the terrain, strategizing. Should she go to Fearworn, we will be sent and she will be in the crossfire. She may yet be among his forces."

No gasp granted William the air he needed. Every burst was too little, then too much. Living out here like this for so long, he saw countless bodies, terrifying deaths. He imagined Charmaine, her body broken, bruised and bloody, twisted beyond recognition, laying in the snow, being dumped in this wasteland rather than taken home where she belonged. He couldn't save her. There was no bully to punch. No kids to snap back to. Only a monster with unfathomable power he couldn't stand against and a world reminding him how ruthlessly cruel it was.

Regardless, William spoke with determination and fear. "We will find her and keep her away from battle until we find the cure."

"Our focus must be on Fearworn."

"Fine, do that, but I will find her. I will save her, no matter what." He searched Nicholas' eyes for recognition, anything to show he understood. "You don't understand. I cannot lose her."

"Then explain. Tell me why you will risk so much, your life even, for one person."

"Because I am selfish. All those years ago when I helped her, I really did it for me," he muttered. Every word caught in his tightened throat. The tears came and they would not stop. Nicholas saw all of it again. He saw far too much, but William could not withstand the worry, the mounting fear of finding Charmaine's broken corpse and being unable to mend her.

"You were right," he wheezed. "I have killed the men I swore to save, and I do not regret a damn thing. Mortals are as cruel as fae, if not worse, for we pretend not to be. Children taken from their homes, sent to fight and knowing they may die, it is not strange to think that they will be angry. I told you the others took their ire out on me. They called me names, stole my food and belongings, beat me when bored. Finally, some raped me. A bunch of angry children far from home taught how to maim and kill, of course they would spoil. They would rot and fester into cursed beasts because that was how we survived. Except I knew I wouldn't live much longer if they kept it up. After I was assigned the title of medic, the beatings stopped. Healers determined whether they lived or died, so when they begged me for help like I begged them to stop, I could spit in their face and say no. That's exactly what I did. When the perfect opportunity came in the middle of a battle, I took their lives or let them bleed out. One begged as I stood over him, and I laughed, then I cried because I should have felt better."

Nicholas' thumb brushed the tears from William's cheeks. "Why didn't you?"

"Because I loved who I was before, and I hate who I have become. I am scarred, mentally and," William dug nails into his shoulders, recalling the scars along his back. "They marked me. I will never forget what they did. They made me this way, the military and those boys. I am not stronger because of this. I am angry and hollow and tormented, barely much of a person at all. And after all that happened to me, I heard someone screaming for help and they sounded like me. A terrified child who needed help in a place that sought to tear you apart."

He heaved a rattled breath, overtaken by more than tears. All of it, every memory swimming in and out of his vision, as if it happened yesterday. He yearned to scream, to cry, to throw a fit, to cling to Nicholas like a dying breath. None of this should have happened. He should have grown up happy with his family, but he hadn't, and it was one of many reasons he couldn't have faith like so many others. Who could believe in an afterlife, in merciful gods when reality is merciless?

"All I could think about was how no one stepped in to help me," he whimpered. "So I ran, and there Charmaine was, beaten bloody. I saw myself in her, the fear in her eyes. Those bastards laughed, as my tormentors had. I made them regret it, and I taught Charmaine to make them regret it. I went after any piece of shit who dared to do the same because I found the world is a better place without them in it. I did not help Charmaine purely out of the goodness of my heart. But I love her dearly now, even as the monster they made me to be."

"Monster," Nicholas echoed. He caught William by the chin, forcing their gaze to meet, capturing him within burning fuchsia light. "Listen well, William Vandervult, for I cannot lie. You are kind and vicious, cunning and infuriating, loyal and fierce. You are wholly wonderful and you are strong. You were before them, as the boy who helped the suffering and gave his family all the love in the world. And you are after, as the man protecting those he loves, regardless of how that love came to be, and protecting yourself by any means necessary. They deserved what they got. What you did was a mercy, for had I heard this and they lived, I would have shown them suffering, pain beyond comprehension, my wicked. I would have done anything you asked and more."

Nicholas' fingers traced the lines of his face to memorize every surface. His thumb brushed a trembling bottom lip, then a chilled cheek and around William's ear. Nicholas' fingers fell into William's hair and he whispered against parted lips, "This may mean nothing to you, but I adore the positively wicked little thing that you are here and now, even if you do not."

William kissed the troublesome bastard for making his heart ache, for making him believe every word, for letting him feel like he wasn't utterly broken and deprived. They did deserve it. He was strong before and he is now. Hearing that from Nicholas meant more than he could explain, more than he could show, but he tried. He clung to Nicholas, tasted his lips, kissed him over and over, each more brilliant than the last.

As Nicholas held him, he cried. Nicholas gave him peace and affection in the soothing motion of his hand against his back, then kissing his temple, his cheek, his shoulder. It was too much. It wasn't enough. He wished to stay here, to fuse, to burrow beneath Nicholas' skin and feed off his fire, to never separate.

"We will search for the cure. I can promise that much," Nicholas said.

"Thank you." They stayed like that, cuddled beneath the fading moonlight, and he thought spending more nights like this for a long, long time wouldn't be so bad.

29

Charmaine

Charmaine faded in and out of consciousness. She spied on the world in intervals, observing a dank cave and rusting metal. Violet eyes peered down at her. A blinding light burned her irises. Pain surged in her arm, then she fell into nothing. She hovered within an inky night, where she stuttered through every breath.

Was this death? Had the Broken Soul judged her impure, and she was cursed to drown in the waters of Elysium? She couldn't see or hear anything. The world became a vast void. She thought of home, of her mother, of the future she wanted and how it faded from her view.

Whimpering, her eyes opened. She inhaled realizing she had not died, but the pain echoing through her limbs made her wish for death. She took in the unfamiliar room that settled a biting fear at the base of her spine. Ancient chains, thick as her wrists, hung from the ceiling. Their sharp hooks held dissected bodies up by their torn muscles. Blood stained the floor, discoloring the rock a dull red. Everything had a metallic scent and a sticky surface. Along the opposite wall, broken jars containing peculiar green liquid lined the shelves alongside preserved limbs and medical supplies.

She dared not to speak, even as she gazed at the unfamiliar writing scratched into the walls. Considering what little she remembered—the military encampment and hurting soldiers—she theorized where she was; Fearworn had her. She hadn't died. Yet. The future she wanted still had a chance.

She was alone. The room had a single exit, a metal door to her left. A desk cluttered with papers sat nearby. Books towered on the desk and along the shelves secured to the wall. The chair had fallen to the floor by an aged grate covered in grime and a peculiar wet substance. Groaning, Charmaine pressed her hands to the wall and pushed herself onto throbbing feet. She gaped at the sight of her clawed hands. Thick nails pierced the tip of her fingers, making the skin raw and bloody. Strange scales ruptured through the shedding skin of her arms. She tugged at her clothes finding the scales along her sides, thighs, then beneath her eyes. The infection, whatever Fearworn did, changed her. She did not know when she would lose herself again. Her mind felt like her own, but she sensed another voice squirm in the back of her head. This voice, this creature, craved to take hold.

If she escaped, she may hurt the people she cares about most. There was no telling if this monster forming within her had her memories or not. What if it returned to her homeland and attacked her mother? She wouldn't be able to live with herself, so rather than running to the door, she searched for the cure they hoped Fearworn had.

Charmaine ripped through the papers on Fearworn's desk. He wrote in the language of fae. Not understanding a word, she snarled and threw her attention to the shelves. Her shaking hands flicked through them, longing for a sign while knowing she had no clue what to look for.

Please, don't let me die here like this, she pleaded to the Holy Soul, or any deity willing to listen. She would give anything to be given a chance at a better life, to be happy, and not feel as if the world tormented her for its own amusement.

"My pet, you are awake."

Charmaine froze. Slow steps approached her, then a gentle hand fell on her shoulder. Every instinct told her to run, yet her legs refused to budge.

"Look at me," Fearworn ordered, and she obeyed. His voice commanded her. The last time she saw Fearworn, he had nearly killed them. He was exactly as she remembered, pale skinned and donned in fine silks. The bloodied floor stained the trail of his blue robes. He paid the mess no mind. His inquisitive attention inspected her thoroughly, excited. Fearworn pressed the sharp nail of his thumb against her chin to push her head from side to side.

"I am surprised you are of sound mind, that you are so inquisitive of your surroundings," Fearworn spoke with the awe of a child, one whose mind finally tasted their own thoughts. "My creations often suffer from a great deal of ailments to the mind."

Charmaine was uncertain whether he wanted her to speak. His eyes narrowed, and she took a chance, asking, "That is not your intention?"

"Of course not. I want them to be real and grand and strong. This," he gestured to the laboratory as if it were a glistening gem rather than a festering hole of gore. "This is my dream, creation."

"And destruction."

"Life comes from death, does it not? A fire scorches the forest and the forest regrows. Nature is a powerful and merciless thing."

Fearworn shuffled to his desk where he scribbled notes, muttering softly to himself. Watching Fearworn tug the chair up to take a seat felt odd. For the monster that had been tormenting so many lives to perform mundane tasks, like sitting at a desk looking through papers, was a peculiar sight. If one ignored the chaotic room, he appeared normal, little more than a man hard at work. She wondered when his life changed. If he was ever someone others conversed with and asked questions without worrying about losing a limb.

"You are staring," Fearworn said.

"Sorry... sir," she muttered.

"Do you have questions for me, my pet?"

She clasped her hands behind her back to pinch her fingers together. She disliked being referred to as a pet, though she disliked everything about the situation at hand. A sickness grew, knotted by fear and pointless hope that William and Nicholas would show up, that they would save her.

"I, uh, I know little about shades, sir, so it's curious to see you work," she replied. If a miracle happened, if she survived, she could bring information back, so she may as well take advantage of speaking with Fearworn. She didn't know of anyone to have done so and live to tell the tale.

"Shades." He chuckled. "What do you know of them, then? I haven't met many mortals to ask."

"We know very little. Shades appear among rare fae children, and they are stronger than most."

"Stronger is a stretch. There are many High Fae capable of winning against a shade. We are not invincible. We're not what you mortals may call gods. We are no different from a volcanic eruption relieving pressure or an avalanche whisking away snow. We are born when magic grows too heavy for the world. That magic must go somewhere, so it goes to us," he said, as if the answer should have been obvious.

"If that is the case, why are there no shades among mortals?"

"Because this realm has little magic as is and I want to know why. I want to see what the other realms offer, the ones I have found and those that remain. Would you like to hear of them?" Fearworn lurched out of his chair. It toppled to the floor while he grabbed books upon books to throw at Charmaine's feet, uncaring of the blood seeping across the covers. He fell to his knees, hands twitching in the air like he clung to the fabric of the world and wished to show her all of it.

"I have already proven there is another realm, and I will prove there are more. Each differs from the last, but there are similarities, strings that connect us all, magic and life and death. It's all there at the tip of my fingers," his voice abruptly fell to a low growl. "But these bastards continue to halt my plans. They stand in my way, in the way of grand discoveries. They do not understand. They don't see what's out there."

Fearworn waved his hand, and the books opened. Their pages fluttered to unveil scribbled images in frantic charcoal. Charmaine's curiosity got the better of her. She fell to a knee and ran a hand over the drawing of a humanoid creature constructed of water surrounded by Fearworn's unreadable ramblings.

"Beautiful," Fearworn whispered while tracing the art. "I have seen glimpses through the scars of these other worlds. They're in reach and we should try to find them."

"Why? What if there is something out there that can hurt us?" she asked, choosing not to mention how he brought plenty of monsters to hurt them already.

"To discover it, of course. Don't you understand?"

She feared what he would do if she said no, fearful of the storm raging in Fearworn's violet eyes. Purple hued tendrils wormed beneath his skin. They sank under his eyes and slithered around his neck. As if the magic within him became a web, it crisscrossed over his body, and undoubtedly into his rotting mind.

She dared to pity him. The magic coming so naturally to fae betrayed him. Nicholas could follow in those footsteps. Shades were sad, in a way she hadn't thought of until she sat before one. Fearworn could have been a brilliant researcher, potentially one to discover other realms and travel them safely. His work may have helped the world, if only he had a grasp on himself, on the curiosity and power battling inside of him.

"I understand," she whispered, and he smiled.

"Good, good, you see." He gripped her chin, then ran a finger along the scales on her cheek. "Now, tell me how all of this feels. What changes have you noticed? Give me every little detail."

He spoke as if she should be excited to share. When she hesitated to respond, the room darkened. His brows furrowed, creating deep lines in his forehead, and a vicious sneer spread over his features. She sensed if she did not share these details, he would force them out of her in any way necessary.

Charmaine shared anything that came to mind. The more she spoke, the wider Fearworn's smile became until the expression was painful to gaze upon. What he had in mind couldn't be good and all she could do was hope she lost herself to the monster before Fearworn's more physical experiments began.

30

Nicholas

Fearworn had Charmaine. Nicholas saw her through the bastard's eyes, possessed by the virus within. A black void replaced the brown of her eyes. Beneath her eyes and around her mouth, the skin peeled and a leathery pattern like that of snakeskin appeared. She stood motionless under Fearworn's scrutiny. His claws gripped her chin, pushing her head from side to side. Her fingers twitched, but she dared not raise her hand against him, even when he commanded her to lie on the table. Fearworn grabbed a scalpel and cut into her leg where the beast had bitten her. The virus sprouted from there, now thick, black roots tangled in through the sinew.

Fearworn muttered to himself and took notes, sounding pleased. He inspected her newly formed claws, so thick they broke through skin. Blood stained her fingers and gums where her teeth sharpened to points. Then he sewed Charmaine up and shoved her aside. She stood in the room's corner, dull-eyed and motionless.

If William saw this, if he knew, he would be indisposed. Nicholas never cared about the thoughts of others. He spoke cruelties like a politician spewing lies, but the desire to stir trouble had dulled. He would not bring this news to William. More accurately, he couldn't.

Nicholas returned to himself, seated cross-legged on his bed. Laurent informed the generals where Charmaine went earlier that morning. The generals ordered Nicholas to monitor Fearworn while the army prepared for what they hoped to be the end of this war. With the last batch of recruits having arrived hours ago, the final string hung in their grasp. A string that, when ripped, would unravel all Fearworn crafted. It'd be a two-day march to Fearworn's hideout, and they had to get there without arousing suspicion. If Fearworn slipped away, it didn't matter if the army decimated his hideout. He was the source, the infection that needed to be cut out.

"Nicholas?" Arden munched on a tray of cheese and crackers on the floor. "Are you feeling alright?"

"Fine. I'm going to take a walk," he replied. Arden watched his departure. His duty was to ensure Nicholas didn't lose himself in the many hours he spent sharing Fearworn's eyes. And if he did, he wasn't certain what his father would order, if he told Arden to sink an iron dagger into his heart or not.

"Where will you be going?" Arden inquired.

"Wherever I please."

"To your mortal medic, then?"

Eerie silence draped over them. Arden bathed his impish grin in red from the wine in his goblet.

"What mortal medic do you speak of?" Power surged at the tip of Nicholas' fingers, yearning to sear the grin off Arden's pale features.

"William, of course. I expected you were toying with someone, seeing as you called none to your bed, but this was unexpected." Arden knocked back the last of his beverage and smacked his lips. "Lord Darkmoon doesn't believe you, by the way, that William is merely a plaything."

So Laurent informed Arden of what he saw. The question became; what were Arden's orders? Was he to prevent Nicholas from seeing William? Or worse?

"My father believes nothing I say, so I often wonder why he bothers to ask," he said.

"Then I will ask, is William merely a plaything?"

"That is none of your concern."

Arden knew evasiveness as well as he. His avoidance gave way to an answer that made his kin laugh. "Should Evera, or better yet, your sister, hear of this, they will have a lot of fun with him."

Nicholas caught Arden's neck, squeezing so tightly saliva dribbled over his lips. "They will hear nothing of this," he warned, voice hostile and foreboding. Fuchsia light illuminated the veins beneath his skin, brighter than a summer sun. His nails pierced the skin of Arden's neck. Blood tickled the tip of his fingers. He pushed and pushed until Arden's neck craned back at an odd angle and he gagged, fingers clawing at Nicholas' wrist. "Should any learn of William, I will suspect you to be the culprit. My wrath will be unforgiving and relentless. You know that well, don't you?"

"I do," Arden wheezed.

"So you will ensure no one learns of this, won't you?"

"Of course."

"Or I could make this much simpler and be rid of you now." Nicholas held tighter. Arden dared to summon a vine between the cracked stones. Nicholas caught his wrist and snapped the bone. Arden couldn't cry out. The hold around his neck was too tight, strangling words and breath from his lungs. When Nicholas released him, Arden plummeted, heaving and coughing. He cradled his bruised neck. Blood slicked the back ends of his hair. Amused ruby eyes fell on Nicholas as he went from coughing to chuckling.

"Do not toy with me again," Nicholas warned.

Arden raised a hand in surrender and laughed louder. "Would only ever dream of it."

Then Nicholas stalked out of the room. He may as well have hung a sign around his neck that read *soft*. Arden saw through him the moment Laurent revealed who his so-called plaything was. Then Arden put him in a position where he couldn't lie. Any words he shared would be seen as avoidance. He made his threats, though that did not guarantee Arden wouldn't speak on them. If Blair learned the truth, she would seek trouble. Evera could learn the truth, or worse, her mother. Alvina had plans and she would destroy anything in her path.

Nicholas nearly pivoted to finish the job, drive an iron dagger through Arden's heart and be done with it. But that would prove to a far worse party that they were right to assume William might have meant something, something mystifying and dangerous. He walked faster, heading for the very person Arden had accused him of. There was no point pretending not to.

The citadel grew into a frenzy ever since the mages of Heign visited. Although a rare few knew of what the mages learned, the soldiers understood they wouldn't visit without enormous news. Rumors spread that a way to defeat Fearworn had been conjured. Gossip elated the troops, sent them buzzing about the camp, working more fervently both in celebration and nerves. If the rumors were true, the last battle was soon, and they were right to worry.

Fearworn would go down fighting. The battle would be bloody. Such thoughts often put a smile on Nicholas' face. However, now he thought of William on the battlefield, surrounded by Fearworn's beasts. Hands bloodied from saving one poor soul after the other, his eyes cold, distant and unsettled, like they would be upon learning about Charmaine.

Damn it. Concern did not suit him.

Nicholas came upon the med bay where soldiers coughed or laid motionless, eyes lost. William toiled among them, a cloth wrapped around his face. He handed foul smelling medicine out and made sure they kept the liquid down. Nicholas wished to waltz in, grab William, and take him wherever he pleased. William would be cross if he made them appear too friendly, especially after having met Laurent. He did not blame William for his paranoia. He was smart to be worried, so Nicholas entertained himself in the hall by freezing any water on the floors to make soldiers trip and stumble. The men would hop up and wander off, thinking nothing of it.

He snickered in secret. The hair on the back of his neck stood high. He caught sight of William. The cloth William wore around his face now hung on his neck, revealing the grim line of his lips and the bags beneath his eyes. Ah, his wicked caught him playing games.

William exited the med bay to enter the supply room. Nicholas scurried after him. William opened a crate to push through vials in search of more rancid medicine.

"Don't trip the soldiers" William chided. "You're too childish."

"Fun," Nicholas corrected. He caught his prey in a fierce grip, then nuzzled his nose along the back of William's tempting nape, savoring the shiver he shared.

"I have no time for you, trouble. The ill require my attention." Humor filled William's voice, much to his relief.

"I am an ill man for you, William Vandervult." He burned one ravenous kiss after the other along William's neck. "Give that attention to me."

"If by ill, you mean rabid, then I suppose you are." William spun in his arms for a kiss. He wanted nothing more than to drag William to bed. Damn it all, they didn't have to do anything, so long as William kept looking at him like that, like there was nothing else in the world.

"And whose fault is that? You are the greatest temptation there is. How am I ever meant to resist?" Nicholas asked.

"Is that so?" William ran his hands down Nicholas' chest to knot his fingers into the belt loops of his pants. "Maybe I'll tempt you tonight."

"Now." Nicholas growled.

William released him. "Tonight, or nothing at all."

He pressed another lingering kiss against William's temple. "You are cruel."

"There is a reason you call me wicked."

"Indeed, there is."

William draped his arms around Nicholas' shoulders, fingers lazily playing with the fae's hair. He couldn't shatter this moment by telling William about Charmaine. He would keep him distracted, do anything to prevent William from asking or thinking of her and all the worries.

"You are staring," William stated.

"Admiring."

"You needn't sweet talk me. I have already agreed to share a bed with you tonight."

"I am sweet talking because I want to." Because he didn't wish to leave. Even if William would slip into his room and warm his bed, he wanted to spend this time together, too. An odd, albeit welcome, sentiment. He couldn't recall wanting to be with someone for no reason. Everyone offered something, laughter, booze, violence, sex, something, but William merely being in his arms meant far more. He hoped William felt the same, that he wanted Nicholas around, not the powerful shade, just Nicholas.

William stepped closer, so they were chest to chest. Nicholas' thumbs brushed his bulky uniform aside to rub soothing circles atop his skin. The tension William always had slipped away and his enchanting lips pulled into a smile.

"Sweet talk some more, then," he said.

"Why?"

"Because I want you to." Or needed him to. William hadn't been sleeping well ever since Charmaine was lost and Laurent learned of them. On the nights they shared, William laid awake for hours. If sleep took him, he'd awake soon after, sweat coating his brow and breaths panicked.

Nicholas tugged him into bed and ran his fingers through William's hair, easing the man into a restless slumber.

During those moments, when William looked lost, Nicholas didn't know what to do, and that irritated him. So, he did what he could, and clung a little tighter, hoping his touch would be enough to be of some comfort. If sweet talk would help, then he would give that, too.

"You are a beauty this world does not deserve," Nicholas said.

Pink tinted William's cheeks, and he licked his lips. "More."

"There is not enough time in this life or the next for me to commit all the carnal acts I wish to do with you." Among other things.

"More."

"Tonight," he teased. William rewarded him with laughter, sweeter than sugar, addictive and enthralling. He wished to capture the sound, bottle it so he could take a sip every evening and fall into bliss.

"Touche." William settled his hands atop his chest. "I really should return to work. I am sure you have duties you are ignoring."

"Not ignoring, but avoiding. I would rather torment you."

"I know. You are exceedingly good at that, trouble."

"I like when you call me trouble."

"Then I shall never call you trouble again."

Nicholas caught those charming lips, leaving one peck after the other, making William smile wider between every breath. "Go away," he said, but didn't release Nicholas' shirt.

"One more minute." An hour, a month, a year, a lifetime, none of it was enough. William made him feel something dangerous, something he liked and disliked craving more of.

Unfortunately, William pushed him aside and gestured for him to leave. He grumbled a curse and wandered toward the door, stopping when William called, "Nicholas... have you seen her yet?"

He froze with his hand on the doorknob. He dared not meet William's gaze when he replied, "My father has informed the generals of Fearworn's whereabouts. We will leave soon."

"You didn't answer. Have you seen Charmaine?"

Nicholas turned the doorknob. William's hand fell on his shoulder. The shade pushed the door open, knowing William would let go. He wouldn't want anyone to see him alone in a room with Nicholas. He used that to his advantage, even if it hurt, slipping into the hall and away from William. Nicholas hurried past the med bay. A nurse moved toward storage, muttering a list to herself.

"Oh Doc, a soldier has come in with an awful rash. The other nurses could really use your help on it," she called, distracting William further.

Nicholas released a slow breath. William would ask again tonight. He would do anything to avoid answering, save canceling their rendezvous, of course.

31

WILLIAM

IF NICHOLAS SAW CHARMAINE and refused to speak, the truth had to be grim. What had Fearworn done to her? Was she still alive? Were they too late? William fell into a chair adjacent to the cots, wishing more than ever that Charmaine was here. She had optimism and hope. He tried so hard to be the same, but every word felt like a lie. A voice, sinister and merciless, uttered cruelties; *Charmaine is dead. Neither of you will see your families again. Her body will rot here, and so will yours.*

He wrung his hands together, raw from a long day of work. The nurses were no better. A young woman frowned over the water bowl, gently scrubbing her pained hands, but another soldier needed attending to. Many caught shimmer sickness, some overcoming it in a few days, while others laid motionless in bed. William monitored them, keeping Montgomery updated since some may have to be moved outside of the citadel, otherwise they would never wake.

William rose when a wind kicked through the room. The nurses shrieked from the chill. A note fell at his feet. Cocking a brow, he retrieved the letter written in flourishing handwriting.

Meet me in the grove from the other night.
Trouble

The note might have made him smile if he weren't mildly irritated with the sender. He stuffed the letter in his pocket.

After his day ended, William slipped on the ring and fled to the grove. Nicholas avoided him, which meant he had answers he didn't want to share. He would get those answers, one way or the other. The night had a brittle chill his jacket couldn't keep at bay. Without his military boots, his feet would have been wet even with shoes and two layers of socks. The light of the camp faded behind him. Pale moonlight flickered through the branches, scarcely illuminating the trees. An orange glow upon the skyline guided him into the grove.

Nicholas waited on what once were boulders now shaped into a bench by his fae magic. A fire roared in front of him, spitting sparks and crackling. His steps alerted the fae, who raised his attention from the flames reflecting in the expressive pink of his eyes.

"Why are we meeting here?" William asked.

"I thought we both should get away from camp as often as we can. This place proved rather nice." Nicholas presented his hand. William shivered from the touch he came to know better than his own. They fit too perfectly together. He fell beside Nicholas, their bodies close and heated by more than the fire.

"If you believed this would distract me from asking you about Charmaine, then you were sorely mistaken."

Nicholas sighed. "Do not ask me to upset you."

"You have had no issue upsetting me up to this point."

"I do not wish to upset you any longer, so do not ask it of me," he admitted the words like a curse. William dared to think they were. They played a dangerous game from the beginning and the match felt soon to set.

"It is too late for that. Your avoidance says enough." He released Nicholas' hand to pace by the fire. "She is alive, but alive means little in these lands. I've had countless men breathing and begging for death."

"Let's not linger on these thoughts tonight."

"How am I meant to think of anything else?" William countered.

"Pay attention to me."

"You are cockier than I realized, if you think that is enough." But he could not stop the smile from forming after Nicholas took his hand and urged the other to his shoulder. Nicholas caught his waist and swayed.

"What are you doing?" William asked.

"Dancing." Nicholas grunted from trying to move them, but his feet stood firm. "This is the part where you move your feet."

"There's no music."

"I could sing for us, though I fear I do not know songs of Terra, or any in your tongue."

"But you can sing in your language?"

"Most fae can. We love our revels, the music, the lights, the dancing, and the booze, especially the booze." Nicholas grabbed his hand and spun him. He stumbled, then laughed when Nicholas tried again and succeeded. "I will make a dancer out of you yet."

"I can dance." He joined Nicholas, swaying to a rhythm they somehow knew. "My tutor found me more tolerable than my brothers."

Nicholas' hum sounded unconvinced.

"It has been many years," he added. "I may have forgotten a few things."

And he never danced with a man. His instructor, and any partners during the summer seasons, were women. Dancing was one of the few ways for him to survive parties and political gatherings. He struggled around the other boys, frightened they may notice his attention lingering on them. Speaking with women had always been easy and fun, but he feared they would notice too. As if a word or a move would spill his secrets. While they danced, he could lie that he was a horrid dancer and needed to focus. Most of the girls laughed and let them sway until their conversations lulled.

Here, caught in a peaceful dance under the stars on a winter night, he didn't worry about what any one would think of him. Nicholas had him enraptured by the deliciously dark magic of his eyes. Their hands soothed one another, their bodies, too. Forehead to forehead, Nicholas' scent of wildflowers and wet earth cradled him, held him closer and dear. His eyes fluttered close, daring to imagine the two of them dancing in his home's garden or at a boring political function without care of what others would think.

Nicholas set a hand beneath his chin. "Look at me."

His eyes opened. "You are ever so needy."

"Yes, I have always craved the world's attention, but now that I have yours, I want nothing more."

"Careful, trouble. You sound as if you care for me."

"Wouldn't that be tragic?" Nicholas kissed him and he tasted like desire. "Let us be at ease tonight. There are so many marvelous things we can do together."

"That we have done many times before."

"And is each moment not better than the last?" Nicholas kissed him harder, fervent and intoxicating. When they broke apart, the fae breathed deep. "Believe this, William, I am capable of worry, and I worry about what is coming. Yes, the future battle against Fearworn excites me. I cannot cease that feeling, this part of me." Nicholas placed William's hand over his chest. "This power within me yearns to be set free, and Fearworn will be a battle of agonizing beauty, but I understand I may not win. That I may not end this war."

He refused to imagine that. The image of Nicholas lying broken and cold had been one he desired when they first met. He did not know when that changed.

"Would that not make you happy? You love battle," he muttered.

"As do you, deep down, in the darkest recess of your mind, you know that, and I have seen it. Still, we understand this war must end, albeit for different reasons. I hope the next battle will be our last and I worry, too, but I wish not to worry with you. Let us," Nicholas licked his lips, sounding so much younger. "Let it be only us tonight. Let us be lost in one another."

He should have hated the thought, should have told Nicholas they got too close, that this had gone far past bedding partners, but the words wouldn't form. They vanished the moment he dared to conjure any, replaced by a single word.

"Let's." He clung to Nicholas' waist as if tonight would be their last, because it might be.

They kissed and danced, enthralled by the other. Nicholas hardly left his lips. The shade's fingers played with the hair on the back of his neck, then Nicholas set a hand to his chest. A playful glint flashed in the fae's eyes. Nicholas shoved him onto the seat, then fell to his knees. Fuchsia flames fluttered to life around them, heating the air. He still shuddered from Nicholas pushing up his shirt to kiss his abdomen. He freed himself of his jacket and shirt. Nicholas kissed lower and lower, palm rubbing his arousal through his pants, encouraging pleasure to build at the base of his gut. He lifted his hips, allowing Nicholas to yank his trousers to his ankles. The fae teasingly kissed around his rosy arousal, nuzzling his nose in golden curls.

"Keep this up and I'll use my hand tonight," he warned, but didn't sound the least bit convincing. Nothing lived up to Nicholas' attention.

"That sounds rather nice." Nicholas' voice grew seductive. "Can I watch?"

He hated to admit that Nicholas could do whatever he wanted and William would be thankful for it. Gripping his cock, he pleasured himself, finding it far more arousing with Nicholas' admiration. The fae's breath caught. His hands ran along William's thighs and cradled his balls. He pumped faster, cursing when Nicholas' lips brushed his tip, but no more.

"How stunning you are like this." Nicholas kissed his chest hungrily. "Makes me want to eat you up."

And Nicholas finally took William's cock between his predatory lips. He was a blissful indulgence, every moan encouraging a ravenous desire. He released himself to bury his fingers in Nicholas' hair, savoring the sweet sensations of being lost.

The night's bite was nothing in the face of their wanting, the heat of Nicholas' mouth, the fire roaring at his back, and the desire in his hands spreading William's thighs. It was truly unfair what Nicholas was capable of, how he drove him wild. His hips undulated, wanting more, to go deeper, to never leave the bliss of Nicholas' mouth. But then the fae dared to depart, leaving him desperate.

"I want you, my wicked," Nicholas said, licking his lips.

"You have me."

"I want you inside of me." Nicholas smirked at his swift intake of breath.

"Truly?"

"Can I lie?" Nicholas stood to undress, revealing his body in all its glory. Beneath the moonlight, he was ethereal, better than any dream could dare to conjure. There was certainly far too much leering on his part, taking in every piece of Nicholas' body, thinking of all he wanted to do. Cradling his neck, Nicholas fell into his lap and brought their naked bodies together to form a glorious harmony of ecstasy.

"Tonight, I want you to have your way with me. Give me everything," Nicholas said.

Nicholas had no idea what he offered. Out here, William accepted that most wanted a replacement for who they missed from home. He faulted no one for that because he played pretend, too, acting like the man he laid with could be someone he loved, that they were far from a battlefield, content and safe at home. But there was never any pretending with Nicholas. Even at the beginning when they hated each other entirely, they didn't pretend they were with anyone else. They were fine as they were, together, always a match in some way or the other.

"What if tonight isn't enough?" He grabbed Nicholas' backside, hips moving faster, continuously building upon their unrivaled fever. "What if it will take many more evenings to give you everything?"

Nicholas chuckled. "I could hope for nothing better."

He caressed Nicholas' goosebump covered skin, curious if the cold or his presence brought about such a reaction. He hoped for the latter, that Nicholas reacted as desperately as he did, that he wanted to freeze this moment in time so they'd never leave.

Nicholas held strong to William's neck and rolled his hips in a maddening rhythm. He devoured Nicholas' pulse, sucking against his pale nape. His hand slipped between Nicholas' cheeks, circling his hole. The fae mewled and rubbed against his curious fingers. His heart palpitated from more than their physical intensity. It was Nicholas, the way his touch had William painfully yearning for more.

Nicholas' sweet laughter tickled his ear when he flipped them, so the shade laid in the corner of the stone seat and William leaned between his legs. Grass sprouted beneath Nicholas' fingers, then crawled over the stone to create a smooth surface. By then, William had fallen to his knees and taken hold of Nicholas' brawny thighs.

"Are you going to stare all evening?" Nicholas asked with his nimble fingers wrapping around his arousal. "Or are you going to get to work before I change my mind?"

"I don't think you would."

"Do not test me, William Vandervult."

"That's unfair. You tease me all the time." William spread those beautiful legs and pressed his tongue against Nicholas' hole, savoring the sweet moan he released.

"This isn't teasing." Nicholas released an enchanting gasp, eyes glowing under the moonlight when William's tongue breached him. "This is torment."

Chuckling, he ceased the so-called torment and gave Nicholas what he desired. He found the motions Nicholas liked best, the ones that had his moans growing high, carrying the beautiful pitch of his voice. The ones that had him shaking and pushing William closer, encouraging him to lick until his jaw ached. He departed once to admire his work, the flush creeping along Nicholas' body and his eyes alight with lust. His chest heaved for breath and begged for attention. William was more than happy to oblige, kissing across his partner's chest, tasting his sweat and leaving his marks. He caught Nicholas' nipple between his teeth, wetting it until his mouth descended upon his cock.

His world became the man panting his name like a silent prayer. He stayed like that, fingers replacing his tongue to thrust inside Nicholas, feeling his partner's pulse humming against his fingertips. Twisting his wrist and curling his fingers, Nicholas' legs shook until the orgasm took him, sending his body into a quivering fit.

Nicholas looked glorious, covered in sweat that he tasted along his lover's thighs, over his chest to the mess made. He tasted salty, delicious, and William wanted more. He slipped his mouth over Nicholas' cock, taking his time to let Nicholas' pleasure heighten. William kissed the base of his cock, whispering against the hot flesh, "The sounds you make are driving me wild. I want inside you so bad."

"Then what are you waiting for?"

Nicholas cursed when William leaned over him to toss both legs over his shoulders. The fae mewled, pawing at William's hips to take hold of his ass and push him forward. His cock thrust into Nicholas' heat, taken by bliss that nearly made William's resolve snapped. His teeth tore into the beautiful leg over his shoulder, soothing the skin with his tongue.

"Don't be gentle with me. I want your everything tonight," Nicholas demanded, eyes clouded by lust.

"And you will have it, whatever you want, trouble." William kissed him and pulled away to slam back in. Sheer ecstasy overtook Nicholas' expression as William's hips drove into him. His cries crescendo, releasing one beautiful note after another. Nicholas' eyes pinched shut as William's power held him down, hitting harder and harder against him. But William wanted to see the pink hue of his eyes overshadowed by lust. "Don't look away from me," he said.

Nicholas' pupils dilated so the fuchsia hue was like the light of dusk. "Who is needy now?"

He was needy. He wanted more. There wasn't enough, even as he kissed Nicholas' legs, pushed his thighs to his chest and fucked him harder. He needed more. A string of words, dangerous and deadly, nearly fell from his lips. He retreated and Nicholas fell against the seat, heaving, eyes no more than ravenous fuchsia embers. He lugged Nicholas onto his feet, kissing him, addicted to the taste of him. Then William turned him and Nicholas fell forward, legs spread and hands caught on the back of the seat.

William returned to Nicholas' embrace, holding hard to his hips, knocking every breath from the fae's trembling form. His hand ran up Nicholas' back, savoring the shiver of his muscles, the sweat along his back that he tasted with a kiss and another. He thought these feelings would settle from this position, that not allowing Nicholas' enraptured expression to take him would let the emotions fade, but nothing worked. The sound of his partner's breath taken between pleas, the heat of his body burning beneath William, the way he twitched and withered from their shared pleasure, it made his insides boil. Like nothing he ever felt and was frightened to keep feeling this strangely peculiar but wonderful thing.

Slowing his hips to a crawl, he caught Nicholas in a kiss. Nicholas gasped against his mouth, hair still caught in his hand. When they parted, he saw himself in Nicholas' eyes, far too open then he should be, far too obvious. But he kept moving his hips as if the lust would overshadow the truth. William grasped Nicholas' cock, enjoying the sweet noises he made. He pumped faster. Then Nicholas' eyes fluttered closed, and he moaned William's name, his orgasm sending his body into a fit of shivers that William soon followed. Nothing else existed, only the two of them and their bliss beneath the stars.

Nicholas' knees buckled when William stood them upright. His arms held tight to Nicholas' waist while he kissed and bit at his partner's neck.

"And you dared to call me rabid," Nicholas laughed, but leaned into his voracious attention. William fell onto the seat, bringing Nicholas into his lap. The fae grunted and he massaged the hips his hands had bruised, though the color faded in a flash. It saddened him. He wanted his mark to remain on Nicholas for a long, long time.

They sat in silence, hearing nothing more than their labored breath slowing and the crackling fire. Nicholas laid against him. His gorgeous eyes opened, the brightest shade of enticing pink. He caught William's hand, not needing to say more. They kissed, slow and serene.

"You will be fucking me much more often from here on out," Nicholas muttered against his mouth.

"I'd be more than happy to, trouble."

Even if they may not have much time left. Soon, the generals would have them march on Fearworn. Nicholas worried he would lose, but for once, for the first time in so long, William wanted to hope that they would win. But winning meant this would be over. They would end. He and Charmaine would return home. Nicholas would return to Faerie.

He would forget about William, just a mortal fool who entertained him in the evenings.

Nicholas knocked his temple against William's. "How can anything bother you after such a tremendous performance?"

"Thank you for the kind review."

"I am nothing if not honest." Nicholas detached himself to dress, unfortunately. William knew he should do the same, but he preferred admiring Nicholas for as long as possible.

One day, he wouldn't be able to admire Nicholas at all.

"Will you forget me?" the question escaped his mouth before he thought of the consequences.

"Forget you?" Nicholas whispered.

There would be no point trying to evade, but he stalled. He retrieved his clothes, feeling Nicholas' questioning gaze. "When this war ends and we return home, will you forget me?"

"Never." Nicholas gripped his arm. Their eyes met and he dared to believe Nicholas looked hurt. "Do you ask because you hope to forget me?"

"No, I fear I will carry you with me always."

He brushed his cooled fingers along William's neck. He feared Nicholas would feel his erratic pulse, how even after they've calmed his heart refused to steady. Nicholas' presence was enough to make him soar, to make him desire in a way unlike hunger or greed, but a taut and perverse urge to ravage.

Nicholas' eyes went abruptly dark, and he stepped aside. He hadn't the time to ask why before a fae emerged from the forest. The stranger had a blood-chilling look, eyes of pure white without pupils and ashen gray skin. Nicholas shielded him from the stranger's firm gaze. The fae's bitter attention swept over them, seemingly uncaring, but he knew better. The stranger could ruin him, let the soldiers know of his rendezvous with a fae, and a shade, no less. They may not have to worry about a last battle if he were to die by morning.

"No one should leave the encampment, especially at night," the stranger spoke calmly.

"I can take care of myself," Nicholas replied. "I'm assuming you came to find me because you need something."

"Yes. Finish this affair swiftly. The generals require your presence. It is time." With a nearly unperceivable bow of his head, the stranger left.

Though he understood what the stranger meant, he still asked, "Time?"

"To face Fearworn," Nicholas replied.

This could be it. They knew where Fearworn was. They knew how to close a shimmer for a short time. They had Nicholas, the power capable of truly standing up to Fearworn. The war could end. He could go home, and he would be taking Charmaine with him.

"We will search for her," Nicholas said, as if he read William's thoughts. "But do not expect everything to go as planned. We are suspecting there to be a cure and suspecting she can be saved."

"I will save her."

"William." Nicholas caught his hands and held them fiercely. "I will help look for her, but you must promise me something in return. If she is lost, you must accept that and let me finish her. You will not get in the way. Swear it."

He refused to imagine such terror.

Nicholas cupped his cheeks. "Swear it."

He forced a nod and bit back a whimper when Nicholas kissed him, quick and sweet.

"The generals will give orders to march. It should take two days to arrive. They'll keep me busy during this time, so we are unlikely to see each other. However, when we arrive, I will find you." Clutching one of his hands, Nicholas walked toward the forest. "Come, you must try to get some rest."

That would be impossible. His thoughts had become an unforgiving current of anxiety, even if they defeated Fearworn, going home meant facing his family. They'd have questions and he wouldn't want to answer. If they played pretend, like he had never gone to war, he would know they were tiptoeing around him, that he caused them discomfort. No path would be easy and he didn't know what to do.

"What of that fae?" he asked. "Will he not speak of what he saw?"

"I will ensure that he won't."

No one could ensure anything with fae, but he hadn't the power to argue. Their night together without worry did not go to plan, regardless of how phenomenal it had been while it lasted. Neither spoke a word, captured by an eerie reticence. Close to the camp, he slipped on his ring and the two separated with only a look. Then he dragged his feet to the hall outside his room and removed the ring. Inside, he fell into his sleeping bag where he lay awake in the consuming gloom.

Two days. They would fight Fearworn in two days. Charmaine had to survive. Nicholas had to win. Luck had to be on their side. Pity that he didn't believe in luck. Barely an hour later, horns blared. Confused soldiers lurched to their feet, unaware that this may be the final battle, one way or the other.

32

William

William knew Death, and she traveled with them. She trailed their steps and shared their breath. The stench of death had yet to take, but it would in two days. One day. An hour. A minute.

Oscar's teeth chattered louder than a fork scraping against a plate. His rifle rattled, captured beneath his pale fingers. The gray sky greeted them, somber as days prior. Snow coated their uniforms, dampened their hair, and bit at chapped, peeling lips. Death would drown many in the cold, biting at exposed skin and curling around those in hiding, hoping being still would spare them. The rest would be lost to the beasts Fearworn set in their path.

"Never stop moving. A moment of hesitation will get you killed," he warned. The battle horns raged. Thousands of soldiers pushed through the trees. "Stay with a group and if you thought you heard something, you did."

Oscar nodded, eyes wide with fear, as if he had seen the future, and it was bleak.

"Do not rely solely on your guns. They will fail you more often than not. You have a knife. Use it."

Oscar patted his side in search of the blade. Another blast of the horn in immediate succession. They had arrived. The ground shook and cracked open like the undead came to reclaim the living world. Oscar clung to William's arm with bruising force. Beasts known and new burst from the soil to color the sky in inky gloom. Fearworn had hidden himself underground. His monsters scurried to the surface like ants protecting their hill. A musky scent permeated the air, followed by gunpowder.

Thunderous cracks, and the sting of metal against bone, engulfed the once silent terrain. Bodies crushed together in their attempt to flee. Soldiers screamed to calm their nerves, or they saw excitement in the coming bloodshed. Beasts cut through their ranks, picking up men to rip in half. Blood rained upon them, streaking winter with crimson.

Oscar's rifle fired. A grump fell, shrieking from the bullet in its chest. Another lunged over soldiers, claws and fangs bared. William shoved Oscar aside. He was too busy deciding to load his gun or use a dagger. William caught the grump by one horn and rammed a blade between its ribs. The grump yowled, then he twisted, and the creature fell dead.

"If you aren't sure whether to use a gun or a knife, use your knife," he said, unclear if Oscar listened. His dim eyes fell on the grump, then the surrounding chaos.

A boisterous roar hurtled toward them. He leapt away from a debrak, dashing through the soldiers. Its heavy steps crushed unfortunate souls in its path. The beast flailed its head, sharp horns tearing soldiers apart. The debrak caught men in its paws and shredded them faster than a toddler with wet paper. Guns fired, bullets pierced its abdomen and shoulders. One arm swatted at the soldiers as if they were no more than flies. He shifted further through the ranks, knowing he'd die too if he stayed crushed like this, but he lost sight of Oscar.

"Oscar!" He called to no avail. The young soldier vanished. All he could do was hope Oscar survived long enough for Nicholas to end this war.

William swerved around battles to find ailing soldiers. Those with minor injuries capable of healing were taken care of, then returned to the fray. Mages and fae battled with all their might. Towers of flame touched the clouds. Howling gales swept beasts off their feet to impale them in trees. A fae confused a group of grumps with copies of herself that burst into a puff of smoke when they landed an attack. Everyone fought hoping this would be the last.

Through it all, fuschia light edged closer and closer. A burst of energy severed a dozen grumps at the torso. Their ruined bodies joined countless others. Nicholas lurched through the masses, his eyes joyful in a way William could not comprehend. He came to William's side, lips sharp and hungry, as he said he would. How Nicholas found him was beyond him, or rather, he didn't want to ask.

"We must hurry," he said. "I know where to go, and we must accomplish this swiftly lest we risk Fearworn's beasts overtaking us."

"Where do we even sta…" William's question fell silent when spotting Charmaine over Nicholas' shoulder.

She prowled over the dead. Wild eyes, black as night, observed her prey. Shadows squirmed beneath her brown skin, now scaled around the edge of her eyes, lips, and hands. Skin peeled from her cheeks, molting like a reptile. She had the movements of a predator, low to the ground, shoulders high, and nostrils flaring as if she could smell everything. Including William and Nicholas. Her gaze shot to them. Head cocked, she simpered with a row of dreary red teeth.

She leapt. William's hand trembled, refusing to raise his revolver. Nicholas caught his hand and sprinted. They swerved past battles and jumped over corpses. Behind them, Charmaine shrieked. Her scream sent many, even the beasts, howling and falling to their knees. A debrak crushed a handful of soldiers and others fired their rifles, shredding a herd of grumps.

"Where are we going?" He held tight to Nicholas' hand, cold as winter.

"Fearworn is below, somewhere in the citadel, no doubt close to a scar. I saw shadowed disciples earlier. I think they emerged from an entrance nearby," Nicholas replied. "Our best bet for finding a cure is in Fearworn's workshop. I saw glimpses of the interior of this citadel, but perhaps not enough."

"Some is better than none."

Though they needed more. They needed proof, hope, a miracle. William stopped putting faith in miracles. There was skill and luck. If you didn't have either or both, you died, like Oscar. William saw the poor boy through the crowd, half his corpse in the hand of a debrak, and the other lying broken yards away. His face held fear, his last moments of pleading that were never heard. Oscar's death felt like an omen, the world trying to tell him that nothing mattered. Today would be his last, too.

"This way," Nicholas demanded. They veered around a group battling spions and ran for a large boulder covered in gore and snow. On the other side, a smaller boulder had been tossed aside, half of it uncoated by snow and covered in dirt. It had been used to hide a stairwell into the earth.

"This is where the shadowed disciples came from. It must lead to the citadel below." Nicholas snapped his fingers.

Two flaming spheres hovered. The spheres descended into the tunnel and they followed. Impatience bristled, prickling cold, a biting anxiety that had William twitching and groaning. It was unlike him. If Nicholas noticed, it did not encourage him to hasten their steps. That was for the best, regardless of his nerves. There was no telling what would meet them at the bottom of the cracked stairwell.

Blasts overhead caused dirt and debris to fall. Cracks formed along the walls. Nicholas hopped over the last two steps. He presented a hand that William accepted. The press of Nicholas' fingers along his callouses urged a sense of calm, and they continued through the narrow halls.

The citadel had been made with haste, rooms and halls carved out of rock leaving behind uneven and sharp surfaces. Crooked doorways led into wide rooms reeking of rot. Maggots and flies hovered over the carcasses fed to the creatures. Other rooms contained makeshift bunks constructed of rock and covered in moth-eaten rags.

Growls emanated from the shadows at their back. He nudged Nicholas' side and held a finger to his lips. Nicholas listened. Low growls headed their way. He settled a hand in front of William, waiting for a group of grumps to burst out of the darkness. One wave of his hand and the stone embankment expanded into spikes, piercing the yowling beasts. Their bodies fell limp.

William and Nicholas stepped forward, though stopped at the sound of another growl. Nicholas sent a ball of flame forward, slipping around the grumps' corpses. Behind them, camouflaged by the shadows, were a pair of black eyes. Charmaine.

Nicholas gripped his hand tighter. "Move."

Shrieking, Charmaine slammed against the spikes, shattering them left and right. Nicholas burst into a run, surprising William. He expected the fae to stand and fight, to raise his hand against her since they were in close quarters. He admired Nicholas' back, his heaving shoulders and serious eyes, beautiful even when shadowed. He liked to think Nicholas didn't hurt her because he may not understand their relationship, but he respected it. William appreciated that, more than he could ever say.

They sprinted through the halls. Nicholas led the way, albeit haphazardly. Neither was certain where they were headed. A wall of webs nearly caught them. The thick, slimy substance hung from the ceiling. Countless bodies had been trapped within, some wiggling. The giant oval room reeked of burnt flesh and dozens of spions crawled about their nest.

They raised their clawed legs and hissed. William shot two that dared to leap at them. Nicholas sent the nest up in flames. The heat brought a sweat to William's brow. Memories bombarded him, thoughts of Hugh and his last moments, that William may follow, and nothing would be left of him to bury.

But Nicholas had his hand. He sprinted out of the room through the only other hall, dragging William with him. Behind them, Charmaine shrieked. Her heavy steps bounded after them. Nicholas swerved left and right, stumbling upon a room that stopped them. His eyes widened, then he ran with newfound vigor.

"This way!" Nicholas called.

He and William lurched through a dining area far cleaner than the rest of the rooms. This had been carefully crafted, each surface smooth with clasps on the walls for torches. Six long tables filled the circular room. Chipped bronze cups and silverware adorned the tables.

Charmaine entered behind them. Her wild eyes had no recognition. Her head twitched atop her shoulders like a fluttering insect. She jumped over the tables and ran across them. One clawed hand swatted at William, barely missing his shoulder. Nicholas waved and the table she ran across lurched up to throw her aside.

William winced at how she landed but bit his tongue. He could not complain. Nicholas was keeping them alive and he could have done far worse. They sped out of the room. Nicholas blocked the entryway with enough rock to give them time to find Fearworn's workshop.

The battle above raged on, making the ground shake. Ahead of them, a metal door waited. Nicholas clenched his hand and the rocks around the door crushed it. He kicked the door in, then they stumbled into Fearworn's workshop. The rancid stench sent William to his knees. That was more than death, it was decay and unforgivable torment. His eyes watered and he gagged, then vomited.

Countless dissected bodies hung from hooks along the walls and ceiling. Blood stained the room and calcified along the grates on the floor. Shelves lined two walls full of jarred specimens and preserved body parts. Limbs fell to the floor from the ruckus. A strange green liquid leaked from the jars. Fearworn's sporadic ramblings had been scratched along the facade and floor. Papers laid scattered about his desk full of markings and plans.

"We don't have much time." William coughed and staggered to his feet. He wiped his mouth with the back of his sleeve. "There has to be something in here for Charmaine."

Nicholas blocked the entryway with a wall of rock and caught the torches aflame. Light filled the crevices of the room, revealing more of Fearworn's victims. Monsters laid about, cut open or crudely sewn up. One wiggled atop a slab, trapped by iron chains that burned its skin. William had seen no creature like it, something scarcely human but with too many limbs and eyes. Nicholas killed the beast, likely less to do with mercy than their survival.

"Did you ever see him working on antidotes?" William asked from the desk. His brows furrowed, perplexed by the peculiar symbols. They were a mystery, and the symbols worsened his mounting anxiety.

"I saw him working on a great deal of things, but nothing he did reversed any of the effects he set upon his victims."

William deemed the desk a lost cause and dashed toward the specimen jars. He cautiously stepped over broken shards and unknown fluids. He scoured the shelves, then came a weak snarl. Dust fell from the ceiling. Charmaine beat against the doorway. William hastened his search. Nicholas joined him.

"What if it isn't here? Where are his personal chambers?" William asked, tossing jars haphazardly when they did not give him what he desired.

"Through there." Nicholas nodded at the blocked entrance, where a long crack formed. Charmaine's growls grew closer.

"What if he has the antidote on him?"

"Or there isn't one?"

William glared, then the walls groaned. Charmaine burst into the room. Nicholas ripped a table from the floor and swung at her. Charmaine caught the opposite end. She tore the metal into pieces like it was nothing more than melted butter. She leapt toward them. Nicholas ripped the legs off the table to hit her temple. Blood seeped from the large cut on her head.

"Don't hurt her," William demanded, heart lurching.

"If I don't, she'll kill the both of us." Nicholas threw the table legs aside.

William returned his attention to the jars. There had to be an antidote. There had to be answers, the ones they needed.

Behind him, Nicholas battled against Charmaine. She was little more than brute force and rage, more intelligent than the monsters, but easily antagonized. When Nicholas landed a punch, she yowled and thrashed about. His flames sparked around the room, hissing by and encircling her. She ran past the flames, uncaring of how they caught her clothes alight. She rammed into Nicholas, sending him into the wall with a low grunt.

"Fuck, fuck!" William aimed his gun at her. Nicholas was holding himself back. He could have killed Charmaine six times over. William wouldn't let Nicholas be harmed, either. Charmaine raised her arm, moments from piercing Nicholas' shoulder. William fired. The bullet shot clean through her bicep. She screamed, and Nicholas kicked her away.

William would apologize later, after they healed her. He had to. His jittery hands continued the search. The jars either had no label or scribbled words he couldn't understand. A rare few had drawings that looked like creatures, perhaps depicting the ones Fearworn created or planned to.

Nicholas held out a hand. Rocks tumbled from the ceiling. They fell upon Charmaine and pushed her to the floor. Her eyes raged, muscles twitching as she fought against Nicholas' power.

"Find something soon or we will have to end this," Nicholas warned. "She will break her damn neck at this rate."

Charmaine's struggles wouldn't cease. Nicholas raised his hand. The rocks dispersed. When Charmaine stood, he sent them hurtling at her. She flew into the wall where the rocks pressed against her once more.

William fell to his knees to investigate the bottom row. He ripped out a jar, and a breath caught in his throat. The jar had a label, a drawing similar to the beasts that took them from camp but in their perfected form.

Charmaine shrieked and put her full power into ripping free. Rocks crumbled when she crushed them. A bone snapped loud enough to hear and Nicholas' power was relentless. Her heels pressed against the wall and sent the rocks scattering. She hurtled forward to grab Nicholas, catching his arms and his side and squeezed. With such a grip, she could break bones.

There was little more to be done. They either saved her or lost her.

William searched for a way to inject her. He couldn't possibly get her to drink this. A needle sat on a table nearby. Behind him, Nicholas shook in her grasp, cursing at her. William grabbed the needle and stabbed the top of the jar. He took as much as he could just as Nicholas shouted, "Hurry up, I am not interested in being crushed!"

Charmaine screamed when William pierced her leg. The needle went deep, and he injected as much as he could. She vaulted away to rip the needle free. Her bleak gaze fell on him.

William's hands shook, wishing, praying to the Holy Soul he hadn't spoken to in years that this worked, that she'd be okay Nicholas shielded him, hands raised to continue the battle.

Charmaine approached, then her knees gave out. Coughing, she clutched her throat and fell to her side. William ran for her, but Nicholas caught his waist. He clawed fruitlessly, kicking and cursing at Nicholas to let go. The fae stayed silent, eyes firm and lips set into a grim line.

Charmaine kicked and squirmed, breaths ragged, then silent. Murk swelled beneath her leg, breaking through skin to release a black puss. More slipped out of her ears, nostrils, mouth and eyes. She heaved a gurgled breath and gagged on it, rolling onto her hands and knees to vomit shadows.

"Let go," William demanded, desperate and pleading.

"Not yet. We do not know what that is and if it can affect you," Nicholas countered.

He hated how Nicholas became the voice of reason. He hated standing there, watching helplessly as Charmaine withered.

Nicholas' attention strayed between the entrance and Charmaine. With the battle continuing above, there was no telling who or what may come below seeking shelter. William understood they shouldn't be here waiting to see how things play out, but he would not leave without Charmaine. If she did not survive, he would take her corpse out of here. He would give her a proper burial, at least.

Charmaine scrambled away from the puss to press her back against the wall. The black of her eyes dulled, revealing their natural brown. She held up her hands as if she had never laid eyes upon them, then whimpered, "William, what...w-what's happening?"

That was her voice, and those were her eyes, brown as an autumn forest. William shoved out of Nicholas' hold, running around the mess to fall at Charmaine's side.

Nicholas inched closer, one hand behind his back. "Do not touch any of that." He nodded at the fluid. "That could have been what she was infected by. The same may happen to you."

"Infected," she echoed in a hoarse voice.

William wanted nothing more than to hug her and tell lies, that they would be okay and everything would be better. Instead, his hands shook, hovering near her. "What is the last thing you remember?"

Charmaine pressed a hand to her temple. "Uh, we...we were in a room? A storage room with some men? I was arguing with..." Her eyes widened. "I killed them. Those men. I killed them."

"That wasn't you. It was this infection. You didn't mean to."

"I killed others. Out there, the battle, our soldiers... while chasing after you, I killed them."

"Don't think like that."

She may not be thinking much of all, mind far too rattled to comprehend much. Charmaine's attention strayed from one item to the next, eyes rolling in her head. He wished to comfort her. He went to lay his hand on her shoulder and Nicholas hissed.

"There is no time for this. We must get her out of here. She is in no condition to be on a battlefield," Nicholas said.

"And where can we take her, especially if we cannot risk touching her?" he countered.

"I'll find something to cover her, then we'll figure out the rest."

Two small lights blinked in the darkness. William cursed too late.

"You won't be going anywhere," Fearworn said from the entryway, eyes of seething violet. Snapping his fingers, the ceiling caved in.

33

Nicholas

He couldn't breathe. Pressure weighed upon him. An inky gloom consumed all. Dirt stung his eyes, clogged his nostrils and lungs. He was trapped, encased, buried.

Let me out, Nicholas yearned to scream, but soil filled his lungs, weighed him down. He was a child again, taken, terrified, whimpering in the dark. There were no flames to conjure, no tears to cry, no fear to scream into the endless void. This void took and took, cementing around his flesh, creating a tomb where he would rot for eternity, no more than food for the worms.

Back then, Nicholas did not believe he would survive his capture. Laurent would be sorrowful of the loss of a shade, not a son. He had others that did his bidding, and probably with less fight. He laid there, believing he would never escape, that his life would end before it began and no one would miss him. No one would care. He could scream and scream, but no one listened, and he had never felt so pathetic, so little, so helpless and pointless.

He felt the same now, confined by an earth promising an eternity of silence, but then warmth squirmed in his grasp and he remembered; William. Nicholas lurched for him when Fearworn entered the room.

He grabbed William's hand. The ceiling collapsed. They were dying together. In a way, nothing sounded more beautiful, but Nicholas had never felt so determined to survive, to escape, and he was not that child anymore.

Power singed his veins, shrieking, amplified, ready to burst, then it did. A blast sent Nicholas hurtling from the debris. Chunks of earth rained around him. Snow stung his cheeks and hands. He rolled through it, falling to his hands and knees. He spat soil across bloody snow. Noise pounded his eardrums. Explosions. Gunfire. Screaming.

He blinked the soil away. The battle raged in a field like the end of time. Beast, mortal, and fae tore each other apart. Blood, guts, and limbs scattered the landscape like bursting roots. William strangled a cough at his side, shivering on his back. Nicholas forced him onto his knees so he could spit up the soil he breathed in, then he took an agonizing breath. Charmaine laid beside them, trembling under the falling snow and wiping her face clean. William must have had a hold of her, too.

"Fearworn," William coughed. "Where..."

The ground trembled. Dirt rose from the hole Nicholas created for their escape. As if a monster lived and breathed beneath the surface, the ground swayed, rising ever higher. Then the soil cracked. Fearworn ascended within a turbulent violet mist that matched the fierce glow of his eyes.

"You, again," Fearworn said softly, almost kindly. His gaze fell to Charmaine. "You came to steal my creation."

"She doesn't belong to you," William snarled, voice hoarse. He tugged on Charmaine's arm to cradle her against his chest. She tried to speak but coughed up more dirt instead.

"She was the first. I had many more tests to conduct, experiments to try, and you have ruined her." Fearworn's calm expression twisted into a fearsome rage. The skin of his face cracked like broken pottery, revealing vibrant violet lines the same colors as his wide eyes. "You've ruined her and now I must try again. I shall try on both of you. You will make wonderful subjects."

The snow came to life around them, icy tendrils that cut and grabbed. Above them, countless knives formed from scattering snowflakes. They descended like a hale storm. Nicholas raised his hands, creating a pink-tinted shield. The knives shattered, and the tendrils slithered over the shield, searching for a way to break through.

"Find the generals," Nicholas ordered. "Tell them to do what they must and find as many fae as you can. Order them to fight with me."

"Fae will not take orders from me," William argued while slipping Charmaine's arm over his shoulder. She was on the verge of blacking out.

"They will see my battle with Fearworn if they haven't already. They will listen." Nicholas winced from a blast of energy that shook their haven. Fearworn sent another and another, each threatening to break through. "Go. Now!"

"Be careful," William whispered.

A path opened, letting William and Charmaine stumble out of the shield. The icy tendrils lunged at them. Nicholas released the shield to melt them in a wave of heat. The last he saw of William was his back as he and Charmaine forced their way through the battle. He could think of them no longer. His prey hovered before him, enveloped by a bristling power that sang an eerie tune.

"Do not look at me as if I am not the reflection of your future," said Fearworn. Lightning danced at his fingertips, a deeper shade than wine. "Speaking from a shade to a shade, this is our glorious end, the path we all must take. One day, you will let go, as I did, and you will find magic like no other."

Fearworn spoke of temptation, of what Nicholas felt from the moment his abilities came into being. There had always been an energy coursing through the earth beneath his feet, the surrounding air, the water he drank and the food he ate. Everything felt connected to him, somehow. He could reach into the world and pluck at the strings of her heart, make her sing exactly what he wanted, but at a cost.

"I find my current self positively superb company, so pardon me if I do not leap with joy from your comments," Nicholas replied and commanded flames to lurch at Fearworn.

Lightning crackled in the surrounding storm. The flames flickered into nothing. Lightning broke forth. A jolt pierced Nicholas' gut. He hurtled through the air and fell, breathless and spasming.

Arden dashed out of the fray, a dagger of harsh vines in each hand. He swiped at Fearworn, who retreated into a pair of vicious jaws. A fae morphed into a wolf tore through the tendons of his ankle, releasing when Fearworn raised a hand. Arden and the wolf, presumably Amos, circled Fearworn, and Nicholas joined them.

"What is the plan here?" Arden licked his crooked lips.

"Exhaust him," Nicholas replied.

He would not mention how they could close the scar for a short time. Arden knew of it, having been around Nicholas and Laurent, so when the time came, Nicholas and he would do what they had to. He couldn't risk Fearworn hearing and thus losing their opportunity. If they wore Fearworn out and he hurried to the scar to escape, they would have a moment of his surprise upon realizing he had nowhere to go. That small window could be enough, it had to be enough.

After each of Nicholas' attacks, his kin responded. More and more joined, they swiped, scratched, and stabbed at Fearworn whenever he stumbled or got a smidge too close. His shadowed disciples came to his aid, but bullets rained upon them from the mortal soldiers. Another fell dead at Nicholas' feet, a gunshot wound through their neck. In the mass of warring bodies, he made out William's eyes, calculating and watchful, his guardian.

Fearworn held his hands high. The sky lurched down like a crumbling tower, then broke apart in fearsome sparks. Spears of lightning rained from above, stretching far as the eye could see. His enemies and monsters alike fell to the attack.

Nicholas swerved around the assault. Fearworn concentrated above. Violet overtook his eyes. Nicholas sent anything he could: fire, ice, rocks, fallen blades, anything and everything at Fearworn. He narrowly shielded half his body from Nicholas' attack. Sparks devastated Fearworn's shoulder, singing the cloth from his left arm and eating the skin from his cheeks. Snarling, he sent that fire back and Nicholas deflected the blaze, leaving it little more than a hot puff of smoke.

Fearworn became the eye of a storm, and the world reacted to his presence. He commanded the elements with such fluidity that Nicholas hardly kept up. He wouldn't, if not for his kin standing guard. They slipped in when they could, distracting Fearworn for brief moments where Nicholas attacked. The teamwork helped because Fearworn had slowed down and not one of them was short of breath yet.

In the distance, a scar shimmered, little more than a single thread peeking out of the cracked earth. Fearworn retreated toward it. Nicholas sent Arden a look, and the fae understood. Arden surged away from the battle in search of the mortal mages. The last attack had to be now. Fearworn was lashing out, desperate against the onslaught of attacks from all angles. His monsters fell in droves, incapable of withstanding long assaults. Most didn't have the minds for strategy. They did well with unexpected attacks, using their massive forms and fearsome claws to tear soldiers apart, then retreat. Here, there was nowhere to retreat to.

Nicholas kept at Fearworn. He threw everything he could think of. Fearworn's snarls grew until he was barely more than a growling beast like the creatures he loved to create, but nothing was more frightful than a cornered animal.

Fearworn lashed out in a wave of energy that sent the world to its knees. His shrill shriek, like Charmaine's, had everyone screaming in agony. Nicholas' ears rang, a pressure pierced him and sent his thoughts scrambling. The earth shook, breaking apart in jagged points that cut through skin and trapped others behind swollen embankments.

Nicholas hissed when two rocks joined to lock his ankle in place. Another rose at his side. He kicked out of his constraints, then rolled away, cursing when another rock wall rose at his back. The earth cut his back. He pressed his hands to the rocks and commanded them to wither. Scrambling out of the dust, he scarcely avoided being impaled by a final spike springing forward from where his body once laid.

A debrak stormed out of the soldiers. Nicholas couldn't dodge its wide swing. The beast caught him and squeezed tight. He screamed and summoned a blast to tear through the beast's forehead. The debrak fell, and Nicholas shoved his way out of its grip. He thought himself safe until the hair stood along the back of his neck. Fearworn hovered nearby. He pointed his hand at Nicholas' back.

"Nicholas!" William screamed and shoved him.

Nicholas fell. A siege of violet light threw William aside. Nicholas tasted blood that did not belong to him. Time stopped. The world faded. All he saw was William's limp body drowning in red snow. His right arm laid a foot away. Cracked bone peeked through ruined flesh, hanging like loose strings from an old coat. His William didn't move and wouldn't respond to his name no matter how wildly Nicholas called. On hands and knees, he scrambled to William's side. Blood caked his fingers, William's blood, hot and sticky. The flesh along the right side of his neck and cheek hung like wet paper, hair laying in clumps of blood. When he breathed, his chest oozed, the skin blackened and torn.

Nicholas' kin called for him. Their desperate pleas meant nothing, not as he held William, heard the blood gurgling in his throat. He coughed and a spittle of crimson stained his lips. Each breath came smaller than the last, strangled, scarce, eerie. They needed a healer, but moving William resulted in a high-pitched whine. Nicholas cursed when his fingers felt the bone of William's spine. Fearworn tore him apart.

They couldn't move. None heard Nicholas' pleas for a healer, even when he knew mortal magic could not fix this. William would die and he could not stop that.

Fae, with all their natural talent and power, were helpless in the face of death. Mortals could spare one another. Fae could glamor, lie, trick, and steal, but when the time came that they needed power more than anything, it laughed in the face of their desires.

"Why would you do that?" Nicholas croaked, wondering if what he felt on his cheeks were tears.

William did not answer.

Whimpering, Nicholas pressed their foreheads together, willing William's heart to continue beating. "Why would you risk your life for me? I'm just a tool to kill Fearworn, to warm your bed at night. You shouldn't have. You are a fool."

"You are the fool," William croaked. "You are so much more than that to me, trouble."

Then his eyes closed, and chest stilled.

"Do not leave." Nicholas' words came out panicked and choked. "Wait for me."

Nicholas would give *anything, anything, anything*, to spare William. He would find time's strings and unfurl them. He would chase after Death itself and pluck William's soul from her bitter grasp. He would tear this world apart.

Power slithered beneath Nicholas' skin, whispering and promising the end he desired. He always said no, always strangled that indescribable need, but today, he accepted. He gave in. For William.

34

William

William dreamed of a black sea and eternal pain. Sea foam filled his lungs. Further and further away, he slipped. Memories of laughter, what he remembered to be his family's voices, whispered against his ears. He thought what they said was kind, but could not process their words.

Was this it, Elysium? Had the Broken Soul deemed him unworthy and dragged him beneath the waters to suffer?

Then the sea burst into deep blue and he sat up in a hospital bed coughing.

"Nicholas?" Shouldn't have been the first name uttered from his chapped lips, but he wanted nothing more than to see him But the fae was not there. No one was.

"Nurse," he called, but the word fell silent when he caught sight of his right arm, or what should have been his right arm. He urged the appendage to move, and the metal monstrosity obeyed. The smooth metal curled as fingers should, although it was cold to the touch. He ripped his hospital gown from his body, revealing the metal fused with his shoulder. Strings of silver spread like unsettling cobwebs through his skin, then faded.

Memories flooded in of Fearworn, screaming, blood, smoke, fire, and pain. His arm lay in the mud, ruined. This was not a prosthetic. It was wild fae magic. He did not know what to think of the arm. Grateful to move the limb as freely as before, others were not so lucky, but he was angrier, infuriated that no one asked if he wanted this contraption. Frustrated that he awoke to some *thing* connected to him, replacing what had been lost that he strangely wanted to mourn. And worried that Nicholas was not here to explain.

Erratic breaths tore through his chest. His lungs burned. His eyes strayed about the room. Familiar medical supplies laid atop shelves along the pale blue facade. The paint had chipped and the wooden floor held countless scrape marks. William was utterly alone until the door opened.

"You're finally awake, Mr. Vandervult," the nurse said. Her eyes lingered on the silver appendage. He covered himself with the blankets. Heat pooled beneath his cheeks that couldn't be described as embarrassment or anger. This was different, deeper, more.

"What happened?" he asked, voice grumbled and rough. "To Fearworn, to everyone, where am I?"

"Fearworn is dead."

William laughed, causing a cough to rattle his chest. The nurse shuffled toward the sink. A glass sat on the edge that she filled and offered him. He chugged the cool water, then whispered, "Say that again?"

"Fearworn is dead, sir."

"How?"

The nurse shuffled her weight from one foot to the other. She spoke carefully, as if worried her phrasing would upset him. "Well, I know little more than what I have heard. Rumors say a shade obliterated Fearworn. Every time I hear a story, it is a little different from the last, but they always say it was a battle of shades that no one could contend with, and we won, thanks not only to that effort, but yours and the other soldiers as well."

We won. He never thought he would live to hear those words. They were beautiful, unbelievable, a promise of hope finally brought to fruition.

"You are in Millbury Hospital. Our town is the closest to the Deadlands," she continued.

"How long have I been asleep?"

To have traveled out of the Deadlands would have taken time. The generals would have been careful with the wounded, so it would have been a slow march. More importantly, his wounds were great, the pain even more so. He should have died.

William's fingertips danced over his chin, sensing neither wound nor scar. This healing was not mortal magic. Wounds such as his were a death sentence, and he swore his heart had stopped, that Death finally got her claws in him and swept him away. To have survived, a fae, a powerful one at that, spared him and connected this peculiar appendage. That couldn't have been Nicholas, could it? If it were, he would have been here. He would be at William's side where he needed the fae most.

"About four days," she answered while carefully inspecting him. She refused to touch the prosthetic

"That can't be. It'd take longer than that for our wounded to get here." As he said that, the nurse tugged an envelope from her pocket.

"I will call for a doctor. He will be here momentarily. Until then, this was left for you." She dropped the envelope into his lap and took hasty steps to the door. She pressed two fingers to her heart and prayed. William needn't hear her to know what she said; *fae-cursed.*

William set the glass aside and ran his left hand over the metal arm. When others saw the prosthetic, they would mutter the same. Everyone knew what happened when a mortal dealt with fae. No one would miss that his arm was fae magic. He would be seen as cursed, as someone foolish enough to deal with fae and potentially a threat, depending on what sort of deal he made. Many tales claimed fae objects were possessed by wild magic, that they'd come to life in the night and kill their owners. Once, he believed all that, too. Now, he wasn't so sure.

Sighing, he grasped the letter that had neither a name nor a seal. His breathing came fast from a hope that this would be from Nicholas, that even if he had not been here, at least he had visited. Upon opening the envelope, William found nothing. No letter, nothing more than the scent of fresh earth.

He jolted at the rattling of the window from a breeze. Branches covered in leaves hit the glass. Green. Color. He hadn't seen a blue sky in so long that the beauty of it mesmerized him. All he wanted was to throw open the window and pinch a leaf between his fingers to remember what they felt like. He craved to run barefoot through the grass and curl his toes into the soil. He wanted to feel the sun on his cheeks, to lie beneath its rays and bask in a summery heat.

"Mr. Vandervult."

William shut his eyes and breathed deep. Neither the door nor window had been opened, yet Laurent Darkmoon stood at his bedside. The perfect depiction of a fae, so eerily breathtaking that William believed himself dead and this to be the drowning sea of Elysium.

"Lord Darkmoon." If he could have run, he might have, for Laurent's presence brought out an instinctual need to flee.

His gray eyes raked over William, and he frowned. "Are you displeased with my work?" Laurent asked.

"I beg your pardon?"

Laurent's nimble fingers caught William's arm and forced it free from the bedsheets. The metal reflected Laurent's apathetic expression.

"Beautiful, isn't it?" He ran his fingers over the metal that William couldn't understand. Somehow, he felt Laurent's touch and even the softness of the sheets.

"They are, but I do not know why you gifted them to me." He chose his words wisely because Laurent wouldn't take kindly to his uncertainty.

A voice told him to be grateful. He still had an arm, but another screamed at the loss of his body. Of something that belonged solely to him and he had no say on whether or not they could be "replaced." This prosthetic was not his, not a part of him. He wanted his body, the piece of himself taken. He wanted his body the way it was before, then he wondered if that was foolish and cruel to think.

"Nicholas informed me of what happened on the battlefield," Laurent replied. "You saved him and would have died from doing so. A debt was owed that he could not repay. There are not many fae who can heal. Did you know that?"

"Yes, sir. I hear that High Fae, those such as yourself, sometimes have healing abilities."

"Luckily for you." He released William's arm. "I repaid you in his stead and brought you here to heal."

"I appreciate the work you put in, but...where is he?" William asked. The abrupt narrowing of Laurent's eyes warned him to tread carefully. "You may have repaid his debt, but I saved his life. He should at least visit to thank me, wouldn't you agree?"

Laurent approached the window. Outside, the trees responded to his presence. The branches stretched. Their shivering leaves brushed against the glass. Laurent pressed the tip of his finger upon the window. The tree burst with life, doubling the leaves and shuddering, as if to thank him. It was strange to see such a detached creature create beauty in a delicate touch.

"He has more pressing matters," Laurent replied. "Nicholas may have slayed Fearworn, but many of his monsters and disciples survived. Upon his demise, they fled like the cowards they are. There are those among them who would seek to continue Fearworn's destruction, albeit not nearly with as much success. Regardless, we must get rid of them all to ensure the end, and work toward closing the Scars he opened permanently."

Nicholas had truly succeeded. He would be celebrated, even by mortals. They may yet write his name in history books. He would love that level of attention, that no one would ever forget him, and whether they wanted to admit it or not, be forever grateful. William imagined Nicholas in his hospital room spouting his brilliance, power, and greatness, spinning on his heels and grinning ear to ear. It hurt that William couldn't see that in person, that he wouldn't get to hear Nicholas share the story in elaborate details no doubt exaggerated in any form he could manage.

"Since he is so busy, it seems I will not hear from him," William muttered, heart aching.

"You will not." Laurent's words were heavy enough to bury. "After the courageous battle and your wounds, your generals have agreed to have you honorably discharged alongside your friend."

He sat taller, hands clenched. Her name nearly slipped from his parched lips. "Albie? Do you know where he is?"

Laurent gestured to the door. "He is resting down the hall. Now that you are awake, it won't be long until the two of you return home. I believe this is a congratulatory message."

A mixture of both. As excited as William was about returning home, he also wanted to speak with Nicholas. At the very least, he wanted to see him. He yearned to bask in the light of Nicholas' crooked smile, his devious words, and avid touch. Though he would never say it aloud, he even wanted to hear Nicholas' bad riddles accompanied by a charming laugh that rattled his bones. He missed Nicholas. He wanted him near so badly, a craving like no other, and he felt he may stop breathing without him. They were ridiculous thoughts, childish ones he had while flipping through the silly romance books he once read. He had ceased believing in their theatrics, and yet, he felt it all now, crushing him.

"Yes, I appreciate what you have given me," William managed to say.

"As you should. You will not receive such grand gifts again. Now that I am certain the debt has been paid, this is goodbye." Laurent smiled, but his eyes were devoid of life. Looking into them made their emptiness peer back into you. Then he vanished.

Alone once more, William wondered why his heart hurt when the impossible had happened. Fearworn was defeated. Charmaine not only survived, but they both were honorably discharged. Their service ended. Soon, they would return home. His injuries, meant to be fatal, were healed. His arm, though lost, was replaced. As Laurent said, he brought a congratulatory message, but why did William feel so hollow?

He stifled a cry, then another, then he couldn't stop. William fell upon his bed, haunted by sorrow. Every breath became strangled, choked between sobs and hiccups. He wiped at his eyes, desperate for the tears to stop, for the pain to cease, but it grew and grew, like a sinkhole taking on more ferocious water that eroded away the walls. The lack of Nicholas brought such anguish that William thought he would rather die on that battlefield again. At least there, he believed Nicholas cared, that Nicholas loved him.

"Love," he whispered.

"Love," he cursed.

He slammed his fist on the railing of the hospital bed, the silver one, the cursed one. Pain ripped into his nerves, making his arm and shoulder twitch. The power in that arm cracked the metal off the bed to clatter on the floor.

What a fool he was to stand up to Nicholas.

What a fool he was to respond to his taunts.

What a fool he was to care, to fall in love with a creature incapable of feeling the same.

Tears did nothing. They would not summon Nicholas. They would not change the past. They were a waste of time that brought about a headache, but William could not stop. He wished he could erase all of this. He wished to bottle every moment they shared, weigh that bottle down, and toss their memories into the sea. His feelings would sink and sink, buried under shivering blackness. He hadn't even the ring to toss, that wretched, wretched ring, not in his gown or on the bedside table, not anywhere. Nicholas left nothing behind but a used toy.

The door creaked. "William?" Charmaine whispered.

She stood in the doorway. Her left arm, wrapped in a cast, hung from a sling. A thin layer of black curls sprouted along her scalp. Scars lined her eyes and mouth where the scales had been, but her face was healing nicely. In another month or so, the scars may be gone entirely. She looked good. She looked like herself, and when she smiled, he smiled back.

She dashed across the room and captured him in a fierce embrace that he was more than happy to return. Right now, he loved that she sought comfort through hugging. He needed one, especially from her. She was warm and alive. His hand slipped around her neck to feel her pulse, to savor the beat against the pad of this thumb, then pulled her back to whisper, "Don't you dare frighten me like that again."

She laughed between tears. "Trust me, I have no intention of being transformed into a mindless beast ever again."

William kissed her forehead. "I love you so dearly, Charmaine. I thought I lost you and I..."

"Oh, I love you, too, you crazy fool," she interrupted. "You actually came for me."

"As you would have done for me."

"Without hesitation." She blinked the tears from her eyes and settled comfortably along the edge of his bed. He did not miss how her attention trailed along his arm. The silver caught in her eyes, but there was no judgment, no fear, more of a relief that William wished he could feel too.

"Did you hear?" she asked. "We won. William, we won. Fearworn is gone. We're going home."

"We're going home," he repeated, but the words did not sound as sweet without the thought of Nicholas. "Did Nicholas ever show? Did he visit you?"

"No, I'm sorry. The last thing I remember is you injecting me with the antidote and a little of us running through the battlefield. Then I woke up here. I have seen no one other than the doctor and nurses. I take it he has not visited you, either?"

"Lord Darkmoon was here a moment ago. He claimed to have saved me in exchange for saving Nicholas' life. Now, Nicholas is to ensure none of the surviving shadowed disciples try to take Fearworn's place. I will not see or hear from him again."

"Does that pain you?" she whispered. It would not matter how he answered, because the tears came when they wished.

Charmaine eased him into her arms and said nothing of his stupid choices and foolish heart, though he wished she would. Scold him, call him an idiot, tell him he should have seen this coming, make him *feel,* feel anything other than this.

William got what he always wanted and lost what he never realized he needed.

Epilogue

Matilda Jessica Vandervult would not allow William to return to anything less than perfection. She raised her boys to be more than needy and demanding lords. They could sweep and dust alongside everyone else. She toiled away in William's room, ensuring all of his books sat neatly on the shelves, and all the new titles waited on the bedside table.

Arthur took the carriage to retrieve William from the port. Matilda wanted to join, but Arthur convinced her to stay home and ensure everything was perfect for William's return. Richard and Henry took a trip into town days ago to purchase clothes for William, enough for him to rest before they took the trip themselves. Oh, Matilda had a list of all the places they would visit.

A new amphitheater had been built near town square, where the local theater and musicians put on plays and shows every week. A bookstore was built a whole three stories high with a small cafe that William could spend his afternoons in. A string of restaurants opened over the years that became family favorites, but the family had never been whole. Even dinners at home were a cold reminder because the Vandervults always set the table for William, too.

Matilda wiped the stray tears from her cheeks. They had consumed her since Robert dashed out of his office a month ago. She lectured him about running. His knee went bad over a decade ago, but he hadn't heard a word. Robert swooped her up in his arms and declared the war was over. Fearworn was dead, but most important of all, their baby would board the first ship home. They fell to the floor together and wept.

A month of worry passed. The sea was treacherous, but none dared speak of the potential hazards. William could not be lost when he was so close to coming home. And finally, the day had come. Arthur stayed at a hotel near the port for a week, and a good thing, too. The ship arrived a day early. Arthur sent a letter that he and William would take the evening at the hotel to rest, then come the following day, so the estate had time to prepare.

In truth, preparations started the moment William left. Asiatic lilies overtook the garden, William's favorite, and Matilda would not have any other flower planted. She enjoyed having tea out there, pretending William sat across from her with his nose in a book or toiling over the stitching of his clothes.

Robert didn't enjoy sitting in the garden. He mourned differently, in avoidance. His actions initially infuriated her, but as the weeks, then months, and years went by, she understood why. If Robert looked into William's room, if he entered the library or the garden, he withered. He became a shell of his former self, overridden by guilt, then rage. He drank when he wasn't a drinker and it was unpleasant, so she made sure William's bedroom door was closed and the staff got books Robert needed from the library. He did better working, waiting, preparing for William's return rather than lingering on him being gone.

Matilda halted outside Robert's office at the sound of voices.

"I worry about her," Richard said. The heels of his shoes clicked across the floor in a regular pacing pattern. "Mother is excited to have William back. We all are, but he will not be as we remembered. Henry has told us as such."

Matilda wrung her hands together, recalling Henry's return from the front lines. She was desperate to hear from him because the army stopped sending personal letters once they went into the Deadlands. Robert wrote to the king, but they received nothing more than a statement that William was alive. Henry saw him, spoke to him, and assured Matilda that he was doing well. She was not foolish enough to believe Henry didn't carefully choose the best words to reassure her.

Richard continued, "We can't expect our lives to return to what they were once. He has been gone for so long and been through more than we'll ever know, and none of us are certain of what he needs."

"Your mother is more than capable of understanding that," Robert countered.

"Of course she is. We all are, but that means very little. We're all excited to see him and we're likely to make mistakes."

"Which we will fix," Henry said. "And we will ask William what he needs, and he will answer when he is ready. He's tough, Rickie, tougher than all of us."

Richard's pacing escalated. "Maybe we should see him one at a time so as to not overwhelm him."

Robert laughed. "I am beginning to think you are worrying most of all."

"For now, our best option is to give William an ardent welcome, and let him rest," Henry said. "Now that he's home, we'll be able to work at this little by little."

Richard groaned. He hated not knowing what to do because he normally always had a path forward, especially in social situations. Matilda couldn't fault him for that. She worried, too. She thought of all this, hoped that she could restrain her own overbearing emotions so as to not smother her son the moment he arrived.

"My lady," Marshall, their head butler, announced. "The carriage is approaching."

Matilda clutched the hem of her skirts. "Good. Tell Robert and the boys to meet us outside. We should all be there to greet him."

She hadn't considered opening the door to the office because she was already hurrying downstairs. Her baby, finally home. She hadn't dashed down the steps so swiftly since she was a little girl. Even then, her parents scolded her for being improper. She believed they would let this moment slide.

Two maids waited at the door, throwing them open for Matilda to sprint into the afternoon sun. They could not have returned on a more perfect day, warm and light. The Vandervults never had vast land. Matilda and Robert disliked being so far away from others. An iron gate surrounded the estate, primarily to protect against monsters, and a short drive led from the entrance to the street. The carriage moved slowly across the gravel, each second ticking into an eternity.

Henry, Richard, and Robert stepped outside. They agreed William would meet the newest additions to their family another day. The girls thought that may be too much for William and believed they should visit after he settled.

And so the four stood together. Matilda's arms rested at her waist, where a single finger tapped anxiously against her glove. Richard took her hand when the carriage lurched closer, closer, and finally pulled to a stop. The thick curtains concealed the interior. All she wanted was to rip them aside, to throw open the door and drag William inside, where she would keep him safe.

Marshall opened the door. Arthur exited first, all charm and kind greetings. He approached her for a brief hug and kiss, then stepped aside in time to view William coming home.

William stood tall as she when he left. He had full flushed cheeks, thin limbs, and a natural smile. The moment he entered a room, the world shined a little brighter. He trembled when the carriage came to take him away. She clung to his cheeks, peering into eyes, shedding streams of tears. She still saw her baby, a precious little thing that had barely begun to understand the world, but that was not the William in front of them.

He stood as tall as his father now, if not a little more. Once full cheeks had sharpened, and thin limbs grew muscular. Though he smiled, the kindness did not reach his eyes. There was a coldness to his gaze, an overgrown chill. He stood perfectly still, gloved hands placing themselves swiftly at his back in a military stance. Matilda cursed the king and Fearworn, and every war ever started. Her precious baby came to understand the world in the most violent of ways. She saw in the way he held himself, in the careful way he approached, how his gaze swept around them like he expected the worst to befall them, but he was here, he was home, and she would never let go.

Matilda hugged her youngest who had grown far too much in the time that passed. William flinched. By the Holy Soul, she wanted to scream, but then his arms took hold of her and held so tight she might have broken if she hadn't wanted this moment for years.

"Welcome home, sweetie," she whimpered.

"I'm glad to be home, Mother," William replied.

Deep down, everyone knew William hadn't really come home.

About the Author

Twoony is a queer geek with a love for storytelling. They write young adult and adult stories ranging from the always enjoyable teen rom-com to fantasy romances. At the age of twelve, they posted their first story online and have been addicted to sharing ever since. Although Twoony graduated from California University of PA with a Bachelors in Graphics & Multimedia, their true passion has always been writing. After creating original novels and comics on sites like Tapas and Wattpad, amounting over 105k subscribers and 7m+ reads, they have managed to live their dream. They are a full-time writer with three needy cats and not enough bookshelves. If you're interested in their work, they have a completed romantic trilogy called Speak the Truth and multiple stand alone novels available at most major retailers. Otherwise, subscribe to their newsletter or follow their social media to learn more.

Newsletter: substack.com/@twoony
Instagram: twoonyauthor
Tiktok: twoonyauthor
Tapas: Twoony

Printed in Great Britain
by Amazon